Fire Horse

ALSO BY BILL SHOEMAKER

Stalking Horse★

★*Published by Fawcett Columbine*

Fire Horse

Bill Shoemaker

Fawcett Columbine

New York

A Fawcett Columbine Book
Published by Ballantine Books

LIBRARY OF CONGRESS CATALOGING–IN–PUBLICATION DATA
Shoemaker, Willie.
p.   cm.
"A Coley Killebrew novel."
ISBN 0-449-90596-9
1. Private investigators—California—Los Angeles—Fiction.
2. Horse racing—California—Los Angeles—Fiction. 3. Los Angeles
(Calif.)—Fiction.   I. Title.
PS3569.H5716F57   1995
813'.54—dc20   94-25365 CIP

Manufactured in the United States of America

First Edition: February 1995

10 9 8 7 6 5 4 3 2

*A lot of people have helped me through
more than 40,000 races during my career as a jockey.
This book is dedicated to them.*

Fire Horse

1

DRIVING WEST FROM Los Angeles along the Santa Monica Freeway there's a spot right around the Cloverfield off-ramp when the Pacific Ocean breezes drop the temperature about ten degrees and scatter the smog enough to give your lungs a fighting chance. I turned off the Cherokee's air-conditioning, pumped up the gain on Chris Connor's supremely depressing rendition of "Cottage for Sale," lowered the windows, and let the cool, damp wind whip through the vehicle. It smelled of brine and coconut oil.

Just when it looked as if the freeway might shoot out into the Pacific, it took a dip and made a roundhouse turn north, suddenly melding into the Pacific Coast Highway. To the right was a slowly but continually eroding bluff as high as a five-story building. To the left was a series of ramshackle cottages price-tagged even in those cautionary times at a million bucks apiece, give or take a hundred thou. Past them was a blazing white beach dotted with humans who were as concerned with skin cancer as I was with the threat of medfly infestation. And beyond them was the quirky ocean, changing in the blink of an eye from a calm, benign playmate to a surly, impatient bully that sent squealing swimmers toward the sand with a mighty slap.

Some spraypaint tagger had given the sign for the Bay City Beach and Cabana Club a contemporary update. With its Day-Glo pink additions it now read BAG CITY BITCHES AND BANANAS CLAN, NEXT LEFT.

By any name, I thought, and turned in. The club was a two-story wooden building. Its paint job had been recent enough to still look fresh, regardless of the beating it took from the sun and salt air and the occasional earthquake. It was chalk white with a dark green trim that matched the awning that led to the front entrance.

I braked the Cherokee behind a tomato-red classic Alfa that was baking in the sun and causing a parking-lot detour. "Won't it start?" I asked the young carhop who was standing beside it.

"Lady got it for her birthday a couple months ago. She don't trust us to drive it," he said without rancor, as if he'd grown used to the idea.

"Well, feel free to drive mine," I told him. "Especially if you can find some shade to park it in."

He nodded, then did a double take before pointing his finger at me. He said, "Hey, you're the jockey. Coley Killebrew."

Nature hadn't had longer than sixteen or seventeen years to work on his tanned pie face, and his sun-bleached crew cut made him look even younger. What with one thing or another, I hadn't donned silks in over seven years. "You don't look old enough to have seen me race," I said.

"Me? Naw, I never even been to the track. But there's a picture of you and my old man on the wall in our place. From Santa Anita. Or maybe Santa Rosita."

"Is your father in racing?"

He shook his head. "He ain't in anything. He bought it a couple years ago. The Big C. Went out with a smoke in his hand. He wasn't never in racing. But he probably put in more time at the track than most of the guys worked there." He squinted, either from the glare or from the exercise of his memory. "There was a Superfan ticket, something like that, is how he met you and the picture got took."

"That was at Santa Rosita, the Superfan stuff," I said. "The hundredth guy through the gate got to meet a jock. What was your father's name?"

"Herman Moss," he replied, neither proud nor ashamed. The name rang no bells. "I'm Herman Junior."

"I'm sorry to hear he's gone," I said.

He stood beside the door of the Cherokee and continued to squint at me. "You a member of the club, Mr. Killebrew?" he asked.

"Can't say I am."

"I didn't think so," the kid replied. "Uh, don't take this the wrong way, but if you're going in to lunch, guys are supposed to wear a jacket in the dining room."

I grinned at him and reached into the Cherokee for the blazer I'd thrown on the backseat a few months ago, for just such an occasion. Then I slipped a couple of bucks from my pocket into the kid's hand. "Thanks for the tip," I told him, "and I meant it about the shade."

"Got a special palm tree all picked out," Herman Moss, Jr., said. He navigated the Cherokee around the untouchable Alfa and I strolled under the awning to an oiled walnut front door with a polished brass plate that read FOR MEMBERS AND THEIR GUESTS ONLY. I didn't fall into either of those categories, but I didn't let it slow me down a bit.

The conditioned air in the club's lobby was not only too cold, it was heavy with a chemically produced piney odor that smelled like urinal incense. I wondered if the members had voted on that pine stink. They voted on everything else. As any longtime resident of the area will tell you, they were all white male Gentiles, and would remain so as long as the board of directors could stonewall the efforts of the city, the state, and the nation to make them conform to the antidiscriminatory laws of the land.

With all of its restrictions, the place apparently was open to owners of Vegas casinos, for Johnny Rousseau was seated at a table near a bay window in the dark-wood-and-forest-green wallpapered dining room. A see-through drink rested untouched on the green tablecloth in front of him. He was in his midforties, a man of average height, deep-tanned, well groomed, handsome, I suppose, though his thin lips gave him a slightly sinister cast. That day he was garbed in earth colors—a cocoa-brown silk jacket, light brown trousers, a brown-and-white striped lisle shirt.

With some reluctance, he shifted his wistful blue eyes from an array of well-turned-out young women draped around the outdoor pool to the snooty maître d' and me as we bore down on him.

"Here is your party, I believe, *sir*," the maître d' informed him through curled lip, before doing an about-face and heading back to his preening post near the entrance. Johnny smiled lazily and said, "I knew a guy like him back in Jersey once. Wound up trying to swim the Hudson with cement in his Johnson-Murphys."

"That snotty doorman's in his element," I said. "What're *you* doing here, Johnny?"

"I'm a guest."

"That's how you got in. What are you doing here?"

He shrugged and gave me a sheepish smile. "You know me, Coley."

I knew him, but I didn't know him well. We'd met a dozen years ago, when my career was at full gallop. He'd just bought a Vegas casino, Moore's Utopia, from its then owner, Matty Moore, a former button man for the Giordino family of Newark. Moore had been forced to sell when his underworld ties became so well-known the gaming commission could no longer pretend they didn't exist. The general assumption was that the Giordinos had financed Johnny, too. But his claim was that the loot for the Utopia had come from the sale of a chain of men's stores along the East Coast that he and his brother Phil inherited from their haberdasher father.

Nearly eight years ago, when my career fell apart and the people I thought were my great friends suddenly disappeared into the woodwork, Johnny paid a call. "Now that the jockey thing's done," he said, "what're you going to do with your time?"

I didn't have any ready answer. I was too busy feeling sorry for myself, or guilty, or something equally productive.

"You got *any* green left?" he asked.

"Some," I said, guardedly.

"There's this L.A. lady," he told me. "She thinks I ought to spend more time here. She don't like Vegas. Weird, but there you are. So what I was thinking is this—how about me and you starting a little bar and grill together? A kind of hangout for the racing crowd. The sports crowd."

"I don't have that kind of cash," I answered.

"Don't worry about the loot. I'll front most of it. You'll be doin' most of the work, 'cause when I'm here in L.A., I'll be with the lady, capiche? But with the bar and grill goin', it'll be like a business trip. It'll be good for me, it'll be good for you. Okay?"

I stared at him. "This is a crazy idea," I said. "The only customers we'd get would be wiseguys and cops."

"How do you figure?"

"We don't have the greatest reputations in the world," I told him.

"Reputations?" He chuckled. "Look, I grew up with Dorie Giordino, but that don't mean I ever got into bed with her or any of her relatives. I'm my own man, and there ain't a guy or a broad alive can prove otherwise."

"That leaves *my* reputation," I said.

"Did you throw the race?"

The memory of that fateful day was still vivid. I'd been up late, drinking. My reflexes were so out of whack it took me two tries to get my boots on. I should never have put those boots in the stirrups that afternoon. But I did. And heading into the home stretch, I saw a space between horses that didn't exist.

"No," I told Johnny. "I didn't throw it. But I was careless. A jockey got hurt and a horse had to be destroyed." And I was banned from racing.

"The fans still like you, pal," Johnny said.

"I don't know why." Those days I didn't like myself. I hadn't discovered that a woman I'd trusted had bet against me and drugged me to insure her bet. Even that knowledge probably wouldn't have improved my mood, since I had no proof.

"Look, I may not sound like it, but I'm a businessman," Johnny said on that long-ago evening. "This isn't just some screwball idea. I know how a kitchen operates. I know how to make a bar pay off. And I think I've got a handle on people, too. I'll teach you everything I know and we can make this work. Me and you, Coley. Fifty-fifty, right down the middle."

So I became half owner and general manager of the Horse's Neck, a more or less traditional bar and grill that, in a land of constantly changing hip-restaurants-of-the-month, continues to do a healthy business every night of the week, except Mondays when we're dark.

But that fine day, instead of making sure our brand-new bartender was quenching the thirsts of the lunch crowd, I was sitting in a segregated beach club wondering why.

Johnny sighed again and said, "You want the whole story?" I wanted to be back at the Horse's Neck. I said, "Is that water you're drinking?"

"A G and T. Want one?"

"If it's going to be a long story."

"I'll make it a double," he said, and waved for the waiter.

I should have been able to figure out the bottom line. Woman trouble. But past that general topic, I would never have guessed the details.

The woman, Johnny explained, was the twenty-two-year-old daughter of Wilton Dresner, a newscaster and political pundit who was popular enough among the more conservative-minded to have his own top-rated syndicated talk show.

"Cronkite's daughter was too old for you?" I asked.

If Johnny heard the question he ignored it. He was too anxious to unburden his romantic soul.

He'd met Paula Dresner and her older brother, Neil, only a few weeks before, when they'd dropped in on his Vegas casino. "My PR gal told me Dresner's son and daughter were in the house," Johnny said. "The brother had that rabbity look. You know, Coley. Nervous. Couldn't keep his eyes off the crap tables, all the time licking his lips like Death Valley Scottie passing a Coke machine. Paula wasn't all that worked up about craps. She wanted to see the way the place operated. So I gave her the hundred-dollar tour through the back of the house."

"I assume she didn't inherit her father's looks." Dresner resembled the American eagle wearing a mouse-brown rug.

He gestured with his head toward the bay window. "That's her on the diving board."

Paula Dresner was of average height, but that was the only thing average about her. She was a stunner, with shag-cut black hair framing a sun-bronzed cover-girl face. Her figure was healthy and athletic and very visible above and below the tiny teal-blue spandex suit she wore.

She walked out to the edge of the board and called down to a group of young people who were seated at a poolside table. Once she had their attention, she backed away from the edge, paused, and raced forward. Her perfectly shaped legs tensed as she bounced and took flight temporarily. Her body arched and then, arms extended and head down for the decline, it went arrow rigid. She knifed into the pool, raising barely a ripple.

"So you showed her your casino," I said to break the mood. Johnny sipped at his gin and tonic and said, "While Neil was dropping roughly ten grand, Coley, I was losing my heart."

I studied him to see if he was being facetious, but there wasn't the hint of a twinkle in his eyes. The hard-nosed Vegas gambler who was about as street savvy and cynical as any man I've known had actually said that he'd lost his heart. To a very young woman whose father was somewhere to the right of Cardinal Richelieu.

"How did *she* feel?" I asked.

"Instead of flying back the next morning, she decides to be my guest for the weekend. That's great for us. But not so great for Neil. While we're getting to know one another, he's bouncing checks all over Vegas. Serious loot. Some of my competitors don't like being stiffed. So as soon as I get wind of the rubber, I call the old man. You ought to meet him, Coley. He's some piece of work."

I didn't want to meet him. I didn't even want him on my TV set, twisting facts, insulting honorable men and women, preaching intolerance and stupidity. "Is that your problem?" I asked. "Clearing the kid's credit?"

"No," Johnny said. "Wilton's got a money fountain in his backyard. Hell, his business manager, a guy named Ed Fein, had just skipped after tapping a serious amount of his loot. But the geetus is flowing in so fast from radio and TV and his books and speaking gigs, the vault is self-filling. Wilton had all the cash he needed right on hand. He wired it to me pronto and I collected Neil's markers and shooed away the leg breakers. Then I sent Paula and Neil on their way home."

"There are planes leaving on the half hour to Vegas, as you well know."

"Look, Coley, Neil is Neil. It's Paula I'm concerned about."

"Okay," I said. "Let's hear about Paula."

Johnny didn't answer. Instead he stared into his gin and tonic. I'd never known him to have such trouble getting to the point. "What's the deal?" I asked.

He frowned. "I, uh, sort of committed myself with her."

Committed himself. "What kind of commitment?" I asked.

He gave me one of those mirthless smiles that say, "You're going to think I'm an idiot, but I know what I'm doing." Then he told me that he'd asked her to marry him.

I tried not to wince. "This was when?" I asked.

"That last night in Vegas. She . . . didn't say no. But she didn't say yes, either. She wanted to think about it. For nearly three weeks I don't hear a word. But I know that phoning her isn't a smart play. So I sweat it out. The Utopia coulda burned to the ground and I wouldn't have known it, that's how out of it I was.

"Then, two days ago, she calls. Says she wants to see me.

"She picks me up at the airport. Big kiss. We're gonna have such fun. Yada, yada, yada. I ask her if she's ready for the white dress and she says not to rush her. We drive to this humble little twenty-room shack Wilton's got up on the cliff, looking down on this place. I'm telling you, Coley, it's got everything including a bowling alley."

"The master of the house there to greet you?" I asked.

"Wilton? He was very grateful for the way I handled the Neil thing. After getting burned by this Fein, he's probably feeling a little short on guys he can trust. We get along pretty well. Better than I thought we would. He lends me a Mercedes sedan, gets me guest privileges to his club. The old boy's a damn fine host."

I didn't have the heart to point out that the old boy couldn't have been more than five years his senior. Instead I asked, "What's he think about you and Paula?"

Johnny shrugged. "It hasn't come up. He must know the situation. I expected to have one of those awkward 'what are your intentions?' scenes. But he's just shined it on, which I take to be a good sign."

"Avoidance doesn't always mean approval," I said.

That earned me a frown. "Yeah." Then, proving my point, he added, "Maybe we should order lunch, huh? I hear the kitchen in this joint is pretty good."

So we ate. We watched Paula and her pals frolic by the pool. We watched the maître d' seat a few captains of industry, a bishop, and a retired Western-movie star who had been my boyhood hero. The latter didn't seem to know or care where he was, as long as there was a dark brown cocktail in front of him and guys at his table to laugh at his jokes.

I asked Johnny why there were no women present and he informed me that we were in the men's grill. Women were not allowed.

"That's a quaint concept," I said. "Why did we have to meet *here*? Wasn't there a spare table at the White People's Party lunchroom?"

"This is better for our purposes," he said, not smiling. "I wanted you to get a look at Paula without her seeing you."

"Why?"

"Because I want you to follow her for me."

Ignoring the pained look on his face, I folded my linen napkin and placed it on the tablecloth. "Not my line," I said, starting to slide my chair back. "Hire a private eye."

He reached out and grabbed my wrist like a man grasping at a straw. "Hear me out, huh?"

He was not a teenager with raging hormones who'd been turned down for the prom. He was a middle-aged adult in whom a last, lingering fragment of youth had surfaced and now he was afraid it was slipping away again. And he thought I could help him. That kind of faith deserves a little loyalty. Maybe ten minutes' worth.

I sat down again and waited.

He placed his hands on the table and studied his fingernails as if he expected to find a TelePrompTer on their pink buffed surfaces. He said, "You think I'm being a real asshole, right?"

"It crossed my mind."

"I'm pretty sure she feels the same as I do. She says she does. But something weird's going on and she won't cop to me about it."

"Weird how?"

"I get here and she says she wants my advice about something. She starts to tell me what, but then she clams up. Says it was a mistake to mention it. She can handle it herself. I can't pry it out of her, so I let it slide.

"But I walk into a room and she hangs up the phone. And our stroll along Rodeo Drive suddenly gets canceled because 'something's come up.' And she's an hour late for dinner last night and says she was with a girlfriend."

"Maybe she was."

"Coley, I don't think she's got any girlfriends."

I gestured with my hand toward the gang by the pool.

"Those are just . . . people she hangs out with during the day. They're like kids. She's light-years beyond 'em."

The words *wishful thinking* came to mind but they did not pass my lips. "What's your theory?" I asked.

"I don't have one. That's why I called you, Coley. You're the smartest guy I know at figuring this kind of thing."

The lunch had been lousy. Overcooked and underseasoned. An ache was making a slow move up my neck into my skull. I said, "From what you've told me, I can paint you a pretty broad picture."

"Great. Give." He leaned forward eagerly.

"If there *is* a problem, chances are it has something to do with the brother, since he's the joker in the family deck. You're the guy who smoothed things out for him before, so she gets you on the scene. But she has a change of heart. Maybe the situation has altered. Maybe she just doesn't want to bother you with another of little brother's cock-ups. In any case, she no longer thinks of you as part of the solution. I suggest you make a move to go home. If she stops you, fine, stay. If not, adios."

"She didn't want me here, she'd tell me to split," he shot back, testily.

Nobody really wants advice from friends. They want reassurance. Regardless, I said, "Some people are uncomfortable being that blunt."

He slumped back in his chair, sulking. "She wouldn't have asked me here if she didn't want me here."

"She changed her mind. That's her call. Respect it. Women like to play their own hands these days."

"She's been sheltered by the old man's power and dough," he said. "She doesn't know how to deal with anything too rough. In Vegas, she wanted to tell those guys to eat Neil's notes. Can you imagine Joey Pagan eating a guy's bad marker? If she's trying something like that now . . ."

"So you want me to follow her?" I asked helplessly. "Why not one of your casino cops? They like that kind of work. That's why they went into the business."

"But they're not as smart or as trustworthy," he said. Then he looked away, adding, "And I didn't help them out of a spot when they were down."

The headache nestled in just over my right eye. Across the room, my movie idol was so falling-down drunk it took two waiters and the maître d' to steer him to the door, not that anyone else seemed to notice. I thanked Johnny for the fine lunch and told him I'd follow Paula Dresner. He nodded, but he couldn't look me in the eye.

Outside, the owner of the classic red Alfa was chewing the ear off of Herman Moss, Jr. The sports car had been out in the sun so long the leather seat was like a fry pan. Did Herman want her to burn her legs? But, the boy protested, didn't the lady take her key so that they couldn't move the car? She had, but didn't he have the common sense to cover the seat with a towel? She was going to take the matter up with the club manager.

I waited under the awning until the discussion ended and the Alfa was on its way. Then I joined young Herman near the parking area. "Life's never easy, is it?" I said.

"Not when you have to put up with people like that."

"Will she really report you to the manager?"

"Absolutely," he said. "But he won't do nothing. She complains about everything. If her old man wasn't so famous on the TV, they wouldn't even let her through the front door."

"Is her old man the one who gave her the car for her birthday?" I asked.

He nodded. "She's got everything she wants, but she's still gotta gripe and complain all the time. Lucky everybody knows Paula Dresner for what she is—a troublemaker."

Not everybody, I mumbled to myself.

2

THE TROUBLEMAKER AND I began our distant relationship the following morning, less than an hour after I'd found a nice waiting place down the road a piece from the main gate of her father's Bay City Heights estate. I was glad she got an early start on the day. One tends to feel a little conspicuous in that neighborhood sitting in a vehicle that isn't carrying lawn-mowing equipment.

The Dresner home, squatting precariously on a grassy cliff up above Pacific Coast Highway, was concrete proof that radio ranting pays. It was not as grotesquely ornate as the beach "cottage" William Randolph Hearst once built for Marion Davies, but it was from the same era. It was almost as tasteful as it was big, surrounded by trees and brightened by colorful flowers.

Architecturally, it looked more East Coastish than California ranch style. It had that touch of dignity that a former fish peddler named Ike Marcus was seeking back in the late twenties just after his Global Studios celebrated its first multimillion-dollar year. Ike visited the track every day of his retired life, which is how I met him. He loved horses, but he loved his house more, with its bowling alley and man-made babbling brook. He must've flipped over in his coffin hard enough to cause a blip on the Richter the day that anti-Semitic broadcast demagogue Wilton Dresner moved in.

Ike, who never lost his eye for the ladies, may have felt differently about Paula Dresner. That morning she looked spectacular, expensively sunglassed and dressed to the nines, not sparing a glance for the parked maroon Jeep Cherokee as she roared by. She appeared not to have a care in the world. Whatever problem she was concealing from Johnny, it wasn't adding even one frown wrinkle to that lovely brow.

The first thing I discovered about the lady was that she led a charmed life behind the wheel of that tomato-colored tin can she was driving. At the foot of the hill, she got tired of the red light and ran it, crossing two very busy lanes of the Pacific Coast Highway. I waited for a considerably safer break in traffic and followed.

That was just the first indication of the kind of driver she was— aggressive, daring, and unforgiving, navigating Southern California like it was downtown Rome. She didn't always signal her sudden lane changes, and any motorist who put a crimp in her forward progress could expect the finger in retaliation. If I had ridden horses that way, I'd have beaten Ike to Forest Lawn.

All things considered, the last thing I expected her to do on that sunny morning was go to church. But her first stop was a Unitarian/Universalist sanctuary where the marquee out front said they were holding a class in inner peace. It may have involved yoga or meditation or something even weirder, like rock-candy crystals. I didn't get close enough to find out.

If the booster shot of inner peace had any influence on her aggressive driving style, it was not apparent. She continued to aim the Alfa like a bullet, miraculously finding parking spaces whenever she wished to stop and shop. Maybe that's how she picked her boutiques, by their available parking spots. In any case, more than once, I wound up double-parked with drivers honking and shouting at me to move on.

Finally, Paula decided she was hungry and we coasted into a parking lot belonging to Chirashizuki, a hot new Japanese restaurant on Melrose where they served raw fish and pickled vegetables in lacquer boxes. I waited in the Cherokee as she hopped from the Alfa. Before her feet touched the asphalt, the doors of four other cars, a Porsche, a Ferrari, and a couple of Range Rovers, had opened. Their half-dozen inhabitants dashed over to greet her with hugs and kisses. It was the star treatment. Luncheon didn't start until Paula got there.

The friends were what I would have expected. Young. Stylish. Sophisticated. Wealthy enough that they could spend a few hours chewing raw sea scrod without worrying about getting back to an office. Like the crowd around the pool at the Bay City Beach Club. Probably some of the same ones. They were the sort of group that used to be called a set but was then referred to as a posse. It was hard to imagine Johnny Rousseau being comfortable around them. His kind of people come in parties and groups and even gangs, not in posses.

I didn't try to follow Paula and her pals into Chirashizuki. Instead I drove the Jeep into an empty slot that afforded a clear view of the restaurant's door and stayed behind the wheel.

It took the carpark five minutes to join me. He was a tall thin lad with a bad haircut, a thick Middle Eastern accent, and an attitude. "You going to restaurant?" he asked.

"Nope," I said.

"You can not park here, you don't go into restaurant."

I passed him a five-dollar bill. That seemed to satisfy him, but he asked, "Why you do this?"

"I'm eccentric."

He scowled at that and went off scratching his bad hair.

He parked a few cars and came back. "Why you no go into restaurant?"

"I thought we went all through that," I said. "I'm a guy who likes parking lots better than I like sushi."

"Taste like wet rubber," he said, and grinned suddenly.

"What do you eat?"

"Big Mac," he said, and went off to relieve a couple of their Lamborghini.

I decided I'd never make it as a cop or a private eye. The waiting game was definitely not for me. I almost convinced myself that I should just prance into the joint and put on a feedbag in the stall next to the posse. Sure it'd be risky. But I'd had a light breakfast and was growing dizzy from lack of chow. And this crowd was so self-obsessed, they wouldn't notice me if I were wearing an Abe Lincoln stovepipe hat.

But I didn't go in. I tapped the horn and waved the now friendly carhike over. "Yes?" he asked.

"How far is it to the nearest Big Mac?"

"Just down the block."

"Why don't you go get us each one?" I asked.

"I could not desert my post," he said.

I gave him a tenner. "One for you, one for me and keep the change."

He grabbed the bill and was off like a shot. While he was gone a Bentley and a Beemer drove in. I hopped out of the Jeep and parked them. Then I paused at Paula's Alfa and took a peek in the glove compartment. An unopened pack of cigarettes, scattered gas-station receipts, several pens, and a business card belonging to one *Jerry Woo, Photography—By Appointment Only.* There was a phone number but no address. Jerry Woo evidently didn't want anybody just dropping by.

I was getting back into the Jeep when the lot attendant returned with a big brown bag with red-and-yellow arches on its side.

"You park my cars?" he asked, alarmed.

"Yeah," I told him. "But don't worry. I'm a professional."

He handed me a soft drink, a burger, and a tiny doll that looked like Arnold Schwarzenegger in a space suit, with a little suction cup attached to his space shoes. "What's this?" I asked.

"This from a new motion picture. They give free with the Big Mac," the attendant told me. "I have one, too. See?"

"What I see is a Jag over there that just drove in," I told him, and he raced away.

I stuck the little Arnold on the dash and devoured my Big Mac and laughed at all the people who were inside Chirashizuki stuck with eating trout tartar, or whatever was the raw catch of the day.

Somehow Paula's crew stretched out the meal for over two hours. Then they came bursting through the door, knocking each other out with bad sushi-chef imitations. An unnaturally thin bunch, I realized, like many of the Southern California rich. Strikingly handsome from a distance, but gaunt and undernourished up close. That kind of svelte means you eat about as much as a jockey with a weight problem and you don't drink at all. Maybe you get a little dietary help from something filling but nonfattening, like drugs.

I was surprised to see the posse saddling up and moving out before Paula. The guest of honor is supposed to depart the party first after arriving last, and judging by their attitude and hers, Paula was life's guest of honor. But somehow she managed to convince them to abandon her at the door of the restaurant. After she'd waved good-bye to them, she ducked back inside.

When she came out fifteen minutes later, I had a surprise. Apparently Chirashizuki provided dressing rooms for its key customers. Gone was the flashy outfit, replaced by a pair of jeans and a black turtleneck. She still looked ready to send a *Vogue* photographer into Kodak heaven, but this was her version of dressing down. I dared to hope that we might be moving on to a destination that would prove more fruitful to my investigation.

No such luck. The Horseshoe Theater was a tiny building on Santa Monica Boulevard. I was familiar with the place. I knew the guy who ran it, a racing buff named Gus Hosmer who taught acting classes to pay for his experimental stage productions and even more experimental handicapping.

I gave Paula a few minutes after she strolled into the building. Then I slipped out of the Cherokee and followed her in. I was taking a chance, getting that close to her. But if I continued to stick to my car, how much useful information would I get? Besides, I was damned fed up with the waiting game.

Gus was in his office, which is the size of a ticket booth and actually doubles as one when he's got a play on the boards. He was sitting at a laptop concentrating mightily on something on the screen. I knocked and said, "Is this where Dustin Hoffman got his start?"

Gus was wearing a Shakespeare sweatshirt over paint-stained denims. The hair on his chin was bushy, on his head marine-corps short. He looked up at me over his granny glasses and smiled broadly.

"Coley Killebrew!" he said, getting to his feet, wiping his hands, and extending his right for a shake. "Lookin' good, guy. You oughta get back in the saddle again so I can blow some more money on you."

"Been away from it too long to go back, Gus."

"Bullshit. Didn't you see where Bill Harmatz took a mount down at Del Mar last season?"

"Sure. One mount."

"But the guy's sixty-two, hadn't ridden a race since 1971. You're still a young guy, Coley, and you haven't been away that long."

"He ran seventh."

"So? You can't blame that on him. Nag was forty-seven-to-one."

"Who do you think talked Harmatz into doing a crazy thing like that?" I wondered.

"The way I heard it, some trainer friend told him he should come back and exercise horses to keep himself in shape. Harmatz decided dodging green exercise riders in the morning was so dangerous, he might as well ride a race in the afternoon. It seemed safer to him."

"Sounds like he lost a bet with somebody to me," I said. While we were talking a few more young beauties of both sexes walked past the window, waving to Gus as they went by. He checked his watch and said, "Wish I could jaw some more, Coley, but I got a class of budding thespians waiting for me in there."

"Any with talent?" I asked innocently.

He wagged his eyebrows like Groucho Marx. "Some of the ladies got talent they've barely begun to use."

"But can they act?"

"One or two aren't that bad. Come and watch the class if you want."

"Can I?" I acted surprised, but it was what I'd hoped for.

"Sure. Look, it'd help my scam if they think you're a producer."

"Do I look like a producer?" I asked. "Where's my backward baseball cap or my tailored denims?"

He nodded. "Yeah, maybe we'd better hide you in the back row. If they see you, let 'em try to guess who you are."

So I got to watch from the shadows as Gus put the lovely Paula through her paces along with four men and three other women, none of whom I recognized. This was quite a different crowd from Paula's lunch mates. For one thing, they looked less affluent; it was probably a struggle for some of them to scrape together the money for Gus's acting lessons. For another, they looked dedicated and eager, even if such eagerness was for the most part not merited.

They spent some time pretending to be trees, then birds, then lizards, before Gus had them read two- and three-character scenes from plays I'd never heard of. I reminded myself not only to stay away from police work but never to take acting classes.

I could tell from the opening tree sequence that Johnny's girlfriend was a long shot to finish in the money as an actress. One of her classmates, a tall, skinny redhead, had the talent to go the distance, but she lacked Paula's push and determination. And family money.

Regardless of how stiff and awkward Paula was, she behaved as if she was certain she was going to be the next Julia Roberts, and Gus, who had the artistic integrity of an infomercial pitchman, did everything he could to encourage her delusion. He favored her shamelessly, giving her twice as long as anybody else to do her readings, all of which were, in a word, lousy.

In the middle of a scene involving a married couple sharing the Sunday paper, Paula stopped and addressed her mentor.

"Gus, when my character asks her husband to pass the TV section, where's she coming from? I'm not finding her inner life here."

"Sometimes you have to provide that," Gus said carefully. "Out of your own experience."

"I think I have a take on her motivation, Paula," the guy playing her husband said.

"Oh, really?" she replied, doing a fine job of registering bored exasperation.

"Yeah, she wants to look at the TV section." Some of the other students laughed. Paula certainly didn't, and Gus tried not to.

"Look," Paula said, "she's trying to convince her husband to steal from his boss. The section of the paper she asks for has to mean something. The playwright wouldn't just pick a prop at random, would he? The television section has to have some significance about her state of mind. Like the word *television*, broken down means teleporting your vision, looking into the future. Just like she's plotting out the course of the conversation, the perfect way to get him to steal the money so that she can be happy. With him or without him."

"That's good, Paula. Inventive," Gus said quickly, before anyone could jump in with a withering remark. "I think you should go with that. Pick it up from that line."

The male students seemed amused by Paula. The other women obviously resented her. Especially the redhead, who was getting tired of looking at the back of Gus's haircut.

The session finally ended. A few of the students cast their eyes back into the shadows where I was sitting, wondering who I was.

No one attempted to talk to me, though, to slip me their agent's phone number, or whip out a portfolio. I needed that baseball cap, I guess. Paula was concentrating so heavily on Gus she never even looked my way.

When the class was over and the students had reluctantly drifted out through the small theater's lobby, Gus asked me if I wanted a couple of tickets to his new production.

"What are you doing?" I asked.

"*Lysistrata*. Greek comedy by Aristophanes."

"Sounds boring. But I guess you don't have to pay a royalty."

"The hell I don't. What do you think, we're doing it in Greek? I have to pay for rights to the translation. And if you think it sounds boring, you obviously never saw *Lysistrata*. The broads are sick of all the fighting, see, so they get together and decide to cut the guys off until they put an end to war. Great, huh? It has classical snob value and potential for all kinds of sex and skin. There was a production in L.A. back in the thirties that was closed by the police, to give you an idea. I'm planning to get well on this one."

We were standing by a small window that faced the street. Through it, I saw Paula Dresner chatting with the guy who'd played her husband in the scene. "Is she in the play?"

He approached the window, looked out and made a face. "Are you kidding? I'll take her loot, sure, but put her on the stage? What kind of theater do you think I'm running?"

"With her looks, she oughta be good for a bit part in a show like that."

"That's the rub, though. She wouldn't settle for any bit part. She'd have to be the star or nothing."

"How well do you know her?"

Gus threw me a sly grin and shook his head. "Sorry, buddy. I can't fix you up with her. One of the others maybe, but with her, you're on your own. Her father's Wilton Dresner. The guy who makes Rush Limbaugh look like a pinko?"

"You ought to try and get him in one of your plays."

"I bet he'd make a damn good Richard the Third, at that," Gus said with a chuckle.

I stuck the tickets in my wallet—maybe I could get a tall blonde of my acquaintance to go with me—and said a quick good-bye to Gus Hosmer.

On Santa Monica Boulevard, some of the students were standing around talking, but the group was breaking up. I spotted the Alfa pulling out into traffic and hurried to the Cherokee.

The redhead broke ranks with the others and moved to intercept me. But I was too quick for her. I was sorry I wasn't a producer who could give her the break she deserved. It was her bad fortune that I was just another fake and that she'd picked a business where luck often counts more than talent.

The rest of the afternoon made the morning seem rife with adventure. But I felt I was getting to know Paula a little better, albeit not up close. Shadowing her was a primer in the rich-girl lifestyle. Wherever she went and whatever she wore, she looked perfect. She moved through every social situation as smoothly and as confidently as she'd made that dive at the Bay City Beach Club. As long as she had her rightful place as the center of everybody's attention, she was downright pleasant and sunny.

We headed back toward Bay City just ahead of the heaviest traffic. I took her as far as the last turn leading to her father's house. Johnny was steering his borrowed Mercedes up the hill a few cars in front of her, so I ducked into a drive, did an about-face, and headed for the Horse's Neck. Let lover boy watch over her for the rest of the night. I had a business to run.

And business at the Horse's Neck was good. My initial fear that we wouldn't draw customers had been dispelled long ago. And month after month we'd made a steady, slightly increasing profit. While I checked in with the staff and glad-handed the patrons, my mind kept drifting back to the weird assignment Johnny had given me.

I was starting to wonder how long I could keep up the surveillance. If Paula Dresner didn't reveal her secret problem pretty soon—and I was beginning to wonder if Johnny was imagining it all—eventually she had to notice me. If a guy in a maroon Jeep Cherokee was on your tail wherever you went, after a while you'd pick up on it, even if you spent most of your time looking at yourself in the rearview mirror. I'd done what I could to blend into the palm trees, but I was no pro at the snooping game. And, at my size, I was not what you'd call average looking.

One thing I could do would be to vary my wheels. Only half seriously, I asked the maître d' of the Neck, a veteran British actor named Jack Hayward, about the availability of his ancient Sunbeam Alpine.

"Borrow my chariot?" he asked in his impeccable British accent. "Coley, my esteem for you knows no bounds, as you surely must realize. But a motorcar is a very personal thing. And as they age, even as we, they take on quirks and odd tempers. Much as I love her, she needs special handing, a certain knowing, familiar touch to achieve maximum performance. Approached key in hand by a driver of a Jeep, how would she respond? Would she satisfy?"

"Jack, I'm asking to borrow your car, not sleep with your mistress."

He laughed, his chubby jowls shaking. "Can't help you there either, I'm afraid. Seriously, Coley, I'll need her tomorrow. My agent called, and I'll be reading for a denture-adhesive commercial."

"Dentures? For a man of your distinction?"

"It helps to recall Larry Olivier's camera pitch at times like this," he said. "What's wrong with your Cherokee, anyway? Confined to its wigwam?"

"No, I just feel the need to be inconspicuous tomorrow."

"Ahhh. Doing a bit of sleuthing, are you?"

"A very little bit."

"Inconspicuous," he muttered. "Hmmm. You must be shadowing someone, eh? A subtle disguise might help."

"Yeah, right. A false nose and glasses maybe?"

"No, no. You can do wonders with much less. Wear a dodger cap, sometimes bill forward, sometimes bill to the back. Makes a world of difference. Take a change of T-shirt, but nothing with a terribly memorable slogan on it. And for heaven's sake, borrow a car more versatile in tight situations than mine."

It was true. I couldn't imagine keeping up with Paula's driving habits in the old Sunbeam Jack drove in such stately fashion.

"Ever do a play called *Lysistrata*, Jack?"

"Oh, indeed, yes. And doesn't that stir up memories? It isn't staged much, you know. Rather controversial. Brings out the censors. I remember a production in Birmingham many years ago. The leading lady's knickers—"

The arrival of a pair of middle-aged diners interrupted the flow of Jack's golden memory. The couple remembered him from his 1950s con-man TV series and were enormously impressed. He's an asset to the business, even if he is a washout as a supplier of surveillance vehicles.

So the next day I said good morning to the little Arnold figure on the dash and made do with the Cherokee.

Paula's and my first stop of the A.M. was an aerobics class at Susanna's Salon, a Beverly Hills health club that catered to body-proud celebrities. This class she didn't dress down for, strolling into the place in a garishly colored spandex outfit Flo Jo might have found a little flamboyant.

She was in the salon for just under an hour, during which time little Arnold and I had several chats about "pomping up." When she exited, the workout garb had been transferred to the sports bag she carried, and her substitute outfit was more along the lines of the shop-and-lunch wear of the day before.

And shop and lunch she did, along Rodeo Drive, where she

spent the rest of the morning trying to use up as much of her father's ill-gotten gains as she could. The salespeople greeted her like their ship coming in.

Luncheon that day was on Beverly Boulevard in a restaurant called Skippy's. That may sound like a forties coffee shop, but as I found out when I was seated at a table near Paula's, the moniker was deceptive. As the menu clearly pointed out, Skippy's was named for the Lab retriever on a popular TV situation comedy and was the creation of the hound's owner, a gent obviously more impressed by the artistic presentation of food than by its quality.

There used to be quite a few of those temples to California cuisine in operation, but tough economic times had thinned the ranks. Skippy's, however, soldiered on, doling out miserly portions so lovingly designed they should have been hanging in the Norton Simon Museum. If the restaurant folded, the other employees might be out of work, but the chef would be a short price to get a National Endowment for the Arts grant. Better that than have him work in a place like the Horse's Neck where the customers like to eat.

After getting a refill of the bread basket, the one saving grace of Skippy's pretentious menu, I glanced over at Paula's table. She was holding sway over a different bunch of friends from yesterday's, but clearly cut from the same cloth. They were a foursome, three quarters female. The other two women were about Paula's age, dressed with a casualness as expensive as her own but outclassed in every other way. The guy had the kind of looks you see on soap operas and the covers of romance novels.

Paula was doing most of the talking. There was a lot of laughter with no urgency to any of it. Whatever her hidden problem was, it had nothing to do with these people. And the cover boy, hunk though he was, was no rival to Johnny. He didn't seem to be paired with Paula, or with either of the others, for that matter.

"What's this we hear about your new *boy*-friend, Pa-ou-la?" he asked, mockingly.

"Hear from who?"

"Clemmie."

"She's so fuckstrated. We bumped into her and what's-his-face, Byron, at dinner the other night. Byron's making like Mr. Groin and she's doing her muffy."

"Pink bow?" the boy asked.

"Yellow," Paula replied. "This late in the season, too. Anyway, to answer your question, my beau is a real hoss. Very male. Industrial. Cranking fun."

"But how well does he hide the salam'?" one of the girls asked.

"You'll never know," Paula said. "That's why I'm not about to intro him to you bozettes. You'd probably go agro and drool on his hand, like Clemmie."

"Clemmie says he's a grayhair," the guy said.

"Clemmy's a C-word, two times over. He's forty-something and you ought to see him in a dinner jacket. Cream-jeans, for true. A real Mel."

Ah, the articulate younger generation. Well, from what I could decipher, at least Paula was taking up for old grayhair Johnny.

A Latin busboy approached their table with a pitcher of mimosa-scented tea while Paula was in the middle of a long description of something inconsequential that happened to her at acting class. He began filling their glasses and Paula paused and stared at him until he'd finished, a rigid smile on her face.

After witnessing her mini-tantrum in the parking area of the Bay City Beach Club, I was surprised that, instead of ragging on him and the other service personnel, she treated them all to a rather bad performance of Lady Bountiful. "Thank you so much for the tea," she told this one as he backed away, smiling nervously. "It's delicious."

I guessed she was on her best behavior with her pals around. But there was an edge to her graciousness. Mount Saint Paula might erupt anytime some menial crossed her, and they seemed to sense it. I hear from my own employees that if you wait on people long enough you develop a nose for customers like that.

The rest of the afternoon added nothing new to my Paula file. All of her usual haunts—stores, restaurants, homes of friends— were in the upscale parts of the city, and her comings and goings had given me nothing to suggest an answer to Johnny's question.

But just as I'd convinced myself that she was nothing more than a carefree rich girl and Johnny was playing a wrong horse, she deviated from her routine. First, she drove to a store on Fairfax called Split Seconds. It was a used-clothing shop. A banner was stuck to its display window that read MOVIE WARDROBE FOR SALE.

Paula opened the Alfa's small trunk and withdrew an assortment of boxes, some of them the items she'd purchased just the day before. She carried them into Split Seconds.

I moved to the storefront window. Past the nicely draped if oddly bald-headed mannequins I saw Paula standing beside a hard-looking middle-aged woman who was examining the contents of the boxes.

The woman didn't seem impressed. Paula removed a bracelet she was wearing. The woman smiled and she and Paula retired to a room at the rear of the store.

I returned to my Jeep. Ten minutes later Paula left the shop. She still wasn't heading for home. Instead she led me far outside her normal sphere, north on the San Diego Freeway to a dreary, run-down suburb in the San Fernando Valley called New Hope. It'd been built to house the families of GIs returning from World War II. But in the intervening years, their upwardly mobile offspring had moved on to fashionable addresses in towns like Encino and Woodland Hills, while New Hope had become the last refuge of the newly hopeless.

At about 7:15 P.M., the red Alfa braked in front of a graffiti-sprayed office building, one of a row of similarly defaced neighbors. Paula got out of the car and walked purposefully through the front door of the building, leaving me in the Cherokee to ponder the graffiti from an eyestraining distance.

I know it's fatal to the tone of a neighborhood, but graffiti with style and originality at least has some entertainment value. The name of one of the taggers was Kid Cliché. I guessed he had more self-awareness than most of his fellow spraypaint Rembrandts.

Paula Dresner was in the building for about fifteen minutes. When she came out, she didn't seem to be the same Paula I'd been tailing for the past few days. For once, she wasn't in control. She was disoriented, like a pedigreed cat shaken suddenly from a tree. She had something clutched in her hand that looked like a glossy eight-by-ten photo. I was too far away to make out the subject.

She seemed to have lost her sense of direction, starting one way, then stopping abruptly, frozen in her tracks. Finally she sighted the red Alfa and rushed to it as if it were a rescue ship suddenly exposed by a lifting fog.

"What do you think, Arnold?" I asked the little plastic figurine on my dash, "do I follow her or do I stay and see what's going on inside the building?"

The answer was easy. I watched her sail away. "Hasta la vista, baby," I said.

The name over the entry to the edifice read, in broken letters, THE LIVELY ARTS BUILDING. A closed and locked Luther's Dance Studio occupied the ground level. It didn't seem the kind of place Paula would choose for fox-trot lessons.

The stairwell smelled like a gym, and I wouldn't have been surprised to stumble over a homeless squatter along the way. But they'd probably found better rest stops.

The deserted Harry Batson Talent Agency—not, I was sure, a major player in the biz—shared the second floor with Lubin Industrials, whatever that might be. Nobody at home in either establishment.

The top floor was split between two minor industries. Eldon's Collectibles had a sign reading WHOLESALE TO TRADE ONLY and a locked door. Judging by the neighborhood, I figured Eldon might

easily be a fence. The other door proclaimed JERRY WOO, PHOTOG-
RAPHY. Bingo. His card had been in Paula's car.

I knocked.

No answer.

The door was unlocked. I opened it a few inches. A dim light
gave the place a shadowy film noir look. I called out, "Yoo hoo,
Mr. Woo." No reply, except my own chuckle of self-amusement.

I opened the door fully and entered as if I knew exactly what
I was doing. The light was coming from a fluorescent lamp on a
chrome-and-glass desk. It illuminated an assortment of framed
horse photographs hanging on the mottled walls and, on the deck,
hundreds of photo contact sheets scattered around as if someone
had been hastily searching for something.

Had Paula been ransacking the place, looking for that eight-by-
ten she'd taken out with her? If she found what she was looking
for, why had she appeared so blown away by the experience?

I focused in on the framed photographs of the horses. They
were all beautiful animals, caught in stunning action. Scanning
them, I noticed a very odd discrepancy in the selection. But I put
that on hold while I did a tour of the Woo suite.

There was a closed door to the right of the desk that led into
what was apparently Jerry Woo's living quarters. Judging by the
stale cooking smells and dust motes, I gathered that the photographer was not a world-class housekeeper. But even with that, the
place shouldn't have looked the way it did.

The sofa bed had been gutted, the cushion covers slit, with
stuffing strewn all over the floor. A couple dozen books had been
thrown from a shelf. In the kitchenette, an empty refrigerator sat
against one wall with open door, its pale light shining down accusingly on ice trays, a milk carton, and broken eggs, all decorating
a speckled blue linoleum floor.

That brought me to the biggest article of debris in the wasted
apartment. He was lying on his back, blocking the entrance to the
kitchenette. His face was twisted with a pain he no longer no-

ticed. One arm was across his chest, the other pointed straight out from his body. There was no blood, no obvious bruises. I couldn't tell what had killed him, but sure as hell something had.

Frowning, I hunkered down beside the corpse. The name Woo had led me to expect a Chinese, but the dead man was a Caucasian. Probably in his late twenties or early thirties. He wore wide sky-blue pastel slacks and a dark blue polo shirt. His body was still warm to the touch, but not warm enough to have been killed in the last fifteen or twenty minutes. The sight of him must have been what had knocked Paula Dresner out of her usual glacial state. I doubted that she'd killed him. For Johnny's sake, I hoped she hadn't.

Something about the corpse's right foot was a puzzler. The sock was turned inside out and a shoe tassel was jammed between the shoe and the sock. No conscious human being could have put up with a lump like that in his shoe. So he hadn't been walking around that way.

Then I spotted the oxblood-colored wallet resting on the floor like a downed bird, wings spread. I pulled out a handkerchief and used it to pick up the wallet. *Jerome Woolrich*, the driver's license said under the dead man's photo; the address was the same as the office/apartment. Also present were thirty-four dollars, half a MasterCard, a press pass to Del Mar Racetrack, and a fifty-brew-free card from the bar at Santa Rosita Raceway, with three beer mugs punched. I put back the wallet.

Beside the sofa bed was an empty plastic folder about the size of a stack of photographs. What looked like its former contents, seven glossies, were on top of the bed. They'd been taken at a stable at various times of the day and night. Horses in their stalls. Stable hands at work. I didn't recognize the location. I wondered if Paula's eight-by-ten had come from this batch and, if so, what it might mean.

Then I stopped asking questions about the photos and corpse and the apartment and asked one of myself. Why was I hanging around and acting like a detective? This wasn't any of my business. Not with a dead body in it. That much I didn't owe Johnny. It was time to get out of there, past time in fact. I stood up, turning back toward the door to the outer office.

I paused by the scattered books that I'd just glanced at the first time through. They weren't photography manuals. They were all on one subject: the Sport of Kings. A couple of recent volumes of the *American Racing Manual*, the industry's reference book of record. Several coffee-table pictorial histories. Handicapping treatises by Tom Ainslie and Andrew Beyer. A biography of Secretariat. I flashed back to those horse portraits in the other room, remembering what had struck me as odd about them.

Returning to Woo's office, I had another look at the photos. All famous runners of recent years. Alysheba, Ferdinand, Winning Colors, John Henry, Sunday Silence. Which one didn't belong? Old John H. was one of the most exciting and versatile runners I ever saw, but he didn't win the Kentucky Derby, and all those others did.

I studied the John Henry photo a bit more closely, examining its frame. Using my handkerchief again, I gently removed it from the wall. There was another photo taped behind it. Of a racehorse and a jockey.

It's not true, as some people believe, that all Thoroughbreds look alike. A horse person can glimpse two virtually identical bays and tell them apart by subtle physical characteristics. I didn't recognize this one, though. I did know the jock, a contemporary of mine named Luis Falcon. The photo was mainly devoted to horse and rider, but over Falcon's shoulder I could see a sign reading LAND O' LINCOLN RACEWAY and, in digital lettering, the time—4:28 P.M., the date— May 19, 1992, and the odds for the sixth race.

Sure, it intrigued me. Why among the racing blue bloods a photo of an ordinary horse snapped after an ordinary race—and why hidden behind another? But, I reminded myself, it was none of my business.

As I was replacing the frame I heard a screech of brakes from the street below. I moved to the window. A police car was parked directly beneath me. Two uniformed cops got out.

One of them looked up toward the window suddenly, and I leaped back out of sight. I didn't think he'd seen me, but I was sure the pair were headed my way, and I wanted nothing to do with them.

Mentally calling myself obscene names for not having left as soon as I'd found Woo's body, and calling Johnny worse names for getting me into this mess, I wiped my fingerprints from the office door and, using the handkerchief, pushed through it and out onto the landing. As I did, the downstairs door squeaked open.

The cops seemed to be moving cautiously. So I had been seen. Time for a bit of misdirection.

Not trying to be quiet, I clumped across the hall to the door of Eldon's Collectibles, raised my foot, and with the help of an adrenaline rush born of desperation kicked in the door. I darted into the shadowy offices.

There were cartons of junk all over the place, and the floor was strewn with those plastic peanuts people use to protect objects from uncaring hands at the post office. I slammed the door behind me and headed for the windows. Through one of them I saw a rusty fire escape. Unfortunately, the window was painted shut.

On a table nearby rested four plaster statues, each of them about a foot and a half high. Elvis. John Wayne. Marilyn Monroe. Humphrey Bogart. Bogey seemed the most likely ally in a film noir situation like this, so hand wrapped in handkerchief, I scooped up his statue and used it to break the window. Hopping out onto the fire escape, I rolled Bogey down the steps while I tiptoed up.

The roof of the Lively Arts Building was simple asphalt. I crossed it carefully and quietly. I could hear the cops clambering down the metal fire escape in hot pursuit of the Bogey doll. That could only deter them for so long. My best course of action was to vacate the premises immediately.

The roof of the neighboring building was six or eight feet lower than the one I was on. It seemed an easy enough leap for a professional athlete, even a retired one. I might not have been in top shape, but I hadn't let myself go completely.

I made the jump in one piece, ending with a kind of self-protective roll we practiced when thousand-pound Thoroughbreds landed us in the dirt. It makes it easier when there's not a field of horses following close behind to trample you. My pants were torn and one elbow scraped, and I picked up plenty of dust, but I did okay.

Panting only moderately, I located my new building's fire escape and descended quickly. As I did I scanned the ground below for any sign of the police. I didn't see them, but I knew they'd be doing something smarter than Mirandizing the Bogey doll. I didn't feel home free just yet, but I was on my way.

I circled the block and strolled up to the Cherokee as if my conscience were as clear as Plexiglas. As I slipped behind the steering wheel, winking at little Arnold, an unmarked police car pulled in next to the squad car and unloaded its team of plainclothes homicide detectives. Jerry Woo would have lots of company that night.

3

ON THE WAY back to the Horse's Neck, I obeyed the traffic laws to the letter, glancing through my rearview mirror for black-and-whites. As I pulled into the restaurant's parking lot, waved through to my reserved space by the valets, almost without realizing it, I made the transition from fugitive to restaurateur. My worries about police apprehension were replaced with the greedy notion that all those cars meant a very good early seating. We were probably at capacity, a matter of considerably more importance than some dead photographer in New Hope. Or so I almost convinced myself.

Ordinarily I would have stopped in the cocktail lounge to talk over tomorrow's racing card with the horse players who hung out there. But that night I sneaked in the back way. I gave myself the excuse that, after rolling around the rooftops, my tattered appearance would be a public-relations mistake. But, in fact, I just wasn't up to the jolly-host bit.

I saluted the kitchen staff and fled up the back stairway to my apartment, an airy two-bedroom space over the restaurant, small, but just right for me.

The apartment would measure up to a pricey suite in a good hotel. In fact, sometimes it reminded me too much of a hotel suite. I hadn't really put much of an imprint on it. There were a few relics of my truncated riding career, photos and trophies, but not many. The best of them were displayed for the customers downstairs in the bar.

Most of the time the apartment seemed comfortable and homey. That night it was a welcome refuge.

A glance at the mirror told me I didn't look quite as disreputable as I'd feared. Still, I tossed my smudged clothes in a corner of the closet and stepped into the shower. While a fine, hot needle spray pelted my body, I sang a medley of pre–Sergeant Pepper Beatles songs. I did my best to behave like a guy who'd never heard of Jerry Woo and hadn't been anywhere near New Hope in months.

Comfortably dressed and in somewhat higher spirits, I began to wonder about the New Hope police. What made them show up at Woo's? Had they been tipped off? By Paula Dresner? What was their take on the body? How had Woo been killed?

This was the wrong thing to be thinking about. What I had to do was to phone Johnny, fill him in, and get myself out of the following–Paula Dresner business.

I was sitting on the couch mulling over how much to tell Johnny about my evening, and how to phrase what I did tell, when the phone rang. As I reached for it, I mentally ticked off all the unwelcome possibilities of who could be on the other end, starting with the LAPD. Owing to my pessimism, the name that should have been on top wasn't even on the list.

"Hi, Coley," my girlfriend Lea said.

"Hello, honey. Never in my life have I been so happy to hear your voice."

"Why's that?"

"Because of who you are. And who you aren't."

"And who aren't I?"

"Anybody else who might have called me."

"Tough day, huh?"

"You could say that," I told her. "Tonight we'll make up for it."

I have to tell you about Lea Starbuck. Since I'd met her about a year before, she'd hardly been out of my thoughts, though not nearly often enough in my company. I think the word might be *besotted*, though it's not one I ever expected to tag myself with again. Not after my painful and educational experiences with women, including the one who'd framed me out of my career as a jockey. When I thought about my feelings for Lea, I could understand better Johnny's thing for Paula Dresner. The difference was I was sure he was going to lose his shirt, but I was betting on a winner.

The Beach Boys might have had Lea in mind when they sang their paean to California girls. She was blond. She was beautiful. And she certainly was tall. Five-eleven. Sure, a jockey pairing up with a tall woman is a living cliché, but look at it this way: almost all women are taller than me, so if I was going to be towered over anyway, why not take it to the limit?

Actually, regardless of size and beauty, she was self-sufficient, smart as a whip, and graceful and athletic and compassionate and . . . but you get the idea. I was besotted.

Still, all that self-sufficiency had its downside. Lea was a loner. So was I. She'd been burned in her past encounters with the opposite sex. So had I. She was afraid of no one and nothing. Except emotional commitment. And I wasn't too crazy about jumping headfirst either.

These were the wrong attributes for a hopeful couple to have in common, but we'd found out early that we laughed at the same things and were serious about the same things, so maybe we could rise above it.

The way I had it figured, our main problem had nothing to do with Lea or myself. Our stumbling block was her father— Raymond Edgar Starbuck, the guy who'd personally banned me from racing. He had been the head of the California Racing Commission at the time. He wasn't in that position anymore.

For the past few years he'd been acting as a sort of trouble-shooter for the racing industry, and during that time the Sport of Kings had had plenty of trouble to shoot, with other forms of gambling putting so much pressure on owners and trainers that some of the levels of morality had worn pretty thin.

Lea worked for her father. The three of us had been involved in a messy job in Louisiana that ended with me in a position to get my jockey license back. If things broke just right, that is, and if I wanted it. I hadn't really come to any definite decision.

Starbuck, not a man to admit when he's wrong, still didn't trust me very much and was about as fond of me as I was of him. We might have gotten along better if Lea and I had not embarked on our relationship. Since his wife's death, Starbuck had come to depend on Lea to be his companion, his confidante, and his good right hand. I could sympathize with that, but I didn't think it very healthy for a parent to assume he would be the sole recipient of his daughter's devotion. Especially since Starbuck was physically sound enough to make a life for himself.

He'd been keeping Lea so busy, she hadn't had much time for me. But tonight was going to be different. Tonight she was having dinner with me at the Horse's Neck, to enjoy the theatrical flourishes of Jack Hayward, to marvel at the culinary creations of Chef Antony, to finish off a bottle of vintage wine from one of the best cellars in California. And then, with a little luck on my part, she would be joining me upstairs. Tonight the lovely Lea was mine. Or so I thought.

"I'm sorry, Coley," she said. "I can't make it for dinner. Working."

How often had I heard that recently? Why did I kid myself it would be any different tonight?

"One of Daddy's undercover missions?" I asked.

"I said I was working. I haven't had a career change since we last talked. I haven't signed on as an Avon lady or anything."

"Avon ladies put their cosmetics back in the boxes every now and then," I told her. "Why does he have to send you on all the night jobs?"

"Because I'm good at what I do," she replied, with a warning note in her voice.

"You are that," I said. The warning note was telling me not to revisit the charge that her father gave her these assignments at awkward times, on short notice, just to keep her away from me. She didn't want to hear it. We'd rehashed the argument too many times, and I could feel our relationship heading for the point of no return. So I just said, "Well, I'm sorry I won't be seeing you tonight" and tried not to sound too pathetic.

Her tone softened a little. "Maybe we could meet later. For dessert."

"Enrico's whipping up some of his rum flan," I told her.

"That'll be nice, too," she said.

4

ASIDE FROM THE pure pleasure of her presence, having dinner with Lea would also have given me an excuse to put off my report to Johnny. Now I had time to track him down and fill him in. I was anxious to get that over and done with before Lea arrived.

The problem was: how would I reach him? I doubted he'd be at the Dresner home at this time of the evening, and I wasn't anxious to make a call there anyway. Then I remembered his cellular phone.

Southern California chic insisted cellulars be part of the wardrobe. If you had the leisure to drive to your destination without being in telephone contact, you just weren't a player. And going for a jog or having a round of golf without offering the world instant access to your power and wisdom suggested that perhaps you might not be the very important person everyone thought you were. For all I knew, jockeys were carrying them so trainers could keep telling them what to do all through the race.

I'd managed to resist the trend. It wasn't the rumors about them causing brain tumors that put me off. The fact was, I considered the absence of a ringing phone to be one of the main pleasures of driving.

When Johnny first got his little talk toy, he'd displayed it proudly. Of course it was top-of-the-line and state-of-the-art. It wasn't just for car use but a little pocket job, no bigger than a pack of smokes when folded, that you carried wherever you went. He gave me his number, in case I ever had to call him in an emergency.

Unfortunately, the only times I'd ever tried to reach him on it, either I'd got a message from the cellular carrier that the phone wasn't available or it had rung its tiny transistors off in a drawer somewhere. But if he was expecting me to call about Paula, he just might have remembered to keep it with him and turned on.

It was a long shot that paid off.

"Coley, you got something?" he asked hopefully.

"Something," I told him. "Have you talked to Paula tonight?"

"A little while ago, yeah."

"How did she seem?"

"Same old same old. A little off, like something was biting her, but I couldn't get anything out of her. She said everything was fine, but she sure as hell didn't sound fine."

"Did she mention anything about being questioned by the police?"

"The cops? Hell no. Why should she?"

"We have to talk. Can you come to the Horse's Neck?"

"No, but why don't you meet me? I'm on my way to a screening. Mark Brittan's new movie."

"You're driving? I can't hear any traffic noise."

"Limo. Soundproof. You oughta see this car. It's Mark's. He sent it for me. Stretch Benz." He chuckled. "The guy's sex happy, you know. There's this pair of panties in the corner under the color TV."

"I bet they're not panties at all," I said. "I bet it's a flag he flies from the radio antenna. Where do I meet you?"

He gave me the address of a screening room in Culver City.

"You may want to skip the movie, Johnny."

"Wouldn't dream of it. Mark's a friend of mine. He's brought me a lot of business and he's a great contact to have. Anyhow, when he says he has something good, he has something good."

"Okay, okay, I'll get going now and maybe we can finish our talk before the screening."

"I'll tell Mark you're coming."

The address Johnny had given me belonged to a small production company that specialized in commercials and industrial training films. The lot had once housed one of the big studios and had included acres of buildings and soundstages that were gradually sold off through the fifties and sixties as the studio system declined and the economics of Hollywood changed. There were still two reminders of the good old days: a grand studio gate and an elderly attendant who checked my identity as gravely and carefully as if I'd asked for a one-on-one with David O. Selznick. Finally, satisfied, he waved me through as if he were opening the door to Oz.

At the screening room, the assembled audience was strictly stag. The guys were still at the standing-around stage, with drinks in their hands, rehashing the headlines in that morning's *Daily Variety*.

Johnny was positioned beside a well-stocked portable bar chatting with the host while a bartender topped his martini glass. I strolled over.

"Coley," Johnny said with a smile, "good to see you. You know Mark Brittan, don't you?"

Brittan was an action star just a little below Clint Eastwood or Harrison Ford in the cinematic pecking order. He was a big guy whose formidable looks were starting to erode around the eyes and neck. I'd never met him, but he seemed to know me.

"Coley Killebrew. I owe you one. Roadside Promise at thirty-two to one."

"You caught us on a good day," I said.

He gave me a male-bonding punch on the biceps, a little harder than was necessary, I thought. "I caught you on a few bad ones, too, amigo," he said, "but who's counting? Anyway, I'm glad you made it tonight. Come on over and I'll introduce you to the rest of the guys, then we'll get it rolling."

"I'm afraid I don't have time to watch the movie," I said, looking uneasily at Johnny.

"Oh, it's not a whole movie. It's a one-reeler, maybe twenty
minutes. Believe me, you'll enjoy it."

"You'll never see this kind of stuff on TV, Coley," Johnny said
with a wink.

After a round of introductions to the mainly industry crowd of
agents, accountants, and gofers, we took our places on the plush
theater seats. No empty popcorn boxes there. No soft-drink-
slimed floor. This was moviegoing insider-style.

The show started and I began to think Johnny had been wrong.
This I *could* have seen on TV. It was a blooper reel, outtakes from
Brittan's latest flick, a historical epic called *Conquistador*. At their
best, and with a few obscenities bleeped, the segments might have
made "America's Funniest Home Videos" on an off week.

Here's how it went. Brittan would have trouble getting his
sword out and everybody would break up. The director would
spot an extra with his reflecting shades still on during the take and
everybody would break up. A supporting player would have repeated problems getting his mouth around an unspeakable line of
dialogue—and everybody would break up. It was boring stuff because it didn't look spontaneous, especially the forced laughter that
followed each goof. It was as though, after the real take was in the
can, they made their mistakes solely for the star's blooper reel.

Eventually, footage of the two female leads began to unspool
and things got more interesting, partly because the performers
themselves were more interesting. One of them was a visually
stunning but nonacting glamour girl, part of a time-honored Hollywood tradition. The other was a slightly older, infinitely more
talented, but equally attractive woman, one of a more endangered
species: the legitimate stage star.

It was obvious the two women weren't finding their sisterhood
powerful, not just because one could act and the other couldn't,

but because they were nursing a real strain of personal animosity barely below the surface.

For some reason—and I hope it wasn't just the physical—I tended to side with the starlet. Some of the outtakes could be laid to her incompetence, but she seemed to be doing her best, while the older woman's celestial petulance alone accounted for some of the other flubs. She seemed to think the younger woman was trying to upstage her, and at their most animated the two of them reminded me of NBA centers working under the basket.

Finally Brittan's home movie cut to the chase: the real reason for the guys-only screening. It showed Brittan and his costar, the older stage-trained actress, in their bedroom scene. It started out mildly enough with PG-rated nuzzles, proceeded to PG-13 steaminess, crossed over into artistic and tasteful R nudity, graduated to an NC-17 full frontal, backal, toppal, and bottomal exposure, quickly dashed through the retired X category to the type of pure let-it-all-hang-out pornography that never applied for any rating at all. No, this would not be on TV, not even cable at its raunchiest.

The reel ended to the kind of thunderous ovation *Citizen Kane* never received. A certain amount of postscreening fawning and ring kissing was obligatory. Some of the select audience were clamoring for an encore showing. Johnny and I would have to forgo the replay, which was fine with me. I already felt I knew the lady better than her gynecologist.

As we were backing out the door Mark Brittan pumped my hand again and said, "You sure you have to leave so soon? Didn't you enjoy the show?"

"I never regret an experience," I told him.

"She's quite a girl, isn't she?"

"Quite a girl."

"I've done some great outtake reels, but my wife says this is the best ever."

As Johnny and I walked across the parking lot to the waiting limo, a white vehicle so long it looked in danger of collapsing in the middle, I said, "His wife liked the movie."

"Mark's wife," Johnny said dismissively. "Queen of the kinks. She'll sleep with anything that'll sleep with her, singly or in pairs. She actually brings women into the house for him."

"Sounds like quite a romance," I said. "Haven't these people ever heard of AIDS?"

"They think it's something other people get—namely gays and druggies. Forget the Brittans, Coley. I pal around with Mark for business reasons. I mean, I don't mind seeing one of his stag films every now and then, but that weird stuff's never been my scene."

The limo had rich, soft leather upholstery. But when I sank down into it, something dug into my bottom. I reached back and withdrew an item that had worked its way between the seat cushions—a small pistol.

I waved it in front of Johnny's nose. "Gee, your host thinks of everything. Not only do you have a bar and TV back here, you can do a little drive-by shooting if you get in the mood."

"It's mine," Johnny said, taking it from me and dropping it into the pocket of his coat. "I don't like to carry it in places where guys are drinking." He added, grinning, "It's my James Bond gun."

His Bond gun. When Johnny had been a teenager in New Jersey, his two most influential role models had been Dean Martin and James Bond, not necessarily in that order. But the glamorous life of a secret agent was not within the realm of possibility for a high-school dropout with no interest in working for the government.

So it had been so long Mr. Bond, hello Dino. Not that he could sing, or wanted to. It was the Martin air of studied casualness that he admired. And the nightlife. He got a job at a club in Paramus, eventually rising to the position of manager. But his father's stroke had drawn him back into the family men's clothing business with his brother, Phil.

When the old man died, he and Phil, who had even less incli-
nation to peddle menswear, sold the string of stores for a nice
piece of change. Johnny's end was enough for him to buy a controlling interest in a Vegas casino. There, with a wardrobe selected
with care before the stores changed hands, he was able to dress and
act with the casual air of Dean Martin while flirting with beautiful
women in his gaming rooms, not to mention dealing with dangerous men, just like the hero of *Casino Royal*.

He had been in Las Vegas less than a year when he bought an
Aston-Martin sports car, though not the one with all the gadgetry
that had been used in the films. He had also picked up a handgun
exactly like the one the secret agent carried, a Walther PPK,
7.65mm. It had been more difficult to find than the Aston-
Martin. Gun owners like big blasting power, and pistols firing bullets of that small a caliber are few and far between in this country.

"You ever use the gun?" I asked, settling back on the limo's soft
leather.

"Me? Hell no." He switched on the intercom and told the
driver to take a walk.

He waited for his will to be obeyed, then lowered his voice.
"Fact is, I'm a lousy shot. I took lessons once and almost plugged
the instructor."

"Then why bother to still carry it?"

"I'm a goddamn public figure, Coley. If not here, then definitely in Vegas. People think I got G-notes in my underwear. I'm
at a certain risk. So I don't mind if it gets around I'm armed. But
it would do me no good if they knew I couldn't hit a billboard if
I was standing only five feet away."

He offered me a drink from a mobile bar that was only slightly
more limited than the one we have at the Neck. We had to fix
our own cocktails, though. We were roughing it.

He waited for me to plunk a few ice cubes into a glass and pour
some scotch over them. Then he said, "So give, Coley. What's the
story with my lady?"

I told him pretty much the whole tale, leaving out my observations of Paula's social life and my appraisal of her character. All that would have earned me was a punch in the nose.

Johnny digested the information about Jerry Woolrich for a few seconds, then asked, "You ever hear of the guy before?"

"Nope."

"How was he killed?"

I shrugged. "I don't know. No blood or wounds that I could see. For all I know, the police may be calling it a heart attack."

"But you said the place had been trashed."

"They could charge that off to a looter who took advantage of Woolrich's bad heart. I, of course, would be cast as the looter. They know somebody was there after his death, and it wasn't Humphrey Bogart."

"Can they identify you?"

"I don't think so, but I just might find out differently."

"But in your opinion, Coley, this Woolrich didn't die from a heart attack, right?"

"Right," I said, nodding. "Definitely he was murdered. For some reason I can't begin to imagine, he was dressed after he was dead. Or at least his shoes and socks were put on by his killer. The socks were inside out. The tassel on one shoe was jammed between the shoe and his arch."

"Maybe he was in the kip with a dame and he shorted out. That would explain the socks."

"That's one scenario," I said.

"I didn't mean he was in the kip with Paula," Johnny added quickly.

"No. I knew you didn't mean that," I said. "In fact, I'm her alibi. He was dead before she got to his office. His body was cool by the time I arrived."

Johnny frowned and was silent for another minute. Then: "Do the cops know she was there tonight?"

"Who knows what they know? She was up there awhile. Since

she came away with a photograph, she was probably digging through the guy's files. She wasn't wearing gloves. Maybe she left fingerprints. But if they haven't talked to her by now . . ."

Johnny was concentrating furiously. "Fingerprints would only mean she was there, not *when* she was there."

"True. Unless she touched something on the body. Like the guy's wallet. But, as I said, if they haven't bothered her by now . . ."

"Christ. No wonder she was so uptight when I talked to her. Walked in on a stiff."

"She seemed upset, all right," I said. "But not upset enough to forget to snatch the photograph. Look, the only way to figure it is that she's been buying stuff on Daddy's credit, selling it to a clothes-and-jewelry fence at Split Seconds, and using the money to pay off Jerry Woo, blackmailer now deceased."

Johnny shook his head. "I already knew she had some kind of trouble, but this doesn't tell me what kind. You got us closer to knowing what's behind it, though." He looked me in the eye. "Find out for me, Coley."

I swallowed the last of my drink and set the glass down on the armrest. "Sorry, Johnny. This is where I get off. Dead bodies make me queasy."

"Coley," he whined, slipping into his con-man mode, "we don't even know if the guy was offed or if he had a heart attack. I'm not asking for anything major. Make a few calls, see what stirs."

"Not this time, Johnny." I really meant it, too. I reached for the handle and swung open the limo door. I was about to step out when Johnny said, "I can make you help me."

I stopped. He sure sounded like a mobster when he said things like that. I answered carefully, "I think I already squared our account."

"No argument. This is something else. How'd you like to be the solo owner of the Horse's Neck?"

That surprised me. I have to admit, though, it was something I'd thought about. Johnny never really interfered with the running of the restaurant, but I'd always been conscious of having a partner, a partner whose vote meant a little more than mine did. I was a free agent on a day-to-day basis, but I couldn't really control my own future the way I wanted. If I owned the Neck, I'd be my own boss. I could start to do some planning. I could burst the bounds of that cozy but confining little apartment. I could get a life, even a family. With Lea. I said, "My cash flow is a little slow these days, Johnny."

"I'll take fifty cents on the dollar. You could refinance the place easy. Interest rates are low, and we've cut a hunk off of the old mortgage."

By now I was sitting down again, with the limo door closed. "What do you want me to do exactly?"

"Find out what's bugging Paula and take care of it."

"No deal."

"What's wrong?"

"The 'taking care' part. Guys my size don't do so well in jail."

"Okay," Johnny said smoothly. "Let's amend the deal. Find out the problem and take care of it *if* it can be done legally. If it can't, tell me and I'll take over."

"I think they call that guilt by association," I said. "Or maybe accessory before the fact."

"Jeezus, Coley. Don't puss out on me completely. Work with me on this."

I felt in my gut it was a bad idea, but the prospect of owning the Horse's Neck outright hung in front of my eyes like the rabbit that makes the grayhound run his legs off.

"If I say yes, I do things my way," I insisted. "No interference from you, no matter what happens."

"Wouldn't dream of it," Johnny said, extending his hand.

I hesitated only a second before I shook it. Then I got out of the limo. Johnny signaled to the driver. By the time I'd walked back to the Cherokee, the long white Benz was on its way out. I wondered where Johnny was headed. I hoped it was to some party or gathering where he might meet other women who'd take his mind off of Paula Dresner. Lovesickness didn't become him.

Me either. I raced back to the Horse's Neck to get ready for my own late date.

I'd expected the dining room to be closed—unlike New Yorkers, Southern Californians usually head for home by ten—but there were a few tables still occupied by couples lingering over their coffees and after-dinner drinks. Jack Hayward eyed them benignly from his favorite table just beside the front door. Like the splendid maître d' he was, his face showed not a trace of impatience.

I paused to ask him if he'd landed the denture-adhesive job. "Alas, no," he replied. "Frankly, I think I registered too young to be credible in the role."

I wasn't sure if he was joking or not, so I let it go. "Anyone come in asking about me?"

"Nary a soul," he said. "Sorry."

"Don't be. That's what I wanted to hear." No visitors meant no connection between me and the late Jerry Woo Woolrich.

The bar was still active and would remain so for another hour or more. I shook a few hands and checked the evening receipts, which were healthy for a weeknight. Cheery news, particularly for a soon-to-be sole owner-operator. Humming a happy tune, I trotted up the steps to my apartment.

Out of habit I checked the messages on my machine, not that I planned on dealing with any of them that night. The good news was that no police had called. The bad news, Lea had. Her assignment was taking longer than she'd thought. Rain check on the dessert.

I sighed and went downstairs to the bar.

5

THE NEXT MORNING I was back at my temp job, parked in the shade of an old Whitebark pine, one block uphill from the Dresner manse. I had a clear view of its impressive front, including the driveway, in a clearing between two neighboring comparatively modest million-dollar Spanish Colonial revivals.

A gardener went to work trimming Dresner's hedges, and a liveried servant hauled out some garbage, but I never saw any of the other inhabitants of the household. Dresner's broadcast schedule probably had him out of the place around dawn, and Johnny's nighttime habits made him a late sleeper. It was odd he and Paula didn't spend more time together during the day, but apparently her daily regimen was as immutable as if it were turning a profit.

Finally, I spied the red Alfa through the greenery as it zoomed across the drive and bounced onto the street. The lady was in her Day-Glo workout garb, with a scarf added to flutter just so in the wind. I followed at a discreet distance. I knew from her outfit where she was probably headed and so I didn't expect the destination to offer any insights into what had happened last night.

Sure enough, after an exciting stunt drive over freeways and surface streets, she pulled up in front of Susanna's Salon. She got out of the Alfa. She did not bother to feed the parking meter before skipping into the building.

Fifteen minutes of watching the ebb and flow of the toned and the tony, and I was having another conversation with my dashboard companion, little Arnold. Waiting is what I do worst. One of the things I love about Lea is that when she says eight o'clock, she's there at eight o'clock. Unless, of course, she calls and says she isn't coming at all.

Waiting *and* thinking about Lea was too deadly a combination. Worse yet, it wasn't getting me any closer to finding out what made Paula tick. "What do you think?" I asked little Arnold. But I knew what he thought. You're this near a gym, you go inside.

Not having the luck of the young and lovely, I fed a couple of quarters into the parking meter before entering the building.

At the front desk, a polite but grim-faced security guard no smaller than Refrigerator Perry gave me the hard stare.

"Yes sir? Can I help you?"

"I'd like to talk to somebody about joining the club."

His look grew harder, as if he were spinning through a mental Rolodex of the Rich and Famous to find a match. Then I saw the lightbulb of recognition come on, and it gave me a little frisson of pride to know that my minor celebrity hadn't entirely faded.

"You're Eddie Delahoussaye, aren't you?" he asked.

"Uh, no, but you're on the right track. I'm Coley Killebrew."

"Oh, yeah, sure." He didn't seem sure at all. So much for minor celebrity. "I'll call somebody, Mr. Killebrew."

He led me through the gate, across a sort of courtyard, and into a reception area that resembled an upscale doctor's waiting room. He told the guy at the counter I wanted to talk about joining.

This second line of defense was a slight, pale, and reedy character who was such a poor example of physical fitness, I wondered how he got the job. He wasn't even a casual racing fan apparently and looked at me with a fish eye, before asking me to sit down. He assured me someone would be with me in a moment.

I sat on a wicker chair among a variety of large-leafed, indoor plants so healthy looking they'd obviously been working out. A caffeine-free coffee table was covered by copies of *GQ*, *People*, *Vanity Fair*, *Los Angeles*, *Daily Variety*, and *Money*. The essentials.

I ignored them in favor of a passing parade of buffed young

women, some of whom looked familiar. They may have been with Paula at the Bay City Beach Club pool. Each was greeted by name by the counter attendant before passing through into the club proper. Without the perfect Paula for comparison, they were an impressive group, considerably more diverting than the magazines.

The woman who finally came to cut our membership deal was even more impressive. She was dressed for work rather than working out, but it was clear she'd done plenty of the latter. She was probably in her late thirties, tanned and muscular, her short skirt showing off bare and well-molded legs.

She gave me a warm smile and shook my hand. "Mr. Killebrew, I'm so pleased to meet you. I'm Susanna."

"Well," I said. "Susanna herself. I'm honored."

She laughed. "I'm the one who's honored, and I respect you too much to try to fool you. I don't own the place. The hostess on duty automatically becomes Susanna."

"What happened to the original?"

"Sold out years ago to Brightwell Industries. I think she lives in Aspen now. Can I offer you a cup of decaf? Or perhaps a drink from our juice bar?"

"No, thanks. I was just hoping for a look around."

"Certainly." She turned to the counterman. "Fred, you know Mr. Killebrew, don't you? One of racing's greatest jockeys." Her tone suggested a slight reproach for not fawning over me properly.

Turning back to me, she said, "I ride myself, so I can appreciate your skill. I exercised horses at Hollywood and Santa Rosita for a while when I was a teenager. I wanted to be a jockey in fact, but I couldn't bear leaving Southern California, and for some reason women jockeys don't seem to make it out here. Do you know why that is?"

The usual reply to that question is that the Southern California jockey colony is the toughest in the country, a challenge to break into regardless of gender. And I knew that if a rider had the talent of a Julie Krone, she could crack the ranks anywhere. But these weren't very tactful answers. So I just said I didn't know.

"It's not as if female jockeys are a new thing," that day's Susanna went on. "Robyn Smith was a top rider in New York years and years ago, till she married Fred Astaire, then she retired. But out here, they don't seem to have any room for women."

I remembered that Astaire had owned racehorses off and on and wondered if he would have employed a female jockey before he fell in love with one.

The pseudo-Susanna had a few more grievances against male chauvinism to get off her chest before segueing into her low-key sales pitch for the salon. Calling it a "salon" turned out to be a rare example of understatement. It was a full-scale fitness center, a country club without the eighteen holes. As we walked around the facilities she pointed out the various aids to sado-masochism in the workout room—rowing machines, stretching equipment, stair climbers, stationary bikes, weight-lifting apparatus.

We proceeded to the squash and handball courts, the Olympic-size pool, and the health-food bar, which didn't seem to stock any of my favorite libations. The operation was so upscale, I don't remember even smelling any sweat.

I saw few male or female bodies of the kind featured in TV ads for more democratic health clubs. I also didn't see any recognizable celebrities, unless you count the chubby second lead on one of the TV cop shows. But Susanna emphasized, carefully mentioning no names, that any number of certifiable superstars were members and that they appreciated the relative anonymity of being surrounded by comparable luminaries. She flattered me as one of their fame-encumbered number, even if you couldn't have convinced the wrestler or the skinny deskman.

We walked up a carpeted back stairway. It was lined with photos of movie Tarzans. There were Elmo Lincoln, Johnny Weissmuller, Lex Barker. They even had Herman Brix and Glen Morris, so the decorator was a real film buff.

At the top of the stairway, she led me through a door onto a balcony, promising me a dazzling view. The balcony extended around the edge of the salon's largest room, a regulation-size basketball court.

"I'll bet the Lakers practice here," I said. Susanna smiled at me but revealed nothing.

Nobody was shooting baskets at the moment, but we could look down on a prancing and jiggling aerobics class. That was where I would have expected to find Paula, but she wasn't part of the show.

"And finally," that day's Susanna said, leading me down a flight of stairs, "our most popular new addition." She opened the door on a ground-level handgun firing range. The noise of the gunshots was intense, but I hadn't heard a sound as we approached.

"That was the most difficult part," Susanna told me, "containing the sound."

There were eight alleys, each occupied by a woman who'd added plastic goggles and noise-reducing headsets to her spandex workout tights. Paula Dresner was third from the door. I swallowed as I watched her bullets tear a small circle out of the forehead of the pistol-wielding thug on the target at the far end of her alley.

"Nice placement," I said, and Susanna followed my glance.

Seeing Paula, two expressions crossed her face in a split second. First came a trace of distaste, as if she were remembering unpleasant run-ins with Wilton Dresner's little girl. Then the mask of businesslike friendliness reasserted itself. "Ah, yes. Well, a few months ago, she'd have had trouble even hitting the target."

"I notice that all of today's shooters are female," I said.

"We've found that most of our women members want to become more proficient with arms," Susanna said. "I'm not sure what that tells us about our society."

As we finished the tour and edged back toward the reception area, my hostess asked me into her office to work out the details of my membership application. I really wasn't considering joining, but I asked her for a ballpark figure. The down payment was about three times the ballpark I had in mind—I was at the old Gilmore Field, she at Dodger Stadium—so I told her I'd have to think about it.

She handed me her card, which remained coy about her real name but did have her Susanna number on it. She was Susanna 5, a sort of science-fiction touch. I wondered how many Susannas there were on the payroll and whether the number indicated rank or seniority. I was not to find out. Number 5 opened her office door and bid me farewell. I passed through the reception area to an obsequious "Have a nice day, Mr. Killebrew" from the desk-man and, from the security guy, a hearty "See you again, Mr. Desormeaux." He just couldn't keep his jockeys straight.

Surprisingly, Paula's red Alfa was no longer parked near the salon. That meant she'd satisfied her gun lust for the day, turned in her weapon, and skedaddled during the ten minutes I'd been in the room with Susanna 5. It didn't necessarily signify that Paula had recognized me and purposely ditched me. Maybe she'd suddenly remembered some forgotten errand she had to run.

Little Arnold gave me his most skeptical look.

Regardless of why she'd left so hurriedly, the fact was I'd dropped the ball. I had no idea where she'd gone or what, aside from a photo taken from the files of a murdered photographer, she had to hide.

6

I DECIDED I was going about this the wrong way. Following Paula around had been an obvious approach. But it had run out of steam as a useful strategy. By ditching me, on purpose or not, she had brought the truth home. Maybe I should have thanked her.

I had to come up with an alternate plan. But which one? It was a given that Paula's problems had something to do with the late Jerry Woo. And his office-apartment had been lousy with clues that came from a world I knew well. It was time to focus on the horse-racing angle. So, when I got back to my apartment, that's what I did.

"Santa Rosita Raceway, the friendly track where the horses pay you back, how can I help you?" chirped a cheery female voice. It was a familiar one, too, but I hadn't heard it for years.

"Hi," I said. "Don't you guys ever change that slogan? It sounds like the horses take a dump on the customers."

She giggled. She always had been a great audience. "They make us say that. During the actual season, we have to say even more. Like Merry Christmas, free Best Pal beer steins for Oktoberfest, and every Wednesday is Senior Citizens' Day."

"You ought to vary it a little. Try something like, 'Santa Rosita Raceway, where the windows clean the people, what can I do you for?'" It was an old line I once heard Milton Berle use, but she loved it.

"You should be grateful I'm a person and not voice mail," she said.

"When you put people on hold, do you still play that song from *Guys and Dolls*?"

She sang a little for me, then asked, "Am I speaking with the infamous Coley Killebrew?"

"Yeah, and you knew it all the time. How are you, Deena?"

"Off-key as ever, right? It's not the same without you, Coley."

"You could have fooled me. Is Roger Willetts in his office?"

"I think you're in luck. I just saw him come in a few minutes ago, with that little rain cloud that's always over his head. If he doesn't answer, I'll go tackle him for you."

After a couple of rings, a deep masculine voice that might have belonged to a frustrated newscaster said, "This is Willetts!" The assistant general manager's terse greeting suggested that all the friendliness at the friendly track was front-loaded.

"Roger, it's Coley."

"Oh, hi, buddy," he said. He sounded about as glad to hear from me as if he owed me money, but I knew that was just his style. When you go through what I did, becoming what somebody called the Shoeless Joe Jackson of racing, your supposed friends drop like medflies in a malathion storm. Roger was one pal I didn't lose.

"How're tricks at the track?" I asked.

"Lousy. Racing's dying. You got out at the right time. We were counting on getting the Breeder's Cup, but they gave it to Woodbine or Beulah Park or some damn place. I expect my pink slip any day now."

He'd get his pink slip the day that Clara McGuinn, the president of the track, put a padlock on the front door and threw away the key. Mrs. Mac, who'd inherited Santa Rosita from her late husband, knew she couldn't do without Roger. He was the key to the whole operation. Without him, the track would collapse. So he could get away with being surly and unpleasant. And he saved the worst of his gloomy personality for his friends.

"Roger, I need to get in touch with Luis Falcon," I said, before he got me too depressed. "Any idea where he's riding these days?"

"Nowhere. He retired about a year ago."

"I hadn't heard. Do you know why? Anything shady?"

"Anything shady, you say. And you sound so hopeful, you sadistic dwarf. Yeah, I always wondered about old Luis, too, like he'd peddle his sister or put a battery to his grandmother if the price was right."

"And did he?"

"Hate to disappoint you, Coley, but as far as I know, it was a health thing. The way you bums abuse your bodies, I don't know how any of you make it past forty. Alive, I mean, forget riding horses."

"You pushing a healthy lifestyle these days, Roger?"

"No, I'm pushing what I always pushed. Paper and the little button on the corner of the antacid box. What are you pushing, Coley? A broom?"

"Numbers on the phone, and I want to push some more. You got an address and phone for Falcon?"

While rustling through some papers on his desk, Roger mumbled about how I could call the damn Jockeys' Guild and why was I bothering him with this trivia. Within seconds, he read off an address in East L.A. and a phone number.

I thanked him and hung up, smiling. For some reason, talking to Roger always cheered me up.

Luis hadn't changed his phone number. But my lucky streak ended there.

"Yeah?" The voice was thick with phlegm and suspicion.

"Luis, it's Coley Killebrew," I said, forcing the heartiness. "How you been?"

The barely audible monosyllable was " 'Kay."

"I need to talk to you. Can we get together for a drink."

"Why should I drink with you?"

Unlike Roger's, Falcon's unfriendliness was the genuine article. We'd known each other for years, but we hadn't been what you'd call pals. He'd never had the good mounts or the big purses, and he'd always resented anybody successful. If I'd been somebody *really* successful, like Laffit Pincay or Gary Stevens, instead of a disgraced outcast, he probably would have hung up without talking to me at all.

"Luis, all I want to do is ask you a few questions about one of your races at Land O' Lincoln back in ninety-two."

"Get fucked!" Falcon said, and broke the connection. I toyed with phoning him back to add, "You, too." But it didn't seem worth the effort. Instead I tried to think of who else I might prevail upon to get me information on that race. Lea's father could probably do it with one phone call. But I hated to ask him. Either he'd turn me down, or he'd do it and I'd owe him. A no-win situation. But I didn't seem to have a choice.

Not wanting to confront the bear on an empty stomach, I went down to the kitchen for lunch.

Surprisingly, it was my old brother on horseback, Luis "Get Fucked" Falcon, who saved me from having to deal with Starbuck. An hour after he'd hung up on me, while I was going over the evening's specials with my head chef, Antony, he called back.

"Hey, man," he said. "You caught me at a bad time. I was feelin' kinda lousy and I took it out on you."

"It's okay," I told him.

"You wanna talk, I talk," he said. "But I need some money for my time."

"How much?" I asked, guardedly.

"Depends on how long," he replied.

"Half hour."

"Fifty bucks and I tell you whatever you wanna know."

"Where? Your place?" I asked.

"No. You know a cantina in East L.A. called Arriba!?"

"I can probably find it," I told him.

"Well, try finding it by nine tonight," he said. "I be there then."

．　　．　　．

Arriba! turned out to be a hundred-percent Chicano bar, which
I might have expected in that part of town. But the joint had a
touch of class, as they say at the track. The outside was dreary and
uninviting, with an ugly neon sign featuring a burro wearing a
sombrero; but the interior had its points. There was a big ornate
mirror behind the oak bar, the kind that, in an old Western B
movie, two bit players would carefully take down before the
shooting started. All the beers and spirits you could think of were
lined up below the mirror, presided over by a chubby barkeep
with a Pancho Villa mustache and a face that was probably naturally friendly but that clouded with suspicion when he spotted me.
The unbroken line of muchachos standing at the bar looked me
over less with hostility than curiosity.

Feeling a little like the house freak, I moved on into the dining
area. Arriba! was twice the size of the Horse's Neck. There were
thirty or more tables in the front room and another ten or fifteen
through an arched passageway. The day's specials were marked on
a blackboard on one wall. The opposite wall held an eclectic mix:
bullfight action photos; portraits of Hispanic heroes ranging from
labor leader Cesar Chavez to boxer Julio Cesar Chavez; and prints
of paintings by the three great Mexican muralists, Orozco,
Siqueiros, and Diego Rivera. Arriba!'s owner was clearly a Renais-
sance man. There were no racehorse shots, so I guessed Luis Falcon must not have had money in the place. Or if he had, maybe
he hated horses, which is something I'd always suspected.

That I was the only gringo in view didn't seem to throw the
pretty waitress who gave me a dazzling smile and showed me to a
table in the rear of the room. Luis Falcon was sitting with his back
to the wall, engaged in serious eating. From the looks of him, that
was now his main occupation. He'd grown so grossly fat since I last
saw him, I barely recognized him. He had one leg propped up on
a chair, the foot encased in a dirty white sock. A pouty young

woman in a flower-patterned and very low-cut dress sat at the table with him. She had a tostada in front of her but wasn't doing anything with it. Watching Luis eat probably didn't help her appetite.

"Sit down, Coley," Luis said, barely looking up from his heaping plate of enchiladas, guacamole, and refried beans.

"Thanks, Luis. Good to see you."

"Liar," he said, adding a chuckle to show he didn't mean to offend. He was trying to be pleasant.

I took the one vacant chair. Having my back to the room didn't bother me. This wasn't really an Old West saloon after all. Still, there seemed to be a touch of hostility in the air. I spotted a pair of eyes one table over to my right that were fixing me with a cold and steady stare. Their owner was rapier thin, with tufts of hair at each corner of his mouth and on the point of his chin. He lit up a crook cigar. When my eyes met his, he looked away but was in no hurry about it.

The waitress returned to the table and asked if I wanted anything. Watching Falcon shovel in the cheese, salsa, and sour cream didn't do anything to stimulate my appetite either. *"Una cerveza,"* I said.

Moving from the table, she brushed against the chair on which Falcon's foot rested. *"Descuidado puta!"* he shouted at her. Then he looked at me and shook his head. "I got diabetes, man. That's what stopped me from racing. The way you gotta treat it, I couldn't keep my weight down, y'know? Hotbox, flipping, fasting, all the stuff we all used to do to keep the fat off, just don' work with diabetes. Messes up your blood sugar. You gotta eat regular meals."

I doubted eating them in such quantity was part of the recommended regimen, but that was his business.

"So I'm out of racing, prob'ly for good. I used to think I had luck with me, but I turned out to be about as lucky as you, amigo."

"What have you been doing since you quit?" I asked.

"Eating. Sleeping." He chuckled. "Making friends with pretty little girls like Louisa here. Say hello to Coley, Louisa. He used to be a big shot."

Louisa said, "Hi," without enthusiasm. Falcon shoveled in another load and I looked away. The waitress brought my beer.

"I remember a race we rode at the Pomona fair one year," Falcon told his girl. "Coley di'n't ride much at the bullring, did you, Coley? Used to go to New York or take a vacation."

"I rode there quite a few times," I said.

"Those turns were really tight," he explained to Louisa, illustrating with a sharp hand movement and showing her a mouthful of partly chewed food. "Back then, before they made it longer, it was a half-a-mile track, you know. Most tracks, they're a mile. Took a real *race* rider to handle the bullring, Coley, no?"

"Absolutely," I said. It helped if you liked to ride Arabians, Appaloosas, and quarter horses as well as Thoroughbreds.

"One time Coley had this two-year-old in a stake there, supposed to be a real prospect. What was the name of that two-year-old, Coley?"

I'd ridden lots of two-year-olds, even a few at Fairplex, which is what they call the L.A. County Fair track in Pomona now, but I knew the race Falcon was about to describe. Listening to this story was going to be one of the prices, along with the fifty bucks, I'd have to pay for whatever information he was going to give me.

"His name was Speculation," I said.

"Yeah, that's right, Speculation. He's odds-on. Goes out by himself, five, six lengths, but he's wide on every single turn. Remember my mount's name, Coley?"

"Nope," I said, and it was true.

"Boodle Bailey. Almost like the comic strip."

I nodded. "Sure, I remember now."

"Boodle's a cheap gelding, not worth a fuck anywhere else, but loved to run at Pomona. Not 'cause he wanted to run in front, either, though you figure with the short stretch, the bullring favored speed. He was a plodder, never in his life beat a horse to the first turn. This race he runs last the first half mile but hugs the rail the whole way, holds on to it like a man hugs a woman. Th' other horses start slowin' down just as Boodle Bailey starts rollin'. I come inside the whole field, baby, the whole fuckin' field, eight of 'em, scrapin' the paint the whole way. Coley's easin' up his blue blood in the last furlong, thinks he's left us all back in the slop. Doesn't know I'm coming till it's too late. I nail him at the wire. Musta been that much," he said, holding up a thumb and forefinger with the width of a tortilla between them.

"You were great at the bullring, all right, Luis," I said, trying to be agreeable. I could have argued with his description of the race, but what was the point?

"So whattaya think my man Coley did? Huh? Claimed foul on me. Says I knocked him off stride, lost him the race. We barely nudged each other."

"I didn't claim foul, Luis," I said. "It was a steward's inquiry."

"But they didn't take my number down, did they, amigo?"

"No."

"And your blue-blood two-year-old, Speculation, won the Santa Anita Derby the next year, but you weren't on him, were you?"

"No, I lost the mount. That's the way it goes sometimes." The truth was I hadn't eased up on Speculation at Pomona. He'd just gotten tired because he didn't like the muddy track. Boodle Bailey, as well as being a bullring specialist, moved up about ten lengths on an off track. And Speculation hadn't been wide on all the turns. He'd just drifted out a little in the stretch, again because he was tired.

It was true Falcon had gotten through inside me—it was one of his more competent rides, and I didn't blame him for remembering it—but I doubted he'd scraped the paint on the whole field. And I still thought he'd fouled me, but the call could have gone either way.

It was true I hadn't been on Speculation in the Santa Anita Derby, but it wasn't because I'd given him a bad ride the year before. It was because I had a better three-year-old to ride on the same day in Florida.

Other than that, Falcon's account was pretty accurate. I didn't bother to straighten him out, but I couldn't resist a slight needle. "Was that the biggest race you ever won, Luis?" I asked.

"Hell, no," he growled. "Thirty-thousand-dollar stake? I won lots of those. Biggest race Boodle Bailey ever won, though. He'd stink up the place all year long. But every year at Pomona he'd win, cheaper and cheaper company every year, but he'd win. Still ran there when he was ten, eleven years old."

The whole time we talked, I was conscious of the thin man at the next table, though his interest seemed to have shifted to another part of the room. I saw him inhale his crook cigar, but as long as I watched, I never saw him exhale. I was fascinated, wondering where the smoke was going. But I pulled myself back to my business with Falcon.

Still trying to keep it casual and friendly, I asked, "What kind of work are you doing now? Trainer?"

He looked me in the eye for the first time. "I meet people in restaurants."

He put out his hand. I covered it with the promised fifty.

"*Gracias,*" Falcon said. "Other than these little moments of employment, I am a gentleman of leisure." As he put the money away I noticed his worn wallet was stuffed with cash, and he noticed me noticing. "I made good money when I was riding. You know how it is."

I knew how it was with Falcon, all right. He had been one of the crowd, a journeyman jockey with few big paydays, and what money he'd made he'd blown on booze and women. That roll he was carrying hadn't come from his riding career.

"So, what do you want to know, amigo?"

"I saw a picture of you on a winning horse at Land O' Lincoln. The date was May nineteenth, 1992. The sixth race."

"So?"

"Remember anything about it?"

"Like what?"

"Let's start with the name of the horse."

Falcon shrugged. "I rode a lot of animals at that track," he said. "It's a long season. There's too many to remember 'em all."

I was skeptical. Falcon rode a lot of horses, sure, but not so many into the winner's circle that he'd forget one. His memory of Boodle Bailey certainly hadn't faded. I let my suspicion show on my face.

"Wait a minute, though," he said, much too casually to be convincing. "I think I do remember that one. That one was something special, a great filly. Bathsheba, that was her name. Carew family in Lexington owned her."

"What else can you remember about that race? Anything unusual?"

Falcon spread his hands. "Nothing unusual, no. She won the race, but that was not so unusual for her."

"Do you remember being photographed?"

"Sure. They always take pictures in the winner's circle, Coley. You been there once or twice."

"What about the photographer? Remember anything about him?"

Falcon blinked at that. Then a smile returned to his face. "The photographer? No, man. How the hell would I remember the photographer? All them guys look alike."

The thin man got up from the next table and headed for the door. When I was sure he was out of earshot, I asked Falcon, "Did you notice the skinny dude who just left?"

"Sure, I saw him. So?"

"Do you know who he is?"

"What do you care?"

"He was watching me."

He laughed nastily. "You scared of somethin', Coley? People out to get you? Maybe comin' to the barrio makes you nervous."

"The guy kept staring at me."

"I don' know how to break this to you, man, but you sorta stand out in here. You're a minority. People gonna look you over. So what?"

"You don't know who he is?"

Falcon shrugged. "A Latino. Like photographers, we all look alike, too."

I tried the girl. "You know him, Louisa?"

Falcon gave her a hard glance. "She don' know him," he said with finality. "She don' know nobody but yours truly. Right, baby?" He grabbed the girl's jaw and gave it a little squeeze. She tried to smile.

"If you finished, Killebrew, I got me a big evening planned with Louisa. She's gonna help me bathe my foot and put on a new sock. I'd invite you, but it's a kinda personal thing."

"That wasn't much information for fifty bucks," I said.

"Just like the races, amigo. You pay your money, you take your chance. I told you what I know."

Falcon swung his bad foot down from the chair and got to his feet. Louisa, who hadn't eaten a bite as far as I'd noticed, got up, too. I didn't envy her the evening ahead, but it was clearly more a business deal than a love match.

With a brief good-bye to my charming old riding buddy, I walked out of the bar.

It had turned dark while I was in there, and I wished I'd parked closer to the building. I started across the lot toward the Cherokee, passing a horse van on the way. It was carrying an animal, too. I could hear it moving and grunting softly on the other side of the metal wall. It seemed like an odd vehicle for an urban parking lot. Where were the closest horse farms? The Valley?

As I walked past the van I sensed something wrong, something vaguely threatening that I couldn't put my finger on. A movement in the shadows? A stirring of the air? Then I caught a whiff of the sickly-sweet smoke from a rum-soaked crook cigar. Like a doofus, I stopped walking. Nothing like making it easier for an assailant to deliver a blow to the head.

7

I AWOKE BECAUSE I was having difficulty breathing. Something was covering my face. I tried to remove it, but I couldn't lift my hands.

And I couldn't breathe.

A full-blown panic overtook me and I shouted.

Someone next to me laughed and said, "Shorty's got a real air problem."

"Punch some holes in the bag," a man with a Latin accent answered. "It won't look good if he chokes. They want it to look good."

The man next to me grunted. I felt him press against me, a hot, beefy body. We were sitting on something soft. A sofa?

The beefy man tore the bag just under my nose. He smelled of hamburger grease and beer and Dentyne, but I breathed in greedily all the same.

Then I poked out my chin and tried to look down through the hole in the bag.

It was dark, but I could make out the curved worn leather seat and the floor of an automobile. I was leaning my head farther back when I heard the car door open and I was yanked roughly from the seat.

That's when I discovered my hands were tied behind my back. My fellow passenger followed me. We'd been sitting so high up I realized we'd been in a truck, not a car. The cobwebs started to clear. I remembered the horse van in the Arriba! parking lot. The memory, for whatever it was worth, came to me just before I was pushed to the ground. I rolled back and felt earth and leaves under my fingers.

Where the hell was I?

The Latin said, "I need some fucking help here, Howard," and his buddy joined him.

I heard a metal clang. Then the unmistakable whinny of a horse.

I looked at the world through my paper-bag hole and saw night. We were in a wooded area. I made out the dark shapes of two men among the trees—Howard, big and slow, the other wiry and quick. And a horse. It was impossible to be any more specific than that.

The wiry man was carrying a long solid object. A lead pipe?

"What're you doing with that?" Howard asked.

"Whaddaya think? I gonna break the horse's fucking leg."

"You ain't gonna do that to no horse while I'm around. That's too cold. Shoot 'em, if you want. But none of that leg shit. That's . . . uh, sadistic."

"It's just a goddamn horse, man."

"You ain't breakin' his leg, Ramon. No way."

Ramon hesitated, as if he might have been thinking of using his club on Howard. Then he dropped it. It landed with a dull thud. "I never knew you was such an animal lover," he said nastily. "Okay, we'll let the horse do it to itself."

"What about Shorty? We don't have the battery and clips."

Ramon turned to look my way. I knew for sure now it was the crook smoker from the bar. "So we gotta improvise. He usta be a jockey. This gonna work out fine."

He moved toward me. I lowered my head and went blind again.

When I chanced another look, they were saddling the animal.

Then the big guy walked toward me. I tucked in my chin as he yanked me to my feet. "He don't weight much more'n a coonhound," he said, laughing again.

He carried me toward the horse. Then he lifted me high and swung me into the saddle. I let him put my feet into the stirrups.

In spite of the circumstances, the animal felt good under me. A big Thoroughbred, I presumed.

Something hard pressed into my back. "You awake, yeah?" the Latin asked. When I didn't answer, he poked the gun harder into my back. I nodded.

"Awright. You be a good boy now. I don't wanna have to shoot you."

There was pressure on my tied hands and then they were no longer attached to one another but were hanging at my sides, limp and useless. When the circulation returned to them, it was joined by a thousand points of pain.

Before my fingers could progress past the tingle stage, I was pushed forward until I was hugging the animal. My hands were tied again. The rope joining them was looped under the horse's neck.

The animal was skittish. I was a little skittish myself.

"Tie his feet, too?" the big guy asked.

"Naw. What do we care if he falls off? The horse just drags him."

He led the animal and me through the woods. I could hear creatures of the night scurry away as if they wanted no part of our fate. A bird let out a strange coo-coo sound. "Why are you doing this?" I asked.

"Shut up," Ramon answered.

I sensed a change in the atmosphere around us. Sounds were no longer sharp and intense but flattened and dulled. "Go get the van ready," Ramon told the other man. "This is gonna be down and dirty. Mainly down." His words seemed to lose themselves. No echo. No more trees overhead.

The horse balked.

Ramon pushed against its rump, trying to move it forward. Not a prudent thing to do. The horse whinnied and kicked back. The kick did not feel as if it hit its mark, but Ramon cursed anyway, probably from surprise.

There was a moment of total silence. Then I heard the spang of a metal spring. It was a recognizable sound, even for a nonsmoker. The opening of a Zippo lighter.

"Look," I pleaded, "don't do any—"

I was interrupted by a rasping noise. The striker wheel spinning against the flint.

Then the horse let out a horrible wail and leaped forward, away from the Zippo's flame.

Into space.

It seemed like another minute before his front hooves struck earth and we were heading down sharply. Moving with too much speed. Skidding. His rear end was moving faster than his front.

The animal dug in his hooves and kept his body from bending and sliding sideways. By some miracle he remained upright, but his natural braking system wasn't working. I rubbed my head against his rigid neck, rumpling the paper bag.

We hurtled down faster. The horse's whinnies were almost continuous.

I finally got the bag loose from its string tie. Then over my head.

I could see. But the moonlit view gave me little hope. We were skating on dirt and rock down the side of a steep canyon. There were only a few trees near us, but farther down, it was heavily wooded. The horse had lost all control. We were like a pinball destined to slam into one thing or another before the game was over.

I'd talked to horses for years, and I did my best to calm this one by whispering gently in his ear. His ears were flicking back and forth in panic, but I sensed he was trying to listen to me.

"Easy, boy. Take it easy, boy." I hoped I didn't sound too panicked myself.

The horse stiffened his legs, trying to stop his downward momentum, with no success. I was afraid he'd go down on all fours or pitch me over his head. To give the animal more confidence, more sense somebody was in control, and to avoid becoming airborne myself, I pressed my calves tighter and tighter against his sides. I don't know how I avoided sailing into space. He saved me a few times by raising his head just enough to stop my forward momentum, as if he were trying to help his partner.

An immense California pine, wide as a steel drum, loomed up to block our way. I was sure we were going to hit it head-on, but I managed to steer him to one side. The horse's haunch connected with the tree trunk as we went by, bouncing us off to the left but also slowing us down some. We took a few more glancing blows, slowing us even more.

At last I managed to get him under control. The terrain was starting to level out. The exhausted horse's natural instinct was to stop and do his shaking in one spot. I kept whispering in his ear, trying to keep him as quiet as I could. I knew I had some bruises, and the horse must have had some, too, but I didn't think either of us was too severely damaged. He was puffing, sweating, trembling, and jittery after the experience, but he was no shakier than I was. He was a fine, smart animal, and I was proud of him. The two of us couldn't have managed it better if we'd been steeplechasers instead of flat racers.

We weren't out of the woods yet, though, literally or figuratively.

The road at the bottom of the canyon was in sight now, and sitting there, waiting, was the horse van. The two men had driven down. I could hear them climbing up the canyon and I saw a flashlight blinking through the trees.

Fortunately, they were downwind of us, and there was enough of a breeze to rustle the pine needles, masking the sound of the horse's blowing. They passed within twenty feet of our position but didn't spot us.

"We should be getting the hell out of here," Howard whined. "It's crazy, trying to find 'em in the dark."

"I want to make sure," Ramon said. He was the one holding the flash.

"There's no way the horse didn't break a leg up there somewhere, Ramon."

"We gotta make sure it did and that Killebrew is dead, or on his way. And we gotta get rid of the ropes on his hands."

I was relieved to see the light move away up the hill. My best plan now was to get off the horse, though the process would be much harder than usual. It was a miracle he hadn't caught a leg in the hanging reins on the way down and killed us both. I didn't want to risk any more riding with my face pressed against that sweaty equine neck.

Taking it slowly and carefully, I slipped my right foot out of the stirrup, then the left foot. I slowly lowered myself to the ground, edging forward on the horse as I did so. The rope that tied my hands under the horse's neck shifted. When my feet were on terra firma, I got him to lower his head enough to work the looped rope free.

I took a step away from the animal. My hands were still tied, but with four feet of hemp between them, they had plenty of freedom of movement.

I led the horse down the hill to the road, weighing my options. If I tried leading him away, the two men could just get in the van and overtake us. No good. The other option was the only viable one: we had to use the van.

I looked up the canyon wall. I could still see the light from Ramon's flash, and it was heading up.

The back of the van was unlocked, but there was no key in the ignition. I had to gamble I could jump-start the thing. First, though, I spent precious minutes getting my four-legged friend into the van. He was obviously a good shipper and did his best to make it easy for me. We were working well together out of mutual gratitude.

I closed the back of the van and walked forward to the cab, sliding into the passenger seat. I glanced up the canyon again, looking for the light of the flash, but I couldn't see it now. As if to underline what bad news that was, there was a loud crack and the roof of the van was dented by a tremendous force just inches from my head.

I jumped over behind the wheel and reached under the dash for the starter wires. It surprised me they were already hanging loose and exposed. Obviously the idea of stealing this van was not original with me.

Ramon and Howard were running down the canyon now, shouting at me. The next shot was from closer range. The side window exploded, sending a shower of glass over my lap. The passenger behind me whinnied in renewed terror.

Somehow warding off my own instinct to panic, I managed to connect two of the bare wires and the van's starter turned over. But when I pumped the gas pedal, the motor wouldn't kick in.

Ramon was closer still, taking aim. I connected the wires again, and this time when I pumped the pedal, the engine roared into life. I put it in gear, hit the accelerator, and the van leaped forward with a jolt.

Ramon got off one more shot, but it was a futile gesture. My passenger and I were on our way. We'd helped each other cheat death.

8

GRATEFUL WHEN THE road signs finally offered a clue to our location, I steered the van up and out of Mulwray Canyon to the Ventura Freeway, following it to the Golden State. Then we worked our way through the familiar maze of downtown Los Angeles until, at last, we arrived back in East L.A.

That may sound like the easiest part of the job. And this was an hour of the night when the traffic was relatively light, though somebody's always going somewhere on California freeways. But with the adrenaline rush subsiding, the trip seemed almost as treacherous as the skid down the hillside.

Objectively speaking, I wasn't happy with my motoring prowess at the moment. I wasn't used to driving a horse van, but that wasn't the real problem. I was dizzy and my head ached from the knockout blow. I wondered if I didn't have a concussion.

But why think about that when I didn't have a choice?

I kept flashing back to my last day as a jockey. My last race. The one where I'd been so woozy from drugs, my reflexes so shot, I tried to go through a hole that wasn't there.

"Snap out of it, Coley!" My own voice came like a whipcrack. I'm not sure if I said it out loud, but I said it and it had its effect. No blackouts allowed now. Get the job done. Even if all I wanted was home and sleep, there were loose ends I had to tie up—and tight ends I had to loosen up, those knots around my wrists.

I felt safe from Ramon and Howard, at least for a while. It should take them some time to walk out of the canyon and find another vehicle to steal. I wanted to retrieve my car and do some self-medicating, but I had my pal in the back of the van to take care of first.

A few blocks away from Arriba!, I pulled the van in behind a service station that had closed for the night. Nearly invisible to the sparse small-hours traffic, I eased myself out of the cab, showering broken glass onto the concrete. I picked one of the bigger shards to cut the ropes from my wrists, a delicate operation that I managed with only a few minor scratches.

My next problem: whose van was this and whose horse was I chauffeuring around in it? I saw nothing in the cab but some reasonably fresh food scraps in a grease-stained Taco Loco bag, a half-dozen empty beer cans, and a pack of cheap rum-soaked crooks with three of the cigars missing. Nothing, that is, that would lead me to anybody but the two guys I least wanted to be led to at the moment, Ramon and Howard.

I walked around to the back of the van, a painful process. I could feel the contusions on my side and legs as I walked. They must be colorful. I'd find out later. My bones weren't broken, and I'd learned to live with bruises.

When I opened the back of the van, the horse shuffled his feet nervously. I patted him and whispered, "Okay now, fella. Just want to get you home, okay?"

On the floor of the van was a discarded horse blanket. I reached for it. There wasn't much light to read by, and my head was swimming a bit, but it was stamped in letters as big as the top line of the eye chart, PROPERTY OF CLOVERFIELD STABLES, OXNARD. Even in my present dazed and battered condition, that was a clue I could follow up.

There was a pay phone outside the service station, and I was amazed to find it in working order. Even the phone book was intact, but it didn't include Oxnard, so I got the number for Cloverfield from Directory Assistance.

The phone was answered on the first ring by a gruff-voiced

gent who identified himself as Shep Collins, Security. Not wanting to play my hand foolishly, in a way that could harm my partner in the van, I did my best to sound like somebody in authority
making a routine check.

"Everything secure over there, Shep?" I said matter-of-factly.

"Who the hell is this?" he demanded, not fooled for a second.

"You missing a big bay?" I asked in a neutral voice.

"You know we are, you son of a bitch," he growled. "What's
your deal?"

"What's yours?"

Shep started to reply, but another voice cut in, shaky and nervous. "This is Cap Tyler. I've been authorized by Candy Dan's
owner to offer you a hundred grand, unmarked bills. No cops. No
reprisals. Just bring the animal back."

That wasn't quite enough for me. I said carefully, "You sure you
don't want me to break his leg first?"

"Break his leg? Jesus, no." Tyler sounded so genuinely distressed,
I was sorry I had to put him through this. "Look, I . . . I can
throw in another twenty grand," he said. "But that's it. Just bring
him back. Unharmed."

That satisfied me I wouldn't be turning the horse over to the
people who wanted him injured. I gave Cap Tyler quick directions
to find the van and the animal, advising him unnecessarily to get
there in a hurry, and hung up without further conversation.

Resisting a sentimental impulse to say good-bye to the horse—
we'd been through a lot together, and until now I hadn't even
known he was named Candy Dan—I used my shirt to wipe the
steering wheel and the door handles. I knew I was getting rid of
Ramon and Howard's prints, too, but that couldn't be helped.

That accomplished, I jogged the few blocks to Arriba!. I guess
I jogged. I know I got there as fast as I could, and I know every
step hurt in three or four different places.

The building was shuttered, the neon sign dark, and my Cherokee was the only vehicle left in the lot. It had changed a bit since

I'd last seen it. My radio was too inexpensive to bother breaking a window for. But the hubcaps were gone and one bumper. At least the thieves hadn't stolen the engine. It started right up.

As lousy as I felt, I decided a little chat with Luis Falcon would not be a bad idea. It seemed pretty damned obvious he had set me up. So I drove to the address Roger Willetts had given me, a pale yellow stucco apartment building not far from Arriba!.

At Apartment 2-A I pushed the doorbell a few times. Nobody answered that or the heavy knocks I tried in case the bell was out of order. I decided Falcon was probably at Louisa's, and I had no idea where she lived.

By this time the energy born of fear and danger had worn off completely and I was feeling my wounds more than ever. Enough detecting for one night.

I might have been kidding myself, but I felt less woozy at the wheel of my familiar Cherokee. Still, I was relieved when the Horse's Neck came into sight.

It was closed for the night, too. The whole county was closed for the night. Was Candy Dan tucked away in his stall by now, at home in familiar surroundings? He should at least be well on his way. Nice horse. I'd have to send him a bouquet of carrots.

I had enough unscrambled gray matter left to check the locks very carefully before I entered the building. Ramon and Howard knew who I was and could find out where I lived easily enough. It didn't seem too likely they could have beaten me there, but events of the night had put me in a cautious mood.

As I reeled into the apartment I remembered spills gone by and thought about how to treat my injuries. Ice? Hot packs? Hell with that. I was okay, had been through lots worse than this, just needed some sleep. Something on the scratches and cuts? Naw, I wasn't going to bleed to death and the sheets would launder.

Nothing to do but grab a quick shower, take some aspirin, and go to sleep. Nothing to do but go to sleep and take some aspirin and one other thing first.

Call Lea. Wake her up. She won't care. Love her. Want to hear her voice. Punch out those numbers.

And there's her voice. Nice voice, but not her. Her machine. Nothing to tell her machine. Go to bed. Sleep.

9

IF I WERE still an active jockey, would I have ridden my mounts the next day? It depends. If I had the favorite in a half-million-dollar Grade One stake, absolutely. If I had a bunch of outsiders in twenty-thousand-dollar claiming races, I don't think so. In my present situation, though, the option of staying in bed with the covers pulled over my head didn't even occur to me.

The first thing I did was to drag my aching body out to the Cherokee and drive it to the dealer for a new bumper and hubcaps. The guy who wrote up my service order shook his head and admonished me to stay out of bad neighborhoods.

"Yeah," I said, "Rodeo Drive is getting worse every day. I just parked it for a second, in broad daylight, to run into Armani for some new shirts, and when I came out, this is what I found."

The guy looked so shocked, I was sorry to be putting him on. But then, these days in Southern California with the fires and mud slides and earthquakes, we have to find our little amusements where we can.

While waiting for the job to be done, I walked to a chain restaurant down the street to have breakfast. Fergy's is never haute cuisine, but it's pretty reliable. They'll serve you the same breakfast whether you're in Hollywood or Louisville or Boston.

A leggy young blonde whose name tag said she was Trudy greeted me like an old friend, established my smoking or non-smoking preference, led me to a red-upholstered booth, offered me a caffeine fix, and handed me a menu. She gave the impression it was all a rare privilege, not something she did a hundred times each morning. She seemed so natural and genuine, my mood turned a few degrees happier.

While I was studying the culinary form the radio station that had been providing mellow and tranquil elevator music suddenly negated all of its good work by offering the decidedly unsoothing daily commentary of Wilton Dresner. I wondered if Fergy's headquarters in Normal, Illinois, knew what this far-flung franchise was foisting on its diners.

Maybe it did. I was definitely in the minority. The place was full of Dresner fans, staff and customers alike.

The great man's face and voice were familiar to just about everybody in North America, barring a few Amish farmers without radios or TV sets, and even they could hardly avoid him if they came to town for provisions. He'd started as a radio newsman some thirty years before, moved to TV as a local anchor in L.A. around the time of the "first" riots, that is, Watts in 1968.

Finding his strongly jingoistic conservative opinions too dynamic to suppress in a daily news format, he'd moved to talk radio, first local, then syndicated; a newspaper column, first local, then syndicated; and finally to the TV talk show, never local, always syndicated, that had been his main platform for the past decade.

He seemed to be everywhere and unavoidable, especially for those of us who couldn't stand him. He'd been essentially a TV personality for years, but he'd kept doing the daily AM commentaries to keep touch with his radio roots.

That morning his subject was illegal immigration. But he never confined himself to hitting one hot button at a time. "It's easy to say our borders have to be controlled more closely. And it's easy to turn around and lay the blame for illegal immigration on honest and struggling small-business operators who need in any way available to them to get around the oppressive governmental bureaucracies that threaten their existence. It's so very easy, my friends, for liberals"—the way Dresner said it, the word might have been *child molesters* or *devil worshipers*—"who don't really want to solve the immigration problem to waltz all around it and ignore the one obvious solution.

"We need not just a controlled border but an *armed* border. Illegal immigrants need not to be politely turned back to try again another day but to be shot the second they set their feet on American soil. Just a few dead wetbacks—oh, excuse me, that's not politically correct terminology, is it? A few dead undocumented workers should be enough to send a message to those who would follow them.

"And before anybody starts calling me a racist pig who hates the Mexican, let me point out what all my fans already know. I'm talking here about the illegals. Our good, honest, God-fearing friends who have made the effort to enter our borders legally, who have struggled and succeeded in becoming United States citizens, are as welcome at my table as any stuck-up politician whose ancestors came over on the *Mayflower*. Even more so. The Mexico-born American is better company.

"And all Americans, wherever they were born, deserve the chance to profit from their labors. We can give them this chance by getting rid of the socialist programs that don't work and letting capitalism, the system that made this country the richest and most powerful and, yes, I'm not afraid to say it, *best* country on the face of the globe, flourish once again."

He railed on and on about the "tyranny of the minimum wage," dope smokers, the evils of MTV and "Beavis and Butthead," and welfare freeloaders. A couple of guys at the booth behind me were lapping it up. It was all they could do to keep from applauding every sentence, like they were Congress and Dresner was giving the State of the Union address. I must admit, he had a great radio voice, and his delivery was as surefooted as an upper-class con man's.

He went on to blithely attack abortion, gays in the military, gays not in the military, the president, the vice-president, the governor of California, the governor of New York, and unless I'm mistaken, Mother Teresa. Then he wrapped it up with, "This has been Wilton Dresner, with today's Modest Proposal."

A couple of commercials and the elevator music was back.

"Love that Dresner man," Trudy gushed when she came back to take my order. The smile and the legs hadn't changed, but somehow she didn't seem like such a sweetheart now.

I was hungry enough to merely mutter something noncommittal and order breakfast. It tasted okay. Ham and eggs and coffee know no politics.

Before I bid adieu to the little hotbed of right-wing brimstone, I stopped at a pay phone and tried Luis Falcon's number. He either wasn't there or wasn't picking up.

Seeing the Cherokee back in form made me feel a little better. But I wasn't satisfied with that. I wanted to feel delirious, and the key to that was Lea.

I aimed the Jeep toward the Santa Monica Freeway, checking the rearview mirror to see if any cars were in pursuit. I took a few unnecessary twists and turns. If anybody was tailing me, they'd have had to be a damn sight more subtle than Ramon and Howard.

Relaxing a bit, I rolled onto the freeway, heading west.

Lea lived in Venice, a beachfront community that had had its ups and downs since the days of the early twentieth century, when developers tried and failed to make it a California version of its namesake in Italy, complete with canals. Now it was a patchwork of the shabby and the elegant and the funky, home to a Bohemian crowd of artists and other creative types as well as the oldest living hippies known to man.

Lea's apartment was just off an extended alley improbably named Speedway. A few unanswered stabs at the doorbell convinced me she wasn't home. Her neighbor, trotting past with his Great Dane, Duchess, slowed down enough to tell me that Lea had gone out early that morning.

"Any idea where?" I asked him.

"Do I look like her social secretary?" he asked.

Duchess was wearing just a dab of perfume. I sniffed. "L'Air du Temps?" I asked her owner.

"I should say not," he replied. "Obsession, and nothing but."

I'd been guessing wrong all morning, so I decided to extend that run by heading a little farther down the Pacific Coast Highway to Lea's father's place in Marina Del Rey. Maybe I'd find her there.

Raymond Edgar Starbuck's house was right on the sand, an impressive two-story structure of sun-bleached wood. Choo Choo, the Asian butler, gave me a friendly greeting at the door.

"Is Miss Lea here, Choo?"

"No, not today," he said, shaking his head regretfully. "Sorry."

"Starbuck?"

He nodded.

"Then he'll have to do," I said.

Choo Choo nodded, ushered me in. "I'll tell him you're here, Mr. Killebrew."

He left me briefly in the entry hall, where pictures of famous nineteenth-century jockeys lined the walls. Tod Sloan, who'd been the fictionalized subject of a George M. Cohan musical comedy and had inspired the song "Yankee Doodle Dandy," was one of them. Snapper Garrison, the Eddie Delahoussaye of his day, whose fast-closing riding style was known as the "Garrison finish," was another.

Then there was Isaac Murphy, the black jockey who'd had a knack for winning Kentucky Derbies. I tried to remember when I'd last ridden against a black jockey. For whatever reason, they were rare today, but they'd been a dominant force in racing of the Reconstruction period.

Why all the old-timers in Starbuck's jockey gallery, I wondered? Why no Arcaro or Longden? I knew the horse portraits in the living room included some reasonably contemporary champions, including my onetime mount Spectacular Bid, but Starbuck didn't go in for depictions of living jockeys—even guys from fifty and sixty years ago like Earl Sande and Johnny Loftus were apparently too recent for him.

After a couple of minutes Choo Choo came back and invited me to follow him. We found the lord of the manor on the massive deck outside his office, where he was intently applying varnish to a birdhouse.

Starbuck was a big man with a square face, looking at the world over Ben Franklin half glasses. At the moment he was dressed in his usual at-home outfit of stained, faded polo shirt with the horse and rider almost worn away, flip-flops the size of tennis rackets on his big feet, and khaki walking shorts. I thought of the article I'd read recently about all the historical tyrants, Hitler included, who favored khaki.

Choo Choo had told him I was there, so he must have agreed to talk to me, but he still felt obliged to act as if my appearance on his deck was an unwelcome surprise. Regarding me as if I were something that just crawled out of a seashell, he asked, "What the devil do you want?"

Freed by the greeting of any obligation to common courtesy, I got right to the point. "I want you to stop interfering with me and Lea."

"You want me to what?" He forgot all about his birdhouse for the moment and gawked at me.

"You heard me."

"Lea's an adult, Killebrew. I don't interfere in her life, and God knows I haven't been interfering with yours. I haven't even seen you in—I don't know how long, but not long enough. Why don't you just get off my property and take your sophomoric fantasies with you?"

He picked up his varnish brush again, a gesture of dismissal. But I wasn't ready to be dismissed.

"Not until we talk about this. Are you going to deny that you've been keeping Lea so busy we can't get together?"

"Will you listen to yourself? You sound like a high-school kid.

I'm in business, Killebrew, and my daughter is not just my daughter but a very important part of my business, the best damned operative I have. The assignments I send her way have nothing to do with how I think it will affect her social life. If the jobs she does for me are putting a crimp in her personal affairs, all she has to do is tell me."

"Bullshit. She'll do anything you say, Starbuck, go where you want her to go, do what you want her to do. And you can take advantage of that any way you choose."

"So my daughter's an unthinking robot, huh? Why are you so attracted to her, then?" He sighed and put aside his brush. "Come with me."

He led me into his office and plunked down behind the big black oak desk, strewn as always with papers. He directed me to take a chair. Then he picked up a bulging manila file folder, like a district attorney brandishing Exhibit A in the face of the jury.

"These are Lea's current reports," he said. "She is involved in a very complicated job, and it's getting more and more complicated every day. And we don't have all the time in the world to get it done. I'm sorry if this is interfering with your romance but . . . hell, I'm not sorry at all. I don't like my daughter hanging around with riffraff. But I know her well enough that I'd never tell her that."

I was still skeptical. "Those sheets of paper packing the file folder could be your bird-seed inventory for all I know," I told him.

"Believe what you want. But I don't make up her schedule. She does that herself. If she's working late instead of putting up with you, that's her decision, not mine. Talk to *her* about it."

Now I was really annoyed. With myself for busting in like an idiot and with Lea for stringing me along without explanation. But most of my annoyance was aimed where it belonged: at Starbuck. He was trying to make me doubt Lea, make me think she had been purposely avoiding me with all the broken dates. He was still trying to drive a wedge between us, and I told myself I wouldn't let it happen.

I must have sat there for a minute or two processing everything. Finally Starbuck broke the silence.

"As long as you're here, why don't you tell me what that wiseguy partner of yours, Johnny Rousseau, is doing in town?"

"What makes you think he's in town?" I said warily.

"Little bird told me."

"Don't listen to little birds. You can't trust them. They just love you for your birdhouses."

Ignoring that, he said, "Do you know if Rousseau's making any investments? Like maybe buying a horse or two?"

"Not that I've heard."

"You'd know, though, if he was?"

"I think so. What's this all about?"

He didn't answer right away, but when he did, he had my full attention. "Your pal Rousseau is getting mixed up in something very nasty. Maybe he knows what he's doing, but if not, you can help him and you can help me."

I was hooked. Starbuck might know something that would tie in with Paula Dresner's problem, and I owed it to Johnny to find out all I could. "What's up?" I asked.

"I'm going to tell you everything I know about this business, Killebrew," Starbuck said. "I hope you'll return the favor by being equally candid with me."

"You're going to tell me as much as you think it's to your advantage to tell me," I corrected him. "And I guarantee I'll do the same."

"Okay, put it any way you want. My client is Bright's, Limited. You've heard of them?"

"Sure. British insurance company. They specialize in horses."

"Right, they like to call themselves the Lloyd's of London of the Thoroughbred bloodstock business. But they have something else in common with Lloyd's they don't like."

"Paying out on claims?" I guessed.

"No insurance company likes to do that. But the occasional big payoff is good for publicity, brings in business. It's the claims that don't fit their extrapolations of acceptable risk that really piss them off. More than piss them off. Some of the payouts they've had to make over the past few years have brought them to the edge of bankruptcy."

"How did that happen?"

"Too many of the animals they've insured have been dying. It's thrown their actuarial tables into the toilet."

"And they suspect fraud."

"Hell yes, they suspect it. They've pinned down some clear cases. But they don't know just how extensive the fraud is. They've put me to work checking out some of their bigger payoffs on the West Coast."

"Is this what Lea's working on?"

"Let's leave Lea out of this discussion," he said.

"She's the only reason I'm here."

"Don't try to put me in the middle of you and her, Killebrew. If you want to know what she's working on, talk to her about it."

I restrained myself from continuing on that tack. I may have come here looking for Lea, but at the moment I was working for Johnny, not sorting out my own love life. "What do you want from me?" I asked.

"Find out if Rousseau is cutting a deal on a racehorse. Let me know the details."

"There must be more to it."

Starbuck hesitated a moment, then said, "Okay. Let me explain it to you."

He mulled over his next words, like a professor in the classroom trying to decide how to convey information to a class of dumb undergraduates. Finally he said, "Let's say you wanted to pull an insurance scam with a horse. What's the first thing you'd do?"

"Take out a policy, I guess," I said.

He matched my sarcasm. "Uh-huh. Good thinking. For how much?"

"For the value of the horse maybe?"

He sighed. "And what determines the value of the horse?"

"The price tag the owner puts on him."

"Yeah? And how would you prove the value you put on him is what he's really worth? If you have a ten-thousand-dollar claimer that you feel is worth a million, do you think any insurance company is going to let you insure him for a million?"

"I guess not."

"So I ask you again—how do you demonstrate the value of the horse?"

"Has he done anything on the track?" I wondered.

"Let's say zilch."

"Then the price I paid for him is the only measure of his value, I guess."

"At last we're getting somewhere. And if you're running a scam, you want the amount the horse gets insured for to be as high as you can get it. So what do you do to pump it up?"

I was getting sick of Starbuck and his patronizing attitude. I said, "We'd get through this a lot faster if you ditched the Q-and-A approach and just told me what you know."

"As thick as you are, maybe you're right. Here's how it works. Several people are involved in the scam, not just you."

"You didn't mention that before."

"I'm mentioning it now. Before you pull the scam, you do everything you can to jack up the value of the animal. That's accomplished by several paper sales among the involved parties. A Thoroughbred is sold for a hundred and fifty thousand, then resold for two hundred thousand, then for half a million, and on and on. Only no money changes hands.

"But not everybody involved in this artificial escalation of price is in on the scam. Every now and then a mark is dragged in, just in case the scam falls apart. The mark thinks he's making a legitimate investment. And he may come out of it a few thousand dollars richer. Then again, he may be left holding the reins on a dead animal with the cops at the door."

"You think Johnny is playing the mark?"

"That would be the more charitable interpretation."

"Another interpretation being that he's one of the guys running the scam?" I asked.

Starbuck shrugged his brawny shoulders. "You tell me."

I shook my head. "If it helps, I can tell you this much. Johnny Rousseau did not come to L.A. to buy a horse."

"How sure of that are you?"

"Pretty damn sure."

"Do me a favor and get absolutely damn sure, okay? You'll be doing him a favor, too."

"Okay," I said. "Why not? But I'd like you to do something for me in return. I need some information I could ferret out for myself, but I think you can get it a lot faster than I can, with all your gizmos." I waved a hand at the computer terminal, copier, and fax machine on his desk.

"What do you want to know?"

"Everything you can find about the sixth race at Land O' Lincoln on May nineteenth, 1992. I'm especially interested in the winner of the race, ridden by Luis Falcon. I've been told it was a filly or mare named Bathsheba, owned by the Carew family in Lexington, but I want to be sure."

"That should be easy enough." Starbuck looked interested and a little suspicious. "I know the Carews, but I don't remember Bathsheba."

Neither did I, and Falcon had made her sound like the second coming of Regret.

"Does this have something to do with Rousseau?" Starbuck asked.

"No." It wasn't exactly a lie. As far as I knew, it had nothing to do with Johnny.

Starbuck opened his mouth to ask another question but decided not to. He must have realized that I'd told him all I was going to. He picked up the phone and started punching buttons.

"Chicago," he muttered. "You don't mind running up my phone bill."

I didn't reply. I knew he was curious enough that he'd have made the call on his own behalf as soon as I was out the door if he hadn't made it for me.

He got through to his contact at Land O' Lincoln, and in less than two minutes of the track's computer time, he had the answers. A chart of the race came curling its way out of his fax machine.

"First of all," he said, studying the chart, "Falcon's mount was named Briarpatch, not Bathsheba. And the horse isn't owned by the Carews. His owner's an Illinois breeder named Bricknell." He passed the chart over to me.

Evidently Luis Falcon had lied about everything. According to the chart, there was nothing particularly eventful about the race, except that Briarpatch, a sixteen-to-one shot, had won in a walk. According to the index column on the left side of the chart, he hadn't had a previous race in the United States. The note on the winner's connections showed he'd been bred in Argentina.

"Import, huh?" I said.

"That's not so unusual. More horses than ever are coming up from South America. You ever watch 'Murder, She Wrote' on TV, Coley?"

"I've seen it," I said, noting the sudden first-name chumminess and wondering where he was going.

"They did a show with a racing background. Mickey Rooney played a trainer who gets murdered. The plot turned on a ringer, like stories about racing often do. Supposedly a great horse got his identity switched with a cheap one, and the great horse wound up running in South America and making big money. That gave me a laugh."

I knew what he meant. Horse racing had been depressed down there for years. The best Thoroughbreds in South America, running in Grade One stakes races, were going for the same kind of purses as the cheapest claimers at Santa Anita or Hollywood Park. If you had a good horse in Argentina or Chile or Brazil, nothing made better sense than to bring him north. Or her. Argentine mares like Bayakoa and Paseana had made a big splash in North American racing. Moving a decent runner in the other direction made no sense at all.

"So, you satisfied?" Starbuck asked.

I nodded. "Mind if I keep this chart?"

Starbuck reached for it. "I'll make you a copy," he said. Meaning he wanted to keep one for himself. He wasn't convinced this had nothing to do with Johnny Rousseau or his investigation.

When the copy was made and he'd handed it across the desk, he said, "Now, to complete our bargain, you get together with the wiseguy and satisfy me. Okay?"

"Sure."

"Only don't tell him too much."

"Johnny's my friend," I said. "What makes you think I won't tell him everything you've told me?"

He looked at me for a moment before he answered, spacing his words for effect. "I don't much like you, Killebrew. But I don't think you're the kind of guy who'd help scumbags slaughter magnificent animals for fun and profit."

"You know I'm not," I said. Mentally, I flashed back to my adventure with Candy Dan.

"If Rousseau's just a mark, I'll protect him. If he isn't, he'll go down with the others."

"Who are the others?" I asked.

"There's no reason for you to know," he said, turning his back to me. "Now get out of here and let me do some work."

His back was no more appealing than his front. I got out of there.

10

THIS TIME I didn't have to try very hard to find Johnny. My soon-to-be ex-partner was waiting for me back at the Horse's Neck. He was occupying a bar stool, schmoozing with Lew Roselli, the head bartender, and our new midday drink pourer, Al Grady.

Grady was talking and gesturing and making faces, and at the end of it all, the three of them broke into loud laughter. Probably one of Grady's Catholic-priest jokes.

Whatever they were talking about, I was sure it wasn't the business. Johnny's interest in the day-to-day running of the place had never been more than casual.

When he saw me, he waved me over. "Hey, partner! What're you drinking?"

"Nothing at the moment," I said. My aching head wasn't quite ready for any alcohol.

The place was pretty well deserted, and I'd expected it to be humming. "Where's all the trade, Lew? I see two bartenders and no customers. Didn't they used to call that featherbedding?"

"Lunchtime rush is over, Coley," Lew told me. A glance of my watch told me how completely I'd lost track of the time. It can fly even when you're not having fun. With a sidelong glance at his new assistant, Lew added, "Featherbedding, huh? Serve him right if we unionized, wouldn't it, Al?"

"Did I tell you the one about the priests' union?" Grady asked brightly.

"Yeah, you did," I assured him.

"They set up a picket line in front of the confessionals, see—"

"Yeah, I remember," I said. "Great story."

"Can I order you something from the kitchen, Coley?" Lew offered.

"Just bring me some coffee. Let's take a table, Johnny." A chair would be kinder to my bruises than a bar stool.

Johnny was dressed in black trousers, black tennis shoes, and a lime-green T-shirt under a black windbreaker. As we walked to our table I noticed there was mud caked on his trouser legs and clods of mud sticking to his shoes.

When we were seated, he said, "I never heard the one about the priests' union."

I shook my head. "I haven't either."

"Then why . . . ? What's on your mind, Coley? You seem strung out. Something about Paula?"

"Well," I said, "I think she spotted me yesterday. She ditched me."

He frowned. "Jesus, that's no good. What're you gonna do?"

"Be more careful, I guess," I told him. Actually, I was going to keep looking into the Woo murder, but I didn't want to get into that with him. I hadn't said anything to him about my ride down the canyon on Candy Dan.

"You gotta be more careful," he said, worry-frowning.

"I plan on it," I said. Then, trying to sound him out about Starbuck's suspicions, I asked, "Anything new with you?"

"Yeah, that's why I came here looking for you. You busy tonight?"

"I don't know. Am I?"

He nodded. "Yeah, you are. At least I don't think you'll want to pass this up. Wilton's throwing a big black-tie charity deal at the Quarterdeck Club in Malibu. It has a gambling theme. The old man says I gave him the idea."

I winced a little. "Charity deal, huh? What's it going to set me back?"

"Not to worry. Tickets are a thou apiece, but I scored you one. It'll give you a chance to observe Paula up close, in her element. But keep it subtle, huh?"

"I'll leave my leopard-skin cummerbund at home."

"Come on, you can dress how you want. What I meant was, you and me, we don't know each other in front of her."

I didn't really get the point of the deception, but I just said, "If you like."

"It should be fun. Mark Brittan and his wife will probably be there."

"You did say she was into group activities."

"What's that supposed to mean? Oh, I see. Big party. Group. Very funny."

I asked casually, "Where'd you pick up all the dirt?"

Johnny looked down at his trousers and shoes. "Aw, Christ." He tried to slap the caked mud away. "I never can set foot in a stable without looking like one of the mud people."

"I didn't know you rode."

"Me? Ride? I like to watch the gee gees race, but I don't want to get personal with one. This was business."

"You wouldn't be buying a horse, would you?"

"I can't talk about it," he said.

That was ominous. Where should I go from here? Still playing it as light as I could, I said, "If you *are* buying, maybe I can give you a few pointers. I do have a little experience in that field, you know. There are things to watch for."

"Yeah, sure, count the legs, make sure there's four of 'em, I know."

"It's not that simple."

"I know, I know. Look, Coley, if I ever buy a horse to race, you're the guy I'll want to have a look at him. But I'm not buying this horse to race. In fact, I'm really not buying him at all. I'm just sort of investing some money at a high rate of interest."

That sounded like the scam Starbuck had described, all right.

Keeping my voice level, as if only politely interested, I said, "How does that work?"

"Guy who owns the nag needs some fast cash. So he sells it to me for a couple weeks, then buys it back at my purchase price plus interest. Easy dough, huh?"

"Sure. Sounds great. But suppose he doesn't have the loot to buy it back? Then you wind up owning a horse you don't want."

"In this case, that's not possible."

"Another thing is, suppose something happens to the horse while you own him?"

Johnny looked blank. "Like what?"

"All kinds of things can happen to horses. They're pretty fragile animals. A broken leg. Illness."

"Well," Johnny said with a grin, "then I guess it would be the insurance company's problem, huh?"

"I guess so," I said, still straining to be casual.

It looked like Starbuck knew more about my partner's activities in Los Angeles than I did. But Johnny Rousseau was into all sorts of things I knew nothing about and didn't want to know anything about.

So, was Johnny a dupe or was he part of the scam? Could be either one. If he was a dupe, I didn't really trust Starbuck to keep him clear of the fallout. But either way, I decided I couldn't get into it with Johnny. Whether he was innocent or guilty, he'd probably tell the others involved enough for them to realize somebody had an eye on them. If I blew Starbuck's whole operation that way, he'd be even less likely to provide Johnny with an escape hatch.

All I said to Johnny was, "Just play it safe, partner. I wouldn't want you to get stuck."

"When did I ever not play it safe? I know my way around deals like this. You just worry about what's up with Paula, and pretty soon"—he cut the air with a wide sweep of his arm—"all this will be yours."

11

A BIG PLACARD outside the door of the Quarterdeck Club's ballroom welcomed me to the party, proclaimed the new name for the room would be Casino Dresner, and informed me that all proceeds would benefit the AEF, whatever that was. I checked in at a table where a young woman with dazzling white teeth was greeting every guest as if they were royalty. Maybe some of them were, so it was smart of her to play it safe.

When I stepped inside the room, I was impressed. They must have hired a studio set designer. The ballroom had been transformed into a Mississippi gambling boat, with a giant flowered paddle wheel decorating one whole wall. The grand circular staircase in the center of the room could have led to Captain Andy's command deck. There were roulette wheels, blackjack and crap tables, and other standard casino features, all of them apparently irresistible to the crowd of men in look-alike tuxes and women in a stunning variety of evening gowns.

At the bar, also well attended, there didn't seem to be any money changing hands. "Drinks on the house?" I asked another stag male who'd arrived the same time I had, a young black-haired guy with a jaded manner that seemed to belong to somebody much older.

"You better believe it," he said, like it was expected. "You go to many of these shindigs?"

"Not many," I said with a smile.

"Well, there are very firm and sensible rules about when there's an open bar and when it's strictly 'no host.' "

"Sounds like you're an old hand."

"They invite me and I'm here," he confided. "Not a guest, exactly. Working press. I'm with the *L.A. Sun.* Frank Sanchez."

"Coley Killebrew."

"Thought you looked familiar," he said, shaking hands.

"You a society reporter?" I ventured.

"No, but I know the rules of charity clambakes like this. If all you're offering is entertainment and conversation, you soak the patrons for their drinks, at the rate of, say, five bucks for a thimble-sized glass of vino."

I nodded. "That's what I expected."

"But this is the other kind, where they're going after the really big bucks. If you want to loosen up the old inhibitions, make them gamble their money away or make bids on items way past their real value at an auction, you're well advised to keep the alcohol flowing freely."

"If you're not a society reporter, what are you doing here?" I asked.

"I'm working on a series of articles on Wilton Dresner. May even turn 'em into a book if I get lucky. I'm following him around like a shadow. Interesting guy. More complicated than you'd think."

"Favorable articles?" I asked.

Sanchez laughed. "I don't know what your connection with Dresner is. . . ."

"None."

"Well, I'm keeping an open mind," he said. "At least until I'm through following him around. I need his cooperation."

"Do you know his daughter?"

"Haven't been able to get to her. Or the son. They're both kind of hard to pin down. And Dresner hasn't given me any help there.

I get the feeling he'd like me to keep away from the family, though he hasn't said it in so many words."

"Do you think there's a story in the family?"

Sanchez grinned. "There's always a story in the family. I can tell Dresner's crazy about the daughter. She grew up with her mother, but came to live with him when she was eighteen. He gives her anything she wants. The son, on the other hand, I get the feeling is a disappointment to him. Sort of a playboy type, can't settle down to anything. What I get from other people, not from him, is that he'd rather I didn't talk to the daughter because he wants to shield his innocent flower from the evil influences of the world and doesn't want me to talk to the son because he's ashamed of him."

"I suppose they'll be here tonight."

"I'm counting on it." Sanchez glanced over his shoulder to where the evening's host was standing in a circle of admirers. "But for now, I better keep close to my man, memorizing his every word for posterity. That's my excuse for being here, after all. Just call me Boswell."

The reporter moved toward Dresner's circle while I drifted on to the corner of the room where the evening's prizes were displayed. The largest of them was a new jet-black Jaguar sedan, and I wondered how they had gotten it into the ballroom of the Quarterdeck Club. Taken it apart and reassembled it maybe? Or perhaps the building had a removable wall, or at least a garage-sized door hidden by some of the gambling-boat decorations.

There was a young woman in an abbreviated outfit watching over the car and describing it and the other prizes to the gathered suckers. She'd have been right at home at an auto show. I asked her what I had to do to win, and she gave me a practiced spiel.

Casino gambling, of course, was illegal in Malibu, as it then was in most of California. But they circumvented the laws against gambling because this was all for charity and because the guests weren't gambling real money. Or not exactly. What they were doing was the same as what patrons of casinos do every day—they were buying chips. In this case, the chips had been manufactured especially for the affair. Stamped *Casino Dresner*, they came in three denominations—hundred-dollar whites with a caricature of our host's mug in the center, fifty-dollar reds bearing Paula's picture, and twenty-five-dollar blues carrying the drawing of a long-haired male, undoubtedly Neil.

At evening's end, the chips could be exchanged for the donated prizes, which included a big-screen color TV—she indicated it with a Vanna White–like gesture—and other toys in addition to the car.

"But," I said to her, "couldn't anybody in a position to plunk down the thousand-dollar entry fee buy any of those things for themselves?"

"I guess they could," she said with a smile, "but that doesn't seem to be hurting business, does it?"

She was right. The social elite that filled the hall clearly had a touch of gambling fever.

"What's the AEF anyway?" I asked her.

"The what?"

"The outfit we're gambling all this dough to benefit."

"Oh, dear," she said, "they didn't tell me. I know all about the prizes and how to win them, but they didn't tell me that. I probably ought to know, shouldn't I? You might ask—"

"Never mind," I said. "It's more fun guessing."

I hadn't contributed diddly to the cause, and I wasn't about to even if I knew what it was, so I had no play money to squander. But I could take full advantage of the open bar. I spent the early part of my evening sipping a very fine California Chardonnay and watching the tuxedoed and gowned gentry cast off their reserve.

Finally I managed to meet my host, who had undertaken the task of shaking hands personally with everybody in the room. With his fierce, slightly protruding eyes, his small hooked nose, and his otherworldly toupee, Dresner was an imposing figure, not quite as mountainous as his soul mate Rush Limbaugh but on his way there.

"Mr. Killebrew, of course," boomed that great radio voice. "Delighted to have you with us. I've certainly enjoyed your exploits on the turf." His voice and manner were enthusiastic, but the look in his eye suggested I was just another empty tux. Challenged to describe any of my exploits on the turf, I doubted he'd be able to come up with one.

A few other partygoers, obviously people he knew from way back, struck up a conversation, and I hung around on the periphery, looking politely interested. Frank Sanchez was there, too, not taking notes but taking it all in. He must have had the reporter's well-trained memory.

"Have you had any word from Ed Fein, Wilton?" asked a neatly mustached, stocky guy in his late forties. He had an English accent that went well with evening clothes and that blandly deadpan delivery that let the world know he was applying the needle.

Dresner accepted it from him in good spirits. Either they were very good friends or the Englishman was somebody with power or money that Dresner thought he might make use of. "No," the big man replied, "I have not heard word one from Fein. And if I ever get my hands on that deceitful bastard, I'll cook him with his books, I can tell you. I should have known what kind of skunk he was when he admitted he voted for Clinton."

The whole group had a hearty laugh at that.

"I can introduce you to my guy," another of the group said. "He's a crook, too, but he voted for Bush."

"Who's Ed Fein?" I asked innocently.

"A former associate of mine," Dresner said. His voice and manner indicated he was being a good sport, but, again, the lightheartedness didn't extend to his eyes. "Took me for . . . well, let's say a lot of money and vanished off the face of the earth. And he had the bad form to do it on my beautiful daughter's birthday."

"One of the great disappearing acts," said the British needler. "It should rank with Amelia Earhart and Judge Crater."

"I hope to hell Ed Fein doesn't turn into a legend," Dresner growled. "I'm sick of hearing about the bastard."

"He's probably dead," suggested another of the tuxes in our circle.

"That would be comforting," Dresner said. "But I'd sure like to know what he did with my money."

That was when somebody, probably thinking Dresner would appreciate a change of subject, mentioned how close the Quarter-deck Club had come to destruction in the recent Malibu fire. Instead of allowing our host to slip from center stage, the new topic sent Dresner off on a choice right-wing tirade.

"I lay that right at the door of the environmentalists," he pronounced.

"I thought it was an arsonist," the needler interjected. "I didn't know he belonged to the Sierra Club."

"Arsonist or no arsonist—and when they find him, he ought to burn along with Fein's books—but arsonist or no arsonist, the fires would never have spread the way they did if it weren't for those goddamn touchy-feely cottontail kissers who care more about some tree rat than they do about people. People who got burned out couldn't even clear the brush around their houses because some fuzzy or feathered friend had his goddamn habitat there."

"I know that was the case down in Laguna, but Malibu—"

"Don't burden me with details. The principle's what's important. Those environmental types believe in nature and Darwin and evolution. God doesn't come into it. But use their own logic and their whole argument falls apart. Nature determines what species survive and what species go under, and we have no business trying to short-circuit the normal processes of nature."

His needler, whom I was starting to suspect of environmental leanings, said, "Well, isn't that the whole point?"

"Of course it's the whole point."

"I mean, surely that's what the environmentalists want. For things to take their natural course without interference."

"Right. But what the environmentalists choose to forget is that we're all part of nature. You're part of nature. I'm part of nature. The real-estate developers are part of nature. Everything created as a result of our natural human brains, whether it's plastic or chemical or so-called synthetic, is just as much a part of nature as the goddamn gnat catcher and whatever he does in his precious habitat."

The British needler said, "You continue to surprise me, Wilton. I'd never in a million years have thought you'd support genetic engineering."

"I'd support what?"

"Well, if every human achievement is part of nature, you must think scientists who alter human genes are part of nature, too. Or that doctors who figured out how to do safe abortions are part of nature."

"If they are, then it's *my* nature to fight 'em every inch of the way." Dresner roared with laughter, poking his friendly adversary on the shoulder with a fist. "You know what I was doing, don't you? Using their own reasoning to defeat them. If you think like we do, that God created everything and made man special, gave us dominion over the animals, then it's a lot simpler. My habitat outranks the gnat catcher's and that's that."

Dresner suddenly became conscious he'd drawn quite a crowd around him. What had started in a group of four had now expanded to more than a dozen.

"Seriously, folks," he told them, "I'm no ogre. I believe in doing what's best for my fellowman, and even my fellow animal. The cause we're here to serve tonight should tell you that." And what cause were we serving anyway? I'd have to find out. "It's just that it should all be left to the private sector," Dresner droned on. "It definitely should not be entrusted to governmental bureaucracy, which tells a homeowner he can't clear his brush because that'll make it hard on rats."

With that, he drifted along to greet another group of guests. I turned to the Britisher who'd been having fun with him and said, as if I knew what I was talking about, "Too bad about that Ed Fein thing."

"Oh, I don't know. Wilton was getting a bit too complacent. He'd invited the accountant to attend a little family birthday party for his daughter, Paula, but Fein had begged off, saying he had too much work to do. The bugger's work was the theft of five million dollars. He made off with it that very night. When Wilton discovered the theft a couple days later, it certainly woke him up. I must say it woke me up, too. I had Fein picked as a stable, reliable chap. Not at all the sort to take your money and run to South America or wherever. Have you known Wilton long?"

"Not very," I admitted.

"He's quite a chap. Talks a load of rubbish, of course. But not everything he says is wrong. Some of it makes a good deal of sense."

"Some of it," I agreed. That was one of the things that made him so dangerous.

The room was getting more and more crowded. The AEF, whatever the hell it was, would be getting a nice infusion of dough out of this. I didn't notice Johnny Rousseau arrive, but after I'd been there about half an hour, I saw him discreetly drifting in my direction. He didn't greet me as a friend but nodded tentatively like a stranger striking up a conversation with a fellow guest. I could tell right away his mood was far from cheery.

"You should feel right at home," I told him.

"No way," he said. "I like to see real loot on the table."

"Where's the real loot going, by the way?"

"The AEF," Johnny said.

"I saw the signs, but as a freeloader, I didn't get the pitch literature. I've been trying to figure out what the letters stand for."

"You coulda asked anybody," Johnny said.

"Not quite anybody. The girl guarding the prizes didn't know. Anyway, it's more fun trying to dope it out. I know it's one of Wilton Dresner's causes so . . . Americans for Emasculating Flagburners? Abortion Elimination Fellowship? Advocates of Ethnic Fumigation? Abolish Environmental Fuckheads?"

"Funny material, Coley," he said without a hint of a smile. "You want me to book you into the lounge at the casino? There's nothing political about the AEF. It's the Anti-Endotoxemia Foundation. You know about endotoxemia?"

"Sure," I said. "It kills horses."

"It's the *number one* killer of horses," Johnny recited, a note of sarcasm in his voice. "I know all the stats. The Dresners are yakking about it all the time."

"I didn't know Dresner was a horse lover."

"Maybe he isn't, but he's sure propping up the AEF."

"Why?"

Johnny said sourly, "There's this guy, a friend of the family, who heads up the foundation and oversees a research lab where they're trying to come up with a cure."

"Friend have a name?" I asked.

"Dr. Charles Lavery." The way he pronounced the name, a stiff monotone with a tightening of his jaw, suggested he didn't feel too friendly toward the family friend.

"I've heard of him," I said. "He's a vet."

"Yeah," said Johnny, biting off the word. "He'll be here tonight. He's the fuckin' guest of honor." He clearly had a problem of some kind with Lavery, and I wondered what it was. Something to do with Paula, of course. A rival? That question would answer itself when Lavery arrived. I had another one for Johnny.

"Does Dresner own any horses?"

"The old man? No."

"What about the son, Neil?" I asked.

"I think he may, yeah."

I looked at him for a moment without speaking, hoping he'd add something more without my having to press him. Then I smiled and said, "Come on, Johnny, you know my next question. Is Neil the one selling you a horse?"

Johnny shook his head vehemently. "Leave that alone, Coley. It's got nothing to do with your job for me."

Ignoring that, I went on, "Because if he is, that may be the real reason his sister asked you to come here, so you could buy little brother's horse."

Johnny chilled me with a look. "I'm gonna do my best to forget you said that," he told me. "Because if I . . ." Instead of finishing the thought, he gave me a casual nod and a clap on the shoulder, then walked away.

I wondered why he'd left so abruptly until I noticed Paula Dresner looking in our direction. It was my first Paula sighting of the evening. She created such a presence in the room, she must not have been there for long. She appeared considerably more relaxed and in control than she had running from Jerry Woo's office. Considerably more attractive, too, in a tight and filmy black gown that was no more revealing than her workout outfit, but in context a definite attention grabber.

Through no plan of mine, our eyes met. Eyes will do that. She smiled at me. I nodded and smiled back. She walked over. I didn't sense any recognition in her face. Unless she was a much better actress than she'd appeared to be at the playhouse, she really had no idea I'd been tailing her.

"Hi, I'm Paula Dresner. I don't think we've met."

"Coley Killebrew," I said, extending a hand. "Some party."

"You're a jockey, aren't you?"

"Past tense. I'm retired now. Do you go to the races?"

"Once in a while. My brother, Neil, has horses."

I noticed she was speaking English, not that schoolgirl slang I'd heard her use at the restaurant.

"Is your brother here tonight?"

"I haven't seen him. I think he'll be along later." She looked me over, wetting her lips with a pink tongue. I suddenly knew how a yearling at auction must feel. Finally she said, "You know, I've always wondered. How do you control a big, heavy animal like that. Is it the hands?"

Almost involuntarily, I held out one of mine, the one that wasn't holding the wineglass.

"The hands are important, sure. But it's not all physical. You have to have a certain rapport with the horse."

She took my hand and squeezed it. Her eyes were fixed on mine, a teasing smile on her face. She said, "Rapport is all very well. But I'm sure strength is more important." She let my hand go. "I bet your legs are strong, too. I bet you're a wonderful rider. I'd love to see you in action."

"There are videotapes of my rides available," I said.

"I was thinking of a more personal demonstration."

"Do you ride yourself?" I asked her.

"I'd never ride myself," she said, with a suggestive laugh. "How boring. It's so much more entertaining to let others do the riding."

I won't pretend I wasn't feeling the effects of the number she was doing on me. I didn't know if she had anything specific in mind, or if this was just how she dealt with every male who crossed her path. I flattered myself that it meant I'd made some kind of imaginary first cut. Given my relationship with Johnny, as well as what I knew about her real personality, I wasn't going to let it go any further, even if it had that potential.

Before I could decide what innocent statement to challenge her one-track mind with next, she started pulling me toward the door of the ballroom. "My brother Neil's here," she explained. "Have you met him?"

I shook my head.

"Well, you must," she said.

I got my first look at Neil Dresner as we headed across the room. He was a man in his twenties, dressed in a rumpled tux and tennis shoes. Lank black hair bothered his forehead.

The stereotype that came to mind may have been unfair, but I was pretty sure I was right. I'd seen plenty of young men like him, children of wealth and privilege who haven't been broadened by their advantages. Instead they become moody and bitter and, in many cases, addicted to booze or drugs or gambling or a combination of all three. I knew Neil had a gambling problem, and I wondered which of the other vices helped him fill his days. And nights.

His handsome sullen face surveyed the party. It apparently wasn't where he wanted to be. When he looked across the room at his father, who was laughing heartily at some comment just uttered by the state senator standing beside him, he couldn't conceal his scorn. But when he spotted his sister rushing toward him, there was a big change. His face shone and came alive. One thing Johnny had neglected to mention was the genuine fondness the two Dresner offspring had for one another.

At first I'd thought Neil had arrived alone. But apparently his companion had been hanging back. The girlfriend Neil brought forward was something to see, a dazzler in Paula's league, or maybe in a league of her own. She was tall and blond and beautiful, with an intelligence that shone through the beauty.

She was Lea Starbuck.

12

"PAULA, YOU REMEMBER Roz?" Neil asked, indicating Lea.

"Of course. Roz *Holbrook*, right? How nice to see you again," his sister replied. There was more noblesse oblige in her manner than genuine feeling. In fact, I got the idea Paula would like to set Lea's coif on fire.

"Neil," Paula said, continuing the amenities, "this is Coley Killebrew."

"Hey, the old jock," he said. "How ya doin'?" I shook Neil's hand, which was soft and limp.

"And Roz Holbrook." I nodded to Lea. There was a slight flash in her eyes and a little twitch of the corners of her mouth. Nobody would have noticed it but me. She had a great poker face.

Neil looked around the room and said loudly. "Alllll right! I can hear those dice hitting the pad. Let's get some of those chips and go do it." He put his arm around his sister and they rushed off to the table where genuine cash and checks were being exchanged for Casino Dresner chips.

"What was your name?" I asked Lea. "Roz, was it?"

"Roz Holbrook, Mr. Killebrew. I'm such a great fan of yours."

I looked around to assure myself no one was listening and said, "Well, Roz, here we are, alone together. For the first time in a week."

She didn't seem too pleased to see me. "What are you doing here, Coley?"

"Johnny invited me."

"Ah. Of course." She relaxed.

"Since you're using an alias," I said, "I assume you're working and you're not really under the spell of that young jackass you're with."

She threw me an enigmatic smile. I think it was supposed to make me jealous or at least make me wonder, but it didn't fool me. Neil Dresner wasn't somebody I had to worry about, at least as a rival for Lea.

"If you'll excuse me," she said, "the young jackass expects me to bring him luck."

She walked away in the general direction of the crap tables. While my instinct was to follow her, I didn't want too much attention from me to put a crimp in whatever her game was. Is that true love and consideration or what?

I continued my desultory wandering around the room.

They had a pretty authentic casino atmosphere going. Certainly the croupiers and dealers had that practiced air of infinite boredom as they raked in the chips from the excited guests.

A big redhead, middle-aged and plump but still impressive, was whooping like a banshee on every turn of the roulette wheel. She looked vaguely familiar, a former second-line movie queen maybe. When I recognized the tuxedo to her left, it dawned on me she was Mrs. Mark Brittan. I gave her a wide berth.

A few moments later a sudden hush dropped over the room, beginning at the entrance door and spreading across the floor like a football crowd doing the wave. I looked toward the entrance, wondering if Madonna had suddenly shimmied in, and saw Wilton Dresner pumping the hand of a handsome man in his late forties. The newcomer's hair was silver at the temples, his face tanned and rugged, his teeth white and gleaming. He wore evening clothes like he was born in them.

A rumbled comment from nearby clued me in. This was the guest of honor, Dr. Charles Lavery.

Charisma is an overworked word but a relatively rare quality. It's hard to pin down why some people have a commanding presence, a magnetic charm that makes you want to befriend them. Lavery had that quality in spades. From the way he was greeted by men and women both, I saw he had that effect on almost everybody in the room. I remembered Claude Rains's line about the Bogey character in *Casablanca*: "If I were a woman, I should be in love with Rick."

"Big fucking deal," said a voice right behind me.

I turned around and said to Johnny, "I've heard of superstar athletes and politicians, even doctors. But veterinarians?"

"Ain't he just grand?" Johnny muttered bitterly. He was quite a bit drunker than the last time I'd encountered him, but certainly no happier.

"What's with you?" I asked.

"I been hearing about this guy till it's coming out of my ears. '*Vanity Fair* called him Saint Charles, the horse's savior,' " he said, in falsetto mimicry of a fawning society woman. "More than the horse's patoot."

"What's his deal?" I asked.

Johnny took a healthy pull at his drink. "The fucker was born with a mountain of dough and he's *doubled* that. He's the vet with the magic touch. Saudis send planes for him to fondle their stallions. But he devotes most of his time in the lab working on this cure for endotoxemia. He hasn't cured it or anything, oh no, but just saying he *might* cure it has people eating out of his hand and stuffing money in his shorts."

"Is he engaged?" I asked. "I'd like to marry him."

Johnny glared at me. "That ain't funny," he said, and stormed away. No, I suppose it wasn't. I decided to try no more humor on Johnny that night.

Over at the craps table, Lea was standing beside Neil, cheering him on. I knew this wasn't the real Lea, but she threw herself into her part so totally, it would be pretty convincing to a stranger. Apparently it was convincing enough to Neil.

I wondered how somebody as independent as Lea could do a clinging bimbo so effectively. And I also wondered if she enjoyed it, if she got a kick out of exerting control over men. Whoa, back off, Coley. I was starting to pick up on Johnny's sour mood.

I looked over at Saint Charles, who had worked his way to the center of the room. He stopped pressing the flesh with the wealthy patrons of AEF long enough to allow himself to be greeted by Paula Dresner. They embraced each other rather fondly I thought. Paula whispered something in his ear, and he let loose a loud, manly laugh. Johnny was watching them without expression. Lavery was a rival, all right.

His face turning more somber, Lavery asked Paula something in a low voice, and she pointed in the direction of the craps table where Neil was doing his thing. The vet shook his head, heaved a somewhat dramatic sigh, and strode purposefully toward the table. Ignoring Lea, he put his hand on Neil's arm and said something softly to him. Neil looked around, a little annoyed, and shook his head. Lavery wouldn't be put off. He gripped Neil's arm and pulled him away from the green velvet just as he was about to roll the dice.

"Hey, Charlie," Neil said, audibly to half the room. "I'm just going good here. Did you see—my picture's on the chips. I'm worth twenty-five bucks, Paula's fifty, and Dad's a hundred. That's how it goes."

Lavery draped a comradely arm over the young man's broad shoulders. "Come on, Neil, there are things we need to talk about."

Neil looked torn for a moment, as if deciding whether it was worth making a scene over. Apparently not. He tossed his dice back onto the table and yelled to Lea to gather his chips for him.

"Sure, baby," she said. She'd chosen a little girl's high-pitched voice that was just right for the role she was playing.

As Lavery guided Neil toward the men's lounge, nodding to other guests with a fixed smile on his face, I casually moved in their direction.

When they walked into the lounge, I didn't follow them, but I hovered near the door, my ears pricked for whatever I could pick up. The noise from the gambling and partying didn't allow me to hear every word of the conversation, but I could tell Lavery was laying a heavy lecture on Neil.

"It's not my fault," Neil whined. His voice came across more clearly than Lavery's softer tones. I strained to hear the vet's reply.

"You have to learn to live up to your responsibilities, Neil."

"This guy Joey Lunchbox won't listen to reason."

"Guys like him never do. Either you live with his insanity, or you pull out. It's your decision."

"Either way, Daddy dear will think I'm King Asshole."

That was a great opening for an overly frank crack, but Lavery played it safe. "Listen, I'm just a friend of your sister's but—"

At that moment two other guests sailed past me and entered the lounge. When the door swung open, Lavery, just inside, looked at them and past them at me. Reluctantly, I moved away.

I saw Lea coming down the circular stairwell. I wasn't the only man in the room watching her, but I was the one she winked at. I took that as a signal to join her.

"I think we should talk," she said to me when we reached the foot of the stairs. Before she could say any more, though, Neil was moving toward us. She whispered, "Later."

"Hey, Roz," Neil demanded, "you got my chips?"

By the time Lea resumed her role as Roz Holbrook, I'd done my best to disappear into the crowd.

Paula and Johnny were sitting at a table at the edge of the room. They didn't seem to be involved in any intimate exchanges, so I thought it safe to join them.

"Johnny, do you know Coley Killebrew?" Paula said.

He was a little too tipsy to remember the game plan. "Oh, yeah, sure," Johnny said. "I mean, we didn't but we do. We talked a little earlier. How ya doin'?" I could see he was about three cocktails over the line. His tan had faded. His eyes were red, and he was slurring his words.

"Did you meet Dr. Lavery, Coley?" Paula asked me.

"No, but I sure was aware when he came into the room. The roulette wheel stopped in midspin, and the dice stood up and saluted."

"He does have a powerful effect, doesn't he? He's a wonderful man."

"*Won*derful man," Johnny echoed. "Wonderful, wonderful man."

Paula gave him a sidelong glance of annoyance. "I approve of men who do things," she said pointedly. "I think that's the most important attribute in a man. The things he does and how he does them."

"I do things," Johnny muttered.

"Why, darling, I never said you didn't." The words didn't sound quite as conciliatory as they might have. "Coley, I'm sure Charles would like to meet you. Maybe I can catch his eye."

Catching a man's eye would never give Paula any problem. A moment later Lavery was strolling over to join us.

"Paula, this is such a stunning evening. I'm overwhelmed. You and your father deserve the gratitude of the whole Thoroughbred industry. If the horses I work with every day could talk—"

"They'd be makin' rap records," Johnny said.

Lavery stayed hearty with an effort. "How are you, Rousseau?"

"Doing things, Lavery. Doing things the way a man should do things."

"Haven't had a bit too much to drink, have you?"

"Haven't had enough."

"Charles," Paula said, "I want you to meet Coley Killebrew. The jockey."

Lavery obviously had heard of me. His greeting was polite enough, but his reserved attitude gave off the kind of chill I sometimes get from people in the Thoroughbred industry. Casual fans don't always remember how my career ended, but Lavery did. And he had no reason to doubt I had irresponsibly endangered some valuable horses. And a jockey or two, if that meant anything.

We shook hands. I was used to cold receptions, and as long as he didn't push the point with any overtly offensive remarks, I wasn't going to make an issue of it.

His personal charm was so strong that I wanted him to like me. I wanted to explain what had really happened that day, but this wasn't the time or place. Johnny, on the other hand, was immune to the handsome vet's potent brand of charm.

"How's the casino business, Rousseau?" Lavery inquired.

Johnny shrugged. "It's a business. Like any other business. Like your business."

"I hardly think it's like any other business. And it certainly isn't like mine. It must be exciting at times, though."

"It ain't exciting. If it gets exciting, I'm not doing it right."

"And I'm sure you do it right," Lavery said, a hint of sarcasm creeping into his delivery. If charisma didn't work on Johnny, he'd try something less amiable. "The edge is always with the house, isn't it? The customer does the gambling, but the house always wins."

"It's the same with racing," Johnny said. "Ain't it, Coley?"

"Well, it's only fair," I said. "You provide the room, the deck, the wheel, the field, whatever, and you get your cut."

"But there's cuts and cuts," Johnny said. "The house gets the whole take tonight." His mood was getting darker and darker and I tried to think of a way to bail him out. It wasn't helping his cause with Paula, though in the great scheme of things, I didn't necessarily find that bad news.

Lavery looked openly contemptuous now. As another way of

demonstrating it, he casually draped a proprietary arm over Paula's shoulder.

Johnny's drunken lassitude left him, and he stiffened threateningly. "Get your arm from around her."

"If Paula doesn't like my arm where it is," Lavery said quietly, "I'm sure she can say so for herself."

Paula, who had probably been in situations like this before, looked from face to face with an "Aren't men silly?" grimace and slid away from both of them. She glided across the room to talk with some other guests, leaving the three of us in a happy little group.

I was about to say something witty to break the atmosphere, but I wasn't quick enough. Johnny leaned into Lavery and snarled, "You touch her again, you slimy bastard, and I'll break your arm."

"You'll actually do it yourself?" Lavery asked. "You won't use hired muscle? Gee, I must be special."

Johnny drew back to direct a punch at Lavery. I grabbed his arm and inserted myself between the two men. I looked Johnny in the eye, asking him to cool it with a shake of the head. The look he gave me said he'd like to beat Lavery to a pulp but would back off for now. I loosened my grip on his arm.

The little incident was over quickly and quietly. I could tell, though, that some in the crowd around us had picked up on the hostility. They were edging away from us. Our host, however, was walking in our direction. A warm smile reasserted itself on Lavery's face as he moved away to greet Wilton Dresner. Johnny and I were still within earshot.

"Charles," Dresner asked him, "what's this I hear about you and Paula flying to Chicago on Tuesday?"

Johnny looked like he'd been struck with a 7.2 migraine.

"Oh, just a day in the Windy City," Lavery replied airily. "Then we might finish up the week in Florida. That's if you don't need her here, of course."

"Take your time. It'll be good for her to get away from that wop. . . ." That's when he noticed Johnny standing nearby. His face reddened.

Johnny stepped forward. "Hey, Wilton, you callin' me a wop?"

"Rousseau? No, you misunderstood. . . ."

"Did I misunderstand it about you telling this asshole it was all right for him to go runnin' off with Paula?"

"You're drunk, Rousseau," Dresner observed.

"I am not drunk," Johnny roared with boozy dignity. "I'm pissed off is what I am."

His voice was loud enough to still the room. The only sound was a roulette wheel finishing its spin. Paula came rushing over to try to intercede.

Johnny turned toward her too quickly. Losing his balance, he staggered and sat down on the floor. Every eye in the room zeroed in on him with shock. Wilton Dresner looked disgusted.

Lavery grabbed Paula and pulled her to him, as if to save her from any involvement with the drunken bore. That sent Johnny's anger into hyperspace. Struggling to stand, he said through clenched teeth, "I told you to keep your hands off her."

"You'd better leave, Mr. Rousseau," Dresner ordered.

The room was deadly quiet. Even the roulette wheels had stopped spinning.

Johnny looked hopefully—and pathetically—at Paula. She looked miserable. She started toward him, but it was a halfhearted attempt. Johnny was expecting more.

"I want to marry you, honey," he told her.

Tears filled her eyes, but she didn't say a word.

"Your presence is no longer welcome here, Mr. Rousseau," Dresner said.

"Go back to your party, Wilton," Johnny said. "This isn't any of your business. It's between me and Paula."

"That's where you're wrong," Dresner replied, his voice booming out now. "My daughter may act foolishly from time to time.

But as long as I am alive, she will live by the rules and standards I have set."

"You won't live forever," Johnny said. Though his voice was soft, it carried like a stage whisper. Half the room must have heard him.

He looked for Paula, but she had allowed Lavery to take her away. All the fire and passion suddenly seemed to drain out of Johnny. Shoulders slumped, he staggered out of the room.

"He shouldn't try to drive," I said to Dresner. "I'll give him a lift."

"Take him to a hotel to sleep it off," Dresner directed. "I'm phoning my butler now. Tell Rousseau his bags will be packed and waiting for him in the morning."

13

I FOUND JOHNNY in front of the Quarterdeck Club, leaning against a lamppost and ignoring the stares of departing party-goers waiting for their cars. He looked at me miserably and said, "Dammit, Coley, what did I do?"

"*Screwed the pooch* is the expression that comes to mind."

"What else could I do? I love her. I couldn't stand by and let that bastard Lavery paw her. It was just too much, Coley."

"Sure, Johnny."

"What do I do now?"

"You're asking the wrong guy. I've got problems of my own."

"What would you do?"

"Well, I wouldn't go back in there tonight for one thing. I might send the old man a box of illegal Havana cigars and Paula a dozen roses along with your best wishes for the future."

"Best wishes for the future," he echoed, turning the phrase over in his mind. "What does that mean? You telling me to give her up?"

Give her up? I said, "Think of it as retiring gracefully from a game you can't win."

He sucked in a deep lungful of ocean air. "I don't think I can do that."

"You have no choice. She's not the lady for you, partner. You don't have a limo driver waiting tonight, do you?"

"No, I drove myself. In Wilton's Mercedes."

"Then I'm your designated driver. Now thank the nice lamp-post for holding you up, and come along with me."

"You taking me back to Dresner's?"

"No, you've been booted out."

"Huh?"

"I'm not making this up," I told him. "The butler's packing your bags as we speak."

"Shit," he moaned. "You gonna drive the Mercedes?" he asked.

"Hell, no. If that car leaves the Quarterdeck, Dresner's the kind of gent who'll report it stolen. You're seriously out of favor."

When the valet parker arrived with the Cherokee, I helped Johnny onto the passenger seat. I was betting he'd be asleep by the time I got around to the driver's side.

He fooled me. He was still awake, miserable, and surprisingly sober.

I tried talking to him, but he seemed distant and distracted. When we'd talked at the Horse's Neck and he'd invited me to tonight's shindig, I'd held back telling him about being kidnapped at Arriba! and the horseback ride down the canyon. I'd wanted to figure out the extent of his involvement in Starbuck's investigation first. I figured this would be a good time to fill him in.

It got his attention. "Describe the two men," he said in a cool and even voice, sounding entirely different from the sloppy drunk he'd been just minutes before.

I gave him a quick thumbnail of Ramon and Howard.

"I'll take care of it. I'll pass the word that you're no longer interested in Luis Falcon or anything to do with him." Then he frowned. "It *was* because you were bothering Falcon, wasn't it?"

"I suppose so."

"But it could have had something to do with the fact you were at Jerry Woo's."

"Uh-huh."

"You think Paula's in any danger?"

"I didn't see her riding a horse down a canyon while I was there," I said. "By the way, the horse was named Candy Dan, and he was from Cloverfield Stables. That mean anything to you?"

Johnny looked blank. "Should it?" he asked.

"That horse you're buying, it isn't from Cloverfield by any chance?"

"I'm not buying any horse," Johnny said flatly. "That deal's dead in the water as of tonight. But *our* deal is still in place. You did what I asked, the Neck is yours whenever you get the papers going."

"I didn't find out what was troubling Paula Dresner," I said.

"I guess I know now what it was," he said. "I guess I know what to do about it. You were right. My only play is to get the hell out of this town."

"There's still the matter of the dead Jerry Woo," I reminded him.

"Not our concern anymore. You and me, we're out of it."

Johnny considered my assignment finished. I wasn't so sure.

14

WE FOUND HIM a hotel for the night. It had to be first-class, of course, though in the shape he was in, a Motel 6 would have done just as well. His brief return to sober clarity had subsided, and he stumbled along like a zombie as I herded him across the lobby, ready to explain his lack of luggage and plead for understanding with a show of cash. It turned out that he was known there, however, and the staff gave him all the deference due a visiting Las Vegas sultan.

In his room, he managed to struggle out of his tux. Then, dressed in socks, shirt, and boxers, he flopped down on the bed. I picked up the tux, put the pants and coat on a hanger. I left him flat on his back in the bed, staring at the ceiling.

Relieved to have him off my hands, I briefly considered going back to the party. But what was the point? According to Johnny, my job was over. I was willing to take his word for it. Yes, I wanted to see Lea. But I didn't want to queer her act.

So I drove home to the Horse's Neck. It was only a little after nine-thirty, meaning I was in time to get back to my regular duties as genial host and new sole owner-operator. At least during the final minutes of the dinner hour.

As soon as I walked in the door, Jack Hayward approached. "Well, don't we look rather elegant tonight," he said, picking an imaginary bit of lint off of the lapel of my tux.

"You mean this isn't Rick's Café Americain?"

"Oh, you romantics are all alike," he said. "And speaking of romantics, I have a couple in the dining room celebrating their fortieth anniversary, the Danzigers. The gentleman is a devotee of the bangtails and a particular admirer of your endeavors on the course. No sooner had I rescued them from the bar and got them comfortably seated at table nine when Mr. Danziger began asking if you would be on hand this evening.

"I, of course, was obliged to inform him with expressions of great regret that I did not expect you."

He leaned toward me and added as if sharing a confidence, "They are still in there, lingering over their decaffeinated coffee and gazing into one another's eyes like newlyweds. I believe it would put the crowning touch to their evening if you could drop by their table and say hello."

"Jack, in the time it took you to tell me that, they might have paid their check and gone home. Lead the way."

They were a handsome couple in their sixties, clasping hands across the table. She was still pretty and must have been sensational when she was younger. I flashed ahead to a view of Lea and me celebrating a special anniversary some years down the road. Probably would never happen, but it was a nice thought.

Danziger—his name was Harold—had won a bet on me once. My mount had been a turf specialist named Times of Gold and I'd ridden him for Charlie Whittingham in the San Juan Capistrano Handicap at Santa Anita. We'd led every step of the way but never by more than half a length, and we'd won by a long neck.

"That horse was a miler, Estelle!" Harold Danziger insisted. "And this man held him together somehow for a mile and three quarters."

"My goodness," his wife said. I sensed she really wasn't that interested in racing but enjoyed his enthusiasm, liked to see him having a good time.

"How in the hell did you ever manage that miraculous ride, Coley?" he asked me.

"I guess it's the clock in my head," I said. "The bad thing is that the ticking keeps me awake at night."

Danziger laughed a lot harder than it was worth, then said, "But seriously, that's what sets the great ones apart. Being able to judge pace. I hear the American jockeys who've gone to ride in Europe, guys like Steve Cauthen and Cash Asmussen, have taught the European riders a lesson about judging pace."

I grinned. "I guess Lester Piggott and Yves St. Martin and Willie Carson might have really accomplished something if they'd been able to judge pace." I wasn't sure if the guy knew I was being gently sarcastic or not, but a smile in his wife's eyes told me she suspected.

"Styles of riding in Europe are different," I said, "but that doesn't mean the jockeys are any less talented."

"Did you ever ride in Europe, Mr. Killebrew?" the wife asked.

"Coley rode everywhere," Danziger said.

"I rode in France a few times, once in the Arc de Triomphe. The main difference is they don't go out and set fast fractions like we do here. Instead they all tend to hang back early, sort of like a bicycle race. And they run in a tighter group than we do, crowding the rail and each other most of the way. When it's time to do the real running in the stretch, they start fanning out. That's as much of a cue to the horses that it's time for business as showing them the whip."

"How did you do in the Arc de Triomphe?" Estelle Danziger asked.

"He ran fifth," her husband replied before I could. The guy was such a fan, I could easily forgive his underrating European jockeys.

"That's right, fifth," I said.

"And this was on an American horse," the husband said, defending me, as if he were afraid mentioning my out-of-the-money finish might have offended me. "And running in a foreign country, in the wrong direction, clockwise instead of counterclockwise, taking the turns the wrong way, right instead of left."

I should have been impressed with the guy's turf knowledge. But what really impressed me was his wife, the way she looked at him. I felt he was one of the luckiest men I'd ever met. And then I thought of Lea again.

I must have stood there for twenty minutes telling war stories. When it was finally time to break away, I wished them a happy anniversary and ordered them an after-dinner drink on the house.

There were only two other tables still occupied. I visited both, but it was a quick hello–hope-you-enjoyed-the-meal–good-bye. None of them wanted to know about European riding styles or the clock in my head.

I spent the rest of the evening in the bar, sipping soda water and making small track talk. At midnight, I lent a hand in closing up the place. I was putting the receipts in the safe when Chef Antony came to tell me Lea was in the kitchen.

Antony's attitude toward Lea was both wavering and complicated. He'd been deeply suspicious of all women since his painful divorce, but Lea, particularly her long and beautiful legs, awakened an unconcealed and more selective lust in his hard heart.

She was still in her ball gown and still looking sensational, hunkering on the floor with a new member of the cleanup crew, showing her how to change the filter in an industrial vacuum cleaner.

She saw me and stood up with a weary smile. "I'm worn-out, Coley," she said.

"Shall I carry you upstairs?"

"I think I can make it on my own," she said. "Barely."

We didn't say another word until we were in my apartment. She kicked off her shoes and stretched out on the sofa.

"How'd you manage to slip from young Neil's clutches?" I asked, more sourly than I'd intended.

"Tell you all about it later," she said, waving a dismissive hand to indicate she didn't take my show of jealousy seriously. "We have something much more important to discuss."

"Mutual funds?"

She made a face. "Us." That was followed by a long, infectious yawn.

"Our relationship is so important, it makes you sleepy?" I asked, pretending to be offended, but not being able to keep a straight face. I was too happy to be with her.

"If this weren't so important, I wouldn't be yawning," she said. "I'd be snoring. Now give me a break; this is serious."

I didn't say a word.

"I know I've been busy, Coley. And I know I've been breaking dates, but I don't want you to get the wrong idea."

"Your father said you asked for the work," I said.

"I did. And I didn't. It's an important case. Dad has several people assigned to it. And I'm in charge of the whole operation." Her voice was a little unsteady, in a way that surprised me, and her eyes pleaded for understanding. "It's the first time Dad's put me in charge of anything of this scope. So in that respect, I did ask for it. But I didn't ask for it to interfere with us."

Standing by the sofa and looking down at her, I said, "I got the idea you might be trying to take a few steps back and night work was the way to do it."

She reached up to touch my face. "I can't deny I've had those feelings. I know you care for me and I for you. But I don't know the extent of that caring. And maybe I'm a little bit afraid to find out."

"Why should you be?" I asked.

"There's something more I want to tell you." She made room for me to sit down beside her on the sofa. "About the last time I was involved with someone."

I nodded. But I really didn't want to hear about it.

"His name was Clint," she said.

"Was it before or after he was mayor of Carmel?"

"This isn't going to work," she said, starting to get up.

"No. No," I protested. "I'm sorry. I feel awkward and confused, and when that happens, I slip into my smart-guy mode."

She stared at me, still slightly annoyed, slightly hurt. "I'm just trying to explain why . . . I do the things I do."

"Tell me about Clint," I said.

"He was a guy who turned his love for cars into a business. He was a luxury-car broker."

I got a mental picture of a big red-faced wheeler-dealer with a diamond ring on his pinkie and white shoes.

"He was young, just a few years older than I was, and he'd built his business up from scratch. Buying trashed sports cars, fixing them up, and selling them at a huge profit. He kept on the move constantly. He'd be out here for a week or two, then on the East Coast, then the Midwest. He had all sorts of clients among racing people, and they all swore by him, even though they didn't know very much about him.

"Anyway, Clint was handsome and athletic, but those weren't the most important things. He was also kind, considerate, fun. I looked forward to our days together."

Good old Clint, I thought, the Alan Alda of auto salesmen.

She frowned and I wondered if my face was revealing what I was feeling. "I think you would have liked him, Coley," she said. "Everybody did. Even Daddy."

"You're kidding!" I didn't have to fake my amazement.

"No, I'm not," she said, understanding my reaction perfectly. "Dad really liked him. But he did warn me it was a mistake to trust anybody until you performed a background check on them."

I nodded. That was the Daddy Starbuck I knew, all right.

"Well, obviously, I wasn't that cynical. I was in love, and Clint was in love with me. I didn't need any stinking background check."

"So what happened?"

"I wanted to get married. He said he did, too, but he kept putting me off, wouldn't set a firm date. And for all the time we spent together, all the fun we had, I never found out his permanent address. I knew he traveled a lot locating cars for people, and he had this great little apartment on the beach at Santa Monica. But I never knew where he actually lived."

"And you didn't know there was a Mrs. Clint," I said.

She sighed. "In Albuquerque. A couple of little Clintettes, too. I can laugh about it now."

I looked her in the eye. She turned her head.

"No, I guess I can't laugh about it. Even now. And there's more."

"I would have thought that was enough."

She shook her head, ruefully. "He was a grifter. Taking extra commissions off the top. And then half the cars he was selling turned out to be stolen. He tried to sell a classic Bentley to a guy who went over the contract with a magnifying glass and found something that looked hinkey. And it all started to unravel."

I took her hand. "What hurt you the most?" I asked. "The fact that he was married and lied to you? Or his being a crook?"

"I like to think his being a crook would have been enough, but who knows? If he'd been single, I might even be waiting for him to get out."

"We both know you better than that. You'd have dropped him like a hot rock."

"Maybe. Anyway, the real point is, Dad was right all along. He didn't gloat about it, but he was right."

I didn't see what made that the real point. She'd been burned once before and that led her to be gun-shy about another relationship. I could understand that all too well. But why bring Daddy into it?

"I think your father was as fooled by Clint as you were," I said. "It wasn't his keen insight that made him suggest a background check. If John Kennedy had been the guy, he'd have said the same thing. He doesn't want you to leave him, Lea."

"That's your strictly objective opinion?" she asked.

"I admit I am a little biased."

"Enough to ignore the fact that Daddy was right. Clint was the wrong man for me."

"According to Daddy, every man is the wrong one," I said. "If you keep believing that father knows best, he'll wind up being the only man in your life."

"I . . . I'm here now," she said. "So, it looks like I might be making room for one more. But I want us to go slowly."

I looked at her. "Slowly, huh? Coming to my place in the middle of the night dressed like that and you want to go slowly? I've heard of mixed messages. . . ."

She reached up and pulled me to her. "Slowly and surely," she said.

15

I WAS IN a deep, warm contented sleep when something woke me. I stared at the ceiling and was trying to figure out what it had been when a loud clatter sounded almost directly beneath my window. Lea, stretched out beside me, equally awake, looked at me curiously. Before she could say a word, I was out of bed. I grabbed a pistol from my desk drawer, put on a robe and slippers, and went down the stairs to the darkened restaurant kitchen.

I was checking the doors and windows when she joined me downstairs. She was fully dressed, but not in her evening gown of the night before. She didn't have a closet full of clothes at my apartment, but the limited wardrobe included a pair of jeans and a T-shirt.

"Find anything worth shooting?" she asked.

"Not yet."

"It sounded like a cat playing hopscotch on your garbage cans."

"Probably," I agreed, "but I wanted to check the windows first."

She looked at the watch on her wrist and yawned. "Three o'clock."

"Yeah," I said, satisfied that all the windows were secure. "And all's well."

"Then maybe you can lower the rod, Louie. I swear I won't try to escape."

Sheepishly, I tried putting the gun into the pocket of my robe. The barrel caught. I pulled it out and looked at it helplessly. "Could we just pretend it's a flashlight?"

"What's with the gun, anyway?" she asked.

"These are tough times," I said.

"No tougher than a week ago when that champagne bottle exploded and you didn't go running for your pistol."

"Last week you weren't in the middle of a big operation," I said. "Or at least I didn't know you were."

"Nobody knows I'm here," she said. "Anyway, I don't think anybody's after me."

"Half the world's after you."

"I mean to harm me. I haven't put myself in that much danger on this job."

"That you know of."

"Good point. But from the speed with which you grabbed that gun, I wonder if somebody isn't after *you*."

"I still owe you that dessert from the other night," I said, changing the subject. "Let's see what we've got."

"Why not? For some unknown reason, I'm famished."

We raided Enrico's dessert larder in a conspiratorial spirit, like a couple of kids sneaking out of the tent at summer camp. While we nibbled white chocolate mousse at a table in the kitchen, I said, "I have some news you can pass along to your father."

"Yes?" she wondered warily, probably suspecting I was going to reopen our earlier conversation.

"Johnny Rousseau decided not to buy the horse. After that scene at the party, he's dropped pretty definitely out of the Dresner family circle. My guess is he'll be going home to Las Vegas today."

"Thanks for the information," she said. "I'm glad he's out of it."

"Me, too. Now, can you tell me what the Dresners have to do with this thing you're working on."

"Only if you'll tell me why you jumped out of your skin because some tomcat knocked the lid off a garbage can."

One garbage-can lid couldn't make all that noise, I wanted to tell her. What I said was, "It's a deal."

"Okay," she said. "About ten years ago, Wilton Dresner bought a stable in Calabasas." The reference was to a northwestern suburb of Los Angeles where there is still enough open country for horses. "He named it Heartland Farms."

"A fine, patriotic, all-American name."

"Something like that."

It annoyed me that Dresner would be interested in horses. Horses were too good for him, a thought I passed along to Lea.

"Oh, he doesn't care about them," she said. "It's Neil. I'm pretty sure that's why Wilton involved himself with Heartland."

"Horses are too good for Neil, too."

She chuckled. "You're not really jealous, are you?"

I leaned over and kissed lips that tasted of white chocolate. "Everybody's jealous. But tell me more about Heartland."

"Well, a couple years ago, a company called Family Marketing wanted to buy Heartland Farms and Wilton was ready to sell. But he had a special deal in mind. He'd sell the controlling interest in Heartland, fifty-one percent, but only on the condition that Neil could stay on as manager as long as he wanted."

"How did Family Marketing feel about that?"

"They went for it."

"I guess they didn't know Neil very well."

"He's not as much of a dead loss as he seems, Coley." My face must have expressed some doubt. She grinned and added, "Not quite as much. Anyway, the deal was struck, and shortly after, the old man made Neil an outright gift of the remaining forty-nine percent. He hoped Neil's fondness for horses would translate into a sense of responsibility and eventual success."

"A touching fatherly gesture. Did it pay off for him?"

"Not really, I'm afraid. Two months after the official partnership began, Heartland's best Thoroughbred, Pale Fire, died. It was attributed to endotoxemia."

"Ah. And that's how Lavery met the Dresners?"

"You're so clever when you want to be."

"Was Pale Fire insured?"

She nodded. "For three hundred thousand dollars."

"Don't tell me. Bright's Limited carried the policy."

"You called it. And Pale Fire was one of the recent claims Bright's asked my father to investigate."

"Did it check out?"

"It seemed to. The death reports were in order. There was no evidence of foul play. But then Dad discovered that Family Marketing was involved, either as owner or co-owner, with two other heavily insured horses that died recently. They also had an interest in one other that had to be destroyed because of a broken leg."

"What the hell *is* Family Marketing? The name sounds like they should be distributing Disney videos."

"I have no idea if they do anything other than speculate in Thoroughbred real estate and bloodstock. They're a very mysterious outfit. We haven't been able to contact any of FM's six executive officers, not to mention the CEO. And even with all of Dad's contacts, we've been unable to find out the first thing about the company's financial structure."

"If there are so many Family Marketing stables, why spend so much time investigating Heartland?" I asked her.

"Because Neil has been busy buying and rebuying horses. The insurance on various Heartland animals is well over nine million dollars."

"And I guess Neil was the one trying to sell Johnny Rousseau a horse."

She nodded. "But I don't think it was Neil's idea. It was Paula who suggested Johnny."

"The original bad-news princess," I said. "Does she have an interest in the stable, too?"

Lea frowned. "Not officially. But if Neil is involved, she's involved. They're amazingly close."

"Brothers and sisters who grew up together usually fight like cats and dogs."

"But they didn't grow up together. Wilton and their mother have been divorced for nearly twenty years. She's a landscape designer who's lived all over Europe. The kids grew up apart—she with her mother, he with Wilton. They both traveled around a lot, so that neither child got to make many friends."

As Lea described the loneliness of the Dresner children, it occurred to me she could be describing her own life. Or mine for that matter. "Neither Dresner was any great shakes as a parent, although I'm sure Wilton, being a well-known champion of family values, imagines he was. Certainly he expected great things of Neil, figures he's given him everything, and he's been pretty generally disappointed.

"Paula and Neil barely knew each other until she graduated from her school in Switzerland three years ago. That's when Mom decided she'd be better off living in the States at Daddy's place in California. Paula and Neil have been thick as thieves ever since. I'm supposed to be the girlfriend, but Neil doesn't have a light in his eye for me like he does for Paula. When she's not around, Neil goes on automatic pilot."

"Do you think this might be an unhealthy relationship?" I asked.

She smiled. "I don't know how healthy it is, but I doubt it's incestuous, if that was what you had in mind."

"You never know. What's Wilton's relationship with Paula been like?"

"Crazy about her. Nothing's too good for her. Kind of controlling, though. He's the sort of father who wants to call all the shots for his kids, keep them under his thumb."

I wanted to ask her if that reminded her of anyone she knew. But I controlled the impulse. Instead I said, "From what I've seen of Paula and Neil, he's not doing too good a job of controlling them. She seems to do what she wants anyway."

"It's deceptive. They may appear to be on a long leash, but it's still a leash."

"And you're hanging out with Neil hoping that he'll fly you into the heart of Family Marketing."

"That's right. Neil hasn't been very forthcoming about discussing business so far, though. He really likes horses. And he likes working at the stable. But he doesn't seem to know very much about his shadowy partners."

"If he's doing all this buying and selling of horseflesh, how innocent could he be?"

She nodded. "Maybe he's just a stooge. Or a partial stooge. I'm sure he wouldn't go along with the killing or maiming of horses, but short of that, I don't think he'd have any attacks of conscience if he cut a few corners. And of course he'd like nothing better than to make enough money on his own to get out from under Wilton's thumb."

"Lea, at the party last night, I overheard a conversation between Lavery and Neil. They mentioned a hood named Joey Lunchbox."

"He used to work for the Vetticino family."

"Right. He's a particularly effective collector. I got the impression that Lavery's warning to Neil had something to do with money the boy owes."

"Gambling debts, probably," Lea said.

"Who's paying Joey's salary these days?"

"I suppose that would be Huey Grosso," she said. "He became organized crime's numero uno when Romeo Vetticino fell victim to Alzheimer's. Romeo's sister tried to keep the power in the family, but the Mafia isn't what you'd call sympathetic to the women's movement."

"What's the story on Grosso?" I asked.

"A very nasty twerp who graduated near the top of his class at Harvard Law."

"Harvard Law? The mobs they are a-changin'."

"Like everything else. Grosso's been replacing old mustache Petes with a new kind of young thug. They carry beepers instead of guns. The smooth surface is deceptive, though. I hear he's more vicious than Vetticino was."

"That's too chilling a concept," I said. "A really criminal lawyer."

"I hate puns," she said.

"The sport of noble minds."

"Well, use your noble mind to give out with your part of the deal," she said. "Tell me why noises in the night make you jump out of your skin."

"I'm going to tell you, but I've got a question of my own first."

"No fair."

"Just a short one. And I'll connect it up. Is Cloverfield Stables on your father's list?"

"No," she said. She looked at me searchingly for a moment and nodded her head like she'd just made a connection. "But it's funny you should mention Cloverfield. A very odd thing just happened there. A horsenapping."

"Really?"

"Yeah. A three-year-old with a lot of promise named Candy Dan. He was stolen along with a horse van belonging to the stable, which took a lot of chutzpah, I think. A few hours after the horse disappeared, the thief phoned and told them where to pick up the animal, in a service-station parking lot, and it was found, unharmed. Daddy still can't make heads nor tails of it. But you can, can't you, Coley?"

"Mind reader?"

"Face reader. Come on. Give."

"Well, first of all, it wasn't the thief who called the stable. It was me. And I'm glad to hear Candy Dan got back okay. When he races next, I'll get a bet down on him. He gives you everything he has."

"A touching testimonial. Now let's have the whole story or I'll tell Enrico who raided his larder."

So I told her about my late-night ride down the canyon on Candy Dan, not stinting on the dramatic elements. But Lea's a pro. Instead of bothering with expressions of concern—obviously I had survived—she asked for a description of the kidnapper–horse thieves. She then said she would try to get them identified. The same reaction as Johnny Rousseau's, though her sources of information would be different.

"You know," I said, "I just had an intriguing but terrifying thought."

"Terrify me."

"Check on the incorporation date of Family Marketing. See if it coincides with Huey Grosso's appointment as head of the 'family' in Southern California. If Grosso is trying to buy into Cloverfield, destroying one of their champion Thoroughbreds would be just the kind of incentive those guys would think of."

"That would also mean Grosso sent those men to kill you."

"That's the terrifying part."

"What could you have done to make his hit list?"

"It probably has something to do with a jockey named Luis Falcon. Your father knows about it."

"You and Dad seem to be getting rather close," she said, a new hard edge to her voice.

"Getting close? What are you talking about? You know how we feel about each other."

She was suddenly very angry, and it baffled me.

"Palling around with him isn't going to help our situation any," she said.

"Palling around?" I think my mouth was hanging open.

She headed for the back door and hesitated. I was hoping she would turn to me with a smile on her face. But instead she drew a gun from her handbag. I was thankful she didn't point it at me.

"I hope your kidnappers *are* outside," she said. "I really feel like shooting somebody."

She went out through the back door, slamming it noisily behind her.

I watched through a window as she walked to her car, a Saab convertible, holding the gun close to her body. She got into the car, started it, and drove away without incident. I scanned the parking area for a few seconds more. Nothing moved. There was no sign of Ramon or Howard or anybody or anything else.

I went back upstairs to my apartment and tried to figure out what had made Lea so mad. She didn't like it when her father and I were at each other's throats. But apparently she liked it even less when we behaved civilly to one another. My God, life in the mid-nineties was confusing.

16

IT WAS NEARLY four A.M. Could I go back to sleep? I didn't think so, and I wasn't sure it was a good idea even if I could.

I hadn't believed for a moment that clattering I'd heard had been cats attacking the garbage. And Lea, whatever else was buzzing in her beautiful brain, hadn't believed it either. My two friends Ramon and Howard could very easily have been waiting for her to leave before they came after me.

I knew they wanted to kill me. I suppose logically the idea that they might be doing it at the behest of Huey Grosso should not have made matters any worse. After all, you can only be so dead. But somehow it did make it worse. Ramon and Howard, hired hands without a real personal stake in whether I lived or died, might give up. And a less determined employer might give up. But Huey Grosso didn't sound like a guy who forgave and forgot.

Johnny had placed me in this mess. And he might have thought I was finished with my job for him, but I didn't feel I was. Anyway, neither of our opinions was as significant as the opinion of the guy who wanted me dead.

Lying there looking at the ceiling of my apartment, I decided that Johnny was going to have to provide me some kind of bodyguard until I could be sure those two thugs no longer had any interest in me. He owed me that much. I picked up the phone and dialed his hotel.

The night clerk had a lousy attitude for an employee of such a snazzy place. He sounded as annoyed as if I'd interrupted his dog-watch crossword puzzle.

"Would you ring Mr. Rousseau's room please? Johnny Rousseau."

"Mr. Rousseau?" His tone had changed from annoyed to guarded.

"That's what I said."

"I'm afraid Mr. Rousseau is no longer a guest of this hotel."

"No longer a guest?" I said stupidly. "Look, my name's Killebrew. I was there when he checked in about seven hours ago."

"Yes, I remember."

"Then you know what kind of shape he was in. Now you're telling me he checked out?"

"Checked out may not be the precise term."

The guy was savoring the fact he knew something I didn't. "Stop playing with me and spit it out." I snapped.

The clerk paused, choosing his words. "If you wish to reach Mr. Rousseau, I suggest you call the Bay City Police Department. They escorted him from here some time ago."

"What do you mean? What happened?"

"Sir, I really believe that's all I can help you with."

And then he hung up.

Could Johnny in his argumentative, drunken state have raised some kind of hell at the hotel, had a fight with somebody on the elevator, maybe? No. He'd been pretty subdued when I'd left him.

The police had escorted him away. It sounded a little more serious than a brawl. If it was really serious, maybe the radio could answer my questions. I switched on one of the local all-news stations, hoping I wouldn't hear anything relevant but fearing I would. And I did.

After a few minutes of sports scores, traffic reports, and weather, they got back to the big story of the night. Someone had shot and fatally wounded Wilton Dresner.

17

MY FIRST IMPULSE was to drive to the Bay City lockup, but I knew there wasn't much I could do for Johnny in the middle of the night. He had access to the best criminal lawyers money could buy. And I couldn't bail him out, that was for sure, not on a charge of murder. About the only thing I could do, rushing out at four A.M., would be to give Ramon and Howard a chance to spill my blood before the break of a new day. So, while I waited for the dawn and a clear view of the alley and parking lot, I listened to the news stations for more details.

"Millions of fans are mourning the death of popular political pundit Wilton Dresner, who was shot to death in his Bay City home shortly after midnight tonight."

Midnight. About two and a half hours after I'd left Johnny at his hotel with no wheels. How could they pin it on him?

"The Bay City police have arrested a suspect whose name is being withheld pending further investigation. According to a spokesman for the Bay City Police Department, the crime does not appear to have been politically motivated."

That gave me a laugh. So the environmentalists, abortionists, feminists, socialists, unionists, and assorted liberals could breathe easy. While the cops pinned it on a guy with plenty of unsavory connections and a personal motive against Dresner that he'd shared with a room full of Malibu patricians.

Frank Sanchez, the reporter who'd been following Dresner around, was interviewed about his quarry. I'd been convinced

Sanchez was going to do a deserved hatchet ambush on Dresner—not a literal one, of course—but nothing he told the radio newspeople suggested anything but respect and admiration, not to mention astonishment at what had happened to the man. Several well-known people in politics and the broadcast industry had been routed out of a sound sleep and asked for a comment on the fallen giant. From the tone of some of his allies in various conservative causes, his death had the potential for as many conspiracy theories as the Kennedy assassination.

I think I actually managed to get a couple more hours' sleep, though it was barely dawn when I woke. I fixed a light breakfast and went out to the parking lot, looking edgily around every step of the way. Feeling cranky and nervous, I got into the Cherokee and drove to Bay City.

Bay City Police Headquarters, which also includes the town jail, is a newish modern building with tasteful landscaping outside and a computer on every desk inside. But whatever the amenities, it doesn't take a place like that long to look and smell and feel like every police station in the world.

I thought I'd restrained myself admirably by not walking in the door until seven-thirty. I told the cop on desk duty I was with the law firm representing Johnny. He seemed to buy that all right, but he told me no matter who I was, I'd have to wait until eight o'clock to confer with a prisoner. The guests of the city were enjoying their nutritious breakfast, and I wouldn't want to disturb them, would I?

So I spent a half hour sitting on a bench and getting an education on the difference between Chicano and Afro-American gangs from a friendly and talkative Hispanic kid waiting to see his brother who was being held in a drive-by shooting. It wasn't the sort of crime you'd expect to find in upscale Bay City, but the gangs were no longer limiting themselves to just their own turfs.

"When you join a gang, man," my bench mate was saying, "you join for life. Black dudes, they move in and out of the gang. Hell, they'll even move the whole gang to some other city. The Crips, man, they went from L. A. to Seattle, y'know? We stay in the barrio, man. We respect our community. We respect our elders. The old guys, we call 'em *vetranos*, we take their advice. We believe in loyalty, y'know? It means nothin' to them black dudes, nothin' at all. And we dress dignified, same as our homeboys dressed ten, twenty years ago. Black dudes, man, are changin' all the time, dress how some rap singer says they oughta dress, y'know?"

I didn't know, so I just listened politely. I wondered if Luis Falcon had been a gang member. Or Ramon. Maybe they belonged to the same gang.

I wondered how my bench mate would feel about Huey Grosso's sort of gang, how he'd compare the upper echelons of organized crime with his barrio federations, but I never got to find out. At seven minutes past eight, an officer told me I could talk to my "client" now.

I followed him down a long hallway to a small conference room where Johnny sat at a table waiting for me. The officer said he'd be outside, out of earshot, but explained he could see us through the glass window in the door.

Johnny hadn't looked too hot when I'd left him the night before, but he looked really awful now. He'd aged ten years overnight. His eyes were sunken, his mouth a thin white line of despair.

"Hi, Coley. Thanks for coming. How did you know I was here? Is it in the news?"

I sat down opposite him. The chair wobbled, and the wooden table had picked up a lot of carved graffiti considering how new the facility was. Maybe they'd brought it over from the old place.

"No, you're an unnamed suspect so far. I called your hotel last night, and they told me you'd changed accommodations."

"It wasn't my idea."

I didn't want to go any further without asking the obvious question. "Did you kill him, Johnny?"

"Hell, no. Of course not." He grinned without humor. "But there are only about a thousand of the town's most influential people who heard me threaten him."

"You have an alibi, don't you? I mean, when I left you, you didn't even have a car."

Johnny shook his head, as if marveling at my naïveté. "I arranged for one with the rental desk at the hotel. And of course they have a record of just when I took it out and brought it back. Plays right into the cops' hands."

"But you were drunk."

"A murder rap's bad enough. You gonna get me for drunk driving, too?"

"It's no joke, Johnny."

"Yeah, tell me about it." He looked down at his hands for a moment, then looked back up at me, a sheepish expression on his face. "It was a couple hours after you left me. I'd sobered up pretty good by then. Hell, I was sober when you drove me there. Just sort of dazed, that's all, kind of in shock, like. I'd had a tough evening. I couldn't stand the idea of losing Paula. All kinds of things were running around in my head.

"I tried to sleep, but I should have known I couldn't. I tried watching TV, but there was nothing but talk-show crap. All I could think of was, I wanted to bring this whole deal to a close, you know what I mean? So I rented the car and drove back to Dresner's place to get my things."

I let my expression speak for me. It must have called him an idiot.

"Yeah, yeah, it was a bonehead play. But I didn't know somebody was going to ventilate Dresner, did I? I just wanted to put the whole sorry mess behind me. Getting my stuff out of there would be a way of saying, that's it, it's over, go back to Vegas, forget Paula, forget everything."

"You were really ready to forget her?"

"Sure. What choice did I have?"

"Going to her house was a funny way of—"

"Okay, okay, so I'm King Dork. Don't rub it in. Anyway, Dresner wasn't even there when I arrived."

"What time was it?"

"Jeez, I dunno. Before midnight, though, I'm sure."

"How do you know he wasn't there?"

"The butler said nobody else was there but him. And he had orders not to let me in. Just to give me my stuff and brush me off."

"So if Dresner was still at the Quarterdeck Club, he must have phoned the butler to give him the instructions about you."

"I guess so."

"What did you do then? Did you leave right away?"

"Sure. I took my time driving back to the hotel, though. I was royally pissed about the whole thing. I wanted to get my thoughts together."

"So how long *did* it take you to get back to the hotel from Dresner's?"

"I don't know. I just drove around, not paying any attention to the time. It must have been an hour or so at least. After I brought back the rental car, I went up to my room, didn't turn on the TV or nothing, just flaked out. I'd almost gone to sleep—or maybe I was asleep—when the cops came in like gangbusters, yelling I was under arrest for the murder of Wilton Dresner."

"The butler must have told the police you'd been there and were turned away before the family came home."

"Yeah, he did."

"So how do they figure—"

"Their theory is I ducked into the garage and hid out there till Wilton got back. Paula stayed a little longer at the party and Neil doesn't live at home anymore. Wilton sent the butler to the Quarterdeck Club to oversee the cleanup. When the butler left, that's when I'm supposed to have gone in to Dresner's room and emptied a gun at him. Then they say that Paula came in a while later and went straight to bed. When the butler got back, he found Wilton's body and called the cops."

"And how do they figure you got in the house?"

Johnny threw up his hands in exasperation. "I had a key, Coley. I'd been a guest there for weeks, remember?"

"But you rang the doorbell the first time."

"Sure I rang the doorbell the first time. And whaddaya mean the first time? That was the *only* time I was there last night. I didn't off him, Coley. You believe me, don't you?"

"Sure, Johnny, sure. Who do you think did it?"

"How the hell should I know? Somebody who disagreed with him on gun control maybe."

"What are you going to do?"

"I've done it. I got Maxwell Fitzgerald as my lawyer."

"A good man."

"No shit. He was here a half hour after they booked me. That's how I know what happened at the house. These cops don't tell you nothing."

"Fitzgerald's got a lot of clout. Why are you still in here?"

"No bail," Johnny said glumly.

"That's pretty strong, if all they've got is circumstantial evidence," I said.

"Yeah, well, they got a couple other things."

I stared at him.

"Uh, the bullets they got out of Wilton and the wall in his den, they're thirty-two caliber."

"Small," I said. "A woman's gun."

He shook his head. "My goddamned Bond gun, Coley, is a thirty-two caliber."

"Where is it?" I asked.

"I don't know. The last I saw it, it was in my room—the guest room at Dresner's—with my other stuff. But it wasn't in the suitcase the butler packed. And he said he didn't see it. It's missing."

"Do the cops know about it?"

He nodded. "I carry the goddamned permit in my wallet."

"Still, until they find the gun . . ."

"There's the other thing," he said.

I sighed.

"I guess Dresner didn't die right away. The cops say he had one of those phoney casino chips clutched in his hand. They took four slugs out of him, still he has time to grab a chip from his pocket. Naturally, they think he was fingering me, a casino owner, for the job."

"It's still pretty circumstantial," I said.

"To you and to me, but not to the judge who denied me bail."

"And you don't have any idea who—" I began.

"Anybody could have bumped him off. The guy was a number-one prick."

"The killer would have had to know where to find your gun," I said.

"It wasn't with the stuff the butler gave me," he said. "Hell, for all I know, it was resting on an end table."

"Maybe the butler saw—"

"Look, Coley," he said. "Just let it be, huh? Fitzgerald's in charge. He knows what he's doing."

"I wasn't suggesting I go slewfooting around looking for clues, Johnny," I said. "Matter of fact, I have a little problem of my own right now."

"Oh? Whatever it is, don't tell me it's my fault, too?"

I didn't feel like burdening him further, but I really didn't want to spend the rest of a brief life constantly looking over my shoulder. "I think I've landed on the bad side of Huey Grosso."

"That putz?" Johnny said scornfully.

"That putz runs organized crime in Southern California."

"He's a college boy. Surrounds himself with brain trusts in the office, but goes third-class when it comes to muscle. Two-bit dork backshooters." He paused. "Does this have anything to do with those two guys who put the grab on you?"

"Uh-huh."

He was silent for a minute or two. "Yeah," he said at last. "They sound like the kind of talent Grosso uses. Okay. Even from in here, I can get somebody to take care of that problem for you."

"Somebody reliable?"

"Walrus. He can handle anything a little macher like Grosso can throw your way. Don't worry about that. I just wonder. . . ."

"Wonder what?" I asked, as he meant me to.

"If it could have been Grosso who had Dresner killed?" He shook his head. "Naw. Wishful thinking. I don't see any connection."

"Actually, there is one," I told him. "I think Grosso owns controlling interest in Heartland."

"No way."

"Do you know what was behind that horse-trading deal Neil Dresner tried to get you into?"

"I told you, that's all over with."

"Okay. But how did the deal work?"

He spread his hands. "I don't know diddly about it, aside from what I told you. It was a simple paper deal. I put up some money. I make a nice profit. Was it maybe something illegal? Maybe so. I didn't want to ask too many questions. But it was nothing in Huey Grosso's line."

"It was part of a massive and systematic insurance fraud. The horse you were going to buy would have wound up dead." I told Johnny about Family Marketing and their relationship with Heartland and other stables. I also mentioned Neil's fear of the hood known as Joey Lunchbox.

Dazed, Johnny said, "Jesus. Maybe Grosso did have the old man killed."

"You might mention that possibility to Fitzgerald. Maybe he can put one of his investigators on it." I stood. "Just out of curiosity, what kind of chip was it?"

"What do you mean, what kind? A party chip."

"A twenty-five, a fifty, or one hundred?"

"It was a fifty," he said.

"Paula's picture was on the fifty."

"Forget that," he said flatly. "Paula didn't have anything to do with the old man's death. I'm sure of that."

"Maybe I should snoop around a little," I said.

"No." His tone was final. "Leave her alone. If you want to do me a favor, maybe you could see what more you can find out about Grosso and Dresner."

"Jesus, Johnny, I'm already on the guy's hit list."

"This Walrus can take care of whatever Grosso can send your way. Please. See if you can make that Grosso–Dresner connection a little stronger. It's the last thing I'll ask of you."

"I'll consider it," I said. "But only after I've seen the Walrus."

18

WHEN I GOT back to the Horse's Neck, Stan Furneaux, my pastry chef, was out of the kitchen and looming over me before I even got the door closed. Stan, one of the first people on the premises any given morning, normally had the cheerful expression that went with his Santa Claus tummy, but today there was a look of apprehension on his face.

"Coley, somebody tried to break in through the alley window last night. There are scratches on the frame. It looks like they must have climbed up on one of the garbage cans and knocked it over. There's a real mess out there."

We walked around the building to the alley, where I saw the scratches for myself. The would-be burglar had used a screwdriver or some similar tool on the wooden sill of the window. It was a small window, but an agile person could have shimmied through. The rest of the scene was not really as dramatic as it seemed to Stan, who, like many chefs, got nervous around dirt—mainly coffee grounds, eggshells, and used wrappers. Cans, paper, and plastic were still snug in the recycle bin.

"I knew right away something was wrong when I saw this," Stan said, indicating the mess. "You know how proud Antony is of the neatness of his garbage."

"Well, pride goeth before a fall," I said.

"You don't seem surprised."

"I'm not," I said with a sigh. "I heard them last night."

"The thieves?"

"Yeah. I'd been hoping I was imagining things. Thanks, Stan." I shooed him back to his oven and, armed with a cup of black coffee, went into my office to mull.

The obvious choices for the aborted break-in were my old amigos Ramon and Howard. But I didn't really see them climbing up on garbage cans to get to me. More likely, they'd have set the place on fire or come up with something equally fatal. Of course, rattle and rob was one of the games burglars had been playing with great results. You rattle a garbage can or set off a car alarm in the middle of the night, and when the home owner pokes his head out to see what's going on, you show him your gun and accompany him back inside. But Ramon and Howard had seemed too crude for that approach.

Regardless of whether it was paid killers or merely the garden-variety burglar, a point had been made. It was time to install a security system.

Several firms had periodically sent their representatives to harangue me ever since the Horse's Neck first opened. I'd considered it, even discussed it once with Johnny, who thought it was a waste of money and suggested we just hang signs on the front and back doors that read BEWARE OF THE SNAKE.

Not certain that all robbers could or would bother to read, I decided it was time to get an alarm system. I'd kept the brochures that the salesmen had left behind. I got out the file and was comparing the pros and cons of hard-wire systems to wireless when the phone rang.

It was Al Grady, the midday mixologist, calling from the bar. "Uh, there's this . . . fella out here says he wants to see you, Coley." Al sounded a little tense and guarded.

"Trouble?" I asked, expecting nothing else by this time.

"Hard to say . . . uh, just a sec." He turned away from the phone and asked, "What's that?"

The "fella" who wanted to see me replied something in a deep mumble.

"What'd he say?" I asked Al.

"He said he's here to bring peace, like Saint Thomas A-something."

"Aquinas!" I heard a deep voice bellow.

"A-kwi-nas," Al said. "You comin' out?"

"To meet a 'fella' who quotes Thomas Aquinas? Absolutely."

I saw him from the back first, and his back was broad enough to blot out all the sun usually shining through the front window. He looked like Mighty Joe Young's big redheaded brother, dressed in crisp fatigues and high-top boots the size of coal scuttles. He was perched on a bar stool that seemed to be embedded in his wide rear end. The glass in front of him looked like it contained water and a slice of lime. He was holding a hardcover book open in the palm of one hand the size of a fielder's glove. If he crushed it, ate it, or threw it through the window, it would have been all right with me. But he actually seemed to be reading it.

Al Grady, standing respectfully behind the bar, cleared his throat and said softly to the behemoth, "Here's Mr. Killebrew."

The giant turned around on the bar stool. His carrot-topped head was almost normal size, which made it a little small for that body. His eyes were clear and emerald green and he had a wide smile that revealed a slight gap between his front teeth. He looked like David Letterman on steroids.

He dislodged the bar stool from his rump and stood. The ground didn't quite shake. Standing about six-foot-six, he shifted the book to his left mitt and presented me with his right. I allowed him to shake mine, praying that he wouldn't squeeze. He didn't, just gave it a very gentle light pump.

"Mr. K," he said cordially, "I'm John Walnicki. Folks call me Walrus."

"That's a relief," I said. "I'd hate for you to be anybody else."

It seemed that Johnny, even sitting in a jail cell, had ways of delivering fast on a promise.

"If I were—someone else, I mean," he said quite seriously, "it might be a very enlarging experience."

I stared at him, all three hundred plus pounds, and said, "How enlarged do you want to be?"

Al snickered, but Walrus didn't see the humor in my question. "Not physically enlarging. Spiritually enlarging." He bestowed his wide, almost beatific smile on me. "What are your feelings about reincarnation?"

"I don't think I want to be a candidate for it."

"That's not gonna be a concern while I'm around," he said. "But seriously, reincarnation is the central concept of several religions. Even Plato believed in it. And, of course, there's karma. You know, where your soul keeps getting recycled until you achieve perfection?"

"Uh-huh," I said. Behind the bar, Al was rolling his eyes heavenward.

"It's in both the Hindu and Buddhist faiths," Walrus informed us. "You can be reincarnated in any one of five categories—gods, humans, animals, hungry ghosts, or denizens of hell."

"I think I'd hold out for god," I said.

"We don't have much choice in the matter," Walrus replied. "And that's what puzzles me. Why do we come back in the form we do? I mean, we're human, so we must not have done too badly last time around. But what did I do to deserve a stint as, well, a protector?"

"Don't you like your work?"

"Sure. And I'm good at it, too. But it doesn't stop me from wondering."

Walking through the restaurant and into the kitchen, I noticed the title of the book he'd been reading. Mary Baker Eddy's *Science and Health*. Christian Science. I pointed to it and said, "Most of the, ah, protectors I've met have trouble reading *Batman*."

"Yes. That's the stereotype," he allowed.

Having put me in my place, the big man nodded genially at Stan Furneaux, who had paused in his dough kneading to gawk at him as we passed his section of stainless-steel counter and continued on into my office.

Walrus looked at the framed photos, losing tote tickets and other mementos hanging on the dark green walls. He took in the antique desk, which supposedly once belonged to Bugsy Siegel, and the new computer that did everything but chill wine, if you knew how to operate it, which I didn't. "I like this place," he said. "Except there aren't any books."

"Upstairs in my apartment," I told him.

That seemed to relieve his mind a little.

"Mainly fiction," I said and his face fell. "Walrus, would you be offended if I asked who you'd been protecting lately?"

"You mean you'd like references?" he asked.

"Sort of. It's my life we're talking about."

He nodded. "Well, I make it a practice not to talk about my employers. What I can do is assure you they're all alive and well. And I can list my qualifications."

"Please," I encouraged him.

"You name a martial art and I know it. I'm an expert kick boxer. I'm a more than good marksman. You can't see 'em, but I've got three handguns on me right now. Even a professional frisk job will find the first two and miss the third. I don't have to use those very often, but they're there. I don't know what you need protection from, but you got it, sir."

"I believe you," I said sincerely. "How many books do you have concealed on you?"

"I only carry one book at a time," he said with a smile. "I know my priorities, and I don't like to be too self-indulgent when I'm working. But, you know, in the strong-arm business, there's a lot of waiting around, so I have to have something available. Do you read much, Mr. K?"

"Not a lot, no. And you can call me Coley."

"I love to read, Coley. But one of its drawbacks is that the more you read, the more questions you have. Like, how is it possible for a man to be a Shintoist and a Buddhist at the same time?"

"That's as tough to figure as the morning line."

While Walrus tried to explain about the historical attempts made by Shintoists and Buddhists to coexist, I began putting files away and closing drawers. When he was finally convinced that I was nothing like a guru, he clammed up for a few minutes and I used the time to fill him in on as much as he needed to know about Ramon and Howard and their probable connection to Huey Grosso. Then I picked up the phone and dialed a number.

I waited for thirteen rings, then stood and headed for the door.

"Where we off to?" my personal bodyguard asked.

"Since Johnny Rosseau went to the trouble of hiring you," I said, "I might as well get his money's worth by placing myself in mortal danger."

"A pragmatist, huh?" the big guy said with a grin. "Let's use my wheels."

Walrus led me to a fairly nondescript tan Ford that was parked on the street nearly a block away from the restaurant. There was a film of grime covering the car, except for two half-moons above the windshield wipers. When I started to get into the passenger seat, the big man shook his head and suggested I hop into the rear and sit directly behind him. "Don't worry," he said, "the back window is bulletproof."

I hadn't been worried until he said that.

When he'd squeezed his bulk under the wheel and shut the door, he asked, "Isn't she a beauty?"

I looked at the car. It seemed like any ten-year-old Ford I'd ever seen. Resting a little bit lower to the ground, of course, under Walrus's weight. It smelled clean. "Nice," I said.

"Nice? I'd have expected a little more enthusiasm from a man who once raced for a living."

"Horses," I said. "As different from automobiles as, well, Shintoism is from Buddhism."

He turned the key in the ignition and started the engine. The resulting sound was a deep thrumming, almost musical. "This is a GT-40 Mark III," he said. "Ford built one hundred of these to race at Le Mans. Race and win. Less than seventy of 'em are still on the road. I've been offered more than ninety grand for this one."

"Too bad they aren't more like horses," I said. "You could put it out for stud."

I gave him directions to Luis Falcon's apartment and settled back to enjoy the ride.

When we were approaching the neighborhood, I instructed Walrus to bypass the building by a block and let me out. I'd walk to the apartment and he was to follow in the car, park, and wait.

He didn't like letting me out of his sight. He suggested we enter the building together. "The guy hasn't answered his phone in a couple of days, so I don't expect anybody to be home. I'm going to have to break in. I'd like you out on the street where you can honk your horn to let me know if anybody interesting should enter after me, like the cops or the two bozos who tried to kill me."

I gave him descriptions of Ramon and Howard. A few minutes later we passed Luis's yellow stucco apartment building. The street seemed strangely empty. Walrus stopped at the curb and as I got out he said, "If you run into trouble, try to yell or break something. Even if I don't hear anything, after fifteen minutes, I'll come on in."

"I'd appreciate your setting Mary Baker Eddy aside until I'm out of there," I told him.

He shook his head sadly and stared at me. "That's my hobby," he said. "This is my business. I don't get 'em confused."

His solemnity made me a believer. I gave him a wink and took my stroll down the block.

Falcon's building looked less hazardous but considerably more dingy in daylight. There was nobody around as I walked up the outside stairs to the second floor. I hit the doorbell of 2-A a couple of times, then pounded on it with my fist. I wasn't too surprised to get the same lack of response as I had the other night.

Picking the lock was about as hard as getting a horse to eat a carrot. I opened the spindly door cautiously, peering around to reassure myself there was nobody home.

Falcon was no better a housekeeper than Jerry Woo. Dust and clutter aplenty. No cooking smells, though. Luis probably did most of his marathon eating out.

The living room was small and dingy with a cottage-cheese ceiling and bright orange shag carpet that looked like a collection of clown wigs. A grimy gold sofa was pushed against one wall with a matching footrest nearby for Luis's wounded extremity. On a scarred mahogany coffee table were an assortment of empty Carta Blanca bottles, three-day-old editions of *La Opinión*, Los Angeles's Spanish language newspaper, and the *Daily Racing Form*.

A brand-new wide-screen TV was against the opposite wall, under a painting on velvet of a giant game fish leaping from the foamy sea. There was nothing in the room to indicate how Luis had once earned his living. Not a trophy or a banner or a photograph. I didn't waste any more time there.

In the sky-blue bedroom, where a sickly green color peered out from cracks in the wall, I discovered some family snapshots atop a thrift-shop dresser. In one group photo of the guests at a wedding, Luis stood next to the bride with his arm around another man who looked like a younger version of the murderous Ramon.

The bed was neatly made and draped with a blue spread. The closet contained two sets of boots, one new and one very old, both with the right toe cut away, three sets of pressed Levi's on hangers, a raincoat, a heavy cowhide jacket, three denim shirts, two Hawaiian short-sleeve shirts, and an antique sword in a leather scabbard.

In the bathroom medicine cabinet, I found a bottle of prescription pills. Chlorpropamide. Luis was supposed to be taking 250 milligrams daily for his diabetes. There was a bright yellow caution tab on the bottle that instructed the patient of the danger of skipping a dose. I wondered if Luis had another supply with him, wherever he'd gone.

So far I'd spent five minutes. Ten more to go before Walrus barged in, guns blazing.

There was nothing in the apartment that remotely resembled a desk or a filing cabinet. Since there was no reading matter either, apart from the newspapers, it appeared as if the printed word did not loom large in Luis Falcon's daily game plan. Walrus would have pegged him for a wrongo at first glance. Still, the man must keep his important papers somewhere.

Luckily, they were in the first drawer in the kitchen that I tried, right next to the two sets of silver-plated utensils. Hidden under a few bills and pieces of junk mail was a bankbook showing a balance of just under forty thousand dollars. Most significantly, the account had been opened on May 20, 1992, the day after Falcon's winning ride at Land O' Lincoln Raceway. The initial deposit had been five thousand dollars. A series of similar deposits followed at one-month intervals, separated by Luis's withdrawals. He evidently was satisfied spending two thousand a month. As the Dickens character—whatever his name was—said, when income exceeds expenses, happiness.

Luis's jockey license and a few other vital documents were at the bottom of the stack. But no incriminating correspondence. Nothing whatsoever to indicate where the money was coming from. I replaced the bankbook into a pocket and checked my watch. I'd just about used up my fifteen minutes.

I eased the front door shut behind me, and smugly congratulating myself on a job well done, I started for the stairs. Something grabbed my right shoulder and spun me into the wall. A beefy arm pinned me there.

"How ya doin', Howard?" I said, trying to speak normally with his elbow pressed into my stomach.

"Bastard knows my name, Ramon," the big Anglo noted.

Ramon's thin face appeared over Howard's shoulder, glaring into mine. "Yeah, he knows a lot, don't he? Too damn much. Think you wouldn't see us again?"

"I could only hope," I said.

"He knows my name," Howard repeated.

"What happened last night?" I asked them. "You let yourself get spooked by a garbage can?"

"Huh?" Howard asked.

"Just bullshit," Ramon said. "The guy's a real bullshit artist. And a troublemaker." He pointed his crook cigar at me. "You make trouble for everybody. You cost us with our boss, chinga."

"Hard to win back that respect, isn't it?" I asked. Howard just gawked at me. He couldn't understand me at all.

"You *really* fucked it up for my cousin Luis."

Some family. "Where is Luis?" I asked.

Howard's nervous eyes darted to Ramon, who said, "He out of town. An' he likes it so much, he ain't coming back."

"The final commute?"

Ramon shrugged. "Let's just say the man don't have to worry about eatin' sweets no more," he said. Probably not a kidding cousin.

I was tired of being squashed against the wall. If Walrus didn't show soon, I was going to kick Howard in his privates and make a run for it.

"When you see Luis," Ramon said to me with a grin, "tell him for me it was nothing personal." So he believed in an afterlife. I'd have to tell Walrus, if I ever saw him again.

"Let's go, Shorty," Howard said. He spun me around and

grabbed the back of my shirt, lifting me off the ground. Ramon followed us down the stairs to the street.

There was no one in front of the building. I looked up and down the street, hope in my heart. I couldn't see Walrus's million-dollar Ford. Had he gone off for a goddamned taco?

Howard continued to carry me down the block to a green Subaru parked near a fenced-in lot. "You guys didn't really steal a Subaru?" I asked incredulously.

"Steal?" Howard asked. "Hell no. It's mine."

Ramon opened the door to the backseat. "I'm gonna love this," he said, taking a buck knife from his jacket pocket. "I'm gonna whittle on you till you only half your size. Then maybe stomp you some and then whittle some more."

"And then maybe we can feed him to BoBo," Howard said.

"Your brother?" I asked.

"Naw. BoBo's my dawg." Howard was attempting to swing me into the rear of the car when Walrus stepped around the fence.

I felt Howard tense. Then he dropped me and reached for the gun stuck under his belt. He was much too slow.

Walrus's huge hand closed on Howard's and the gun. The bones in Howard's hand crackled like twigs. Walrus ripped the firearm loose and swatted Howard's face with it, doing considerable damage to nose and cheek.

Then my bodyguard stomped on Howard's instep, drove an elbow into his chest and brought the fist on the end of that arm back and up into the battered man's neck.

Howard gagged and staggered, like a drunk looking for a place to sit before falling down. Walrus grabbed him by shirt and belt and threw him at Ramon, who was sliding his buck knife from its sheath.

The two thugs fell to the sidewalk. I looked down the street. It was still empty. But there were faces at the windows of apartments, staring at us.

Walrus lifted the unconscious Howard off of Ramon and tossed him out into the street. The big man didn't even bother to check where Howard had fallen. He was staring at Ramon, who was crawling away on his back, his fingers trying to find the handle of his knife.

Walrus swatted the knife away, then plinked Ramon's nose with his middle finger. Ramon's eyes watered. He started to call Walrus a name, but the big man grabbed him by the ears and yanked him up off the ground until his feet dangled helplessly over the sidewalk. Ramon screamed with pain, his arms flailing. "Try to relax," Walrus told him. "Say ommmmmm."

Then he bounced Ramon's head against the roof of the Subaru. Just one quick plonk, and the killer of man and horse was unconscious.

Still no one was on the street. Except Howard, of course. And he wasn't likely to be getting up anytime soon. But inside the buildings, phones were probably being used to call the police.

Walrus hoisted Ramon on his shoulder. "Car's around the corner," he said, starting that way.

"What about him?" I said, indicating Howard.

"That boy's finished for the day," Walrus said. "We'll just leave him. This one we'll keep with us," he said, indicating Ramon, "for informational purposes only."

Walrus carried Ramon around the corner to where the Ford was inconspicuously parked. He opened the back door and tossed his load in with slightly less care than he'd have given an overcoat. "You can ride up front with me now, Coley, since the danger seems to be past. You get a better feel of the car from up here."

As he started up he said, "I didn't want to use my gun."

I looked at him, puzzled.

"They parked and entered the building so quickly, the only way I could have stopped them was to shoot them. But you weren't in serious trouble up there."

"I wasn't?"

"No. I was on the stairs. If either of them had made any move on you that might have proved fatal, I'd have had to shoot them. I just wanted to clarify that point."

"Consider it clarified." I looked at Ramon, asleep on the backseat. "What if he comes to while you're driving?"

"Won't happen. Trust me. This is my business."

Who was I to argue with a proven expert?

Walrus drove us to a public park I'd never noticed before a few streets over from Figueroa. Like other parks suffering from funding cuts, it was overgrown and understaffed. The homeless had camped out on its northern perimeter, the basketballers on its western side. Walrus held the unconscious Ramon upright by his collar and walked him like a puppet to the south of the park. Ostensibly it was a picnic area, but judging by the gang symbols that had been sprayed on every surface, only the bravest of picnickers would dare to use its facilities. At the moment it was quiet as a church on Monday morning. And a little less populated.

We marched across the empty grounds and Walrus dumped Ramon onto a gang-marked picnic table. "I like this place," the big man told me. "I come here to read."

"What about the gangs?" I asked.

"We get along fine," he said. "We have a spiritual understanding." He walked to a drinking fountain, collected about a gallon of water in his palm, and returned to drip it on Ramon's face.

The thug sputtered and came around. He started to sit up and Walrus shoved him back onto the table, banging his head. "Ow, Jesus, man," Ramon whined. His ears were bloodred. He put a hand to one of them and winced. "Jus' take it easy. We can work this out."

"Sure we can," Walrus told him. "As long as you're ready to answer some questions."

Pigeons were flying in, thinking we'd be leaving crumbs. I'd have settled for a few crumbs from Ramon.

"Yeah, sure," he said. "I tell you what I can. But I don' know much."

"What's your full name, Ramon? Falcon, like your cousin?"

"Naw. Luis on my mother's side. Valdez my name."

"Who hired you and Howard to get rid of me?" I asked.

"Joey Lunchbox."

"And he's working for Huey Grosso now, right?"

"I don' know. Ask him."

Walrus plinked Ramon's right ear and the hoodlum cried out in pain. "Mr. Lunchbox is not available to ask at the moment, Mr. Valdez," Walrus explained softly. "So we're asking you."

"I don' know who he work for. He phones me, says what he wants done, and I do it. He pays me. I don' know where the money comes from."

"Why does Joey Lunchbox want me dead?"

"He don' tell me stuff like that. I sure as hell don' ask. It's a job. I don' have any curious."

"Curiosity," Walrus corrected.

"Did you and Howard try to break into my restaurant last night?"

"Hell, no. We try, we do it. We pros, man."

Ramon was in serious need of a reality check. Walrus gave it to him in the form of another ear flick. When his howl subsided, I asked him why Joey Lunchbox had ordered Luis killed.

"Well, you see, Luis sort of brought me and Howard in."

"Luis was the main contact with Lunchbox," I said.

"Uh-huh. That's why Joey was mad at him worse than us. Joey's a little crazy. You know about the fingers?"

I'd heard the story, possibly apocryphal, that when the hood was collecting for old man Vetticino, he'd carry the bag cash in a kid's lunchbox, which is how he got his name. One day, when he emptied out the lunchbox on the don's desk, there were a few bloody fingers mixed in with the money.

"What's this?" Vetticino is supposed to have asked.

"You said if they was Tap City to collect their valuables," Joey told him.

"So what's with the digits?"

"Jimmy Slide didn't have the cash," Joey said. Jimmy Slide was a car mechanic. His fingers were his most valuable possessions.

I looked at Ramon. "Joey's not supposed to be crazy, exactly. Just very literal. Did he tell you to kill Wilton Dresner?"

"Dresner? The talk guy? Hell, I don't have anything to do with that. Radio says they got the killer. Casino guy. Johnny Musso, something like that."

"You know the name is Rousseau, and you know he's the wrong man."

Ramon shook his head. "Look. Radio says the killer emptied the gun at Dresner. Four bullets into the body, three into the wall. A real mess. Whoever shoots him—maybe this casino guy, maybe not—is fucking *echo chispas*—outta-sight angry at the guy. Pros don't get angry. One shot, boom, the guy's dead."

"Let's hear about the theft of Candy Dan, Ramon."

Ramon looked pained, not only from his ears. "It was too tricky, man. They want a horse messed up, the easy way's to use a lead pipe on the leg. Who's to say it ain't no accident? But this one, we gotta steal the goddamn animal first, and that ain't so easy by itself. Then I guess Luis tells Joey you called him and Joey says we gotta make it look like *you* stole the horse and fucked him up."

"Just because I phoned Luis?"

Ramon grinned unpleasantly. "Maybe Joey don' like you."

"At this point, he can't like you too much, either," I said. "You didn't get me *or* Candy Dan. Some pro."

"Hey, my way woulda worked, man. I break the horse's leg and then me and Howard stomp you into the ground and we make it look like the horse—" He stopped again, realizing that he wasn't making any friends with his thwarted plan.

"Anyway, that bastard Howard, he don' wanna break no horse's leg. Animal lover. And we play too cute and you get away from us. So no harm, huh?"

"Howard probably wouldn't agree with you," I said.

"Yeah, well, he'll just have to take his lumps. Where is he?"

"Lying in the street," Walrus said. "Halfway to Nirvana."

Ramon's eyes were moving nervously. He started to sit up, but Walrus pushed him back down. "How about it, Coley? Did Mr. Valdez answer all your questions?"

"Where's Luis's body?" I asked.

"I dunno."

Walrus reached out for an ear and Ramon jerked his head away. "Out by Pale Rock," he almost shouted. "They puttin' up a shopping center. Luis down in a hole."

"A shopping center covers a lot of territory," I said. "Where is the hole, exactly?"

Ramon hesitated, but when Walrus went for his ear again, he said, "Under where they're building a Taco Loco."

"That's a pretty droll place to bury poor Luis," I said. "Okay, let's move on to Jerry Woo."

Ramon frowned.

"Maybe you know him as Jerry Woolrich," I said.

"Yeah, well," he said, then mumbled something.

"What?"

"Howard and me did him," he mumbled.

"And Joey Lunchbox?"

"Joey was there, man, but you say I told you and I'll call you a liar."

Walrus moved to flick Ramon's ear again, but the Latin said, "You can cut my fuckin' ear off, man. But I ain't puttin' no finger on Joey."

"How'd you kill him?" I asked.

He hesitated. "There's this machine Joey has. It sorta electrocutes people. See, we needed to make him tell us where he was hiding some pictures."

"What kind of pictures?"

"Horses, man. But there were some other pictures, and Joey took them, too."

"Were they in a folder under Woo's bed?" I asked.

He seemed surprised. "Yeah. Stuck in the mattress."

"Now let's get back to an earlier question—why am I on Huey Grosso's hit list?"

"I dunno. Look. You ask me and I tell you everything I know," Ramon whined. "But I dunno this. I swear by the Sacred Virgin, man."

Walrus rolled his tongue around under his lips and cheek, thinking. Finally he said, "One thing I think we're losing in our society is the concept of blasphemy. Nothing's sacred anymore."

"Ramon's no choirboy," I said. "That's for sure."

"He swears by the Sacred Virgin, but I think he's lying. I think he needs to go to confession."

Ramon had been following our conversation like it was a tennis match, but he wasn't enjoying the action. "Whatta you talkin' about? I tol' you everything."

"Let's go for a ride," Walrus said, hooking a finger under the chain on Ramon's neck and encouraging him to sit up.

"Wh-where we goin'?"

Walrus ignored the question. Instead he lifted Ramon from the table by his belt. "I can break your leg," he said, "or you can promise me not to try and run away."

"I promise," Ramon replied immediately.

"If you do try, I'll catch you and break both legs. Are we of one mind on this?"

"Oh, yes," Ramon answered.

The three of us crossed the park. On the way we passed a group of young blacks wearing Crips colors. They waved to Walrus and called him "the stone man" and "Mr. Stone." In a friendly way, of course.

At the car, Walrus handed me his keys. "You drive. Mr. Valdez and I will ride in back."

"Sure, Walrus, whatever you say."

Once we were all seated, Walrus apologized for the chauffeur-passenger setup. "I just need my hands free," he said.

As he directed, I drove us onto the San Diego Freeway, concentrating on the traffic and trying not to think about what might be happening in the seat behind me. I was conscious of shifting and moving. Then I heard a window being lowered, felt the wind whip through the car. This was followed by a shriek of horror from our prisoner.

I glanced at the passenger's side mirror and saw a very large arm dangling something over the asphalt. Ramon's body. Upside down. His face must have been only inches away from hamburger. His high-pitched scream sounded like a siren.

After what seemed a long time to me and must have been an eternity to Ramon, Walrus hauled him back in.

The thug was gibbering. "I swear . . . I don' know why they want him dead. I don' know nothin' else . . . I swear."

"Okay," Walrus told him. "I'm convinced. Coley?"

"You're the expert," I said.

"Aw, Mr. Valdez." The big man sounded annoyed. "You've wet your trousers."

"Oh, Jesus, I couldn't help . . ."

"It's all right," Walrus said. "Just sorta bunch up the material to keep it off the seat cover."

"Coley, what do we do with Mr. Valdez?"

We were just passing a sign for the Temple off-ramp that leads directly to Parker Center. I pointed at the green-and-white billboard. "You'll like this, Walrus. A sign from God."

"That's a rare blessing," he said.

.   .   .

Ramon and I walked into Parker Center, leaving Walrus in the Ford. The civilian clerk at robbery-homicide division, a stern-looking forty-something woman seated behind the counter, cast a skeptical eye at Ramon with his wet pants, but allowed that Detective Wiley was on duty.

She picked up the phone, dialed his office, and gave him my name. She listened for a beat, nodded, and replaced the phone. "He said you were a lecher and a reprobate," she told me, "but to let you in anyway."

"I was an innocent boy before I met Sean Wiley," I informed her.

"I just bet," she said, and unlocked the swinging half door. When we were through, she continued a wary watch on Ramon and pointed to a row of partitioned-off cubicles along the back wall of the room. "Detective Wiley is second office from the left."

Indeed he was, feet up on the desk, studying the NBA box scores in the newspaper and biting into a multilayered sandwich that might have given Dagwood Bumstead trouble.

"Coley!" he said, waving me to have a seat and placing the sandwich carefully on his desk. "Well, this is sure a surprise." Then he saw Ramon, frowned, and gave him the hard eye. The thug was casting furtive glances around the division, possibly gauging his chances of making it to the gate and out before somebody shot him. His chances were not good.

"How's it going, Sean?" I asked.

"Slow, slow day," he replied, still distracted by Ramon. "No points, no rebounds, no assists. Not even a blocked shot. Just looking for something I can get my teeth into. Speaking of which, who's your friend?"

"Ramon Valdez. I'd be surprised if he doesn't have a rap sheet that will make the top forty."

Sean stared at Ramon again. "Needs potty training," he said.

"At the least."

"What mayhem has he been up to lately?"

"He tried to kill me."

Sean shrugged. "Can't fault his judgment there. That time at Hollywood you let Ladybe Good wear herself out and wind up out of the money, I lost thirty smacks and would've killed you myself."

"That was ten years ago," I complained.

"You know what thirty bucks was worth *then*?"

Try talking to a Scot about money. "Ramon works for Joey Lunchbox," I said.

"Ah," Sean said, putting on a wolfish grin. "Lunchbox is one asshole I'd love to treat to a jailhouse enema."

"Poetic," I said. "Well, this may be your big chance."

I told Sean of the probable whereabouts of Luis Falcon's corpse. "This young man killed him and a photographer named Jerry Woolrich and just maybe you can talk him into implicating Lunchbox."

"Never heard of the man," Ramon said.

"What's your interest in all this, Coley?"

"I'm just a taxpayer, trying to take a bite out of crime," I said.

"You a witness to any of these alleged capital offenses?"

I shook my head.

"How do you know this man's guilty?"

"He told me."

"I tol' him shit," Ramon said.

"Well, let me check all this out," Sean said. "Then we'll present this piece of dog feces with a few options on his future."

"Man, I want to call a lawyer," Ramon said.

It was a reasonable request, but Sean looked at him uncomprehendingly.

"It's my constitutional right," Ramon said.

Sean grinned at me. "Nobody knows the Constitution like a crook, you ever notice that?" Turning back to Ramon, he said, "You watch a lot of TV, do you, punk? You think us cops got our hands tied behind our backs? I may surprise you. You have any idea how long I can keep a dirtbag like you circling through the L.A. penal system without anybody even knowing you're there?"

"Legally?" Ramon asked.

Sean shrugged. "Legally enough. I already hold the record, but records are made to be broken. And so are punks like you."

"Sean loves to use the system," I said.

He nodded. "It's a specialty of mine."

"You can't keep me forever, till you charge me with somethin'," Ramon said.

"You're right. We may just have to find a way to deport your ass." Sean grinned. "I've got some real good pals in Immigration."

"He's got a partner, Sean," I said. "I only know him by the name Howard. Last I saw of him he was lying in the middle of Medina Street, not far from Brooklyn Avenue."

When I finished giving him a description of the battered thug, Sean crossed the room and put his hand on Ramon's shoulder. He gave me a wink and said, "Thanks for the business."

Back in the car, Walrus asked, "Did you tell your friend everything?"

"No. Not everything."

"Good. They have their own agendas and you can never be sure what they are."

What I hadn't mentioned to Sean was anything about Huey Grosso or the kidnapping of Candy Dan or the Dresners. Maybe Ramon would tell all, but if the police bulled into Starbuck and Lea's investigation, I did not want to be involved in any way.

"I don't have many contacts in law enforcement," Walrus said. "But a cooperative cop can come in handy."

"Sean and I go way back. Remember the Hap Dunlop murder?"

Walrus shook his big head back and forth.

"Maybe before your time," I said. "Fifteen, sixteen years ago. Hap was a jock who was the victim of a gangland-style killing. Sean was the investigating officer and he spent a lot of time hanging around the tracks. I'd barely lost my bug and was starting to show what I could do. We became friends. We even roomed together while he was between wives."

"Did he ever catch the guy?"

"Hap's killer? No. It was a contract job. Hap made somebody mad and paid the price. Sean gave it his best shot, but he couldn't even get a toehold on that one. And so he moved on."

"There are times when existentialism is the way to go," Walrus said.

"Amen to that," I told him.

19

WE BOTH AGREED that as soon as Joey Lunchbox discovered that Ramon and Howard's mission had been aborted, he would be dispatching two more sentinels of senseless destruction. So instead of calling it a day, Walrus moved into my apartment's guest room.

The bed in there was plenty big for any visiting jockeys that might drop by—not that they ever did—but less than adequate for a Walrus. He told me he didn't mind, that sleeping on the floor might be the kind of ascetic experience that would be good for his soul.

I, on the other hand, was too grateful for his presence not to want to make his accommodations as four star as I could. I called a furniture store that boasted both Los Angeles Lakers and Clippers among its clientele and ordered a bed that Kareem Abdul-Jabbar would have found roomy. By putting just a slightly larger dent in my available credit, the huge frame was delivered and installed within two hours.

I spent most of the evening dealing with the restaurant business and so, in his way, did Walrus. I'd instructed the staff to let him have anything he wanted. Chefs Antony, Stan, and Enrico were more complimented than appalled by the volume of entrées, breads, and desserts he managed to consume.

When not noshing, he established a beachhead in the bar on a stool nearest the cash register, where he could sip his soft drink and, as surreptitiously as possible, study the reflection in the bar mirror of the customers entering the Neck.

Aside from Walrus, the only thing that kept this from being a typical night at work was a call from Frank Sanchez, the reporter from the *Sun* who'd been covering Wilton Dresner. I took it in my office.

"I've been trying to get you all day, Coley. You're a hard guy to pin down."

"All part of my plan."

"Do you have a few minutes?"

"I guess so," I said, resigning myself. I'd tried to maintain good press relations when I was riding, not that it did me that much good ultimately. "What can I do for you?"

"Well, I'm still working the Dresner story, which as you can imagine is suddenly hotter than a jalapeño."

"Got that book contract yet?"

"Prospects are high," he said with a chuckle. "Especially since we're talking true crime instead of biography. I've been trying to get quotes from everybody who talked to Dresner at the AEF party without stepping on the toes of the Bay City police. I hope you can help me."

"If I can."

"I understand Johnny Rousseau is your business partner."

There was no ducking that one. And I didn't think it was the time to announce my new solo ownership. "He and I started the restaurant and I run it. He spends most of his time in Las Vegas."

"But at the moment he's spending his time in the Bay City lockup. The assumption is that he put the bullets in Dresner."

"There's considerable distance between assumption and conviction," I said.

"Then I take it you don't believe he's guilty."

"It would take quite a lot to convince me," I said.

"You heard him threaten Dresner at the party."

"He was drunk and it wasn't much of a threat anyway. I think his words were, 'You won't live forever.' Who can argue with that?"

"Dresner surely can't. What was the problem between the two of them?"

I sighed. "You tell me what you've heard and I'll tell you whether I agree."

"The word is that Rousseau's got it bad for Dresner's daughter. Only at the party, it looked like she had eyes for the horse doctor, Charles Lavery. This set Rousseau off in a big way, and when Dresner seemed to be encouraging the daughter–Lavery linkup, Rousseau flipped and made his incriminating comment. Is that the way you saw it?"

"More or less," I said. "But look at it this way. Lavery's still alive, right?"

"Definitely. I had lunch with him today. Quite a guy. Sort of sucks you in; it's hard to explain. I didn't realize until I left him he hadn't told me a damn thing."

"My point is, if Rousseau was driven to murder because of jealousy, why would he kill Dresner? Lavery would have been a much more likely target."

"Yeah. That point's been raised. But the cops say that they don't think Rousseau really planned to kill Dresner. He went to the house to get his gear and bumped into the man. Maybe they argued. Who knows? Rousseau was carrying a gun and he plugged him. I don't suppose you've talked to him since the murder. . . ."

"Nope," I lied.

"What about the story that Rousseau is mobbed up?"

"As far as I know, Johnny Rousseau is an honest businessman. Last time I looked, gambling was legal in Nevada and they don't have to finesse it the way they do in Malibu."

"Point taken."

"Now, can I ask you a question?"

"Sure."

"Is the police investigation still open? Or are they settling for Johnny?"

"You have something specific in mind?" Sanchez was the reporter back on the attack.

I wasn't about to mention Huey Grosso, Heartland Farms, Family Marketing, or anything to do with Starbuck's investigation. But I thought I might just give his head a little spin. "Don't you think there might be some connection between Dresner's death and the missing business partner, Ed Fein."

He was quiet for a minute. Thinking? Making notes? Yawning? "That's an angle I hadn't considered," he admitted. "Nobody's mentioned Fein at all in connection with Dresner's death. Definitely not the cops. They're very satisfied with Rousseau. But this is interesting."

"What do you know about Fein?" I asked. I really wasn't that curious, but it amused me to misdirect him. "What kind of a guy was he?"

"According to the people I talked to, he was a middle-aged, colorless sort of dude; a numbers nerd. He wasn't flashy. Not much of a risk taker. He sure wasn't a career criminal. Never so much as cheated on his income tax. His work was his whole life.

"His wife died of the Big C a couple years ago, and he never remarried. If he had any women since, they were a secret to people who knew him. He pulled down good money for taking care of Dresner's interests. He wasn't in any kind of financial bind when he split. The evidence was pretty indisputable he'd done it, but people who knew him couldn't imagine what made him go off the rails like that."

"We live in tough economic times," I told him. "Speaking of which, I'd better get back to my business."

"Thanks for your cooperation and your tip on Fein," he said, and sounded as if he meant it. "I may have to call you again."

"Feel free," I said.

•   •   •

In the main dining room, Walrus was in deep conversation with Jack Hayward about Henry VIII's break with the Catholic Church. Jack's knowledge of the event had probably come from an old movie script, but he had Walrus enthralled.

We turned off the neon sign a little before midnight.

As Walrus and I climbed the stairs to the apartment, he said, "I want you to know, Coley, this is the most enriching work experience I've had since I was looking out for Charlie Chaplin when he was here to pick up his Oscar."

"What kind of a guy was he?" I asked.

"You know I don't talk about my clients," he said piously.

Chastised, I dropped the subject. We entered the apartment and Walrus started for his room. He paused and said, "He wasn't what I'd call loquacious. In fact, the whole forty-eight hours I was with him, he didn't say word one."

"That's one of the things that made him a star," I said.

20

THE NEXT MORNING was spent in workaday pursuits. Talking with suppliers. Getting estimates from painters, since I was thinking of brightening the exterior in celebration of my impending ownership. Meeting with my accountant in Century City to apprise him of the change and to get his input. Walrus accompanied me and got a lot of reading done.

When we returned, a message from Starbuck was on my machine, requesting my presence at his beachfront place at two. I wasn't going to make it, even if we left immediately.

At a quarter after, Walrus parked beside a fire hydrant in front of Starbuck's home. He started to open his door, but I assured him I would be in no danger inside.

"It's your call," he said. "Just give a shout or—"

"Break a window," I said. "Right."

Choo Choo ushered me into the study-office, where Starbuck was entertaining a familiar-looking guy who reminded me of a fireplug in a waistcoat.

"This is Channing Hoag, Coley," Starbuck said, not getting up from his seat behind the desk. "He's the U.S. representative for Bright's, Limited."

Hoag extended a hand, saying in a clipped British accent, "Mr. Killebrew, I believe we've met before."

"Sure we have. You were the guy who was giving Wilton Dresner a hard time at the AEF fund-raiser."

"Poor Wilton," he said, grimacing and showing picket-fence

teeth under the neatly trimmed mustache. "The man did a lot of good in his way, but he did have some rather old-world ideas about things."

"You don't hear too many people these days coming out in favor of slavery," I said.

"Oh, he was just having a bit of fun with that. Wilton was a very shrewd man. And he was a decent man, too, as was evidenced by that fund-raiser. He was genuinely concerned about the welfare of horses. In my work, I encounter too many who only regard them as profit-making machines. If they can't earn you enough lolly on the course, you find a way to liquidate them and collect on the insurance. New ways all the time, too."

Hoag dropped into a chair opposite Starbuck and sighed. "Poor old Wilton. I wished I could have been here for the funeral."

"Mr. Hoag's been in Chicago," Starbuck explained.

"A quick visit and not a very satisfactory one, I fear. I just disembarked at LAX about an hour ago." He frowned. "Got a bit tied up at the airport by a very persistent journalist who was waiting to ask me questions about Dresner."

"Hispanic fellow?" I asked with a smile.

"Yes. Enterprising of him to track me down, and he was rather more courteous than I might have imagined, but I had nothing to tell him other than what I've just told you. When I managed to get away from him, I came straight here to bring Raymond up to date. He's been making quite a bit of progress on our behalf."

Starbuck waved off the compliment as if it were a pesky mosquito.

"Another suspicious horse death in the Windy City?" I guessed.

Starbuck nodded. "At a farm in Lambert, Illinois, just outside of Chicago. Owned by a chap named Bricknell." He stared at me without blinking. "The cause given was equine colic."

"Is that usually fatal?" I asked.

"It can be," Hoag said. "And in this case, the veterinarian claims it was."

"You don't sound convinced," I said.

"Well, what can I say? Raymond knows how fishy the whole thing is. But we can't prove a thing. It's damned frustrating." The Englishman got up from his chair and started pacing around the office, his face red with indignation. "Do you have any idea how many ways unscrupulous reptiles can imitate natural or accidental death in horses? They've tried everything. Drownings in swimming pools. A fall from a cliff."

"Tell me about it," I said.

"It's difficult even to talk about. I've seen stabbings disguised as wounds suffered from tree branches or picket fences. They electrocute the poor beasts. Clip a wire to the horse's ear and another to its anus, and the animal is felled in seconds. At least they don't suffer."

"Can't they detect that?"

"Unless the vet knows what to look for, singed patches on the flesh where the wire clips were attached, the death is attributed to colic. Or endotoxemia."

"Did you check for electrocution?" I asked.

"Of course. But there was no sign of singed hide. I had to accept the vet's finding and approve payment. But it certainly doesn't feel right."

Hoag rose from his chair. "Well, Raymond, I know you wish to confer with Mr. Killebrew. You must excuse me. It's been a long flight, and I really should ring my office in London." His expression said he wasn't looking forward to the call.

When the Englishman had left the room, Starbuck got right to the point. "About that horse Falcon rode in Chicago, Briarpatch . . . ?"

"Falcon started a bank account the next day. He's been depositing five grand a month ever since."

He sat back in his chair and looked thoughtful for a few seconds. "Anything else?"

"Falcon is doing his riding in the eighth circle these days."

"Care to translate that?" he asked gruffly.

"He's gone where the roses grow. Below. Below."

"Well, regardless," Starbuck said, unmoved, "I told you Briarpatch was from Argentina. He came to this country as part of a three-horse shipment four years ago. And he was not the big news of the shipment. In fact, he was a throw-in, along for company. The big horse of the trio was named Rebaso."

"That sounds familiar."

"He was a champion down there. Not that he made much money. As we discussed the other day, they don't. That's why he was sent here. He was expected to clean up on American tracks."

"But something happened to him," I said.

"Something. You remember that stable fire at Cedar Point Track in Daytona?"

"Right." I nodded.

"Eighty-five horses burned in that blaze. And one of them was Rebaso. Or so they said."

"You think he didn't burn?"

"I don't think so. For my money, it was Briarpatch that died at Cedar Point. I think the owners collected the insurance—and it was a nice chunk of change—on Rebaso. Next thing you know, the real Rebaso is racing as Briarpatch, ridden by that sterling reinsman Luis Falcon. Since Briarpatch had shown nothing in Argentina, he paid a very nice price."

"A ringer," I said. "Just like the 'Murder, She Wrote' you were ridiculing."

"They still had it backward," he grumbled. "It's the South American who cleans up in the States, not the other way around. And methods of identification are looser down there, too, making a switch possible."

"Hold on a second," I said. "The chart said Briarpatch was a gelding. Wasn't Rebaso an entire horse?"

"He was, yes," said Starbuck. "So big deal. They gelded Rebaso before they started running him as Briarpatch." He leaned forward in mock confidentiality. "One of the first things you learn as a breeder—it's not that hard to make a stallion a gelding. But the reverse is kinda tricky."

I ignored his heavy-handed sarcasm. Something else was tickling the back of my brain. I said, "What was the name of the owner of the stable Hoag said he just visited?"

"You're slow today, Coley. It was Bricknell. Arnie Bricknell. Same guy who was listed as the owner of Briarpatch in that Land O' Lincoln chart. The horse that Hoag just checked out, the supposed equine-colic victim, was Kickstart, another one of Bricknell's best."

"So this Bricknell is probably involved in insurance fraud, among other kinds, up to his neck. And he probably was involved in the Cedar Point fire."

"It looks like it." He stared at me for a few seconds and said, "I could use your help, Coley."

I'd thought he was being unusually chummy. I didn't ask what he wanted from me, just glared at him.

"I'd like you to pay a visit to Bricknell Stables and see what you can turn up."

"Why should I?"

"You did some good work for me before, and my best operative isn't available."

"Lea, you mean?"

"She's on the inside of the Dresner's family, in a key position to find out who shot the old man. She doesn't believe it was your great and good friend Johnny Rousseau." So far so good, I thought.

"Lea might be able to dig up something to get your pal out from under the murder rap. Unless I have to take her out of that situation and send her to Illinois. I mean, nobody's paying me to find out who canceled Dresner's check, and chances are it has nothing to do with my primary investigation."

"No, it was probably some deranged Democrat who just couldn't take listening to him anymore."

"So I guess I'll just pull Lea out and put her onto the Bricknell connection, which seems like a much hotter lead." He paused, waiting for me to say something, but I just let the silence lie there. Why make it easy for him?

"Just a short trip to Chicago," he said. "Of course, if you don't really care if Rousseau spends the rest of his life behind bars . . ."

"What does Hoag say about your switch theory?" I asked.

"I haven't told him about it. I don't like to confuse customers with facts until I'm sure they are facts. That's why I'm buying you a ticket to go and see."

"Is Family Marketing involved?"

Starbuck's face broke into a wide grin. "Thanks for reminding me. That was a lucky guess of yours. It looks like Family Marketing may indeed be one of Huey Grosso's enterprises. But Family Marketing doesn't own any of Bricknell Stables."

"That doesn't make sense," I said with a frown. "Grosso didn't like me talking to Luis Falcon, and Falcon is tied to Briarpatch."

"However," Starbuck said airily, "Family Marketing *is* listed as the former owner of both Rebaso and Briarpatch. The company sold the horse to Bricknell."

The guy sure knew how to drive me nuts. "When," I asked with extraordinary patience and restraint, "were you going to tell me that?"

"I just did."

"And what other information do you have that you haven't chosen to pass along, Starbuck? You sent me into a situation last time without telling me everything and it nearly cost me and Lea our lives. Once bitten, twice shy."

"What's your concern?" he asked.

"My concern is that I am presently on Huey Grosso's hit list and you seem to be putting me in a position where I'll make him even madder."

"Bullshit," Starbuck said. "If anything, I'm moving you out of harm's way."

"You don't think his influence extends to Chicago, of all places. Home of Al Capone."

"You don't know how these things work, Coley," Starbuck said. "The West Coast is Grosso's home territory. If he's gonna try to take you out, it'll be here and not in Chicago, where he'll have to go through seven kinds of explanations to the family there. There's as much bureaucracy in organized crime as there is everywhere else."

I thought that over for a second. I had a tough time trusting Starbuck, but his reasoning did make a certain amount of sense.

"Okay. I'll head out for Chicago in the morning."

"Look at it this way," Starbuck said. "Grosso has already put out a contract on you. If you make him madder, what more can he do?" He blessed me with a merry smile.

"You're right," I replied, putting a smirk on my face that would make even Bruce Willis cringe. "Screw him and his law degree."

Starbuck sobered suddenly and stared at me. He preferred me cowering in fear. "Well," he said, "if you make it all the way to Chicago without Grosso getting his mitts on you, keep this in mind—Rebaso got nicked by a tree branch when he was a yearling. If he isn't in horse heaven, he should have a two-inch scar on his neck, just to the right of his withers."

"I'll check it out. And by the way, I'll need two round-trip tickets to the Windy City. I'm taking a friend."

"A woman?" he asked. "This isn't a goddamn pleasure trip." But I could see his emotions were mixed. He didn't want me to have a good time, but he was hoping this meant Lea and I were going our separate ways.

"Not a woman," I replied, but offering no further information. "And if the seats aren't in first class, I'll upgrade and add it to my bill."

21

THAT NIGHT SOMEBODY succeeded in breaking into the Horse's Neck. And they obviously were not Ramon and Howard.

With Walrus in the next room, I was sleeping like a baby. I wasn't even aware anything was wrong until baby-elephant footsteps on the stairs interrupted my peaceful dreams. By the time I was out of bed and slipping on my robe, the same footsteps had come thudding back up the stairs. Walrus stood in the doorway of my room, a hairless Neanderthal, barefoot in his boxers, with a Dan Wesson Magnum looking tiny in his fist.

"A break-in," he told me, barely breathing hard. "They beat it."

"They? How many?"

"Two, I think. One inside, doing the grab. The other on point outside in the car. The inside man heard me coming, I guess."

"People across the state heard you coming," I said.

"Yeah, well, I figured speed was more important than silence. Anyway, the guy was out the front door by the time I got there and their car was already pulling away."

I opened my mouth and he said, "A ninety-two Electra. Dark color, probably blue. Loose muffler. They'd muddied their license plate."

"Let's go see the damage."

There wasn't much. Nothing seemed to be touched except for the glass trophy case, which Mr. Inside had broken. That was the sound that had served as an early wake-up call for Walrus.

I did a quick inventory of the objects in the case. One seemed to be missing.

"You looking for a small silver horse and rider on an onyx base?" Walrus asked. He was daintily holding the trophy I'd been presented for winning the 1982 Santa Rosita Handicap. "The grabber must've dropped it in his hurry."

I took it from him and stared at it. Luckily, it wasn't even dented. Why that one in particular? I wondered. I had a couple of others that were more intrinsically valuable and several that at least looked more valuable. Something was prodding at the back of my mind about the '82 Santa Rosita. What was it?

Walrus showed me how the thief had entered. Through the same alley window he'd tried the first time around. Hardheaded.

"Too bad you don't sleep with your car keys in your hand," I said. "You might've been able to head them off."

He frowned. "You're not in tune with the concept, Coley," he said. "My job is to protect you, not your chattel. The thieves may have been a diversion to get me out of the way, you know, so somebody else could come after you."

There was some logic to that. Particularly since the thief had gone for the glass cabinet over the cash register and not the register itself. This could have been Huey Grosso's doing, but it seemed excessively elaborate and sneaky, even for a Harvard Law grad.

"Good thinking," I said.

"Protect the Client is the first commandment. Protect Yourself is the second."

I looked at the splintered window lock. "Well, in the interest of protecting my chattel, I think I'll get a hammer and nail this window shut."

The not-so-gentle giant stood there in his shorts and looked sheepish. "Uh, Coley?"

"Yes?" I asked, wondering what philosophic query would spring from his lips.

"Do you think it's too early for breakfast?"

•   •   •

Thanks to the burglary, Walrus and I were fed, dressed, packed, and ready for our Chicago flight a couple of hours before we had to leave for the airport. It gave me time to make a phone call.

It wasn't my pal Deena who answered the Santa Rosita phone but a receptionist who was equally pleasant and managed to put me through to Roger Willetts just as fast.

"Hi, Coley," he greeted me in typical lugubrious fashion. "Guys in your business have to get up at this ungodly hour? You might as well still be racing."

"I have to catch a plane or I'd be deep in dreamland. How goes the battle?"

"One of these days you'll call this number and the cleaning lady will tell you Willetts couldn't take it anymore and hanged himself with the venetian-blind cord during a Bay Meadows simulcast. Did you catch up with Luis Falcon?"

The mention of Falcon's name threw me for a second. Had his body been found? Was Willetts asking me if I'd killed him? No. It had been an innocent question and I replied just as innocently. "Didn't have to, but thanks for your help anyway."

"So what else do you need? Pincay's social security number?"

"No," I said, chuckling. "But I need your memory. There's something about the 1982 Santa Rosita 'cap that I can't quite recall."

"You oughta remember that one well enough. You brought Codswollop in at forty-nine to one, beat Golden Apple by a neck while in receipt of twenty pounds." He paused, then added, "I hope you got your trophy under lock and key."

"Why?"

"What do you mean why? Don't you read the papers?"

"No more often than I have to," I said.

"Somebody swiped the framed winner's-circle photo of Codswollop right off the wall in our Turf Club two months ago. Wonder where it's hanging now?"

"Of course. The picture that disappeared, that's what I was trying to remember," I said, slapping my forehead with the palm of my hand.

"And then last month, Edna Bannon called." That would be Mrs. Thomas Bannon, Codswollop's owner. "Said she needed a duplicate of her trophy from that race, cost was no object. Somebody'd broken into her house and stolen the original, along with a framed copy of the program, signed by you and Hawley and McHargue and Pincay and a bunch of other jocks that rode that day.

"Thieves also took some other racing stuff but left behind a bunch of art and jewelry that was more valuable but had nothing to do with the track."

"I wonder if Joe Bremmer still has his trainer's trophy," I said.

"Far as I know. At least he hasn't asked for a dupe. But then again, Bremmer's such a sentimental devil, he's probably using the thing for a doorstop. No trouble with your trophy, I hope."

"Somebody tried to lift it last night," I said.

"No shit," he replied, neither surprised nor bored. "You know, I keep asking myself why we give away so many trophies for one damn race anyway?"

"Somebody seems to like them. Roger, are these thefts just isolated cases or . . . ?"

"Not at all, pal. There've been more racing items stolen in the last six months than I can remember in twenty years. All kinds of stuff. Saddles, silks, horseshoes. Like somebody's building a private museum."

I didn't know whether to be relieved or not. It was a nutty situation, but at least it didn't sound like Huey Grosso's kind of endeavor.

"Any idea who's behind it?"

"Just rumors about some collector buying up this kind of stuff any way he can get it. The stolen items are so varied, they figure all sorts of different people are doing them. Freelancers. As to what the mysterious collector wants with all the stuff, nobody seems to have a clue."

"Maybe he just enjoys looking at them," I suggested.

"Why not? Collectors are nuts, anyway. Maybe he figures racing is in its death throes and pretty soon any trophy will be a priceless antique."

"But why target particular races?"

"Maybe he's what they call a completist."

"And why *that* race? Codswollop never had another big payday in his life. You'd think trophies awarded to Affirmed or Alydar or Spectacular Bid would be the valuable ones."

"Beats me. Maybe the owner of Golden Apple went over the top, thought his horse had the Santa Rosita Handicap won if the weights had been fair. Golden Apple carried a hundred and thirty-two in that race, you'll remember, your mount a hundred and twelve. Apple was the last horse ever got assigned to carry a hundred and thirty or more at Santa Rosita, can you believe that? If we ran it now, he'd have a hundred and twenty and we'd be down on our knees begging his owner to accept that monstrous impost and not take him out of town. With so many big purses all over the country, if you want a big horse in your handicap, you can't pile the weight on."

"Times change," I said.

"Times change, but racing doesn't change enough, and if it changes, it's in the wrong way. Racing's a dinosaur, Coley, and I'm here at Jurassic Park, waiting to get eaten."

The conversation with Roger Willetts made me feel better. I'd never heard him sounding so cheerful.

I put the Santa Rosita 'cap trophy in my apartment away from public view, then gave the kitchen, bar, and dining-room staff all the instructions they were too professional to need in my absence. Walrus used that time to move his very special Ford next to the Cherokee on the only section of the parking lot that was covered by a roof. Not satisfied with that, he draped the machine with a tonneau cover. When he was finished, we took a cab to Los Angeles International Airport.

Slouching comfortably in our soft, all-leather first-class seats, I tried to sleep while Walrus watched the flight attendant mix drinks. "Why would somebody want to drink whiskey this early in the morning?" he asked.

"Hair of the dog," I said, without thinking. Then, naturally, had to have a discussion about the meaning of the expression.

The service on the flight was excellent; the food would probably have closed an earthbound eatery within a month but, by airline standards, was four star. The movie, the story of three generations of astronauts, was maybe one generation too much. But it was photographed in cool blue colors that were soothing for a man needing sleep. Walrus elected to read the whole flight.

At Chicago's O'Hare Airport, we rented a car—my companion insisted on a Buick sedan—and headed directly to the semirural suburb of Lambert, Illinois. I drove while Walrus pored over an Auto Club map as intently as a volume of sacred scriptures. He wasn't the best guy to be giving directions, though, because he was always able to see several alternate routes and had trouble deciding among them.

Once we got within the town limits of Lambert, Bricknell Stables wasn't hard to find. The spread was doing its best to pretend it was in Kentucky. It displayed an impressive front, with a shiny white, ornately decorated entry gate that would have been right at home in the antebellum South. A gatesman informed us that the stable offices were "quite-a-ways-straight-ahead."

Just inside the grounds was a bronze statue of a horse in the shade of a tree. I couldn't tell if it was a famous Thoroughbred or maybe the first animal Bricknell had put to sleep for the insurance money.

We drove the surprisingly long distance to the office between the traditional white fences of the horse farm. Mares and stallions were turned out, separately of course, in the fields on either side of the drive. One beautiful stallion pranced after us until we pulled up in front of a neat one-story building.

Walrus waited in the Buick with our luggage.

There was a flashy blonde in the reception area. She was a little heavy by current standards, but when Monroe and Mansfield were in their prime, she would have run a close third. She introduced herself as Dixie.

"If you're looking for work," she said, "you need to see the trainer, Gil Westover, or the farm manager, Joe Beck. We've got plenty of exercise riders, but you look like you'd be fun to have around." She said that last with a sexy smirk I didn't flatter myself was exclusively manufactured for me.

"I'm here to see Mr. Bricknell," I said. "Is he in?"

"He hasn't been *in* all day," she said. Was I imagining the double entendre?

"Do you expect him?"

"Sometimes he *comes* when you least expect it," she said. No, I wasn't imagining it.

"Why don't I wait awhile and see?"

"Be my guest, Mister . . . ?"

I'd decided the easiest way to play it was to stick to the almost truth. I identified myself and told her I was from Bright's. Starbuck was working for the company and I was working for him, so technically . . .

She repeated my name a couple of times, then smiled as if it gave her a thrill. She winked and shimmied into the back office, where she no doubt notified Bricknell of my presence.

A few minutes later he strode through the door. He was a

type-A hard charger in his forties. Probably worked out every morning and figured it made him healthy, but one day he'd drop dead from a massive coronary and surprise everybody, himself most of all.

"You Killebrew?" he asked, as if the room were filled with ex-jockeys.

I allowed as how I was and he waved me into his office with the air of a guy who didn't have all day. Maybe his midlife crisis was chasing him.

Aside from the inevitable shots of long-legged foals, rearing stallions, and flower-covered winners, the office was decorated with maybe a dozen shots of an angular, attractive brunette who wore clothes like a *Vogue* model.

"Lovely woman," I said.

"My wife," Bricknell replied dully. Now Dixie's plump presence seemed all the more interesting.

"I recognize your name, of course," he said. "Seen you ride. How long you been with Bright's?" His eyes darted impatiently as he matched me small talk for small talk.

"A few years."

"Well, look, your man Hoag was just here. And the limey left me with the impression that everything was taken care of."

I raised my hand placatingly. "It is. Payment's been authorized. I'm just here to finish up some of the paperwork. Routine stuff mostly. Do you have a certificate of death on the horse?"

"Sure. Thought Hoag had one, but Dixie'll make you a copy."

"It must be tough to lose a fine animal like Kickstart."

"He was a good one. But if there's one thing I've learned, you can't be sentimental in this business. If that's all you need . . ."

There were a few things more, but I flashed him a smile as insincere as his and made my exit. Dixie was waiting with a copy of the death certificate. "You were eavesdropping," I said. "You naughty girl."

"He expects me to be," she said with a grin. "Eavesdropping, I mean."

"Would you do me a little favor?"

"Honey, I might even be inclined to do you a big favor."

Walrus, who'd committed the road map to memory, was behind the Buick's steering wheel when I emerged. As we rolled away from Bricknell Stables he asked, "What'd you find out?"

"That Bricknell is a pretty arrogant bastard, that his assistant behaves as if she spent most of her early years watching old Marilyn Monroe movies. And most important of all"—I waved the death certificate—"that the vet who declared Kickstart's death to be as natural as shredded wheat is named G. T. Hartmann, DVM."

"You're going to want to visit him?"

"What better time than now."

The favor I'd asked of Dixie was for her to look up the address of Dr. Hartmann's office. Surprisingly, it was not in the rural horse country but in Chicago, in a Michigan Avenue high-rise where few of the doctor's patients would be able to visit.

There was a brass plaque in the skyscraper's lobby that proclaimed it the third tallest building in the city. I thought it was odd that in a metropolis with such an inferiority complex that it gleefully referred to itself as the Second City, there would be a building so proud of its third tallest status.

Hartmann's offices were on the twenty-first floor. The pale gray waiting room was small and empty with numbered Leroy Neiman prints on the walls and copies of *The Blood Horse* and *The Thoroughbred Times* on the tables. On the other side of a tiny sliding window, a young woman in street clothes, pleasant looking but no Dixie, told me that Dr. Hartmann rarely came into the office.

"I realize the doctor must make a lot of house calls," I said.

She didn't crack a smile. Beyond her, I could see a compulsively neat work space containing a filing cabinet, a computer, and a huge jug of bottled water. There was no evidence the doctor ever practiced the veterinary art in this place, even on small animals.

I told the receptionist I was a representative of Bright's, Ltd., and I needed to talk to Dr. Hartmann about the horse Kickstart.

"I'll look at doctor's schedule," she said grudgingly. A moment later she informed me, "Doctor will be at Bricknell Stables all afternoon."

Terrific. I thanked her and left the third tallest building in the Second City.

"Guess what?" I said to the waiting Walrus.

The vagueness of the question disturbed him much more than the answer or the drive back to Bricknell's.

22

BRICKNELL WOULD HAVE been happier to see a giant anthrax germ lumbering toward his horse barn than to have me pay a return visit. But somehow he restrained himself from giving me the boot. When I told him I needed to have a word with Dr. Hartmann, he just grunted "Sure," and led the way.

Bricknell Stables was a big operation, and the facilities were as good as I'd seen anywhere. Clean, neat, and efficient. The farm didn't fit the white-collar crime profile, but I'd cast Bricknell as a villain and couldn't shake the feeling.

It seemed like a long walk before we came to a stall where a slender female dressed more for the Turf Club than the barn was examining the legs of a beautiful bay filly.

"How's she doing, Georgia?" Bricknell asked.

The woman turned around. "I'm very pleased, Arnie. That filling in the ankle has practically disappeared. She should be able to resume training in a couple of weeks."

Then she looked inquiringly at me. Startling blue eyes peering out of a face with the kind of bone structure that would still be beautiful at sixty. At the moment the bones couldn't be much older than twenty-seven or twenty-eight.

"Georgia," Bricknell said wearily, "I'm afraid another person from Bright's needs to talk to you about Kickstart. Dr. Georgia Hartmann. Coley Killebrew."

Dr. Hartmann was an incongruous figure. Not because she was a woman. The idea of a female vet, though unthinkable just a few decades ago, didn't seem all that unusual. In fact, for reasons I know not why, women seem to establish a rapport with horses quicker than most men. But Georgia Hartmann was a little short in the tooth to be so well established in her profession. And she was much too expensively turned out to be mucking about in a barn.

"Mr. Killebrew," she said, extending an immaculately manicured hand. She gave no indication that my name rang any bells. But that didn't mean anything. No reason a vet has to be a turf historian.

"That's quite a nice-looking filly," I said.

"Yes, isn't she?" She gave me the full force of her unblinking blue eyes. "Well, what can I tell you about poor Kickstart, other than to repeat what I told the other gentleman, that we tried in every possible way to save him?"

"Oh, I don't doubt for a second you did everything you could, Dr. Hartmann. But an insurance company—at least one like Bright's—has to take the long view of things. We care about the bottom line, of course. But we also have a genuine concern for horses. We want to know everything about Kickstart's unfortunate death, because the slightest thing might help to save other horses in the future."

The glib outpouring of bullshit surprised even me. It didn't cut any ice with Bricknell, of course. But it did get through to Dr. Georgia Hartmann. The blue orbs radiated sympathy for my concern for the Thoroughbred.

"His case was anomalous in some ways. I don't know how much you know about equine colic."

"Just that it sounds painful."

"It's one of the leading causes of death in horses. For Kickstart, the real culprit was endotoxemia. Roughly translated it means 'inner poison.' Bacterial production in the animal's gut increases at an abnormal rate. When the bacteria begin to die in huge numbers, they release a toxin. This can lead to laminitis or enteritis, or, as was the case with poor Kickstart, to death. We did everything we could, but he just didn't make it."

Dr. Hartmann's manner was that of a controlled, no-nonsense professional, but as she got to the point of describing her patient's death, I sensed her control was maintained with difficulty. She really did strike me as devoted to her patients, and if there was dirty work going on, I resisted the idea she could be a party to it.

"Was there any possibility the horse could have been tampered with in any way?"

"Absolutely not, Mr. Killebrew. I saw no evidence of anything sinister, except for the bacteria that took the poor animal's life. There's so much we don't understand in veterinary medicine. But I assure you we are trying."

She continued for a while about other conditions afflicting horses. As I listened I nodded and grunted in all the right places, acting knowledgeable even about the technical details that sailed right over my head. When the recitation was done, I reassured Dr. Hartmann that I was certain she had done everything appropriate for Kickstart and sounded like a godsend to all her patients. Then, sort of offhandedly, I pressed home the real purpose of my visit.

"Mr. Bricknell, you have another Thoroughbred insured by my firm for a substantial amount of money—"

"I have several, yes."

"The one I'm interested in is Briarpatch. I wonder if I could look in on him while I'm here."

"Impossible," Bricknell said.

"Really? Why? Isn't the horse here?"

"Certainly he's here. But he's off limits, not available to outsiders."

"I'm not exactly a tourist," I said. "As an agent of my company, I have a right to make sure he's being well cared for."

He smiled nastily. "You're right," he said. "You can see Briarpatch, Killebrew. All you have to do is prove you work for Bright's."

"Prove?" I asked indignantly.

"Show me something that identifies you as an employee of Bright's or I'll have to ask you to leave my property."

"What's going on?" I asked. "I'm beginning to think you may be hiding something from my company."

"Let me tell you what I'm beginning to think, Killebrew. I'm beginning to think that an ex-jockey with a dicey reputation isn't the kind of employee I'd expect of a staid British outfit like Bright's."

"Bright's is impressed by facts, not rumors," I said, stung by the gall of this horse killer. "And the fact is I know a little something about separating the real from the fake, which is why they hired me. I suggest we put in a call to Channing Hoag in L.A. right now. You can get him to vouch for me, and I, because I'm human enough to be annoyed and embarrassed by your accusations, can prevail upon him to hold up on that Kickstart check until we're all very old and gray."

The atmosphere was getting heavy, and Dr. Hartmann jumped in to lower the tensions. "Arnie," she said cheerily, "could we speak for a moment?"

He reluctantly walked away with her. With her back turned to me, I couldn't hear anything she was saying, only Bricknell's protesting growls. Finally he said, "I'd tell him to go—" He caught himself, shot me a venomous glance, and mumbled, "That's fine. You handle it." Then he stormed away.

Dr. Hartmann walked toward me, poker-faced. "Arnie lets his emotions speak louder than his intelligence sometimes," she said. "But his heart's in the right place."

"Where's that, in a jar in the freezer?"

Her eyes were frosty enough to have been in that same jar. "I don't know if you really are from Bright's or what the story is. Frankly, I don't care. If, as I just told Arnie, you're testing the security around Briarpatch, then you have your answer—we're being very, very careful with him. No unauthorized person sees him.

Tomorrow he will be vanned to the track with the same kind of security measures reserved for an armored-car shipment."

"Very impressive."

"Arnie takes care with *all* of his horses," she said. "It's just a short van ride from here to the track, so they're kept here, rather than stabled at Land O' Lincoln. Not to put too fine a line to it, he is overprotective of his animals. If that's the kind of thing you're checking, rest assured. If you're some sort of impostor out to do Briarpatch harm, that's not going to happen. So, Mr. Killebrew, if you wish to pursue this line of inquiry further, I'm afraid you will have to provide Arnie with some credentials. If that annoys you so much that you'll hold up a check that he needs desperately to keep this place going, so be it."

"Very nicely put," I said. "But it leaves me with the impression you're more than just the vet here at Bricknell's."

"Arnie and I are friends. Not lovers, thank God. Just friends. And I look after the health of his horses. Period. I am talking with you now because he has a temper that tends to blind him to simple solutions. And now I think it's time you were going, Mr. Killebrew."

I thought so, too.

23

WHEN I'M WORKING for Raymond Edgar Starbuck, I believe in going first-class all the way. Which is why Walrus and I were staying at the Land O' Lincoln Inn, a newish luxury hotel a short stretch of Dan Ryan Expressway from the track. It was a place that did its heaviest business during the racing season.

When you had a room on the concierge level, as we did, you not only got a *Daily Racing Form* waiting outside your door each morning, you were entitled to a complimentary continental breakfast in the VIP lounge. The hotel chain would have been in receivership by now if all its concierge-level guests ate as heartily as Walrus. He had scarfed down the complete tray of hors d'oeuvres the night before, getting no more discouragement than a couple of worried glances from the hostess on duty. That morning he was on his sixth Danish when I looked up from my *Form* and asked if he spent much time at the races.

"Fairly often on the job. My kind of clients usually like the track."

"What about you?"

"It's never appealed to me particularly."

"Don't like to gamble?"

"Sure I do. Every day. Everybody gambles. Life's a gamble. But when it comes to what you might call organized gambling, no, it's not my thing. That's not for religious reasons, you understand."

When he said that, I knew what was coming. But I played

straight man. "What do the great religions say about gambling, Walrus?"

"Well, in the Bible, gambling is condemned all over the place. In the Old Testament, in the Book of Isaiah particularly, and even more so in the New Testament. But explain this to me, Coley—if gambling is evil, why isn't casting lots? All through the Bible, they're always casting lots to figure out what the will of God is."

"Sounds like superstition more than gambling," I said.

"Well, yeah, that's true, but casting lots was used for gambling, too, and from Genesis to Revelation there's not a word against it. Now, Buddhism strongly condemns gambling. Hinduism does, too, but with more loopholes if you want to look for them. Where it really gets fascinating is in some of the tribal religions, where they have what's called *sacred* gambling."

Walrus's lecture was almost as interesting as the race card at Land O' Lincoln. Continuing to listen with half an ear, and nodding periodically, I turned back to my *Form*.

There had been a trend in the past few years, spurred mainly by the success of the annual Breeder's Cup Day, to put together super racing programs, cards with no state-bred maiden races, no non-winners-of-two, no cheap claimers, but instead one major stakes race after another. It was the sort of thing that had been done in Europe, in short and prestigious meets like Great Britain's Royal Ascot, for many years, but the usual pre–Breeder's Cup practice in North America had been to stick to a single major race to a card.

Today, as one of several rich preludes to the Breeder's Cup, Land O' Lincoln was putting up a couple million dollars in added money, spread over six races for various divisions. The fourth race, the one Briarpatch would be running in, was the Stovepipe Hat Turf Mile. It didn't strike me as a dignified name for a graded stake—and it wasn't the biggest race of the day, either, despite being worth three hundred thousand dollars—but it was certainly the most contentious contest on the card.

Briarpatch had put together a fine record, mostly at Chicago area tracks like Arlington, Hawthorne, and Sportsman's Park, since that first win under Luis Falcon here at Land O' Lincoln. But today he was up against it, with some highly fancied runners shipped in from both coasts. He would not be the favorite.

Gorgonzola, a fast West Coast sprinter who'd been a tiger on Santa Anita's hillside turf course, was trying to stretch his speed to a mile. If the race was being simulcast to California, the kind of horseplayers who hung out in the Neck's bar would make Gorgonzola a prohibitive favorite.

On the other hand, if the denizens of New York's betting parlors had a chance at the action, the heavy money would go on their hometown favorite, Garment District. Used to going a mile and an eighth or more, that horse would be shortening up a bit for the Stovepipe Hat.

Even in Illinois, both those invaders figured to attract more action than Briarpatch, whose previous competition had undeniably been softer. On the other hand, the one-mile distance was a perfect trip for Bricknell's horse. After studying his record in the *Form*, I marked him down as worth a bet.

Not knowing what the day might have in store for us, Walrus and I turned down the offer of a hotel limo ride to the track and took the rental car. Judging by the traffic jam, today's crowd would be one of the biggest of the year in the Chicago area. We walked through the gates about half an hour before the first race, one of the few contests on the card that was not a battle of top runners.

Thanks to the hotel concierge, we had clubhouse reserved seats. They, like everything else, were going straight on my expense account.

Land O' Lincoln isn't the oldest track in the Chicago area, but it certainly must be the kitschiest, with its log-cabin motif. The various bars, fast-food restaurants, computer betting rooms, and TV rooms were named for figures in Lincoln's biography: Nancy Hanks, Ann Rutledge, Stephen Douglas, General Grant. On a losing day, the whole cutesy layout could be enough to send you looking for the John Wilkes Booth room.

I'd ridden here a couple of times but wasn't used to seeing it from the horseplayer's vantage point. I hadn't been missing much. Apart from the Lincolnesque touches, it could have been any other American racetrack from Aqueduct to Hollywood Park.

With the kind of money on the line today and the caliber of horses scheduled to run, I wished I had a few live mounts to ride myself.

Walrus and I sat in our assigned places for the first couple of contests. Then I spotted a familiar couple a few sections away in the box seats. Paula Dresner and Dr. Charles Lavery. It had been their proposed trip to the Midwest that had set Johnny off at the AEF benefit. I'd naively assumed the trip would have been canceled by Wilton Dresner's death. Apparently not.

I told Walrus to sit tight with his Perrier and volume of Confucius's teachings and went to express my sympathy to the nongrieving Paula.

When I got to the Lavery–Dresner box, the first thing I noticed was a definite coolness between them. Paula seemed pleased to see me, her face lighting up slightly with a wan smile. The charismatic Lavery was uncharacteristically out of sorts and scarcely reacted at all.

"I was so sorry to hear about your father," I said softly.

"Thanks. That's very kind of you." She was dressed in black, with very little makeup, but looked terrific as always. "Won't you join us?"

The invitation surprised me. I think it surprised Lavery, too. I turned and saw Walrus at the clubhouse window, staring down at us. I gave him a broad wink and took a seat next to Paula.

The field for the third race, a hundred grander for two-year-old fillies, was loading into the gate, far across the track in the seven-furlong chute and thus barely visible from the stands. Lavery offered Paula his binoculars. She declined.

The dozen horses broke in an even line, and we watched them speed along the backstretch. I didn't have a bet on the race, or any particular rooting interest—there were no California fillies or others I was familiar with—and neither apparently did my two companions. We watched the race with a calm disinterest unique in the huge crowd of screaming partisans. As the field came down the stretch we stood automatically when the people in front of us did, but the three-horse photo finish had none of us jumping up and down or yelling.

"This whole experience with Daddy has been very painful to me," Paula said when we'd resumed our seats.

"Naturally," I said.

"And the police aren't helping any. They won't stop poking around the house." She made it sound as if they were doing it purely to inconvenience her.

"It's their job to find out what happened."

"Oh, I know that, but can't they just look somewhere else? I wish we could bring a sense of completion to it, you know? Having things drag on this way keeps adding to the pain. You must know what I mean?"

"Sure."

"Charles thought it would do me good to get away for a while. We'd been planning this trip anyway. But I shouldn't have come. Consider how it makes me look."

"Your friends will understand," I said.

"It's not my friends I'm worried about. I know I must appear very callous, as if I didn't care for my father. The fact is I didn't know him very well."

"Is that right? You lived with him, though."

"For four years, yes, but he had such a busy schedule, we barely saw each other. My parents divorced when I was very young, Coley. I didn't come to live with my father until I was eighteen.

He's been generous in many ways, but we weren't really as close as people might think. Still, he was my father and I loved him."

"Do you think Johnny Rousseau killed him?"

She looked momentarily perplexed. "Poor Johnny. I . . . I don't know. If he did, it was all my fault. . . ."

"How's that?" I asked.

"I asked him to come and stay with us."

"You and he were sort of an item, weren't you?"

She gave me a condescending smile. "That's a lovely, old-fashioned way to describe it. An item."

I looked at Lavery. He seemed to have tuned out our conversation.

"What do the police say about Rousseau?" I asked her.

"I'm clueless. They don't tell me anything."

"Can you think of anyone else who might have wanted to kill your father?"

She shrugged. "He had mojo enemies. People he seriously dissed on his shows."

"Anybody in particular come to mind?"

She shook her head. "My interest in party sci is at the zero level."

"Party sci?" I asked.

"Politics. Political science. The stuff Daddy was always talking about."

"How's your brother holding up?" I asked. Finally, one of my questions got a reaction from Lavery. He turned to glare at me.

Tears filled Paula's eyes, and she took a handkerchief from her purse. She could talk about her father's death dry-eyed, but the mention of her living brother sent her over the edge.

She turned to Lavery and said accusingly, "I never should have left Neil."

"He'll be fine," Lavery murmured. "It's good for him to be on his own."

"I feel like I've deserted him. And he needs me. He's such a feeb when it comes to crisis. He's liable to . . . do something dumb. I can't just hang here with you, Charles. I can't. I'm going home."

Lavery looked as if he were about to argue, then decided it wasn't worth it. "I'll drive you," he offered.

"No, I won't hear of it," she said, lapsing into a Joan of Arc impression. "Your horse is running, and you can't miss that. I'll get a cab."

Lavery dug some keys out of his pocket and handed them to her. "At least take the car. You can leave it at the hotel."

Paula bent over and pecked him on the cheek. "Thanks for being so very Charles. I hope your horse does it and that the dinner really clicks bigtime."

She gave me a quick good-bye and strode up the aisle. Lavery sat back down. I probably should have left him. Especially since the person who'd invited me into the box had just run out on him, prompted by my questions. But I wanted to ask him a few things.

There was a sudden roar from the crowd, and I glanced at the tote board to see that the result of the third race had been posted.

Lavery jotted the prices down in his program in a neat hand. "Little Blossom," he said. "A very promising filly. And I'm alive in the pick-six."

The guy's self-control went beyond admirable to near schizophrenic.

Just to break the ice, I said, "I'm sorry if I disturbed Paula. . . ."

"No," said Lavery. "Not your fault. If you hadn't come along, she might have sat it out for another uneasy half hour at best. It was stupid to think I could get her mind off of . . ."

Lavery's train of thought seemed to wander as he stared out at the losers from the third race being led past the stands on their way back to the barn. "I was being selfish, I know. I had to be here, because of this dinner tonight, and I didn't want to leave her while she was so upset. But by bringing her, I upset her even more."

Charm at full throttle now, he gave me a sort of bonded-male, "who can understand women?" look.

"This dinner tonight is in your honor?"

Lavery shook his head. "No, but I am speaking. It's being given to benefit the fight against equine colic. As a former jockey, you must be familiar with the disease."

"More and more every day."

"What sort of work are you doing these days?"

"I keep busy. I, uh, do occasional odd jobs for the racing profession."

"Oh? Well, if you're interested, I just happen to have an extra dinner ticket."

I thanked him but said I had other plans for the evening.

"You may be sorry to miss it. I'm going to shake things up to-night." His mood was shifting once again, from quiet charismatic to wild-eyed zealot.

"Sounds interesting. Any chance of a preview?"

"Why not?" Lavery said, obviously eager to turn over his hole card. He leaned forward confidentially. "At my clinic, we are on the verge of a discovery that has eluded even the venerable Equine Disease Center. We're about to have a major breakthrough in the prevention of endotoxemia."

He paused, evidently waiting for some sort of awestruck response. I knit my brows and said, "Great news," with as much feeling as I could muster.

It was more than enough. "We feel we've discovered the reason for the sudden growth of bacteria that triggers the disease. And," he went on excitedly, "we're on the cusp of providing an inoculation that could very well eradicate the disease entirely."

Then, apparently realizing I wasn't a member of the American Academy of Veterinary Science, he went through another of his

Jekyll-and-Hyde segues. He was Joe Cool again, noble smile in place, as he turned to look at the track.

"Paula mentioned you have a horse running today." I spoke into the awkward silence.

"I don't *have* it," he said. "That is, it's not mine. I've just heard about Briarpatch from an associate who treats the animal."

"Dr. Hartmann?" I asked innocently.

He stared at me. "You know Georgia? I don't understand why *we*'ve never met before, Killebrew."

"It's the way of the world," I said.

"Georgia's terrific, isn't she?"

"So young and so well established," I said.

"She's exceptionally talented. Did you know she's an associate on the staff of my clinic? Her contributions to my research have been considerable."

"I was talking to her today," I went on. "She just lost a patient to endototoxemia and equine colic."

Lavery nodded. "Kickstart, you mean. A tragedy."

That was when the blower of the hunting horn stepped out in front of the stands to play "Boots and Saddles," giving it that little extra flourish they sometimes throw in to herald major stakes races. The field for the fourth race began to parade onto the track.

"There's Briarpatch, number three," Lavery said, his binoculars pressed to his face. "Damn, if he doesn't look magnificent." He shifted his gaze to the tote board. "Six to one. There, Killebrew, is an overlay if ever I saw one. I don't think he'll pay that, though. He doesn't figure to go off at any better than four. But with all the sucker money on those two coastal invaders, I don't think he'll go any lower than that."

"Gorgonzola's a tough customer," I protested. I'd picked Briarpatch myself and already had laid twenty bucks on his nose, but listening to Lavery brought out the loyalty I felt for California horseflesh.

He shook his head. "It's absurd to bet that sprinter down to two to one. Gorgonzola is fast enough, but this is three sixteenths farther than he cares to run. He'll make the pace. But he won't last around two turns. And as for the favorite, Garment District won't be able to keep up with these horses running a mile."

"Maybe if the pace is fast enough," I said, switching my devil's advocacy to the state of New York. "If Gorgonzola and Briarpatch soften each other up, Garment District might take it."

"Briarpatch won't be caught up in any speed duel," Lavery said. "Gorgonzola won't last whether anything runs with him or not, and Garment District will do well to get on the board." He spoke with such feeling, I began to wonder if he'd been protesting too much when he said he owned no part of Biarpatch.

"Garment District is first-time Lasix," I pointed out. Lasix was the antibleeding medication that was legal in Illinois, California, and nearly every other pari-mutuel state but not on Garment District's home ground of New York. Racing programs now informed the bettor which runners were using Lasix, regularly or for the first time, and also which were going off it. There weren't many in the latter category.

"Doesn't matter," Lavery insisted. "Lasix allows horses to achieve their potential, but it can't make them run any faster."

The full field of twelve was loaded into the gate in front of the grandstand. In a mile race on the Land O' Lincoln turf course, the run to the first turn was fairly short, and early position was important. Gorgonzola would break from the extreme outside, while Briarpatch had an ideal number-three post position. Garment District had drawn the rail, but since he figured to drop immediately to the rear in the early going, the draw for him was relatively insignificant.

The top three would be easy to spot. Gorgonzola was a gray, whose coat was getting nearer and nearer white as he grew older. Briarpatch was a huge bay who must have stood seventeen hands, a hand being the same as four inches measured at the withers. Garment District, on the other hand, was a smallish chestnut with a distinctive lowered-head running style that reminded me of the recent champion A. P. Indy.

Gorgonzola's jock did his job, hustling his mount out of the gate, getting clear of the field almost immediately, and crossing over to the rail. The gray had a three-length lead by the time they hit the first turn. Briarpatch was saving ground on the inside, running in fourth place and snugly held by his rider. The New Yorker, Garment District, dropped immediately to the rear as expected. As they turned into the backstretch he was some six lengths behind the eleventh horse and about twenty behind Gorgonzola. To win, he'd have to be Silky Sullivan reincarnated.

As they proceeded along the backstretch Biarpatch gradually, relentlessly moved up. Entering the far turn, he was second, a length and a half behind Gorgonzola, who was beginning to shorten stride. The L.A. horse offered brave resistance to the challenge, running neck and neck with Briarpatch for a few yards, but then he started to drop back.

By the time they turned into the stretch, there was little doubt the massive Briarpatch was the best horse on the track. He'd opened up as much as six lengths as he passed the eighth pole. That was when Garment District decided to give the crowd a thrill. Head down to show he was serious, he did a dramatic number on all the other horses in the field, charging past them on the outside. Though he appeared to be accelerating, I knew it was an illusion. Like nearly all stretch runners, he was merely keeping the same pace he had throughout the race, while the others were slowing down.

It must have appeared to some chalk players that Garment District was going to overhaul Briarpatch, too. They certainly were making enough noise. But that was another illusion. The finish, a one-length victory for Briarpatch, wasn't nearly as close as it looked. His jockey was taking it easy with him through the last sixteenth of a mile, not making him do any more than he had to, while Garment District's rider was pumping and slashing for all he was worth.

When it was over, Lavery turned and asked innocently where Gorgonzola had wound up.

"About seventh," I said, smugly proud of that win ticket on Briarpatch in my pocket. My analysis of the race had been identical to Lavery's, but there was no reason I had to let him know that.

"Killebrew," Lavery said, getting to his feet, "I'm meeting Georgia Hartmann and Arnie Bricknell for a little postrace champagne celebration back at his barn. Want to come along?"

It was a temptation, if for no other reason than to see the look on Bricknell's face. But if he and Dr. Hartmann were going to be clinking glasses somewhere, I wanted to be in an entirely different location, trying to get close to Briarpatch.

"That's nice of you, Lavery," I said, "but I wouldn't leave the rest of this racing card to have drinks with Sharon Stone, Walter Cronkite, and the pope."

"You won't miss any races. There's closed-circuit TV in the stable area."

"Really, thanks. But I like my racing live."

"Well, please use the box then. Hope to see you later."

And he was off, leaving me to pretend intense interest in my program. When the vet had reached the entrance to the box-seat area, I started after him. I looked up at the clubhouse window, but Walrus was no longer seated there. There was no time to wonder about that. Lavery had picked up the pace, and he was my lead to Bricknell's barn. I decided to keep him on a short string. In that crowd, it was easy to stay reasonably close without him spotting me.

On the whole, I had come to Chicago well prepared. True, I hadn't had Bright's credentials to wave under the noses of Hartmann and Bricknell. Posing as the company's rep had been a last-minute inspiration, and not a particularly good one, all things considered. But I did think ahead enough to make sure that Starbuck arranged for Walrus and me to pick up the necessary passes to the Land O' Lincoln stable area.

Mine got me past the guard as I continued after Lavery. From time to time I looked over my shoulder, expecting to find Walrus in my wake. I couldn't believe he'd fallen down on the job. But I also couldn't believe anyone that big could be following me without my spotting him.

According to Dr. Hartmann, Bricknell kept his horses at his stables and vanned them in before a race. But he maintained a good-sized barn at the track and there were several four-legged beasts in residence that looked very much like Thoroughbreds. One more mystery.

Lavery waltzed right past the horses without a second glance. His destination was the office at the end of the shed row. As I neared it I could hear the champagne corks popping inside. Dr. Hartmann and some others I didn't recognize were there to greet Lavery. The main members of Bricknell's party would still be posing for pictures in the winner's circle. As for Briarpatch himself, he had the indignities of the receiving barn still to go through. Take this cup, fellow, and go behind the shed.

I found a comfortable spot behind some bales of hay in an empty stall near the office. Ears open for whatever snatches of conversation I could pick up, I settled in to wait for the celebration to get fully under way. I was also able to shift a few bales to get a clear view of the office door.

After about ten minutes the Bricknells arrived to a round of congratulations. I recognized the stable owner's thin and stylish wife from all the pictures in his office. She had a brittle manner to go with her lean contours, and Bricknell seemed oddly uncomfortable around her. My guess was that old Arnie had married money and was biding his time until he was rich enough on his own to unload the Mrs. Then he'd run off with Dixie or

Georgia Hartmann maybe, though they both seemed too good for him.

There was a male with them I didn't recognize. I assumed it was Gil Westover, Briarpatch's trainer. When Mrs. Bricknell entered the gala, greeted warmly by Doc Lavery at the door, Westover pulled Bricknell aside, fortunately close enough to my hiding place that I could hear their conversation.

"We could win the Breeder's Cup Mile with this horse, Arnie. You know damn well we could."

"But he's not eligible." The tone in Bricknell's voice suggested this was an old and tired discussion.

"We could supplement."

"It's a bad bet."

"He could win an Eclipse Award for best turf horse, Arnie. You know that can't happen if all he does is run in Chicago. You know how provincial the voters are."

"And just what will the Eclipse Award do for me? Briarpatch isn't a stud horse, he's a gelding. With a gelding, ninety cents and an Eclipse Award gets you a cup of coffee."

The trainer seemed puzzled. "But the prestige, Arnie . . ."

"Fuck prestige. It's a bad bet," Bricknell repeated. "I'm not putting up a hundred and twenty grand against the possibility of winning half a mill and then seeing some nag from England or France come and steal the purse. And they always do."

"Then where are we going with this horse, Arnie?"

That was what I wanted to know. But some other guests moved in on them. If Bricknell answered, I didn't hear it.

Eventually, the star of the day, Briarpatch, having been cooled down, was returned to the barn. The champagne crowd spilled out of the office to ooh and ahh appreciatively as he passed by. Then it was back to the party to dish and drink.

Drs. Lavery and Hartmann did not join the other partygoers. They followed Briarpatch and his handler to the awaiting stall. Before the animal entered, they took a closer, more professional look. I heard them conferring, apparently satisfied with the horse's condition. Then she returned to the festivities. Lavery stayed with Briarpatch for a few minutes, running his hand over the animal's body and staring at him in open admiration. Finally, with a "So long, champ," he, too, went back to the party. The patient handler led the horse into the stall.

I was anxious to check out Briarpatch myself. As soon as the handler had strolled away, I made my move. It was risky, but it seemed highly unlikely that any of the partygoers would be wandering out to offer Briarpatch a glass of champagne.

Keeping in the shadows, I skulked along the shed row to Briarpatch's stall. There, I wasted no time. Softly mouthing soothing sounds, I studied the big horse's neck near the withers.

The two-inch scar that Starbuck had mentioned was there. Unless Briarpatch was caught by a similar branch at that similar place in his neck—and I could not begin to calculate those odds—the animal was definitely the supposedly deceased Rebaso. And if Rebaso was still alive, that seemed to indicate that the fire that killed all those animals at Cedar Point had been no accident.

I felt sickened, then furious. I wanted to enter the party and confront that bastard Bricknell in front of all his friends. But that would only have resulted in something fatal happening to Briarpatch/Rebaso, another fire probably, and my either being killed along with the animal, or facing a slander suit. No, the best chance I had of avenging those beautiful, innocent creatures was to see Bricknell and all of his pals thrown out of racing and into prison. And to do that, I had to get the hell out of there with my discovery.

I let myself out of the stall, securing the gate. Two men stood about twenty feet away, watching me. I thought at first they were stablehands. I desperately wanted to believe they were stablehands.

I nodded to the one nearest me as if I had every right in the world to be there. He didn't nod back. He was a large man. They were both large. Definitely not exercise riders or jockeys. Nor were they grooms or hotwalkers. And stablehands didn't stand like that, with their legs apart and arms held out from their sides as if waiting for a fight. These two were in a different line of work altogether.

The smaller man, not less than six-two, wore a scar, much more noticeable than Briarpatch's, that ran from his ear to his chin. His companion was a big African-American with a shaved scalp and one crossed eye. Identifying marks aside, they could have come out of the same stable as Ramon and Howard.

"Clip him quiet, Geo," the one with the scar said.

The black man approached me with not a trace of wariness. I waited until he was standing in front of me and tried to kick him in the groin. He was fast enough to grab my foot and use it to flip me head over heels.

I landed with a thud on the ground and he went down on one knee beside me, his large hand circling the back of my neck. "You a bad little guy, huh?" he asked in a whisper.

As he turned me I grabbed a handful of dirt and hay and tossed it into his face. He released my neck and staggered back. I tried my kick again and this time connected. But I'd lost sight of Scarface.

I felt something like an electric prod touching the back of my head and I pitched forward on top of the moaning Geo.

I can only imagine what happened next.

Geo used his feet to kick me aside and stood up, still hurting. If he was particularly vindictive, he probably gave me a kick in *my* groin. I'm pretty sure somebody did.

Through the pain, I heard Scarface tell Geo to roll me up in a couple of horse blankets and carry me out of there over his shoulder.

I was in no mood to resist. The blankets smelled of sweat and urine and other natural perfumes. I was lifted and draped over the black man's shoulder. We probably passed right by the party with everybody drinking and lying and eating those little hors d'oeuvres that put more weight on you than a six-course meal. "Oh, look," maybe one of them said, staring out the doorway. "Isn't that horse blanket just about the size of an ex-jockey?"

To which Bricknell may have replied, "Very ex-jockey."

24

I WASN'T UNDER wraps for long.

As soon as they left me to my own devices, I straightened and rolled until I was free of the blankets. I was lying on the floor of a dark horse van.

Almost immediately, the back door of the van opened and Geo hopped aboard, outlined by the glare of afternoon. He was carrying ropes. He slammed the door shut and said, "You gonna let me tie you up, little man, or do I have to break your bones?"

I looked around me. Nothing but the blankets and a layer of hay. No sign of a weapon. Geo grinned at me, his wonky eye peering somewhere over my shoulder. I selected option one.

He tied my hands and feet securely and, as an added touch, pulled an oily rag from his pocket and stuffed it in my mouth. Then he left me.

In just a few minutes the back of the van opened, letting in brightness again. Geo and Scarface led the horse they were calling Briarpatch up a ramp until he was standing beside me. He looked down at me as if wondering what the hell I was doing there.

The two thugs weren't handling him with the care a recent graded stakes winner deserved. They didn't bother to position him properly. They didn't bother to do anything except slam the door shut on us, throwing the van into darkness once again.

Briarpatch didn't particularly like the dark. He whinnied a little, and I felt like whinnying back.

Moments later the van's engine started and we were in motion.

Scarface and Geo moved past the gate guard without incident, so they must have checked out as authorized horse transporters. I made a few "mmmffff" noises and even tried banging my feet against the floor. But the hay muffled the sound.

If only the guard had been one of those overconscientious jerks, demanding a look at the rear of the van. "This is a security area. Better check back there to make sure you boys aren't carrying any fruit. Or vegetables. Or live plants. Or bound and gagged retired jockeys."

No such luck. The guard was a pussycat. Moments later we were bouncing along what I guessed was the Dan Ryan Expressway. I was uncomfortable and annoyed. And frightened. I wanted to believe that Walrus had somehow seen everything and was now a few paces back following the van. But it's hard to hold a positive thought when you're tied up and being bounced around in close proximity to an animal weighing about half a ton who might at any moment fall down and squash you like a lovebug.

It wasn't a long ride, and Briarpatch and I managed to coexist throughout. Thank God for pros like Briarpatch and Candy Dan. I'd known plenty of skittish Thoroughbreds who would have had a game of soccer with my skull. This boy was mellow as a moonbeam and I was fleetingly grateful they'd gelded Rebaso when they turned him into Briarpatch. Sorry about that, big fellow.

Our destination turned out to be a cement storage warehouse that occupied most of a square block of downtown Chicago. Geo dragged me out of the van and dropped me on the ground without ceremony. The warehouse appeared to be deserted for the evening.

Scarface and Geo led Briarpatch out of the van. As he emerged the animal stared at me with such profound sadness I felt certain he knew what they were planning for him. For us.

"Where to, Rayno?" the black man asked.

Rayno jerked his scarred chin to a row of metal doors. "The horse goes in bin forty-three. That's where they're set up."

Set up? What did that mean? Did I really want to know?

While Geo took care of the larger passenger, Rayno grabbed the shoulder of my jacket and dragged me to the door of bin 40. He dropped me and got out a ring of keys that were hooked to his belt loop. He unlocked the rusty metal door and opened it onto a cement room of approximately twenty-five square feet. There was a layer of dust on the floor, plus torn newspapers, baling wire, hunks of thick cardboard, and bits and pieces of packing material.

Without a word, the man with the scar dragged me into the center of the room. He hunkered down, felt the ropes on my wrists, and stood. "Mmmmmmuuummmmmmmmum?" I asked. He ignored the question and walked out on me, slamming the metal door behind him. The key made a grinding sound as it turned in the lock.

Enough light crept in around the edges of the door to give me a dim view of my surroundings. Sounds from outside were muffled and distorted. I could hear Geo coming back and saying something incomprehensible to Rayno. Then their footsteps receded. A moment later I heard the van's engine starting. The van drove away and all was silence.

After indulging myself in a couple of self-pitying sighs, I set about figuring how I might get out of there and see what I could do for Briarpatch.

My first move was to work my bound hands from behind my back. I rolled on my side and began to slide my hands down, over my butt. I've always considered myself on the thin side, but my rear end seemed to jut out like a giant promontory, nearly impossible to circle. Grunting and stretching my limbs and the rope to the breaking point, I somehow managed to get past that obstacle. The legs were a snap.

I waited a few seconds for blood to flow back into my hands. I wiggled my fingers, then grabbed and yanked the rag that had been stuck in my mouth. The sudden freedom of tongue and teeth was a benefit more psychological than practical.

A jockey's hands are his most important tools. I flexed my fingers again, making sure they were working properly. They're thin and small-boned. But they're also strong. I reached down and began to struggle with the ropes tying my ankles.

It was a slow and painfully gradual process. How long it took I'm not sure, but eventually I was able to loosen the knots and slip the ropes off my feet.

The binding around my wrists was a harder challenge. First I tried rubbing the knots against the floor, but that got me nowhere. The cement was too smooth to give me any help. Moving around the room searching for a rough patch, I cursed the proficiency of the construction crew. Everywhere you went these days you found shoddy workmanship. But where was it when you really needed it?

I considered the other materials available to me in the cell. The newspapers were no good even for reading in this light. The cardboard and the packing material held no promise. But the baling wire . . .

Once I figured out how I could use it, the wire finally turned the trick. By securing it between my shoes, point upward, I was able to bring the knot of the wrist tie down onto it. I kept digging the tip of the wire into the knot until it started to loosen.

And my hands and feet were free.

A few minutes later I responded to that with a sarcastic "Big deal." Little man, what now?

Covered in perspiration and totally oblivious of how much time had passed while I was struggling with the ropes, I paced off the room. Solid concrete. That left the door as my only hope. And a faint one it was. Solid metal. Locked. With the lock on the other side.

On one level, I pretty well realized that my situation was hopeless. I remembered a cartoon by Shel Silverstein, that strange baldheaded guy who writes children's books and songs like "A Boy Named Sue." In his drawing, two political prisoners are in a dungeon, chained hand and foot to a wall about fifty feet from the floor. One of them says to the other, "Now here's my plan. . . ."

I longed for a plan. Even a crazy one. I took my magic baling wire to the door and poked listlessly at the bolt. No way was I going to be able to slide that sturdy spike out of its hole. My chances of getting out of there on my own were on a par with Silverstein's prisoners.

Then I tried an even more hopeless ploy. I kicked at the door. Except for a muffled clang, it didn't react to my onslaught.

Panting and frustrated, I sat down on the floor to wait, hoping something would happen to me before I was reduced to dry bones.

25

THE DAYLIGHT AROUND the door had almost disappeared when I heard a car engine, the first indication since Rayno and Geo had left that I was in a populated city and not on the moon.

Was it the van returning? Was it Walrus? Since my ear for automotive engines was untrained, the only thing I knew for sure was that I had to be prepared for anything. A big part of that would be to pretend to be a still-helpless prisoner.

I shuffled over to the grimy rag I'd discarded and, with just a slight gag, stuck it back into my mouth. Then I found the ropes and tied my feet with slipknots. The difficult part was wrapping the cords around my wrists with my hands behind my back. I wound up grabbing the loose ends in my fist.

I suppose my plan was to wait for an opening, and then jump up and run like hell.

Unfortunately, nobody entered my cell. At least not at first. There were sounds of scuffling and groaning, which made me think that somebody out there must have been in the same situation as me. But the sounds trailed away.

Time, as they say, passed.

Then another vehicle arrived. A car door slammed. Footsteps. One person. Judging by the heaviness of the footfalls, probably a man. Those footsteps also moved away.

What the hell was going on? Was I the damned forgotten man?

I strained my ears for some clue. Finally there was a cacophony of sounds. Voices. Footsteps. Shouts. A laugh. A movable party was on its way, bringing good cheer and fun, fun, fun.

The crowd stopped before my door. No more talk or laughter. The key turned in the lock, and the metal door swung open. It was night, but the area outside the storage bunker was lighted.

Standing in the doorway were three men outlined in the light. Rayno and Geo were rumpled and shopworn, looking nothing like the mob poster boys of earlier in the day. There was dried blood under Rayno's nose, a red patch on his cheek, and his shirt was ripped. Geo looked marginally less damaged, but the skin of his knuckles was rubbed raw, and he winced when he tried to use his left foot.

The fashion plate with them must have steered clear of the battle, for he was in pristine condition. Five-nine, dark, with Italian features. Armani-clad from ankle to neck. I pegged him in his fifties, but he could have been a few years either side of that. His face was placid, his brown eyes vacant. He seemed so unemotional that, were this about a decade in the future, I'd have wondered if he were real or a Memorex robot. He'd been in the Neck a few times, but we'd never met. Joey Lunchbox.

He and his boss, Huey Grosso, were the very people Starbuck had convinced me I'd be avoiding on this Chicago trip. Why did I ever listen to him?

He walked into the room and stood before me, looking down.

"You guys cook a mean steak in your joint, Killebrew," he said. He turned to the other two men. "You fuckers think this town's got meat, you oughta see the top sirloin at Killebrew's place. This thick. Charred on the outside, pink like your girlfriend in the middle." He put his fingertips together and kissed them.

Geo and Rayno looked as perplexed by this restaurant review as I was. Joey moved toward the door. There, he turned, eyebrows forming an angry V. "Well," he said to Rayno. "You just gonna stand there like a couple of assholes? Bring him."

Rayno gestured to Geo, who hoisted me up and slung me over

his rounded shoulder, toting me out of the room. It was a strain to keep the ropes around my hands and feet, but I managed it. Thanks to the night and their anxiety to be finished with their work, the hoods didn't give my bindings even a glance.

They took me to storage area 43, the number I remembered had been Briarpatch's destination so many hours before. It was twice the size of my cell. Electricity had been brought in via a thick cable, and the rectangular concrete room was well lighted by high-tech metal work lamps.

I lifted my head and twisted my neck to see that Briarpatch was lying on a blanket in the middle of the room. He wasn't moving. In the corner was another motionless mound, not much smaller than the horse. Whatever little hope I'd had drained away at the sight of Walrus, his hands and feet securely bound.

"Mmmmmuummmmmmumum," I complained from Geo's shoulder.

Joey Lunchbox followed us into the room. "They're both alive," he assured me. "For the time being. Just sleeping off some trank."

Geo dumped me on the floor next to Walrus, who was snoring softly. It was then I noticed something unpleasant in the opposite corner of the room. Coils of wire, one pair of ends attached to a large dry-cell battery, the others to metal clips.

"You're a dumb bastard, Killebrew," Joey Lunchbox said matter-of-factly. "All this trouble over a fucking horse. And now we gotta ace the goddamn horse. And you. And your friend. And who the hell knows who else."

"Mmmmum," I mumbled.

He reached out a manicured, almost feminine hand that smelled of cologne and plucked the rag from my mouth. "You wanna try that again without the muffler?" he asked.

"I don't understand what this is all about," I said.

"It ain't that difficult to figure. We was gonna pop you just for asking Luis Falcon questions about the horse. Now you get caught in the animal's stall. Which means you probably saw the scar on his neck. So it's cleanup time. Everybody goes. The Cedar Point fire stays an accident."

"You killed Jerry Woo," I said.

"The pissant paparazzi? Yeah. What the hell's that got to do with the price of beans?"

"Why'd you do it?"

"It was a business move." Joey seemed proud of knowing something I didn't. "The Woolrich character tried to blackmail my boss, for Christ's sake. What an asshole! The guy had a nice little thing going. Lots of customers. Then he tries to take on Huey. Go figure."

"Lots of customers? Who else was he blackmailing?"

"You're just fulla questions, aren't you, Killebrew? Well, as a matter of fact, Woolrich was putting the screws to somebody the boss does business with. By getting rid of the bastard, he was doin' all sort of people a big favor."

"Would I know this business associate?" I asked.

"Could be. It was—"

He was interrupted by the slamming of a car door.

Joey turned from me, facing the entrance to the concrete room just in time to see Dr. Charles Lavery arrive, resplendent in dinner tux, carrying a small black leather pouch. He appeared startled to see me.

"What the hell is Killebrew doing here?" he demanded.

"Don't you worry about it, doc," Joey said. "Just do your thing with the horsie."

Lavery continued staring at me, swallowing hard. "I'm not going to be a part—"

"You're not a *part* of anything," Joey said, a menacing edge of impatience in his tone. "You're here to do a job. Just take care of the horse."

I said, "They're going to kill me and my friend, Lavery. They probably killed Paula's father."

Joey frowned. "Who you got us killing now?"

"Paula Dresner's father. Wilton Dresner."

Joey was the sort of guy who found humor everywhere, apparently. He guffawed. "Wilton Dresner?" He shook his head gleefully. "Why the Christ would we ace him? Huey loved that Dresner, never missed his show. Huey's got a lot of ideas about politics and society and stuff, and Dresner agreed with him right down the line. They got together every now and then. Huey says Dresner was the last real American patriot."

"How'd they meet? When Huey decided to buy Heartland farms from Dresner?"

Joey looked confused. "No. They met at some function. Christians and Jews, something like that. The boss didn't want Dresner to be hip to the fact it was him buying Heartland. I don't think Dresner ever knew they was in business together. I don't know why the boss wanted it a secret."

"Maybe Dresner found out and that's why he was killed."

Suddenly Joey stopped smiling and his face got that cold robot look again. "I swear, Killebrew, you're just like the cops. Every time a white guy eats it, they add him to our account. There's other people out there acing people, you know."

As Joey spoke my attention was focused on Lavery. However deeply he was involved in all this, he seemed very uncomfortable being a party to murder. Murder of humans anyway. His face white with fear and indignation, he said, "I'm not going to stand by and let you kill—"

"I ain't askin' you to stand by, doc. I ain't asking you anything. I'm telling you to do what you came for."

The Beretta appeared in Joey's hand so quickly, it looked like a magic trick. He jammed its muzzle into Lavery's neck and growled, "Do your job and keep your nose out of the rest. Either that or leave and we'll take care of the horse ourselves. The boss won't be happy, but there's other ways to do the job. If it was up to me, the nag'd be dog food by now."

Touching his neck where the gun had pressed, Lavery turned

away from me with a sheepish look. Did he really care what I thought of him? Maybe he did. Winning friends and influencing people was a habit with him.

He removed rubber gloves from a leather pouch. Then a face mask. Then a hypodermic syringe filled with a blue fluid.

Joey watched his preparations with apprehension. "I don't wanna be too close to that stuff."

Lavery ignored him and bent down beside the sleeping horse. He plunged the needle into the horse's backside and injected the blue fluid from the syringe.

He stood and asked Joey to remove a Ziploc plastic bag from his leather pouch. Joey did it charily. Lavery dropped the needle, syringe, and gloves into the bag and pressed it shut. Then he put the bag into his pouch.

"You can take this animal back to Bricknell Stables as soon as he regains consciousness," he said.

"You sure that stuff'll do the trick?"

Lavery nodded his head slowly. "I wish to Christ it wouldn't, but it will. The syrum isn't quite perfected."

"Saint Charles, the horses' savior," I said from the concrete floor.

Lavery wheeled on me. "You don't know anything about it, Killebrew."

"I know you're in bed with Huey Grosso and you've murdered some beautiful Thoroughbreds so that he can collect on their insurance."

"That isn't why I'm doing it. I love horses. I entered veterinary medicine to save them, not kill them. And I still want to save them. What I told you at the track is true. I'm close to a breakthrough." He had that messianic look in his eye again.

"Does Georgia Hartmann know you do this stuff, Lavery?"

"No," he replied, his anguish credible. "Killebrew," he continued, "if I could just explain—"

Joey Lunchbox's impatience cut Lavery short.

"So long, doc. See you in La La Land."

Lavery held his ground for a few seconds. Joey raised his hand and jerked his thumb toward the door. Lavery turned and left the room.

Joey grinned at me, shaking his head in wonder. "Whatta guy, the doc. Reminds me of Harry the Bat. You know Harry, Killebrew?"

"Nope."

"Hit man out of Tampa. Never uses a gun or a knife. Always a baseball bat. Says he ain't no killer, he's an athlete."

"What does Lavery think he is?"

"He used to think he was some holy Joe scientist back when Huey first heard about him. He had this secret sauce he'd been dicking with in his lab. Using it on horses to test it. Stuff was supposed to save their lives. A . . . a . . . inoc . . ."

"Inoculation," I finished for him.

"Yeah. That. It puts germs into the horse that let it ignore other germs. Something like that. Only the doc hasn't got it to work yet. In fact, there are a bunch of horses that were perfectly fine before the doc tried out his inoc—whatever, on 'em. All worm food now. He's been at it awhile. But nobody's got wise because they looked like they died of natural causes. So the insurance companies have paid off. According to the doc, he's been puttin' his end of the action back into his lab. But I dunno if I buy that."

"Where'd he get the horses?"

"Same place he gets 'em now. From owners who're happy to share the insurance in return for him putting the animals to sleep. There are a lot of 'em out there, Killebrew. Times are tough."

"And now Lavery is partnered with Grosso."

"Not exactly partnered. He's more of an independent contractor. He does some things for Huey, and Huey tosses him a few bucks for his so-called clinic. But he better be there when Huey wants his services."

Briarpatch's tranquilizer had begun wearing off. He grunted

and snorted, raised his head. Horses spend more time lying down than most people believe, but in uncertain surroundings, their instinct is to be on their feet. He whinnied and rose shakily. Then he stared at the men in the room.

The poor animal.

"Hey, Killebrew, cheer up." Joey laughed. "The horse's got a slim chance of pulling through. Maybe the doc's blue juice will work this time. Hell, he's got better odds of surviving than you do.

"Put the horsie back in the van, guys."

Rayno and Geo led Briarpatch out.

Joey stared at me. "What's the secret?" he asked.

"Secret?"

"Yeah. How do you get meat like that out in L.A.? Huey has this place, the Finzi Gardens, ever eat there?"

"Once," I said. Lots of white marble and statues and menus as big as surfboards. Lousy food. Cheap wine masquerading as vintage. Surly help.

"The steaks taste like roadkill," he said.

"I'll take your word for it."

"I mean, where you get your meat? Man, those sirloin strips melt in your mouth."

"The secret will die with me," I told him.

He scowled. "Now you're really pissin' me off," he said.

Walrus let out a deep groan and rolled over on his side just as Geo and Rayno returned from the van.

"Looks like the tough guy is coming around," Joey Lunchbox said.

"Bastard caught me when I wasn't lookin'," Rayno grumbled. "Ain't so smart now."

"This guy's good," Joey said to me. "You didn't waste your money with him, exactly. Thing is, nobody's good enough to outfight a shot of trank."

Walrus sat up and shook his head, red hair flying like a flame in an air current. "What?" he asked.

Rayno drew back his leg to kick the big man. Probably in the face.

"Cool it," Joey commanded, and the leg fell.

"I owe him," Rayno said.

Geo, his bad eye staring out over our heads, concentrated on the dialogue between Rayno and Joey.

The L.A. hood smiled suddenly. "Okay. I'm nothing if I'm not generous to my employees. You owe him?" Rayno nodded his head. "Then be my guest. You can put the clamps on him."

26

RAYNO DRAGGED THE battery and cables to where Walrus was lying. He clipped one wire to Walrus's ear and another to his big toe. Walrus struggled some, but he was still groggy and he'd been tied up more efficiently than I.

Joey explained, "We used to get rid of horses with the clamps, but the insurance companies were getting wise, and the doc's method is so much safer. Still, the clamps have their uses. Don't they, Rayno?"

In a sudden flash of insight, I remembered Ramon mentioning Joey's shock machine. And the backward sock on Jerry Woo's foot.

Joey nodded to Rayno, and the scar-faced hood pressed a contact switch on the battery. Walrus's huge body spasmed and twisted. He emitted a horrible bellow and collapsed back onto the floor of the room. Wide-awake now, his face covered in perspiration, he glared at his tormentors.

"What's your point, Joey?" I almost shouted.

"My point is, suppose we up the amps to get you in the mood to talk?"

"I'm in the mood right now."

Joey smiled and nodded. "That's being sensible. Okay. Question one. What tipped you to Briarpatch?"

I took a deep breath, trying to think things through without letting him know I was stalling. What would happen if I told Joey about Jerry Woo's photograph? It had already done its job. Starbuck knew about it and now he suspected a Thoroughbred switch had been made. If I died, it would confirm that suspicion. I decided mentioning the photo could do no harm. Why not save Walrus a bit of pain before we both were killed?

"Jerry Woo showed me the winner's-circle picture of Falcon and Briarpatch just before he died."

"Why? Was he a pal of yours?"

"No. I, uh, do a little private detective work as a sideline. Woo paid me to make sure the horse really was Rebaso."

Joey nodded. Getting paid to do something made sense to him.

"Next question. What's Ray Starbuck up to?"

That caught me off guard. "How would I know?"

"You were over to his place. How much does he know about the Cedar Point torch job?"

"Nothing about it. Jerry Woo hired me, not him. Why would I bring Starbuck in?"

"Don't fuck with me, Killebrew."

"Look, Joey, I only went to Starbuck's to see his daughter." As I said that I realized I'd probably never see her again. The thought hit me like a blow to the midsection.

"She hot?"

I didn't answer him.

"Starbuck's an asshole. Someday I'll take him out for free. He like you screwin' his little girl?"

I glared at him.

"Jeez, excuse me. It's true love, huh? Well, I may have to look in on her when I get back. She'll be pining over her lost short stuff and I'll show her what a man can do. Well, I think that about wraps it up, here."

He turned to Rayno and Geo and said, "Kill 'em," as casually as if he were ordering a hamburger.

"With the clamps?" Rayno asked.

"If you want. Then dump 'em in the lake."

He started for the door.

"You aren't going to stick around and watch?" I asked him.

"Naw. These guys know what they're doing. And I gotta get back home. There's something I hav'ta take care of, if the wind is right."

When Joey got to the door, he turned around and looked my way one last time. "I like the bread in your restaurant, too."

He winked at me and was gone.

Rayno waited until Joey's car started and cruised away to turn to Geo and say, "I'm glad we don't see all that much of that guy. He's a flake. All these California guys are flakes."

He leaned forward over the battery, getting ready to send a final shot of current through Walrus. Geo was across the room. The hand I was holding wasn't all that great, but I had to play it now or never.

I jumped to my feet, easily stepping out of the leg bindings and letting the untied ropes around my hands fall away. I rushed Rayno and kicked like I was going for a fifty-yard field goal. The point of my shoe connected satisfactorily with his chin and delivered him at least temporarily to dreamland. That left Geo.

But I wasn't alone. Walrus emitted a tremendous bellow, and straining his muscles, broke the ropes that were containing him. While scrambling to his feet, he reached over for the battery. He lifted it up over his head and heaved it at the face of the surprised Geo.

The black man managed to feint to one side and took only a glancing blow from the flying battery. It knocked him down but not out. He stood and rushed Walrus, his shiny shaved head lowered like a battering ram.

Bad idea. Walrus stepped aside like a seasoned bullfighter and, as Geo shot past, gave him a little push—headfirst into a cinderblock wall. The noise was like a coconut hitting the sidewalk from a very tall tree. Geo crumpled to the floor.

Walrus staggered over to the black man and frowned. "I think he'll live," he said. "I'm screwing up right and left on this job."

"You just snapped those ropes like they were threads," I said, very impressed.

"Illusion versus reality," Walrus said. "They seemed so thick I never would have even tried if I hadn't seen you do it first."

27

WE LEFT RAYNO and Geo cluttering up the floor of the storage room. It was time we said good-bye to Chicago.

While hot-wiring the van, Walrus was filled with self-deprecation. "I've never screwed up so badly," he said. "I was sitting there in the clubhouse, eyeballing you down in the box, and suddenly somebody's sitting across the table from me. Joey Lunchbox, grinning at me like a jackass. He's got a gun in his pocket, he tells me. 'I can shoot you down and walk away clean,' he said. 'Or we can both walk away clean.'

"So, like a complete doofus, I let this cretin walk me out to his car, where he removed every damn weapon I was carrying. Nearly six grand worth."

I clucked sympathetically as the engine turned over.

"Just a minute," he said, and hopped out of the van.

He ran inside bin 43 and returned a minute or so later. He shut the door and, using Rayno's keys, locked it.

He took his seat at the van's steering wheel and gave me another disgusted look, rattling the keys in my face. "See. I go to all the effort to jump the starter and the keys are available. I'm losing it, Coley."

"You're too young for senility," I told him. "It's the tranquilizer."

"The tranquilizer," he repeated as we drove away. "Joey gets me to drive his goddamned Seville rental out here. Then he tells his lameos to tie me up.

"As a joke, I guess, he puts away his gun. So, naturally, I start smacking his boys around. They're big, but they're also stupid. I'm about to knock every tooth out of that black guy's head when this . . . dart hits me in the back. Coley, that hoodlum shot me with a tranquilizer gun. Damned degrading."

"It could have been a Smith and Wesson," I told him.

"There's that," he said. "Well, I deserved everything I got. I'm just sorry I didn't take better care of you."

"I'm alive," I said. "No complaints."

"I'll do better next time."

I sighed. "Yes, I suppose there might be a next time."

"I hope so," Walrus said.

At the empty Land O' Lincoln parking lot we exchanged the van for our rental, which took us to O'Hare Airport. While Walrus was off booking us on a red-eye flight back to Los Angeles, I made a few phone calls.

The first was to the Chicago police to tell them about two men locked in a concrete bin at Cotter Storage. I'd spotted the name as we drove away from the place.

The second call was long-distance—to Lea in L.A. I briefly filled her in on our Chicago adventures, asking her to relay the necessary information—about Briarpatch, Lavery, and particularly, about Joey Lunchbox—to her father.

"He just left town," she said.

"Left town?"

"Flying to Lexington."

"For the cure?"

Silence. Then: "No, something to do with an ill horse there, another Bright's customer. I'll leave word at his hotel."

I mentioned my meeting Paula Dresner at the track, then said, "She seemed very worried about her brother."

"He broke a date with me tonight," Lea said.

"Now I'm worried about him."

"Told me he was too bummed out by his father's death to party," she informed me. "He certainly sounded bummed out."

"I think he may be a key player in all this. According to Joey Lunchbox, Wilton Dresner wasn't aware that they were in business together. But Neil has been on the scene at Heartland and has to know about Grosso's involvement." A piece fell into place. "At the gambling party, Neil and Lavery were talking about Joey Lunchbox. Neil absolutely knows about the connection. And he's a very weak link. If we have any chance of tying his father's death to Grosso, Neil is the bow on the ribbon."

"Maybe Dad will have some idea how—"

"I don't think we can wait for that," I said, interrupting her. The last thing I wanted was Starbuck derailing our progress. "As soon as we land, I want to go see Neil. Wake him up if we have to."

"I'm not sure that's the wisest move," she said.

"Trust me. Joey Lunchbox is getting rid of people who pose a threat to his boss. Sooner or later they'll get around to Neil. We can't afford to wait."

Walrus was walking toward me with our tickets. He pointed to his wristwatch.

I took one of the tickets and gave Lea our flight number. She said she'd be waiting when we landed at LAX.

When we arrived there at four A.M., it felt like we'd gone back to the Windy City. A dry breeze was blowing, and a warm one, considering the time of year and the early hour.

LAX gets even less sleep than the Los Angeles freeway system, but the waiting room was relatively deserted. My heart leaped as I saw the tall blond Lea standing at the gate blessing me with a dazzling smile.

"I wasn't sure I'd ever see you again," I said softly.

I tried to pull her to me, but she was uncharacteristically rigid. "We're not alone," she said.

I nodded. "Sorry. Lea, this is John Walnicki. Call him Walrus. Walrus, meet Lea."

"Hi, Walrus," she greeted him, and showed no sign of concern when he wrapped his hand around hers and gave it a hearty shake.

She looked at me. "It wasn't Walrus I was referring to," she said.

She gestured to a figure coming our way from the men's room. Channing Hoag, Bright's man in the U.S., looking impeccably tweedy, if a bit sleepy-eyed.

"I got through to Dad. He's flying back as soon as he can. He suggested I bring in Mr. Hoag," she said.

"Didn't trust us to do the job ourselves?" I asked.

She flushed. "Don't start."

Hoag was stifling a yawn as he joined us. He woke up completely when I introduced him to Walrus. "Amazing," he said, staring at the big man so intently it was edging into rudeness. "It's a pity all of our life-insurance policyholders aren't as formidable as you, sir."

"I'm in good shape, all right," Walrus replied, "but I'm probably not the best risk."

As we walked out of the terminal I said, "It's too bad we had to bother you with this, Hoag."

"Nonsense. Glad to do it. I've known Neil for several years, and I think I can convince him to do the right thing."

"Lea can be pretty convincing herself," I said.

"When Neil finds out who I really am," she said, "I don't think he's going to be too receptive to anything I might suggest."

"I was a bit surprised when you called," Hoag told her. Then he turned to me. "I've met Roz—ah, Lea—a few times with Neil. I had no idea who she was. I didn't even know Ray Starbuck had a daughter, much less that she was assisting him."

"Starbuck is famous for his little secrets," I said, prompting Lea to jab her elbow into my arm, nearly knocking me over.

A blast of dry, warm Santa Ana wind was waiting for us when we exited the terminal and headed for Lea's cherry-red Saab. She'd parked it in the passenger loading zone, a chancy thing to do. Even at this hour of the morning, as the annoying electronic voices continued to repeat, the white zone was for loading and unloading of passengers only, no parking. But some of us have never known the heartbreak of the tow-away and I suspected this was the case with Lea.

She had escaped it once more.

Another blast of the red wind blew around the terminal as Walrus tucked our luggage snugly into the trunk. Then the four of us took our places—Lea behind the wheel, the big man in the passenger seat, in deference to his long legs, Hoag and myself in back. Without a word of warning, she propelled us from the curb and away from the airport nearly as fast as light travels.

As we headed north on the nearly empty San Diego Freeway, Hoag yawned and said, "Too bad you gents couldn't have come in at a decent hour."

He rolled down his window, apparently hoping that the fresh air would clear his head. But the Santa Anas were too tepid and dry to be of much use.

The wind bothered me. I was forgetting something important.

Something Joey Lunchbox had said. Yes. Just before he'd left us at the storage room he'd said he had to rush back to L.A. Why? Because he had work to do if the wind was right.

My stomach lurched.

Hoag was frowning at the Sunset Boulevard off-ramp, which we'd just driven past. "You missed the turnoff to the Dresner home," he told Lea.

"Neil isn't there," she said. "He's at the stables."

"I'm sure you're wrong," the man from Bright's replied. "He's been staying at the family home since Wilton's death."

"He's at Heartland tonight," she said. "I talked with him earlier."

Hoag looked skeptical. "If you're wrong, we're going miles out of our way," he said. "I suggest we try the house first. It's on the way. Shouldn't take a minute."

"No," I said. "We're going to Heartland. Even if Neil isn't there."

"What are you talking about, Coley?" Lea asked.

I repeated Joey Lunchbox's comment about the wind being right. "What kind of wind is blowing tonight?" I asked.

"Santa Ana," Walrus replied.

"And what are Santa Anas right for?"

No one replied, so I added, "Think Cedar Point."

"Fire?" Lea asked. Only it wasn't a question, really.

I turned to Hoag. "How much life insurance is your company carrying on the animals at Heartland Farms?"

He looked shocked. "Sizable. In the midseven figures. My God! You're not saying . . ."

But I was. Not long ago, the combination of drying Santa Ana winds and arson had blackened a huge section of Southern California. The area was still devastated. And now, unless I was racing on the wrong track. Grosso was determined to put those Santa Anas to work again, only this time Heartland Farms and the surrounding countryside would be burned. Maybe it would pass as an act of God. Maybe they'd call it arson. It didn't matter to Grosso. He'd collect on the policies in either case.

"You must be wrong," Hoag said. "Who in their right mind would . . . ?" He paused, realizing he'd answered his question. A sociopathic mob boss would.

Lea took us smoothly from the San Diego to the Ventura Freeway. We were only minutes away from the stable.

I said, "We should stop long enough to alert the cops and the Calabasas Fire Department."

"And tell them what?" Channing Hoag asked. "That you think a Mafia chieftain is plotting to set the whole countryside on fire to kill a few horses? By the time they bought into that, the whole bloody city could be up in flames."

That made sense. "Then let's just report a fire," I said, "and not give them any of the weirder details. We can sort that out later."

"Good idea," Hoag said. "We can phone from Heartland. We're not that far away, and we'll be able to warn the people there and set the poor animals free."

28

THE WEIRD THING was that Heartland Farms seemed strangely familiar to me. I'd never been there before, but I recognized the oval driveway, the main building, the barns. A dream? Déjà vu?

The whole place was eerily quiet in the predawn hours. We walked past several horse barns, the night lamps displaying enough Thoroughbreds in residence to merit a No Vacancy sign. Some were asleep, standing or lying, their snorting breath punctuating equine dreams. Others were stall-walking, made skittish by the sound of the wind in the trees and rafters.

Floating on the warm wind was the bracing odor of gasoline. Joey and his men had started their work.

But they were nowhere to be seen. Lea, who knew her way around the spread, led us to the bunkhouse. No smell of gasoline there. Only at the barns. Inside the bunkhouse we turned on the lights and found a skeleton crew of five, all slumped over the dinner table.

Lea lifted one wrist. "Alive," she said.

I pointed to glasses still partially filled with some cola-colored liquid. "Very fast-acting stuff. Nothing but state-of-the-art for Huey Grosso."

"Come on," Lea suggested. "There's a phone in the main building."

It was a two-story, wooden clapboard structure. Two cars were parked near the rear door—a Land Rover that Lea identified as Neil's, and a white Caddy convertible.

Bugs flitted at the light over the back door to the building, some of them darting inside the open door to escape the wind. It looked as if somebody had neglected to secure the screen all the way and the gusts had pushed it wide. I gestured to the others to enter quietly.

The wind was making its own noise. But it wasn't loud enough to drown out the argument going on in a lighted room near the front. That part of the house was serving as a business area. In a darkened anteroom, I paused beside a desk containing a potted plant, a small IBM computer, a lamp, and a telephone.

Just past the desk was the entryway to the lighted office where two men were caught up in heated conversation.

"You gotta stop this," said Neil's anguished, tearful voice.

"Stop it? You got horseshit for brains, kid?" Joey Lunchbox's slightly nasal, smirky delivery.

"But you can't just burn all those horses."

"I'm not burnin' any horses," Joey replied.

"Y-you're not?" Neil sounded incredulous.

"No. Do we look like the kind of guys who'd do that? What my boys are doing is setting the brush on fire. Couple miles from here."

"Bu-bu-but that's the same thing. The winds are gonna blow the fire all the hell over everywhere. The horses will burn. Everything will burn. And not just *this* stable."

"Well, shit. If that's what happens, it's God's way, huh? Not our fault."

"You bastard."

The sound of a slap.

"Watch your mouth, kid."

"You—you—you won't get away with it," Neil sobbed.

"No? Then you'll be right there with me in that courtroom. Your sister, too."

"You leave her out of it."

"She can take care of herself, your sister. Last time I looked, she was doin' *fine*."

Joey began to laugh merrily.

"Don't you say that, you fucker!" Neil screamed.

I looked at Lea, but she seemed confused by the anger that Joey's statement had prompted.

There was the sound of another slap. It seemed like the right time to make our entrance. We walked into the room, Walrus automatically taking the point.

Joey was so surprised he waited a beat before going for his gun. By then, Walrus was able to grab his arm, twist the gun away.

He swung at Walrus's face with his free hand.

The big man dodged the swing and, grinning, placed Joey's gun on the desk. He assumed a fighter's stance.

Joey tried another swing. Walrus blocked it and delivered a punch of his own, breaking Joey's nose. Blood dripping from his nostrils, Joey backed away, woozy. He touched his nose and looked at his red fingers. He screamed and rushed the big man.

Walrus drove his left fist into Joey's stomach. Then used his free hand to slap the hood's face hard enough to deck him. In a mixture of pain and frustration, Joey Lunchbox sat up on the floor and began to sob.

"What a cream puff," Walrus said.

Neil leaned forward at his desk, gawking in disbelief at the weeping Joey. His hand automatically found a nearly empty bottle of scotch on his desktop. I pushed him aside a few inches and reached for the phone. "Time to call in the troops," I said.

"Please replace the receiver, Mr. Killebrew," a polite but commanding voice ordered.

Channing Hoag was pointing Joey Lunchbox's gun at me while carefully keeping his distance from Walrus. "Rise up, Mr. Lunchbox," he said. "There's work to do."

Groggy, Joey got to his feet. He stared at Hoag, as surprised as the rest of us. "You workin' for Huey, too?" he asked.

Hoag smiled. "Not exactly."

"What he means," I said, "is that he thinks he's not working for your boss. He thinks they're equals. Grosso takes out the policies on the horses. Hoag approves the deal and okays the claims."

Hoag watched me with a tiny smile on his face. Joey seemed to be getting back some of his confidence. "Huey don't have any equal partners," he said.

"Tell it to the man with the gun."

Joey looked from me to Hoag and gave him a sickly grin. "I mean," he said, "I guess he's got people he works with."

"As long as he needs them," I said.

Hoag shook his head. "If you think I'm going to get all nervous about an eventual showdown with Mr. Grosso, you're betting on the wrong horse.

"Mr. Lunchbox, would you happen to have any other weapons on your person?"

"Out in the car. A Magnum."

"Not exactly high-tech, but if it pleases you . . . do get it."

As Joey headed away I called out, "Attaboy, fetch."

"Ah, Mr. Killebrew." Hoag sighed. "You never give up, do you?"

"Not when you're going to kill us all anyway," I said, trying not to look at Walrus or think about what he might be planning.

"Good point," Hoag said. "But what a waste of energy."

"Why'd you hire my father?" Lea asked him.

Hoag turned his head to her, and Walrus began to inch forward. "It was the office in London. I did my best to dissuade them. But they were in such distress over their losses, they insisted. It's caused me all sorts of extra precautions. Like having to come up with a reason to get him out of town before the big night. By the time he returns, these pesky Santa Ana winds will have done their damage. Nearly fifty million dollars' worth, as best I can calculate. But he has been annoyingly troublesome."

"Who has?" the returning Joey asked from the door. He had the Magnum in his right hand, not aiming it at anybody in particular.

"Raymond Starbuck," Hoag told him.

"I'd love to pop that smart-guy son of a bitch."

"Good," Hoag said. "I recommend it. It will be the only way to handle him once his daughter dies."

Leering, Joey let his eyes travel over Lea's body.

Walrus made his move. He ran straight to Joey and grabbed the Magnum. He jerked the weapon free and spun Joey in the general direction of Hoag.

Then he shifted the gun in his huge hand and took aim on Hoag. But the insurance man was surprisingly calm and agile, sidestepping Joey's flailing body, and in the same graceful motion firing at Walrus.

My bodyguard grunted and lost momentum as the bullet pierced his side. Hoag took a few backward steps so that he could keep all of us in his line of vision. He was cool enough not to use another bullet on Walrus unless he had to. Not with three more of us in the room.

Walrus stayed standing for a few seconds, then his legs went out and he sat down hard on the carpet. The Magnum was still in his fist, but there didn't seem to be much he could do with it. He turned to me and his mouth formed the word "Sorry." Then he rolled over onto his side and, eyes closed, emitted a loud rush of air that was almost a cry of anguish.

It was the final straw for Neil Dresner.

He rose from his chair, still cradling the now empty scotch bottle. He woozily circled the desk, shouting, "You goddamned . . . fascist. . . ."

"Let's not bring politics into this," Hoag told him.

Neil staggered toward the Englishman, raising the bottle like a club.

Hoag didn't waste a bullet on him. He brought the barrel of the gun down on the boy's head.

Neil staggered backward, tripped on his own feet, and fell. As he went down his head hit the corner of his desk with an unhealthy sound.

Then there was silence in the room. Outside, the wind whipped branches and slammed doors. But that seemed to be part of some other mural.

Lea moved toward the boy, but Hoag warned her off. "Just stay where you are, Miss Starbuck."

Joey Lunchbox prodded Neil's unmoving body with his shoe, then bent and felt for a pulse in the young man's neck. Standing, he said to Hoag, "An impressive two for two. Mister, you're some kind of life-insurance salesman."

29

"WE'VE WASTED ENOUGH time," Hoag told Joey. "Escort Mr. Killebrew out to a barn and tie him well enough to keep him there. Don't shoot him unless you have to."

The last glimpse I had of Lea, before Joey pushed me through the door, was one I will always remember—angry, defiant, and achingly beautiful.

Outside, the midnight blue of the sky was being replaced around the edges by a bright orange. Daybreak. The wind continued to howl, hot and dry. Being essentially lazy, Joey guided me to the nearest barn. The wind whipped at our clothes as we cut across the driveway.

Inside the barn, Joey turned on an overhead light and closed the door. He pointed to a solid wooden beam that ran from the floor to the lofty ceiling. He ordered me to wrap my arms around it. Happy as a clam, he reached into his pocket and found a pair of handcuffs.

"Hoag's a tricky bastard," I told him as he circled one of my wrists with the cold steel.

"So?"

"So he's getting you to do all the slime work. But you're holding all the cards."

He hesitated, frowning, and snapped the other cuff shut, then began ratcheting them closed. "Jesus, you got little mitts, Killebrew." I made a fist and pulled back, forcing the cuff to ride up off my wrist nearly an inch. Joey grunted and closed the bands to their limit. "Yeah, that does it."

He stepped back, surveyed the cuffs, and asked, "Now what was all that about me holding the cards?"

"You just saw Hoag kill two people."

The wind slammed the barn door open and Joey ripped the Magnum from his belt and aimed it at the empty space.

"Who're you afraid of, Joey? Hoag?"

"Not afraid of anybody, chump."

"So, if you're not afraid of him, why don't you squeeze him a little?"

"What're you yapping about?" He slipped the gun back under his belt.

"You know how much this torch job is going to bring in? Fifty million. How much are you getting for all your work?"

"Huey treats me good," Joey said.

"The split will probably be thirty-five for Grosso, fifteen for Hoag," I said.

"So what?"

"So maybe Grosso treats you good, but what about Hoag? He's ordering you around like a goddamn busboy. Maybe you should get a cut off his end."

He stared at me, mouth open. I took that to be a sign that he was considering it. I tried to close the deal. "You keep quiet about him murdering the Dresner kid and he maybe kicks in a couple mil in cash."

Joey shook his head. "Naw. Huey'd hand me my head if I tried to pull something like that."

"Odds are Hoag won't want him to know who killed the Dresner kid, either. Huey would hold him up for more than you would."

"That's too friggin' tricky," Joey said.

"I could do it for you," I told him. "I'll put the screws to Hoag, collect the dough, and then split with you, fifty-fifty. We up his ante to four mil. Two mil apiece and your name doesn't even come up in the conversation."

"Good plan, Mr. Killebrew, except for one particular," a British voice said. "You'll be dead."

Hoag was standing in the open doorway, half in shadow, the wind ruffling his hair.

"Just a passing thought," I told him.

Looking as guilty as a schoolboy who'd been caught dealing crack, Joey went all humble. "I got him fixed up here real good. Just like you said." He paused, then added, "Jeez, what happened to you?"

Hoag's nose was bleeding and there was a red welt on one cheek. Lea would not go gently.

Joey smiled in spite of himself. "The blonde too much for you?"

Hoag glared at him. "Hardly." Then he turned apoplectic. "Handcuffs?" he shouted, looking at my wrists.

"Got 'em from one of Huey's cop pals."

"They won't burn, you twit. Use rope."

Joey looked stricken. "I, uh, don't have a key. That's the way you do it. If you don't have the key, the guy has no chance of getting it from you."

Hoag's face turned bright red, but he held it in. He began to breathe in and out slowly. Finally, when he'd returned to his natural pink hue, he said, "Leave it, then. We'd better take a little trip and see how the other mental deficients are proceeding with their brushfires."

Even before Joey's convertible Seville glided toward the main gate, I began working on the cuffs. They're designed for average-sized wrists and can only be ratcheted down so far. As any cop working gang detail can tell you, kids can slip right out of them. But they were just a fraction too tight, even for my slender wrists.

All I accomplished was to rub the skin raw. That made the cuffs fit even tighter.

When I was riding, I had a clock in my head. I could gauge time almost to the second. But cuffed to the thick wooden post, depressed, worried about Lea, I have no idea how many minutes passed before I started to smell smoke.

30

THE HORSES WERE panicked by the scent and by the relentless wind. They whinnied and kicked at their stalls. I was panicked, too. Burning is a terrible way to die and I was blinded by imaginary visions of Lea and me engulfed by flames. The thought that we'd be dead from smoke inhalation before the fire touched us didn't occur to me. But even if it had, it would have seemed like small solace. I damn well didn't want us to die by any means, gentle or harsh, until we were old and gray and had lived long and well. Together.

I forced the dreadful pictures from my mind. Changed the thrust of my thoughts. Okay, Coley, there are only two ways you're going to get free. Either you break the post or you slip the cuffs.

The post was solid, and held fast at both ends.

That left the cuffs.

My hands were starting to perspire, and this seemed to help. But the metal bands were just too tight. Panic sneaked back in with its close friend insanity. Maybe, I told myself, I could break my thumb in such a way . . .

From the corner of my eye I saw something in the doorway. I tensed and then relaxed. The shadowy hulk was bigger than Joey or Hoag or any other living creature I could think of. He looked like James Arness in the movie *The Thing*. Shoot him, chop him, freeze him, and he'd just keep lurching back for more. That was *The Thing*. It was also my man Walrus.

"I'll get us out of here, Coley," he said, his voice less powerful than normal. "Just leave it to me."

His shirt was stuck to his chest and dark with blood. He was working at about half force. He studied the post for a few seconds, followed it from the stone-encased base to its attachment to the roof with huge bolts. He backed away and drew up a huge leg. He shot it out quickly, in a martial-arts kick that landed solidly on the hard wood. It rattled me and must have hurt him greatly. But the post didn't even dent.

"It's no good, Walrus," I said. "Get me some grease."

"Grease?" he asked, nearly out of it.

"For the cuffs."

He nodded and lumbered off. It wouldn't have surprised me if he'd collapsed in a heap before he got to the barn door. But the guy wasn't going to let one little bullet stop him. He staggered out into the new, windy day.

A few minutes later he was back.

"Will this do?" he asked, showing me a bottle of liquid wax.

"It just might."

The clear liquid was soothing on my raw wrists, but also unpleasantly cold and pungent smelling. I shoved my right arm forward and let the cuff ride up a few inches toward my elbow. Then I positioned the metal band with my left hand and jerked back quickly with the right. The skin over my thumb knuckle ripped, but my hand slipped free!

Yelling loud enough to startle the already spooked horses, I ran to Walrus and joyfully hugged his waist. "I did it for you, right?" he asked, and laughed.

The laugh turned into a cough. He staggered back out of my grasp. "I . . . I . . ." he began, and then he fell.

He was still breathing but unconscious. It took all my strength to drag him out of the barn. I left him beside a thick bush that screened both wind and early-morning sun.

Then I went into the main house.

"Lea," I shouted frantically. I refused to let myself believe that Hoag had already killed her. If he'd been concerned about my handcuffs being found, he wouldn't have done anything foolish like shooting her. But she'd marked his face, hurt him. . . .

I called her name again, moving from room to room.

It was a bigger house than it looked from the outside, a rabbit warren of offices and living spaces. Quickly but methodically, I searched each room for any space large enough to conceal a human body. I was so intent on finding Lea that I barely registered stepping over Neil Dresner's lifeless form.

Upstairs, my progress was stopped by a chilling sight. Through the window I could see a plume of gray-white smoke blanketing out over the not-too-distant countryside. A sudden wind snapped the blanket, sending plumes of white into the air followed by tiny dots of red flame. It was moving fast.

I continued my search through bathrooms and bedrooms and, finally, in a locked closet at the far end of the house, I found her.

Hoag had tossed her in and bolted the door from the outside. She wasn't tied up, but she was unconscious. There was a large knot on her forehead.

I rushed to a bathroom, filled a glass of water, and returned to Lea, dowsing her with it. She woke up sputtering.

She didn't ask, Where am I? or any of the idiotic time-wasting questions. Just: "Did they start the fire?"

I nodded. Following her lead, I didn't spend precious moments on how happy I was to find her alive. I said, "We have to wake up the stablehands and set the horses free."

She allowed herself one touch of her swollen forehead and a wince. Then she was on her feet and headed for the door.

As we left the house a familiar red Alfa came up the drive, screeching to a halt a few steps from us. Paula Dresner jumped out, looking worried and puzzled.

"Coley? Roz? There's a fire. . . ."

"We know," I said.

"The brush was burning on both sides of the road while I was driving up. I've been phoning, but the lines are down. . . . Where's Neil?"

She must have read some of the truth in our faces. Lea put out a hand, but Paula whirled away from it and ran into the house, calling her brother's name.

It would have been a nice humane gesture to go after her, save her from stumbling over her brother's body, but Lea and I had more important jobs to do.

We went to the bunkhouse and started waking the stablehands. Water in the face wasn't enough. We shook, slapped, and shouted, and eventually were able to get past whatever drug had been used. As they staggered woozily from the building we told them about the fire.

There was enough smoke in the air for them to get the drift themselves. As they rushed to free the horses I turned to Lea. "You'd better drive Walrus to the nearest hospital," I said. "And get some treatment for yourself, too."

"But—"

"Don't give me any of your macho Amazon crap."

"My macho what?" She looked furious for a brief second, then burst out laughing. "You silver-tongued devil. And while I'm safe and secure in a hospital nursing my macho Amazon pride, what will you be doing?"

"Helping to get this place evacuated of horses and people. Then I'll try to find some cops who'll listen to me about how the fire got started."

"Mini-macho," she said with mock scorn. She pulled me to her for one brief kiss. Then she ran to her Saab.

She parked next to the unconscious Walrus. With the help of a stablehand, we got the big man onto the passenger seat. His eyes opened and he mumbled something I couldn't hear.

I tried strapping him upright with the safety belt, but it

wouldn't stretch far enough. So I lowered the seat back until he was nearly supine. The whole time he continued to mumble.

I leaned closer and asked, "What is it, Walrus?"

"I'm praying, Coley," he said in a reedy voice. "Praying to Jesus, Buddha, Zoroaster, and Moses." He smiled. "Covering all bets."

"We should go," Lea said.

I backed away. "I love you," I said to Lea.

"And I love you, Mr. Mini-macho."

The stablehands had been sorting the horses. We started loading some of them into the available vans and trailers. I hoped that the hands who knew their stock were loading the animals according to their value. But I wasted no time worrying about bottom-line price. I just wanted all living creatures out of there before the fire swept over everything.

When all the van space was taken, we set the remaining horses free to fend for themselves. With any luck they'd have the sense to avoid the smoke and fire and not run back into any burning barns as frightened horses have been known to do.

With all this activity, I'd forgotten about Paula. But she hadn't forgotten about me. I was sending a gray on its way when I saw her leaving the main building. She stopped at her little red car, reached down, and picked up her purse. Then she headed toward me. Her eyes were red from crying, but she looked as if she'd gotten past that.

When she was within six feet of me, she stopped, reached into the pocket of her jacket, and took out a small pistol that looked very much like Johnny Rousseau's Bond gun. She pointed it at my chest.

"You killed my brother, you bastard," she said. It was all I needed to make my morning complete.

31

"**W**HOA," I SAID, as evenly as I could while staring into the stubby barrel of a handgun that had probably been used recently. "Would I still be waiting around here if I'd killed him?"

"Say if you did or didn't. But don't bullshit me. I know when people bullshit."

Her eyes were glassy and she seemed to be on autopilot. "I didn't kill your brother," I said, slowly and sincerely.

"But you know who did." She held the weapon steady as a rock.

"Yes," I said. "A man named Channing Hoag."

"I know him. He was a friend of my father's. A Brit." She paused, a windup doll waiting for a new signal from her machinery. "Tell me why he killed Neil," she said, with a singular lack of emotion.

"He and another man planned this fire, and when Neil tried to stop them, Hoag killed him."

"Where is Channing Hoag now?"

"I don't know. Somewhere out there, setting new fires, I guess."

"Is this place going to burn?"

"It sure looks that way," I said. "Hoag and his pals primed it with gasoline. You can smell it."

She nodded.

"You'd better drive away now," I told her. "You saw the brush burning. With this kind of dry wind, a firestorm can run right over you. You should get away from here as quickly as you can. We're trying to save the horses. Isn't that what Neil would want us to do?"

"Sure. He wouldn't want them to burn. But I don't want him to burn either."

"He's dead."

"He's not going to burn." Paula put the gun back into her pocket, but kept her hand on it as she walked away from me. She shouted to the stablehands. "My brother is in the house. I need help getting him to my car."

A couple of them followed her. They were in for a surprise. If they'd known they were bringing out a dead boss instead of rescuing a live one, they might have chosen to stick with the horses.

It was an odd procession that went from the house to the bright red Alfa a few moments later. Two men carrying the late Neil Dresner while his sister held his head.

Once they'd put him into the front seat, Paula leaned him back and adjusted the seat belt, holding him upright. "We're going now, Neil," she said, and started the engine. The two hands looked at one another. One of them said, "Miss Dresner, maybe you'd better . . ."

She drove away before he could finish the sentence.

She still had the gun in her pocket. Maybe I should have tried to take it away from her. But I didn't feel like getting shot for being a Samaritan. I turned back to finish up with the horses.

When all the animals had been turned loose, one of the hands asked me, "Think we ought to hose down the roof?"

"Not much point. If the fire gets here, it's going to run through these buildings in a matter of seconds, wet roof or not. You better move the vans out while you can still find roads that are passable."

"Aren't you coming?" he asked.

"I'll be right behind you."

32

DAWN HAD BROKEN by the time the last trailer cleared the property, but you couldn't tell by the sky. The air was black with smoke, and the heat was intensifying. Helicopters were circling overhead. Above the roar of their motors, bullhorns warned people to evacuate immediately. As the last two-legged inhabitant of Heartland Farms I decided to obey the warning.

I'd noticed earlier that the late Neil Dresner had left the keys in the ignition of his Jaguar. It started smoothly. I backed up and was about to drive away when I saw that some of the freed horses had gathered in a tight little group near the barn, an ominous sign that they might reenter. I hopped from the Jag and ran to the tiny herd, trying to scatter them.

They stood their dangerous ground. In frustration, I shouted, "Then burn, goddammit."

As if in reply, a couple of the horses trotted away. But they were following nature's advice, not mine. The wind was blowing the smoke from the southwest, and they traveled northeast with the wind, away from the fire. I followed their example.

I was heading for the Jaguar when a dark Plymouth sedan began its approach down the long drive. Since I was not expecting guests, I ducked down behind a toolshed near the barn.

As the car got closer I recognized Joey Lunchbox in the passenger seat. There were two other men in the back, the torch team presumably. So they weren't willing to let nature take its course after all. They were going to make sure Heartland burned.

The sedan stopped directly behind the Jag and the four of them, including the driver, piled out. Lousy odds, even for Mr. Mini-macho.

Joey's smirk froze when he saw the horses outside of their stalls. Wailing like a goosed banshee, he ran into a barn. Almost immediately he exited, waving his arms. "They're gone! The horses. Killebrew. The whole deal is fucked."

One of the firebugs dragged a gadget from the trunk that looked like a vacuum cleaner with a nozzle. He asked Joey which barn he wanted to hit first.

"Didn't you just hear what I said?" Joey screamed. "There's nothing here. What's the fucking point in starting a fire?"

He led the others into the main building.

That looked like my cue to get a-moving.

But the Plymouth was blocking the Jaguar. And the driver had taken his keys.

Once again, I felt compelled to try my hand at the hot wire. I was approaching the Plymouth when one of Joey's boys exited the back door of the building. He saw me and froze for a beat. Then he yelled, "Hey, Joey. Out here!"

I didn't hesitate. I ran toward the nearest horse, a big roan, grabbing it by its halter. I couldn't mount him from the ground, especially not without a saddle. So I led him to a fence. I climbed the crosspieces and was getting on when Joey took his first shot.

The horse was a little wired to begin with and the gunshot spooked him. He reared up. Even when I was riding every day, I wasn't much used to bareback. I left that to circus performers and Indians. But when your life is on the line, you develop skills fast. Somehow I managed to hang on to the roan. I dug my heels into his side, and we were away.

I heard a car engine kick over but I didn't have time to look back. I moved the Thoroughbred through the smoky morning light, trying to keep the animal on solid ground.

The fire was spreading faster now. There was more smoke and

more heat. We passed hastily deserted farmland, fertile fields about to be burned clean. The Plymouth was gaining. Over the wind, I could hear Joey shouting instructions to the driver. Even if it had been Secretariat under me, there was no way I was going to out-run an internal-combustion engine. On the flat, that is. But there was no reason I had to stick to the roads.

I pointed the horse down a grassy knoll that I hoped we could handle and the car couldn't. The change of terrain transferred the advantage to me. I couldn't hear them behind me. Maybe they'd given up. The Plymouth definitely wasn't an all-terrain vehicle.

Suddenly a huge blaze streaked across the knoll.

Above us, Joey and the man with the vacuum cleaner were walking. The vacuum man aimed his nozzle at the grass and a flame shot out of its tip. Just what I needed.

I moved the roan farther down the knoll and continued on. I didn't see any more flare-ups. I prodded the horse with my heel, and he responded with more speed. The smoke was rolling in like black curtains now.

We'd put a few miles between us and Heartland, but the fire seemed to be gaining. Helicopters zoomed above, and larger planes carrying water. We passed more deserted farms and one where a brave landowner stood on his roof with a hose, evidently waiting until the last minute to keep his property wet.

Eventually, we met up with the road we'd deserted. Joey's Plymouth was nowhere to be seen. I assumed they'd given up. But as we started forward the wind cut a clear path through the smoke and there was the car ahead of us, parked dead center in the road. Empty.

I looked around wildly. Where were Joey and his men?

Then something zipped past my cheek, followed immediately by the sound of a shot. And more shots. I turned the horse and we went down off the road again. Almost tumbling. More gunfire. It was a miracle neither of us was hit. But these were arsonists, not gunmen. Thank heaven we were in the era of specialization.

Still, we were definitely on the run.

I heard car doors slam, then the engine starting.

They were following us off road.

I urged the roan onward, but we had to move cautiously. Too many potholes and potential dangers in front of us. And behind us . . . I couldn't see the pursuing car. But I knew it was still there.

The ground was getting flatter and more even, bad news for us. The sedan could pick up speed now. Sooner or later a bullet would connect.

Of course, something else could kill us first.

I spotted the oncoming hazard just in time. The rolling grass dipped abruptly to a deep ditch. It looked about four feet across. My friend should be able to manage that. I gave him a kick, and he went over the gap easily.

That earned him a congratulatory pat.

Even if Detroit and the Japanese got together for a supercar, it still wouldn't be able to make a jump like that. Assuming they didn't wind up in the ditch, Joey and the boys would not be able to follow us by car. And with them on foot, I wouldn't need Secretariat to leave them in the dust.

There was a loud crash behind us, and a car horn began to blare. Above its sound came a male voice screaming in pain.

I pulled up and made a circle, slowly and cautiously taking the horse back the way we'd come. The wind had blown some of the smoke away, and I saw the sedan nose down in the ditch.

One member of the arson squad had opened the back door and was staggering out. Joey Lunchbox would not be doing that. He had crashed headfirst through the windshield, his face slick with blood. I couldn't tell if he was dead or alive, and I really didn't care much either way.

I wheeled the roan northeast again and we galloped away toward fresh air and freedom.

33

THE NURSE AT the hospital told me that Walrus was rally-ing splendidly, but that I shouldn't stay too long. She was petite, but solid, with curly golden hair that threatened to upset her starched white cap. She seemed to have something on her mind, so I paused before entering Walrus's room.

"Is Mr. Walnicki a clergyman?" she asked.

"In his heart," I told her. "Actually, he's more of a theologian."

"Well, all I can say is that there is an aura around that man. He's the holiest patient I've ever had under my care."

"He'll be glad to hear that," I said and went in.

He was resting in bed, propped up by four pillows, leafing through a Gideon Bible. He dropped the book to the bed and grinned at me. "Hiya, Coley."

I held out my wrapped present. "For the man who has every-thing," I said.

He took it and studied it. It was thin, approximately eight by four inches. He said, "It's too big to be that bastard Hoag's heart."

"Maybe next week on the heart."

He tore the gift wrap off of *The Confessions of Saint Augustine*.

"Gee, Coley, this is swell. It'll be a real relief after this bible. I never have liked any but the Douey-Reims translation."

"I was afraid you might already have the Saint Augustine," I said.

"Not in this edition," he said. He opened the book and studied the print history. Then he yawned and asked, "Well, you gonna tell me what happened after I pooped out on the party?"

"The nurse said I shouldn't stay too long."

"So make it the abridged version."

I filled him in, ending with my leaving the roan at a horse farm that seemed safe from the fires.

"I reported Joey Lunchbox's smashup," I said. "But I think the cops and paramedics had a lot of other things on their mind before they got around to caring for Joey."

"Tough," said Walrus. He looked suddenly glum. "I'm really sorry I screwed up so badly, Coley."

"What do you mean? Without you, I'd only have died about three times in the last forty-eight hours."

"Yeah, well, that's nice of you to say." He yawned and his eyelids drooped.

"I'll come back tomorrow," I told him.

"Wait. What's happening with the fires? I don't have TV privileges yet."

"There are still some hot spots, but they're getting them contained."

"Tongues of flame," he said. "You know, Coley, fire has all kinds of mystical significance. . . ."

But I never found out what they were, because the big guy fell asleep before he could get the lecture rolling.

At the reception desk, I discovered that Lea's bump on the noggin had been judged superficial. She'd left me a message that she could be reached at her father's place.

Using the pay phone on the main floor, I made a silent prayer that she'd answer the ring. Or possibly Choo Choo. Of course, it was Starbuck who picked up the receiver. Fresh off a hurried return flight and angry as a bear with the gout.

As soon as he heard my voice, he launched into a "What the

hell were you thinking of putting Lea in the middle of that fire?" harangue. After a minute or two she took the phone from him and forced him back into his cage.

"Coley, are you all right?" she asked.

"Sure, I'll tell you all about it when I see you. How's the head?"

"Colorful. Dad insists that I keep an ice bag on it to reduce the swelling, but it's so cold it hurts."

I told her I was familiar with ice bags and, in her father's case, windbags. "I've seen Walrus, and he's doing fine. Now I want to see you."

"When?" she asked.

"As soon as I can get to the Neck for a shower and change of clothes."

"A shower? You must love me."

"I may even splash on a little cologne," I said, feeling downright giddy.

34

AT THE HORSE'S Neck, I was met by a welcoming committee of the restaurant's morning crew. They'd gathered in the bar, sipping coffee and sodas in a mood of what? Triumph? Solidarity? I eyed them warily. Had our release of the horses made the TV news? Or, at the other end of the spectrum, were they planning a walkout for higher wages?

I knew I'd been wrong on both counts when my pastry chef, Stan Furneaux, said, "We got 'em, boss!"

"Got who?" I asked.

"You can forget about those security systems," Al Grady informed me. "And give that man mountain his walking papers, too. You don't need outside help when you got us in your corner. Team Killebrew."

"What are you talking about?"

Before I could get an answer, the front door was thrown open and Jack Hayward marched in, hair still damp from the shower, a razor cut or two on his chin. I didn't think he'd been up that early since he worked for John Ford. He trotted over to me, a martyr's expression on his face. "Coley, I'm frightfully sorry," he said. "I'm truly devastated. I had no idea."

"No idea of what, Jack?"

"It was my fault, period. If you tossed me into the cold and rendered me redundant at my advanced age, I would understand completely, and cheerfully accept my fate."

"Jack, I have no—"

"If, however," he cut me off, "through some extraordinary kindness of heart and feeling for the good times we've had, you should decide to retain my services, let me just assure you that nothing like this will ever happen again."

"What the hell happened?" I exploded.

"Maybe we oughta start from the beginning," Stan said. "Except we've all got different beginnings."

"Go ahead. Let's hear yours. Or anybody's."

"Well, first of all, we caught the two birds who've been breakin' in here," Al said. "They're in the back with the kitchen crew sittin' on 'em."

"They're in back?" I asked, matters getting fuzzier not clearer.

"Sure. That's where Stan found 'em this morning when he got here at six."

"It's nine now," I said.

"Well, we weren't sure what you'd want us to do—" Stan began.

"They're crooks," I said. "Call the cops."

"We did that," Stan said, "just a short while ago."

"They changed their MOs, Coley," Al interjected. "Breakin' in through the window didn't work for 'em, so they just waltzed in here last night—"

"An hour before closing," Jack squeezed in. "Ordered filet mignon and seafood pasta. Split a Caesar salad. Crème brûlée—"

"Forget the goddamned menu and tell me what happened," I said, my head starting to hurt.

"They dawdled over their coffees until they were nearly the last table in the place," Jack informed me, "then secluded themselves in the water closets."

"The night staff closed up and went home, leavin' 'em in here," Al reported with unseemly glee. "Good thing the day crew picked up the ball and ran with it."

"So let's go get a look at these burglars," I said.

"Technically, they aren't burglars," Jack Hayward said. "They didn't break in."

"Thieves, then," I said. "But you're walking on thin ice, Jack."

"All my fault," he said, going martyr again. "If only I'd checked the WCs."

I led the procession to the kitchen. It was empty. I looked at Al.

"Upstairs, boss," he said.

"Upstairs is my apartment."

"Oh, Coley," Jack groaned, adding a funereal timbre to his delivery. "They seemed like such wonderful people. And they'd become regulars. They were so disappointed to hear you were out of town. Was your trip successful, by the way?"

"Never mind the trip," I said.

"Well, they were such fans and they asked for a little tour of the building after they paid their tab. And when I showed them your apartment—"

"Showed them my apartment," I repeated flatly.

"Actually, just let them poke their heads in. But I think one of them must have wedged something in the door as we were leaving. And I have been informed they spent the night upstairs."

"These crooks spent the night in my apartment?"

"When we returned to the main salon," Jack continued, "they asked to use the loos and I went about my business showing the last patrons out. I . . . assumed Antony had let them out and he assumed I had."

We were starting up the stairs when the police came through the front of the house. Considering all I'd been through in the past forty-eight hours without one cop poking his nose in, I almost found it amusing that four uniformed policemen had arrived to apprehend a couple of half-cooked yeggs.

"This way, officers," Jack Hayward said, suddenly shifting from Saint Agnes to Sherlock Holmes. "I'll lead you to the miscreants."

We all trooped up the stairs and into my apartment, where five members of the early-morning kitchen staff were guarding the thieves with knives and meat cleavers. One of them brandished a grater.

The objects of their guardianship were an elderly man and woman. I'd met them a few nights before when they were supposedly celebrating their fortieth wedding anniversary. The racing fan Harold Danziger and his wife, Estelle.

They were sitting on my leather couch. Resting on a nearby table was my trophy from the Santa Rosita Handicap.

"Good morning, Coley," Harold Danziger said pleasantly. "I hope your trip was successful."

I didn't reply. Instead I picked up the trophy and stepped away from them while the police moved in.

Danziger peered around one thick-waisted cop and called out, "This is all a misunderstanding, Coley. We weren't actually going to take anything. We think you're wonderful."

Before the cops could get going with their questions, I got in one of my own. "Have you really been married forty years?"

"Of course," Estelle said. "You helped us celebrate our anniversary."

I was sappy enough to hope that part of it was true, that even though they were career crooks, their advertisement for long and happy marriages was still intact.

I stayed in the room long enough to hear Harold's plea of innocence. He claimed that he emerged from the men's room to find that the restaurant was completely empty. He didn't think he'd been in there longer than ten or fifteen minutes—though he and Estelle had had a bit to drink.

He found Estelle asleep in the ladies' room. They really shouldn't imbibe so late at night.

Anyway, they were afraid if they opened any of the exterior doors, an alarm would go off. So they went looking for a phone.

They evidently missed the one in the bar and the main dining area and the kitchen and elected instead to try the door to my apartment, which they found open.

There, since they knew I was out of town, they decided to spend the night, sleeping on my bed, until someone arrived to let them out.

In the morning, they were awakened by the kitchen crew brandishing their weapons.

In their favor was the fact that they had been asleep when Stan and the kitchen crew discovered them, drawn to the apartment by Harold's loud snores. Against them was the fact that they'd been in the rest rooms for well over an hour and a half, the time it usually takes to close the restaurant and the kitchen down.

It wasn't the crime of the century, so the cops got out of there fast. The Danzigers were taken away to be booked. Jack Hayward went with them, representing the restaurant, to provide whatever information the police might need.

One cop stayed behind to do a final check. I told him I was confused as to why the Danzigers hadn't left at night, when they could have gotten away clean.

"We found this by your bed, Mr. Killebrew," he said, holding up a large plastic bag containing an empty bottle of Courvoisier. "Some of these whacks get off on the danger, you know. Looks like these two got so turned on by their theft, they decided to make a night of it in your bed. At their age, too. They probably didn't know how early your staff gets here."

Ah, romance. "Evidently they've been stealing all the trophies from that one particular race," I told the cop. "I don't have any idea why."

"We'll find out, Mr. Killebrew," he said with the air of a wise and patient man. "You have a good day now."

Was it possible to have a good day? It had been so long since I'd known one. I decided to find out. As quickly as I could, I showered, shaved, and donned clothes that smelled nice and fresh and not smoky or sweaty at all.

Stan and Al were waiting for me in the kitchen. They were disappointed I didn't want to hear more of the details of their daring capture of the senior-citizen burglars, but I was in a hurry. "When Jack comes in this afternoon," I said, "tell him I expect him personally to get my apartment cleaned. He can throw the bed linen away."

Lea was in her father's office. So was her father. They were seated on the rattan furniture beside his desk. One of them was glad to see me. Even with the multicolor bruise on her forehead, she looked spectacular.

"What the hell kept you, Killebrew?" Starbuck asked.

I ignored him completely, walked directly to Lea's chair. I bent slightly, took her face in my hands, and planted a lengthy kiss on her lips. Right there in front of God and her father.

"Well, for Christ's sake," I heard Starbuck mutter. Lea stirred, but didn't break the kiss. That made it all the sweeter.

When we finally drew apart, we saw that Starbuck had left his chair to turn on the little TV set that rested on a nearby table.

He returned to his chair with the remote channel switcher and began pressing buttons. One after the other, the local stations were giving full-throttle coverage to the brushfires.

The blaze that swept across Calabasas, the largest of several, was still being attributed to the Santa Ana winds. Firefighters were referring to it as "contained."

Lea told me that it had in fact destroyed the Heartland Farms buildings, but most of the horses had been found and saved.

"Well, now I've got the bastard," Starbuck said, turning to us. He winced at the sight of us, me, sitting on the arm of Lea's chair, holding her hand, she, leaning her head against my hip.

"What bastard is that?" I asked.

"Grosso," he snarled. "As soon as—"

The scene had changed on the TV. Instead of more fire footage, we were looking at the news desk in the studio, where an attractive Latin anchorwoman was frowning into the camera. Above and to the right of her head was an insert reading DAYLIGHT MURDER in bright red letters.

"At approximately nine-thirty this morning insurance executive Channing Hoag was shot as he entered his office building in the mid–Wilshire corridor. A single thirty-two-caliber bullet penetrated his brain. According to an LAPD spokesperson, several passersby heard the shot being fired, though no actual witness to the shooting has been found. Our Greg Brantley is live at police headquarters, where the big news is that the search is on for a young woman observed fleeing the scene. Greg?"

The picture shifted to an LAPD hallway, where a field reporter was shoving his mike into the face of a harried-looking plainclothesman.

"Detective, is this mystery woman a suspect in the Hoag slaying?"

"Well, I wouldn't call her a mystery woman. . . ."

"Then you know her identity."

"No. But we're looking into that. Uh, if you'll excuse me . . ."

The lawman tried an end run around the reporter, but Greg Brantley tagged him at the door. "Will an attempt be made to get a description of the woman?"

For a moment it looked as if the detective might bust out laughing, but he was too much of a pro for that. Instead he simply said that the woman's ID was one of several lines of inquiry they were pursuing.

The field reporter threw it back to the anchor.

"It wasn't a woman who got Hoag with a single bullet," Starbuck said. "It was one of Huey Grosso's enforcers. And I don't think Huey's a big believer in NOW." He scowled at us. "Will you two try and control yourselves while I get some more coffee?"

As soon as he left the room for a moment, I whispered to Lea, "We have to get to the Dresner place. Immediately."

She looked at me curiously. I told her about my brief, nearly fatal confrontation with Paula Dresner at the stables. I explained that I thought the gun Paula was carrying was the same Walther PPK that had fired the bullets into Wilton Dresner. I also described her prowess with a handgun at Susanna's Salon.

"Let's say you're right. Why do you want to get involved?" Lea asked. "I'm not sure I wouldn't have done the same thing if he'd killed my brother."

"Maybe," I replied. "But I think it's time I did something about Johnny Rousseau."

35

WE PASSED STARBUCK on our way out.

"Where the hell're you going?" he asked.

"To solve a few murders," I said.

"Hold on a minute," he shouted. Maybe he thought I was kidding. Maybe he thought we were eloping. It didn't matter what he thought.

"Lea, you need rest," he told her, running after us.

She stopped, wheeled on him. "Do you ever rest when you're on the verge of breaking something big?" she asked. He didn't have an answer. I hustled her out of there before he thought about coming with us.

When we were in the Cherokee, Lea asked, "Murders?"

"Four," I told her.

"All Paula's?" she asked, not without skepticism.

"One or two," I said. "How are you feeling, really?"

"Not so bad considering everything. Turn here. It's a shortcut to the freeway."

I obeyed her and nearly lost the Jeep in a pothole the size of Rhode Island.

"Other than the one Hoag committed, I know of only two murders," she said. "Hoag and Wilton Dresner."

The shortcut really worked. An entrance to the Santa Monica Freeway was only half a block away. "There are a couple others. But let's talk about us," I said.

"There'll be time for that," she said.

"I'm not so sure. For some damn reason, I keep getting into situations where people stick guns in my face. I feel my life expectancy is averaging out at about an hour and a half. So excuse me if I want to cut to the chase."

"Okay, let's," she said. "You love me and I love you. My father is not in the picture. He and I have already had our talk. I won't move in with you at your apartment. I don't want to live over a restaurant. But we might try to find a little Spanish bungalow somewhere.

"Now, tell me about the other two murders."

"Bungalow, huh?" I said, smiling.

"If I have to ask you about the murders once more, the deal's off," she said.

"I'm not sure where to start," I told her. "Okay. Let's take them in reverse chronology. Hoag was shot this morning, presumably by Paula Dresner. Let's skip past her father's death and go back to the killing of the photographer known as Jerry Woo. In Chicago, when he thought I was about to buy the farm, Joey Lunchbox was very candid with me. He said he'd had Woo murdered because he was trying to blackmail his boss, Huey Grosso."

"Woo must have been an idiot," Lea said.

"Just overconfident," I said. "He thought Grosso would be smart enough to respect the fact that Woo had salted away photographic evidence that some of the gang boss's heavily insured horses were alive and well long after the death benefits had been paid. Unfortunately for the photographer, Grosso isn't a very conservative player. He sent in Joey and a pair of skull crackers who tortured Woo into disclosing the whereabouts of his stash of photos. They left one behind—the shot of Briarpatch that I discovered in Woo's office.

"But they found other pictures that Woo was using to blackmail his less aggressive victims. According to Joey, one of these other victims was someone Grosso did business with."

"Wilton Dresner?" Lea asked.

We were nearing the turnoff to the Dresner home. I moved over into the freeway's right lane. "Wilton wasn't actually in business with Grosso," I told her. "Neil was. And he was one of Woo's involuntary customers."

"What makes you think so?"

I told her about following Paula to Woo's place, seeing her leave with the photo.

"But wouldn't that mean *she* was the blackmail victim?"

"Maybe she was," I said. "What confuses me is why she hocked her stuff to pay Woo off."

"She needed money."

"Not if I'm right about the murder that started all this."

The Cherokee bounced onto the drive leading to the Dresner home. Paula's red Alfa was the only car present. She had left it at a careless angle, as close to the front door as she could get. The seat where Neil Dresner had been for his last ride was empty.

"Dammit, what murder are you talking about?" Lea asked.

"Let's ask Paula," I said.

36

THE FRONT DOOR of the Dresner house was wide open. We knocked on it anyway and rang the bell. When no one answered, we walked into a dark entryway.

Lea called out, "Henry?" There was no answer.

"The butler?" I guessed.

She nodded. "He's always here."

"Henry's gone. I fired him," a voice said from the top of the stairs. "'Nobody lives here anymore but Paula."

She descended the stairwell slowly, as if she were a bit tipsy. She was wearing a long filmy nightgown. Her lipstick was a dark color, purple or perhaps black.

Lea softly hummed the da-da-di-da opening bars of the "Twilight Zone" theme. I might have smiled, but as Paula drew nearer she brought her right hand from behind her back. She was holding the same weapon she'd pointed at me at Heartland Farms.

She wasn't aiming it at either of us. She wagged it from side to side, as if she wasn't sure what it was for.

"Have you used that gun, Paula?" I asked.

"Sure. Carpe fucking diem. I had to avenge Neil." Her voice was slightly slurred. She had taken something to bring her down. "Neil was my only real friend from the time I arrived at this dud place. Just think, though, I never would have even known him if my dear sweet mother hadn't wanted to dump me."

"Why did she want to do that?" I asked.

"She said she couldn't handle me." Paula smiled at the memory.

"She couldn't, because I didn't want to be handled. Not by her. But I really think it was this guy named Alois she shacked up with. He started trying to bone me when I was sixteen. After a couple years I finally gave him the big thrill. And good old Mom, not really competitive, you understand, shipped me off to Wilton. Said she was afraid of me."

"Was your father afraid of you, too?" I asked.

"Wilton. No, Wilton was brain-dead where Neil and I were concerned. Now he's all dead." She frowned. "I think you'd better leave. I don't feel like entertaining."

"Maybe we can help you."

She gave that a second's thought, turning the gun over in her hands. I cursed myself for bringing Lea; Paula was too unpredictable.

She said, "I don't know what to do with Neil. What do you do with people after they die? I didn't want him to burn, but maybe I should have let him. I mean, he's gone. It's just his husk left. His pod."

"We can figure something out," I said, edging toward her slowly, unthreateningly. I had to do what I'd neglected back at Heartland: get that gun.

"Can we?" Paula said. "Can we really? People like to help me." She smiled. "Men like to help me."

"We should call somebody," I said.

"You mean like the police? Or an undertaker? Do we have to?"

"We should. Where is Neil now?" She was only a couple of feet away.

"In Wilton's den," she said with a sardonic grimace. "In Wilton's own personal doge's chair that he wouldn't let any of us lesser mortals sit in. Ever. He hated Neil. Neil did everything to try to satisfy him, but nothing was ever enough."

"Why do you call your father Wilton?" Lea asked. Paula looked startled. I think she'd forgotten Lea was there.

In the instant Paula's eyes shifted, I saw my chance to reach out for the gun. I nearly got it. My hand was only inches away when she jerked the weapon back. She shook her head slowly.

"No fair, Coley," she said.

She still didn't point the Walther at me, though. She cradled it to her breast now, like a small child. A lunge forward and I might have taken it away from her, but if I failed . . . I moved back a step, wanting her to stay calm, not to come out of her drug-induced haze and start blasting away.

"Why did you call him Wilton?" Lea repeated, her voice almost soothing.

"What should I have called him, Roz?" she asked scornfully. "Daddy? A man I barely knew. A fucking hypocrite. So moral, with his whores; so sanctimonious, with his scummy crook friends."

"He loved you," Lea said. "Anybody who was around you both could tell that. He'd do anything for you."

"It was all show," Paula snarled back. "From the time I got here, he treated me like his little baby girl. I was eighteen years old. I'd done blow with rock stars and fucked royalty. I'd had an abortion and tried suicide. His baby girl."

"Did you kill him?" I asked as casually as I could.

She hesitated.

"Sure." Her voice was thin, tinny.

"And Channing Hoag?"

"You know I did. But he only killed Neil once. Wilton killed him a hundred times in a hundred different cruel ways. Called him a weakling, an alcoholic, a loser. And he turned Neil into all those things."

She turned to Lea and said with sudden vehemence, "You weren't much help, Roz. With your Little Mary Sunshine 'your father loves you' bullshit."

I held my breath.

Lea began to say something in her defense, but I decided to

change the subject entirely. "You mentioned Wilton's 'scummy crook friends,' " I said. "Who did you mean?"

"That sleazoid Huey Grosso. He'd come here every month or so for some sort of confab. He almost raped me once, for God's sake, then pretended it was a mistake. I ran to tell Wilton and he got all red-faced and he and the gross Grosso went into the study and shut the door. And I heard Wilton shouting. But when he came out, he sent me to my room. And whenever Grosso came over, I'd have to go out or hang in my room until he left. Wilton said he loved me, would give me anything, but if that were true, he'd have done something about Grosso, not made me a prisoner in my own cage. God, I hated that son of a bitch." Grosso or Dresner? Probably both.

"Was Ed Fein one of those 'scummy crook friends,' too?"

She looked at me slyly. "Ed? No, I wasn't talking about Ed. He wasn't a criminal. Not really. What do you know about Ed?"

"I know he stole Wilton's money and disappeared. I know he's never been seen again. He was paid a good salary to take care of Wilton's investments. Everybody thought he lived for his work. What made him suddenly run off with a big chunk of stolen money? If it was a woman, she must've been really something."

She smiled. "Ed thought so," she said.

"Was it your idea for Fein to embezzle the money?"

She considered the question for a few seconds, then said, "It was actually Neil's idea. I mean, it started when I used to flirt with Ed when he'd come to the house. He was this nerdy kind of guy whose wife had died from cancer. And I kinda felt sorry for him and would 'accidentally' brush up against him. You know, turn him on a little.

"One afternoon Ed dropped by and Wilton was out. He started to leave, but he seemed so sad. I . . . took him to my room. He was a little freaked, but he was so horny that didn't matter. And I made him happier than he'd been in years.

"I told Neil about it. He didn't understand. I mean, there's nothing wrong with a mercy fuck. It made me feel good and it sure as hell made Ed feel good. So what was the harm? But Neil is . . . was sort of pure, really. Still, he came up with the plan."

"How did the plan work?" I asked.

She leaned against the balustrade, the gun swinging on one finger now like a pendulum. I leaned toward her, ready for another try at the weapon, but she jerked alert again, gripping the pistol. "Let's go upstairs," she said. "I don't like leaving Neil alone."

I went up with her. I waved Lea away behind my back. But she followed us, her curiosity getting the better of her caution.

Dresner's study was floor-to-ceiling books, an ornate French antique desk, and behind it, a high-backed, green velvet chair holding Neil's body. Rigor mortis had set in and the body was bending. The face looked horrific, lips drawn back to expose the ivory grin.

Soft leather matching sofa and chairs faced the desk. Paula took one of the chairs. I sat near her on the edge of the sofa. Lea remained just outside the door.

"Neil was brilliant," Paula said. "He told Ed what to do. Something about a dummy withholding account. Something like that. Wilton was making so much money he didn't know where all of it was coming from. Or going. Ed got him to sign a few papers and that was that.

"Our goal was five million. Neil was to get two million, which he'd put into Heartland. Ed and I were supposed to use the remaining three to run away together."

"Fein believed you'd do that?" I asked. "Run away with him?"

"Sure. I sort of believed it myself. Ed was very nice to me. Very gentle. But I never thought I'd spend the rest of my life with him. I needed somebody with an edge. Somebody like Johnny Rousseau."

"Or Charles Lavery?"

"Charles? Well, Charles is a homington."

"A what?"

"A queer. Still in the closet, of course. A lot of his funding comes from women who'd like to shack up with him. The weird thing, as beautiful as he is, even if he were straight, I don't think I'd really want to get it on with him."

"That wasn't the impression I got at the party."

"Well, Johnny behaved so badly at the party. I mean, he was drunk and shouting. I didn't want him or anybody else to think I liked that kind of behavior."

Her voice was childish and singsong. It added to her pathos.

"Let's get back to Ed Fein," I said.

"Ed, yes. He had all kinds of crazy ideas of places we'd go, things we'd do. Dumb stuff, like sunsets and boat trips. I can't stand boats. I get sick.

"Anyway, Neil's plan worked. We decided to do it on my birthday. That's when Ed emptied out this bank account he'd set up and brought the cash to Heartland. So much money."

"How did Fein die?"

"It was his own fault. I told him I'd changed my mind and I wasn't going away with him. He thought I was kidding. When he realized I wasn't, he got all bristly. Said he was going to put the money back. He grabbed the leather case and started to leave. Neil grabbed him and he and Ed started fighting in the office."

"What did you do?"

"I . . . grabbed a letter opener from Neil's desk and I'm not sure how it happened exactly, but I stabbed Ed in the neck. It was just an awful mess. Blood all over everything. Even the money. It took us hours to clean up."

I asked her what happened to the money.

She sighed. "We didn't get to spend any of it."

"Where is it?"

"I don't know. Neil hid it somewhere at Heartland. He wouldn't tell me where. He said we had to wait a long time before spending any of it and he didn't trust me to do that. So he took temptation out of my path."

"It could be ashes now," I said.

"No matter," she said. "It's too late. Ed's probably ashes, too."

"You buried him at Heartland?"

"Neil and I. After the hands had gone to sleep. There was this old cottage on the edge of the property. Workers or something lived there a long time ago. Anyway, it was falling apart. That last earthquake, the big one, shook all the bricks loose. So Neil hired these guys to tear the place down and cart the mess away. But the cottage had some kind of grain cellar that was like this perfect grave. That's where we put ol' Ed, and Neil filled it in with mud. It took him hours. Then he drove Ed's car out to the airport with me following in the Alfa. We figured the police would think that Ed had flown away somewhere with the money and that's exactly what they did think."

"You're lucky the stablehands weren't very alert."

"They were asleep when Neil did his digging."

"I mean when Fein arrived. If the police could have placed him at Heartland that night, you would have been in for trouble."

"We didn't even think about that at the time. And none of them paid any attention to Ed. Except for that fucking photographer."

"Jerry Woo."

"Whatever he called himself. He was a goddamned liar. He told Neil he was on assignment to do a magazine article for *The American Horse*, or some such shit. He wanted to spend a week with the stablehands."

I had seen the photos of Heartland scattered on Woo's floor. That's why the place had seemed so familiar to me.

"But he was lying," she said. "That crude thug who worked for Grosso—"

"Joey Lunchbox?"

"That's the one. He told Neil that the photographer had found out that Grosso was one of the owners of Heartland and that's why he was taking pictures of the horses. For some reason, he thought he might use the pictures to get at Grosso. He wound up getting at us as well."

"What was it about your picture that was so incriminating?" I asked.

"It was the three of us together," she said. "Going into the building."

"But couldn't it have been taken on some other night, when Fein had come out on business for your father?"

"No," she said. "It had to be the night he disappeared. The Alfa was in the picture."

It clicked in. When I'd first seen her driving away from the Bay City Beach Club, the parking attendant had said she'd been given the car for her birthday. Ed Fein had disappeared on her birthday. And the car was in the photo.

"So Woo knew you'd killed Fein," I said.

"He most certainly did not," she said. "He just thought we'd helped Ed get away. Thank heaven."

"What difference did that make?"

"If he'd thought we'd killed Ed and had all that money, he would have blackmailed us for much more. As it was, I had to sell some of my jewelry and stuff to pay him off."

"And you had all that cash just sitting there."

"That was Neil," she said. "He was afraid to touch it. Not even to pay his gambling debts."

"You must have been tempted to kill the blackmailer."

"You know it," she said eagerly. "I might have, too. But somebody beat me to it. Grosso's men. I arrived not long after they'd done it. The guy's corpse was still sort of warm. I dug through all the mess and found the picture and ran away with it. I thought that was the end of our problems. But noooooo."

"There were more pictures?"

"One more. An even clearer shot. You could see Ed's briefcase, the one with all the money in it. Just our luck, Grosso's thugs picked it up when they did the photographer."

"And *they* tried to blackmail you and Neil?"

She shook her head. "No. Grosso decided his old pal Wilton

might want to see it. It was waiting for him when he got back from the benefit at the Quarterdeck Club. When I got home, he confronted me with it. He said we'd betrayed him with Fein. I told him Neil had nothing to do with it, that I'd been sleeping with Ed. Wilton didn't care about the money. He didn't even mention it. He just freaked. He started hitting me. He'd never done that before. Neil put up with that kind of abuse, but I never had to."

She paused, frowning furiously as if trying to recall some elusive detail from that night. When she continued, she spoke slower and with less certainty. "I went and got the gun and returned to the den. Wilton was still there, ranting. I shot him and shot him."

"You say you went and got the gun. That one?"

She looked at it and nodded.

"It's Johnny's, isn't it?"

She blinked, hesitated, then said, "Yes."

"Where'd you get it exactly?"

"The guest room where Johnny was staying."

"I thought the butler had already packed Johnny's stuff," I said. "And Johnny had claimed it."

"He must have left the gun behind. It was in the guest room. On a table."

"How did you know it would be there?"

"I just knew," she said, annoyed. "Why won't you let me tell you what happened? Why all the questions?"

"I want to get everything straight in my mind," I said. "Is it possible you took the gun from Johnny's room earlier that night, before going to the party?" I asked.

"Maybe. Maybe Johnny gave it to me. For self-protection. He was very good to me. You know why?"

"Because he cares for you," I suggested.

"Yes," she said. "And because I love him."

"But you let him go to prison," I said. "Blamed for your father's murder."

"But I never would have let them find him guilty," she said. She lowered her voice to almost a whisper, as if making sure Lea couldn't hear her. "Will you do me a big favor, Coley? Something very important?"

"If I can."

"Will you kill me? I'd like to be with Neil now and I don't think I can do it myself." She held the gun out to me. I took it, stood and walked to the door, and asked Lea to call the police.

When Paula realized I wasn't going to kill her, she didn't scream or rage as I'd expected. Maybe it was the drug. She seemed vaguely surprised, as if men rarely refused her anything. Then she drew up her legs under the nightgown and hugged them. She remained like that, rocking slightly on the leather chair, until the Bay City police came for her.

It was nearly two hours before we were allowed to leave the Dresner house. Driving home through the late-evening traffic, Lea asked, "How in the world did you make that connection between Paula and Ed Fein?"

I smiled. "We both heard Joey Lunchbox talking about it."

She frowned at me. "We did?"

"Just before we interrupted them at Heartland, Joey and Neil were having an angry chat. Joey mentioned Paula. Do you remember exactly what he said?"

Lea thought about it. "My head hurts enough without this," she said. "I think it was something about them getting caught. If Joey were to go to jail, Neil and Paula would, too."

"There was a little more to it," I told her. "Joey said, and I quote, 'Your little sister can take care of herself. Last I saw of her she was doin' fine.'"

"Right. Then Joey began to laugh as if he'd said something incomparably clever, but it wasn't very . . . oh, no! Doin' Fein." She winced as if in pain. "A pun?"

"I'm afraid so."

"And you picked up on it?"

"Great minds," I said.

She leaned back against the seat of the Cherokee and closed her eyes.

"Do you hate me?" I asked.

"I'm a little tired," she said. "I was drifting off, thinking about what part of town I wanted to live in."

"I bet we could get Dresner's place for a song."

"You are sick," she said. "Maybe Daddy's right about you."

"Not about anything," I told her.

She sighed and said no more. She was asleep before I got her back to Daddy's house.

37

"I'M STAYING IN Vegas from now on," Johnny Rousseau said. "Not so much smog in the air. Not so much chance of getting in trouble."

"Las Vegas," I said. "What trouble could anybody get into there? The place is like Lourdes."

"You're lucky I'm not sensitive, Coley."

We were sitting at a desk in the office of a title company, drinking weak coffee out of cardboard cups, admiring the realistic fabric-leaved foliage, and waiting for the title officer, a young woman with orange hair and more makeup than a Kabuki actor, to bring back copies of all the papers we'd just signed.

Not quite two weeks had passed since the arrest of Paula Dresner for the murders of her father, Channing Hoag, and Edward Fein. It was obvious hers was going to be another in the seemingly endless parade of spectacular Southern California murder trials. Maxwell Fitzgerald, the same high-powered defender whom Johnny had hired, would now appear as Paula's chief advocate. I supposed Johnny had made the referral.

The media, print and visual, were coming up with new angles on the case daily, a few valid, most contrived, some without the remotest connection to the facts. Network shows were interrupted for special reports on the finding of Ed Fein's charred remains and speculation on the whereabouts of the yet-to-be-discovered money. Screenwriters sat beside their television sets, notepads ready. Court TV geared up for another high-ratings ride. This one had everything. Beautiful defendant. Famous father victim. Dark family secrets.

Frank Sanchez had called to say he'd signed a two-book contract, one a biography of Wilton Dresner, which would hit the stores the day the trial started, the second an account of the trial itself to come flying off the presses within weeks of the verdict. If there was a verdict. Juries get so confused these days.

In the biggest exclusive of the Paula Dresner feeding frenzy, one of the TV tabloids had come up with an interview with Paula's mother, the landscape designer living in Europe. She had no intention of rushing to her daughter's aid. She was taped at a sidewalk café, in a city carefully and mysteriously unspecified. She was an exceedingly handsome woman who looked like Paula might at fifty. Her hair was cut short like Paula's. Had the daughter imitated the mother or vice versa?

"She was a monster. She terrified me," the former Mrs. Dresner said in a curiously dispassionate manner. "It got to the point I couldn't handle her anymore."

"She was wild as a teenager?" the unctuous interviewer asked in a nasal voice.

"More than wild. She was homicidal." Dramatic pause. "I mean it."

"She killed someone in Europe?" Even to a TV tabloid reporter, it sounded too good to be true.

"I didn't say that. She didn't actually kill anyone. But she came close. She tried to stab a ski instructor in St. Moritz who broke off with her. Then there was a schoolmate in Geneva and that sculptor in Rome. I had the money and the connections to cover those incidents up, but I always thought, maybe next time . . ."

"Did you tell Wilton Dresner why you were sending your daughter to live with him?" the interviewer asked.

"No," the former Mrs. Dresner replied, "I didn't. Let him find out for himself. Like I did."

Maybe no one would ever follow up on those supposed incidents in Europe, but the story would live forever.

As for the horse insurance racket, which was strictly page three
material, Starbuck had amassed enough evidence to bring the
whole operation tumbling down. Quite a few people had been in-
dicted, including Lavery and Bricknell. But not Georgia Hartmann. Cynical crime watchers were sure Huey Grosso would find
a way to wriggle off the hook, letting his associates take the fall.
Starbuck swore that would not happen and I was happy he had
something to think about other than Lea and myself.

Luis Falcon's body was found where Ramon had told us it
would be, buried near a Taco Loco emporium at the Pale Rock
Shopping Center. I never heard another word about Ramon or
Howard, a tribute to the effectiveness of my policeman friend,
Detective Sean Wiley.

Walrus was back on his feet but not quite finished with the
medical profession. He and his curly-haired nurse were spending
most of her off-duty hours together.

There was one other good bit of wellness news. Briarpatch.
a.k.a. Rebaso, survived, and may even race again, once they officially unscramble his identity. How he managed to cheat the horse
reaper I'm not sure. Maybe Lavery suddenly and coincidentally
found the miracle serum he was looking for. More likely he'd
pulled his punch at the last moment and injected the horse with
a less-than-fatal dose. He'd seemed genuinely fond of the animal
at Land O' Lincoln. I expect we'll find out for sure when he fin-
ishes the book he's writing in prison.

Harold and Estelle Danziger, despite a lengthy if nonviolent rap
sheet of bunco games, got off pretty lightly and would spend their
forty-first anniversary out of prison, probably running a scam
somewhere. I had to talk Jack Hayward out of giving them
money to help finance an infomercial peddling a book on avoiding con artists.

On an anonymous tip, not from Estelle and Harold who kept

their mouths shut, New Jersey police raided the ramshackle home of a retired pari-mutuel clerk in Atlantic City and found the biggest haul of stolen racing memorabilia ever recovered, including a half-dozen items related to the 1982 Santa Rosita Handicap. The other races the obsessed owner was specializing in spelled out the theme of his collection and the reason for his interest in my victory on Codswollop: long-priced winners. One of the most valuable items he'd had stolen was the program for the 1919 Sanford Stakes at Saratoga, in which Upset had defeated Man O' War. I learned from Roger Willetts that after the owner of Codswollop got her original trophy back, she refused to pay for the duplicate. It's now on display in Roger's office at the track.

Candy Dan won an allowance race at Hollywood Park and may be headed for better things. The horse who carried me out of the Calabasas fire turned out to be named Tuba Fore, a ten-thousand-dollar claimer who'd won once in thirty-nine starts. He'll always be a stakes horse to me.

I wish I could say that the story had a completely happy ending. But there was no way to work that out. As Johnny and I left the title office I slipped the signed and notarized quitclaim deed into my pocket and pointed to a clean little fast-food joint next door. It was called Clarabelle's. "Let's grab a quick lunch here," I suggested.

The place was crowded, but there was an empty leatherette booth along one wall. "Looks like they've been saving this one for us," Johnny noted as we sat down.

"Our lucky day," I said.

We ordered hamburgers, preceded by two beers. After taking his first sip, Johnny asked, "So what are your plans, Coley? You gonna marry the Starbuck lady?"

"We're looking for a house," I said. I glanced at the couple in the next booth. Not a hint of romance in that relationship. The guy was bored, staring at the other diners. The woman was scribbling on a notepad.

"What are *your* plans, Johnny? You going to wait for Paula Dresner?"

He smiled. "Maybe not."

"She told me she loved you."

"Oh, yeah? When was this?"

"About half an hour before the cops picked her up."

He looked rather wistful. "I was crazy about her, as you well know," he said. "But not that crazy. Hell, it wasn't all her fault, what happened. Wilton and that bitch who calls herself her mother have to share the blame."

"They're not the only ones."

"No?" He stared at me.

"Maybe Paula isn't the murderess everybody thinks she is," I said.

He put down his beer glass. "What're you talking about?"

"She probably killed Ed Fein," I said. "Fitzgerald could make a case that Neil stabbed the guy, but Paula probably did it. I know she killed Hoag. And for the same reason, I know she didn't kill her father."

Johnny cocked his head to one side. "What reason is that?"

"She's a lousy actress, but she's Academy all the way when it comes to firing a gun," I said. "She closed out Hoag's account with just one bullet. She wouldn't have had to empty a whole chamber to do her father in."

"You shoot your old man, you get a little nervous," Johnny said. He seemed a little nervous himself, looking around the room, studying the other diners. The couple in the next booth were warming up to one another now, nibbling at their bread pudding.

"On edge, Paula might have needed two shots," I said.

"If she didn't do it, who did?"

"You, maybe."

He smiled. "You got a very weird sense of humor, Coley."

"Dresner grabbed that casino poker chip before he died," I said.

"You know the chip had Paula's picture on it," Johnny replied.

"It was your gun."

"But Paula had it," he said.

"How do you suppose she got it?"

The smile left his face. "Why don't you tell me?" he asked with an angry edge to his voice. He was running his hand along the underside of the table.

"Paula says you left it for her."

"That's her take on it. I frankly don't know how she got it. Maybe she grabbed it from the guest room before the butler—what was his name, Henry?—before Henry packed my stuff. Maybe Henry found it in the guest room and gave it to her."

"Maybe Henry killed Dresner," I said.

"You mean the butler did it," Johnny said. He'd stopped fondling the table. "You wouldn't be wearing a wire, would you, buddy?"

I shook my head.

The waitress approached us with our burgers. She smiled politely as she served them, oblivious of the tension that had built up between us.

When she walked away, Johnny asked, "What do you want from me? You got the goddamned restaurant. What more do you want?"

"I want you to cop to the crime, Johnny. You got angry and shot Dresner. And now you're going to let that pathetic young woman pay for it?"

"She ain't gonna pay for nothing, champ," he said in a near whisper, "if you just keep your goddamn nose out of it. If they convict her, she'll wind up at some country club for a few years. But the conviction rate in this state is nearing ground zero, so the odds are she'll walk. Especially with Fitzgerald at her table."

"What about you? Doesn't it weigh you down, having a dead man on your conscience?"

"Dresner wasn't a man. He was a sorry piece of dogshit."

"There are a lot of guys like that out there," I said. "I hope you're not planning to kill 'em all."

He shook his head. "I don't do murder."

"What do you call it?"

He took a deep breath. "I used my guest key on the front door and snuck up to Paula's bedroom. Oh, I know. It was a bush thing to do. But I was sure that if I could have five minutes, I could . . . Well, anyway, I hear Wilton barge into the house, shouting for the butler to take his car back to the Quarterdeck to crack the whip over the cleaning crew. Then he went into his office.

"Five minutes later Paula's footsteps are on the stairs. Wilton is out of his office and shouting at her to come into his den. I hear her cry out and I join the party. She's on the carpet. The son of a bitch is shoving some photograph in her face and kicking her in the stomach. I shout for him to stop and he grabs a poker from the fireplace and comes at me. The guy had flipped. I had to shoot him. I'm not so good at it, as you know, but I got the job done."

"So it was self-defense?"

He nodded.

"Why didn't you stay until the cops got there, explain it to them?" I asked.

"I . . . You know what cops think of me to begin with. There I was, a trespasser in the dead man's house. He's lying on the floor, with my bullets in him and Paula, my only alibi, is in zoneland, and I don't know when or if she's gonna come out of it."

"So you ran out?"

"I panicked."

"It's a story that's worked before," I said. "But the gun is a problem."

He raised a questioning eyebrow.

"Where did it come from?" I asked.

"My coat pocket."

"You didn't have it at the hotel," I said. "I know, I put your tux on a hanger."

He shrugged. "So what? I had the gun and I used it."

"Here's the *so what*," I told him. "If you just happened to be armed at Dresner's, that would be one thing. But you didn't have the gun on you earlier that evening. As you pointed out in Mark Brittan's limo, you don't like to carry a gun into a place where people are drinking; you leave it in the car. So, if you went to the effort of driving back to the Quarterdeck Club, sneaking into the parking area, retrieving your gun from the car you borrowed from Dresner *before* going back to his house, that, to my mind, suggests a certain premeditation."

"Yeah? To my mind, it suggests I might have remembered a gun I was quite fond of and drove out to the club to get it back before I left for Vegas. I stuck it in my pocket and didn't think about it again, until Dresner came at me with the poker. It was a damn good thing I did go get it or *I'd* be in Forest Lawn and you could be asking *him* your fucking questions."

"How did Paula wind up with the gun?" I asked.

"What do you think?" he asked testily. "That I stuck it in her fist when she was unconscious to lay the blame on her?"

"Is that what happened?"

"Jesus, Coley, you really think I'm some twisted asshole? No, you son of a bitch. What happened was that she started screaming when Dresner hit the deck. I guess I put the gun down when I went to help her. Then I heard the butler coming in downstairs, so I did my fade out the back. I left the goddamn gun there. Paula must've hidden it from the cops."

If she loved him, she might have done that.

"And you're still going to let her be tried for your crime?"

"If Dresner was the only name on her dance card, I'd have confessed as soon as they booked her. But she's on the spot for two guys anyway." He shook his head and mumbled something.

"What did you say?" I asked.

I said, "I don't think she's the one who stabbed Ed Fein. As soon as I read about them finding Fein's body out by Heartland, I remembered something Neil told me when I was out there."

I waited for him to continue.

"Maybe I'm making too much of it, but Neil got drunk one night and was crying in his cocktail and said he'd screwed up a multimillion-dollar deal. I asked him what had happened and he sorta blew it off with, 'I killed the goose and now we can't cash in the golden eggs.' "

"If he killed Fein," I asked, "why is Paula copping to it?"

"Why is she copping to her father's shooting?" Johnny replied. "Because she's a dumb little twist who thinks she's starring in some goddamn tearjerk movie where everybody respects nobility and everything turns out okay in the end."

"Your reaction to her 'confessions' should give her the big picture fast," I said.

"If I stepped into it," he said, "I'd never get out. If I tried to tell 'em what Neil said, it wouldn't cut any ice. It's no confession. It's nothing that'll help her case. They'd probably wind up dragging me in on Fein's murder and I never even laid eyes on the guy."

"So you're not going to do anything to help her?" I asked.

He stood up, ignoring the question. "Are there a bunch of cops outside waiting to cart me off?"

"Not to my knowledge."

"Then I'm out of here. I'd rather spend my time with people I like."

"Johnny, before you get too high on your horse, remember who got me into this mess."

"Yeah, yeah," he said.

"And remember who it was sent me out on a possibly fatal fool's errand to prove Huey Grosso killed Dresner."

He smiled and for a moment seemed his old charming self.

"Yeah, I guess I wasn't such a good pal, myself. Well, keep it out of the mud, Coley."

He sauntered from the restaurant like a man with not a worry in the world.

The waitress bustled over. "You and your friend didn't touch those burgers," she said accusingly.

"We sorta lost our appetites," I told her.

She pulled the check from her pad and held it out to me.

"That goes to my cousin in the next booth," I said, pointing to Detective Sean Wiley, who was in the middle of his third rice pudding. The woman with him had closed her shorthand notebook and was removing the little sound amplifier from her ear. Her name was Lulu Stern and she was an investigator for the DA's office.

"What do you think?" Sean asked her as we walked to the cashier.

"I think he's a very smooth customer and a genuine son of a bitch," Lulu replied. "Regardless, the DA's not gonna bring him to trial on the strength of this," she said, holding up the notebook and the small microcassette machine on which she'd taped Johnny's and my conversation. "A confession of self-defense, obtained in a slightly less than legal manner. And there's the thing about the poker. We did find it, with Dresner's prints on it."

"I didn't see anything about a poker in any of the reports," I said.

"We don't want to make Fitzgerald's job *too* easy," she said. "But the DA was leaning toward self-defense in that one, anyway."

"What about Neil Dresner's comment about killing the goose?" I asked.

"Get serious, Killebrew. Secondhand information of a vague confession from a dubious source. The only thing this little get-together really achieved is that this"—she tapped the notepad—"will probably convince the DA to reduce the charges against the girl to only two counts of murder. That way we can keep Dresner's death open, in case we should ever have any other dealings with Mr. Rousseau in L.A. County."

And that's the way it went. Paula goes on trial next week for the murders of Ed Fein and Channing Hoag. The Fein stabbing will be the tough one for her to beat. There's been a good deal of speculation as to how Fitzgerald is going to plead her. Innocent? Self-defense? Temporary insanity? Regardless, factoring in all the possibilities and the current trend in trials by jury, the Las Vegas odds are six to five in favor of her leaving the courtroom a free woman. I'd like to think Johnny is betting her to win, but about some guys, you never know.